CW00343113

THE PORTAL TO EXE'S PAST MAY JUST
SPELL THE END OF HER FUTURE...

EXHUMED

C. B. ARCHE

Published by Ishkabibble Books.

Paperback ISBN: 978-1-963289-01-5
eBook ISBN: 978-1-963289-00-8
Audio ISBN: 978-1-963289-02-2

IshkabibbleBooks.com

Cover design and interior layout by Miblart.com

 ii

IN REMEMBRANCE

For my wonderful mother —
Monalea Lillian Haag Bartsch
(aka: Ishkabibble; Mahidable; Mom)

Devout Christian, loving wife, devoted mother
of nine, dedicated school librarian, talented cake
decorator, inventive cook, avid reader,
and my best friend.

Without her boundless love and unwavering
belief in me, this book wouldn't exist.

Acknowledgements

Thanks be to God the Father, Son, and Holy Spirit for blessing me with a talent for writing and answering my daily prayers for assistance with my work.

Thanks to my remarkable father — Elroy Erwin Bartsch, for the generous support I needed to finish this book.

Thanks to my eldest sister — Deb Schuh, for her endless encouragement and editing assistance. (And for telling me to indie publish years ago!)

Thanks to my closest sister — Dianne Bartsch for... everything.

Thanks to my amazing beta readers for their perceptive insights and inspiring enthusiasm.

Special appreciation to my dearly departed ancestors who inspired the names of many of my characters:
My maternal great-grandmother: Althea Experience Parsell Gotham
My maternal grandfather: Grover Emil Haag
My paternal great-grandmother: Ella Amanda Althoff Winter
And of course, my mother (See dedication page!)

Thanks to all who've served and sacrificed in the U.S. military. Freedom isn't free. -- John 15:13

Pronunciation Guide

In fiction, you're free to pronounce names any way you please. But for the curious reader, this is how I pronounce these people and places. ~ C. B. Arche

Exe Parsell — X pahr-SEL

Malina Verelustre — mah-LEE-nuh VER-uh-LUHS-truh

Jettani Invidia — zheh-TAH-nee in-VID-ee-yuh

Seren — SER-uhn

Anacapia — ah-nah-CAH-pee-ah

Disimulata — dih-SIM-yuh-LAH-tuh

Rochda Lasis Veresos — ROHK-duh lah-SEES ver-EY-sohs

Fainéant —FEY-ney-ahnt

Gyve — jahyv

Find out more about my fantasy world at: TheExeBooks.com.

CONTENTS

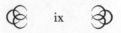

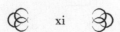

CHAPTER ONE

DEATH WISH

They don't deserve to die.

The words crystalized like ice in Experience's fevered mind, sending shivers down her spine as she raced through the military air base, dripping sweat in the oven-hot heat of Arizona's late September sun.

Rat-a-tat bursts of gunfire from the training range echoed her own ragged exhales as Exe zigzagged between the symmetrical rows of dirt-covered ammo bunkers. *If only I'd run toward the platoons doing maneuvers on the parade ground. Or even dashed back into the crowd of kids saying goodbye to my brothers.* Either option would've thwarted her pursuers, but Exe refused to put others at risk just to save herself.

Pressing herself against the molten metal of an ammo bunker's heavy blast door, Exe strained to hear her stalkers' determined footsteps. The eerie silence was broken only by the blistering breeze whistling through a nearby pipe. The steel door screamed as she eased it open and slipped inside. Cool, stale air shocked her overheated skin as she searched the empty crypt of an armory for a place to hide. The sliver of sunlight piercing her sanctuary through the bunker door set her on edge, but she wouldn't close it. *I left it ajar to throw those prom queen stalkers off my trail.*

"Liar. You're too terrified to shut yourself in completely."

That sneering inner voice was right. The truth was that she couldn't bear to be completely sealed inside. Even now, the cracked walls of the dank, cavernous bunker seemed to close in on her as she hunkered down in the shadows. Hugging her knees, Exe berated herself, *Why did I let those girls lure me away? I should've known better. No one at school would bother involving* me *in a bon voyage surprise for my brothers.*

Quick, shallow breaths and a racing heartbeat threatened to spiral her into a full on panic attack. *"Calm down. You're used to the adrenaline rush of feeling hunted, remember? You've got nothing to fear,"* her inner voice chided.

Nothing, except the fear that I'll accidentally injure my attackers, Exe thought as she hit play on her '80s-era Walkman. She pressed the headphones hard over her ears, willing the pulsing beat of Pat Benatar's "Invincible" to ease her panic. Although she tried to focus solely on the music, the stand-and-fight lyrics wouldn't leave her alone. *It's too dangerous for me to fight back,* Exe admonished herself.

If only it were easier to skip songs on cassette. Typically, Exe took secret pleasure in appreciating things that the rest of the world had forgotten, like her outdated Walkman. (*Do I cling to things from my parents' past because I know so little about my own?*) But at the moment, she found the limitations of her beloved, old-school technology utterly frustrating. Exe bit her lip to keep herself from wishing for the song to be over.

"*It's dangerous to wish for things,*" her irritating inner voice singsonged.

It's dangerous to wish for things, Exe echoed the thought dutifully. As her ragged breathing slowed, she wondered, *Has the bus come yet? Those girls won't miss school just to hunt me down, will they?*

"*You know it's not really you they're after.*"

Exe wiped the cold sweat from her forehead and touched the delicate Art Deco necklace that she'd worn her whole life, marveling at its constant coolness against her flushed skin. The smoky amethyst pendant (that exactly matched her eyes) glittered enticingly. She knew of no one else who wore a mysterious, irremovable necklace with a chain that lengthened to keep the gem hidden under any outfit. But somehow it was always too short to pull over her head, no matter how hard she—or anyone else—tried.

Even though the jewel mostly kept itself out of sight, the stardusted pendant's powerful pull enticed certain people with tyrannical tendencies into attempted thievery. She'd swiftly learned to recognize (and mostly steer clear of) the type: queen bees, cutthroat competitors, brazen bullies, relentless leaders. Once, even a particularly dictatorial teacher had accused A-student Exe of using it to reflect test answers off of a D-student's paper in an attempt to confiscate her necklace.

At the moment, Exe decided that, as much as she loved this lone link to her mysterious past, she'd gladly hand it over to her hunters just to get rid of them. *For their own safety. If only I could...*

How long have I been hiding? Ten minutes? Twenty? Exe reached for her cellphone to check the time, but it wasn't in her back pocket. Scolding herself for losing her only lifeline, Exe peered out the door, bracing herself for the short dash home. Just as she reached for the handle, the dreaded duo stepped into view.

They don't deserve to die, Exe chanted internally as the door clanged open and twenty silver-lacquered nails stabbed into her arms like tiny knives. Eyes closed against the punishing sun, Exe hung limp as the over-glammed girls dragged her out. The two teenagers dropped her onto the hard, hot earth, her head landing near a shallow puddle formed by the runoff from some rusted drainage pipes.

"What is that thing?" The stiletto-heeled leader wrenched Exe's Walkman off, half-strangling her with the cord as she mocked the retro tunes blasting from the headphones. Sneering laughter taunted Exe as the teen ripped the cassette from the player, unspooling the tape maliciously. "Now hand over that necklace—or else."

This will soon end, don't wish them dead, Exe silently recited the phrase, hanging onto the thought as if her attackers' lives depended on it: *Because they do.*

The leader's stiletto heel forced Exe's face into the mud at the puddle's edge as her sidekick's silver nails clawed at her throat, searching for the necklace. *No, not mud. More like dusty soup,* Exe half-smiled, concentrating on slowing her unsteady breaths that rippled the dust across the puddle. *Arizona's dirt is so dry, it rejects water.*

"Break it at the clasp," stiletto chick commanded, ripping Exe from her reverie.

"I'm trying," Strawberry lip-gloss breath hovered hot over Experience's ear as stiletto chick's friend fumbled with the delicate platinum chain. "I can't find it."

"There is no clasp," Exe murmured. "It can't come off."

"Just rip it off her," stiletto chick ordered her lip-glossed sidekick.

Exe's fingers twisted into the wet weeds that had sprung up beside puddle as the unbreakable chain slashed into her flesh—a familiar slice of cold metal drawing blood. *There'll be another scar in a few weeks.* Her neck was a notch post testimony to the number of jealous cheerleaders and bitter rich chicks that had tried to steal the necklace from her over the years.

This will soon end, don't wish them dead. This will soon end, don't wish them dead, Exe's silent chant grew to a whisper as the bloody cut on her neck ripped wider. *Don't* "wish them dead—"

"Are you threatening me?" The gritty stiletto ground into Exe's cheek, forcing her teeth apart until she was sure the heel would stab clean through.

I want them gone. It was a desperate desire so close to a wish that Exe feared she'd give into it in a haze of pain and anger. *But I mustn't wish it.*

"It's dangerous to wish for things."

It's dangerous to wish— Exe struggled to repeat the mantra in her mind, fighting the urge to scream as pain exploded across her face. Desperate to hang on to her control, she traced comforting letters into the dusty mud with the tip of her trembling finger. It was no use. Against her will, she wished.

The deafening roar hit her first. Hot sand rippled. The earth shuddered, knocking her attackers to their knees. A concentrated dust cloud rolled out as the ammo bunker collapsed in on itself, coating them all in a fine layer of grime.

"Hey sis, I know girls wear mud masks, but I don't think you're doing it right," a familiar voice casually joked, cutting through the sputtering coughs of her attackers.

"Easy," Exe wiped the grit from her eyes to find her brother Easy standing between her and her assailants, wearing a roguish grin that didn't quite reach his eyes.

Stiletto chick staggered to her feet, "Easy, it's not what you think. We saved your sister's life. Dragged her to safety just before that bunker collapsed, right?" She nudged her friend, but strawberry lip-gloss breath wisely stayed quiet.

"And just why was Exe hiding in there? Don't bother, I already know," Easy said, smoothly charming even in condemnation. "I hope you enjoyed spending time with my sister, because your social lives are now over. I'll make sure of that."

Easy waited for her devastated stalkers to slink away before turning to Exe. "Rescued in the nick of time yet again. You're welcome."

"How did you find me?" Exe asked, swatting dust from her clothes as she rose.

"It's moving day, remember? We can't move without you," Easy picked up her battered Walkman, respooling the cassette with his pinky. "A Walkman, Exe? Seriously? I think you may be taking this retro obsession of yours a bit too far."

"I know, but this is a big military base," Exe said, ignoring his commentary on her preference for the past as she wiped the wet dirt from her face with the hem of her vintage Led Zeppelin concert tee. "How did you know where to look?"

Easy stilled as if alarmed by the simple question, then shrugged, "I figured you'd only be absent if you were in trouble. And since you never ask for help, I'd most likely find you hiding away in some creephole. The bunkers were the best bet."

Easy seemed satisfied with his explanation, but Exe wasn't so sure. It suddenly struck her that either Easy or one of her five other brothers typically showed up whenever she desperately needed them. *It happens way too often to be classified as coincidence.*

"Why waste time worrying about insignificant details? You should be reveling in the knowledge that you'll never have to see those girls again."

Instantly relieved, Exe smiled—until she caught sight of Easy's stern expression.

"You've only yourself to blame, you know. Nine cities in seven countries over thirteen years, and no matter where we've moved, this always happens," Easy scolded. "If you'd only let kids know that you're a part of the Parsell Pack, no one would even dare to whisper about you, let alone target you like this."

'Just join in.' That was always Easy's advice, but that was, well, easy for him to say. Even Ferris Bueller and his amazing "Day Off" had nothing on Easy. Although only fifteen, Easy had more daring and charisma than all the other Parsell boys put together.

"Why you insist on staying friendless, I'll never understand," Easy said. "It's not like making friends is hard. You wouldn't even have to do anything if you'd let me help."

"Why do I need more friends when I've got six mischief-loving brothers?" Exe joked as Easy gently whacked her back, swirling up a cloud of dust.

"Touché," Easy smiled at her, giving her dusty shoulders a hearty thump. "I guess you're not wanting for companionship with us around. Just don't expect us to braid your hair or paint your toenails."

"When have I ever?" Exe feigned outrage. Silently she warned herself against accepting Easy's tempting proposition. *Friends are out of the question. I'm too dangerous.* Still, she couldn't keep from contemplating Easy's offer as he continued pounding the dust from her clothes with growing enthusiasm.

Exe knew he was right. It would take Easy no effort at all to find her a real friend or two. One word from him and she'd be fighting off potential BFFs. His knack for making friends had earned him his nickname (it helped that his real name was Ezekiel). At every new school they attended, Easy quickly became the leader of the crowd—a fact their other brothers relied on. Because of Easy, friendships with the Parsell brothers became the most sought-after relationships in school. And the kids all fell in line because the Parsell boys treated everyone they met like a long-lost friend.

Part of Exe longed to relax and enjoy the instant popularity she'd have with Easy's help. *Kind of.* She didn't want to be the center of attention the way her brothers always were. She just wanted to laugh and joke and have careless conversations like any normal fifteen-year-old girl. *Normal.* Unfortunately, she was anything but.

"I didn't do anything to make them come after me," Exe blurted out. "It's not my fault! It's never on purpose!"

"I know," Easy said.

Exe read a thousand meanings into the gentle understanding behind those two words. *The rest of the family avoids the topic, but would Easy be willing to talk about my real problem?* No one in her family ever mentioned her wild, unnatural powers, but she desperately wanted to talk about them to someone.

Exe cradled the amethyst pendant in her hand, feeling both comforted and cursed. The dark stone glittered dangerously as she polished away the dust. Deep down, Exe knew that the necklace was connected to her unnatural ability to make her wishes come true. Yes, her wishes all came true, but life was no fairy tale. Her wishes were granted with disastrous results. That's why Exe spent every waking moment focused on suppressing her perilous powers instead of having a social life.

But now her abilities had expanded beyond her control. In fact, her powers were probably the reason why a fortified ammo bunker that had stood strong since the 1940s had suddenly collapsed in on itself to distract her attackers—just what she'd wished for.

"Why are you thinking about this again?" Exe's eyelids sagged closed, but that didn't silence the relentless inner voice that berated her every questioning thought. *"You'll never be normal, even if you wish for it. You tried that once, remember? It didn't work. So quit the pity party."*

"You're a mess, Exe," Easy smiled as he handed back her Walkman. "You'd better get cleaned up. We hit the road at zero seven hundred hours and the 'rents are dropping us right off at our new school. So you can't wait to change at the new house."

With that, Easy pulled out his phone and jogged off toward home, texting without losing his footing or his way. Exe watched him go, trying not to be impressed as he leapt over a curb without looking up. *What I wouldn't give to have a life as easy as Easy's.*

The lure of friends was tempting, but she couldn't risk it. Exe stared down at the letters she'd traced into the mud—U R O K. "I'm safer alone," Exe said, stamping the letters into oblivion. *One dead friend is enough.*

Maneuvers

Exe trailed Easy back to the cookie-cutter army base housing, where a school bus idled beside their moving truck. A pack of students swarmed between the vehicles, mobbing the Parsell boys for a final farewell. The crowd whooped and applauded Easy's return; no one noticed Exe's arrival a few moments later.

Locating her lost phone under a tumbleweed, Exe scanned the area for her assailants. They were already on the bus, cowering in the seat behind the driver. Easy had ostracized them as promised, but it was a hollow victory. Their outcast status wouldn't last without her ultra-popular brothers in attendance at their old school to see to it.

Exe tried to catch Easy's eye to flash him a grateful smile, but he was too busy moving through the crowd with their two eldest brothers. All three were embracing girls as if they were soldiers heading off to war, instead of school boys moving just forty minutes away. At a sharp blast from the bus horn, the students straggled on board.

As their friends waved a final farewell through the bus windows, Exe's six brothers jumped back to work. Forming a human conveyor belt, the boys passed boxes into the truck's cargo area where their uniformed father stacked them with military precision. Tough, tall, and perpetually thin, Colonel Grover "Rove" Parsell could quell the antics of his six growing boys with one look. Only his wildly curly hair stood in complete opposition to his strict disposition. At the moment, he did not look pleased.

Exe could feel her father's eyes on her, questioning her dirty, bedraggled appearance. She averted her gaze, silently begging him not to order an explanation.

The familiar hiss-sigh of the school bus pulling away turned Rove's attention. Exe seized the opportunity and disappeared behind the dwindling stack of boxes, scanning the labels until she found one of her own. While pulling out a mismatched outfit, Exe casually wondered how much easier it would be to simply wish her current clothes clean.

"Don't. It's too dangerous. It's not even safe to wish for little things." Exe felt like screaming at the repressive voice of reason that constantly needled her. Instead, she buried her bubbling resentment and slipped into the empty house to change clothes like any ordinary girl.

There wasn't a box left to dodge as Exe wandered through the tiny, two-bedroom home. Without clutter and curtains, the small house felt like a shell, abandoned and exposed. It showed no sign that it had recently housed nine lively people. Exe caressed the bare walls, curious about the other families who'd left behind memories.

"I think that's it," Ella called out from the empty kitchen, squeezing a sponge with a one-handed twist learned from years of cleaning up after six messy boys and one less-than-neat girl. Ella Parsell's pretty figure had turned plump after having six children, but her soft eyes and warm smile gave her a beauty few people could muster.

"They can't expect any better than this," Exe smiled, finding it easier to relax and be herself in this quiet moment alone with her mother. Somehow, no matter how bad things got, Ella always made Exe feel better. "It's cleaner than when we moved in."

"But you're not," Ella dampened a paper towel and proceeded to wipe Exe's dirty face as if she were a toddler. "What happened this time?"

"Nothing. I just– You know kids. Messy, messy, messy," Exe joked lamely.

"Go clean up," Ella said in a 'We'll talk about this later,' tone. After one last dab at Exe's gritty cheek, Ella headed off to give the bathroom a final inspection.

With all the curtains gone, the kitchen pantry was the only secluded place left to change. Exe had barely stepped inside when the front door opened and she heard Rove's military stride echo through the empty house.

"We need to discuss this move, Ella," Rove called out.

Exe eased the pantry door open just a crack. Her brothers had been competing for months to find out details on the move. Their parents would only say that they were headed for a small town in Arizona. If Exe could find out more intel, she'd pass it on to Easy so he could win the bet. *It's the least I can do to repay him for the rescue.*

"There's nothing to discuss," Ella called out. "You broke your promise."

The tone was familiar. *They're discussing me.* Years ago she had wondered why Rove and Ella fought about her all the time.

She didn't wonder anymore. *Adopted.* Although it was never discussed, Exe had known it for years. She and Easy were the same age and in the same grade, but they weren't twins. They didn't even celebrate their birthdays together. Not to mention that she had freaky powers and he didn't. Yeah, she'd figured out that she was adopted by the time she was in kindergarten.

"She'll have a place to sleep. That's all that matters," Rove was shouting. "I got as much done as I could in the time I had."

Ella's reply was muffled, but Exe knew, *They're fighting over where to stick me in the new house.* She'd probably be stuck sharing a room with her little brothers, or on a cot in her parents' bedroom. That was the worst—listening to the discordant snores of her parents while her brothers whispered and joked in their own private bedroom.

"That's not what I came in to discuss," Rove's explosive response rattled Exe. *He must've come into the kitchen.* "I can't shake this feeling, Ella. We're making a tactical error. I think we should reconsider this move."

Exe pressed herself tight against the wall. Getting caught eavesdropping would result in a month's worth of military-style punishments, like mandatory morning calisthenics or evening KP duty. *Especially since they're talking about me.*

"We've had this same discussion every morning for the last three months, dear," Ella's voice got clearer as she moved into the kitchen too. "You wake up certain that we're making a mistake, but within an hour or two you're back to being convinced that this is for the best. Admit it, you're just having cold feet at the thought of retiring."

"That's not it. You know I was ready to retire long before half of our kids were born. But I kept re-upping and uprooting our family for– who knows what reason. No, it's something else," Rove said. "We weren't ever going back to that town, remember? We swore we wouldn't on the day we got her. Yet now we're moving there? Why?"

Wait, what? Exe puzzled.

"I don't recall that, honey," Ella stared sightlessly out the kitchen window—if she turned toward the pantry, Exe was caught. "Even if we did agree to that all those years ago, maybe we were just nervous because of how quickly Exe's adoption came together."

"Quick? We went there on a day trip with three preschool boys and left with an extra two-year-old girl in tow. Do you even remember how that happened? I don't."

Are we moving to the town where they adopted me? Exe smothered a gasp.

"You know how I longed for a little girl. And with six boys, Exe was our chance to have one," Ella's rote words rang false as she re-cleaned the spotless countertops.

"We didn't have all six yet. We'd just found out you were pregnant with Timothy. For all we knew that day, he could've been a girl," Rove pondered, pacing—a sure sign that he was deeply perturbed. "It doesn't make sense. Any of it."

"Why are we even discussing this? She's been with us for thirteen years," Ella's voice grew fainter. Exe risked a peek and spotted them moving to the front door. "Hold on, is that why you're moving us back there after all these years?" Ella reached for the doorknob. "You want to find her birth parents? Why? Exe may not have been the easiest child to raise, but she's a part of this family."

Rove's reply was too quiet to hear—and Exe desperately wished to hear his answer. *Oh no!* Exe rushed out of the pantry. She was too late.

CRASH! The front door window exploded inward, showering her parents with shattered glass. Shimmering splinters protruded everywhere on Ella's face like prickers on a cactus. Thready rivulets of blood flowed from each tiny wound.

Rove lifted the base of a shattered water glass out of the pile of broken window pane. Exe had wished for a water glass to help her eavesdrop—and they knew it. Her parents shared a disquieted look before turning to her. That awful, familiar look unearthed a dreadful memory:

Ella's eyes growing wide with horror as four-year-old Exe refilled her cup without touching the milk jug. Exe had only done it because no one would pour her more in the chaos that was dinner with her rambunctious brothers and their frazzled parents.

But that look in Ella's eyes. Confused. Wary. As if she were seeing Exe for the first time and not liking what she saw. Both Ella and Rove had that same look on their faces now. Exe whirled and ran.

Rove spent an hour picking glass slivers from Ella's face. The big one under her eye was sure to leave a scar. *I could've taken her eye out*, Exe wallowed. The horror of the incident overwhelmed her, squashing all other thoughts. Only an inkling of an idea remained, nagging at her that she was forgetting something important.

The older boys boarded up the broken window while the younger ones amused themselves by pelting them with spitballs (a game the eldest boys joined once the work was done). Exe watched from the back of their vintage Dodge van where she'd hidden amongst the luggage. *Maybe if Ella and Rove don't see me for a while, they'll forget what I've done.* Given Ella's wounds, that was unlikely, but if enough time passed maybe they'd just punish her without talking about it. The last thing Exe wanted to do was talk.

"How could you forget that you're dangerous? Someone you love got hurt because you failed to keep your powers suppressed for just a few moments."

This all-consuming obsession with her own dangerousness exhausted her. It felt impossible to maintain a constant watchfulness against wishing. *After all, wishing is natural and instinctive for most people,* Exe complained to herself.

"But most people don't have to worry about their wishes coming true."

Her inner nag was right. Lately, these incidents of uncontrolled wishing were happening more frequently, and coming true faster, too. She'd only just wished for a distraction or a rescuer this morning, and she'd gotten both almost instantaneously. And the idea of using a glass to eavesdrop had barely even registered in her mind before one had ripped free from its packaging and hurtled through the window.

Exe risked a peek at her parents. The sight of the blood still streaking her mother's face as Rove tweezed out thousands of tiny glass shards focused her dark thoughts on this single, disturbing fact: *My powers are out of control.*

From that day six years ago when she'd accidentally murdered her friend, she'd kept her powers bottled-up. But now they were almost impossible to contain. *Maybe they're out of control because I've buried the memory of the murder too deep?* Digging into her subconscious, Exe forced herself to relive that horrific day:

Bonnie. The blonde-haired, blue-eyed darling of the fourth grade had taken gangly new-student Exe under her wing. That best friend bliss had lasted for seven beautiful weeks—long enough for Exe to spill all of her secrets. Once, she'd even shown off her powers to her new friend. After that, Bonnie changed.

One day they were friends, and the next she'd turned the entire class against Exe. Girls ran from her, giggling in mock terror, while the boys pelted her with erasers. Out in the schoolyard, Exe had confronted Bonnie. The playground equipment shuddered, shaking children off swings and monkey bars as, in a voice dark and serious, Exe told Bonnie, "I wish you were dead."

One week later Bonnie was dead. Hit by a bus. Rumor had it that Bonnie ran out into traffic because she'd seen Exe coming (although Exe didn't remember being there). *Not that it matters. I wished the girl dead, and she died. It was my fault.*

An explosion of laughter jolted Exe out of her worst memory.

Now that Ella was patched up, her rowdy brothers scrambled to shoot off the last of their spitballs before piling into the van. Buried alone in the back seat with the baggage, Exe watched her good-humored brothers enviously. *How simple their lives are.*

As Rove drove away from the familiar army base and into the big, busy city, Exe tried to pull herself out of her despondency. If only she could remember the one fascinating fact she'd learned from her parents' crushing conversation. *What was it?*

Recalling their discussion felt like sifting through shifting sand. Whenever she got close to remembering, some fierce, unknown wind drifted gigantic dunes of forgetfulness over top of it. Just when she was about to give up, the inkling crystalized into memory: *We're moving to the town I was adopted from thirteen years ago.*

"*That can't be true.*"

The idea that she was born in some tiny Arizona town instantly seemed ridiculously farfetched. She'd been searching a lifetime for someone else with freakish powers like hers, but she hadn't found a single soul. Not one person with powers materialized in any of the exotic countries the Parsells had lived in over the years. So Exe finally gave up. Still: *Maybe someday. Maybe today...*

"*After all this time? It's silly to think that you'll find someone in rural Arizona.*"

Exe pressed her forehead against the van's sun-warmed window, watching the city shift from towering, sparkling skyscrapers to squatter, dirtier industrial buildings. Neither the nagging voice or her inner turmoil could shake her flickering hope. Maybe she was finally going home, where there just might be someone else just like her. *One person. That's all I need. Someone to teach me how to control my powers or even shut them off completely so I don't hurt anyone else. Then I'll finally be normal.*

"*Normal? Impossible.*" Suddenly it felt as if it would be easier to wish the whole world away than to get her wayward powers under control.

But a persistent hope insisted, *Maybe having powers will BE normal wherever we're going.* Exe couldn't resist the familiar fantasy—finding a place where she'd be considered ordinary. A peaceful place where all people had powers, so there'd be no reason to repress her own. A place where no one would be afraid of her. *Even me.*

Her imagination ran wild with the possibilities of such a place, until a murky mist of yearning and regret unfurled within her. That bleak longing blotted out her happy dream—a wholly unfamiliar, darkly desperate desire.

"Home." That one word triggered a multitude of images flashing through her mind like computer virus popups. A phantasmagoria of shimmery lands, impossible buildings, and fantastical fauna flew by so fast that Exe couldn't hang on to a single picture—save one. For a moment, the vision of a glistening, gorgeous fence topped with elegant curls of vicious barbed wire hung in her mind.

BANG! Their old red Dodge van tilted off-kilter and skittered to a bumpy halt. A luggage avalanche slammed Exe against the seatback and launched a heavy footlocker at her head, stinging the fresh cut on her neck.

Exe's youngest brother howled in the aftermath, hanging awkwardly on the arm of the booster seat that had skidded out from under him. The other two younger boys rubbed the bumps where their heads had collided over a video game. Behind them, the eldest worried that the impact of his shoulder with Easy's might've wrenched his throwing arm, while the second oldest re-ruffled his perfectly-mussed rock star hair.

Her brothers didn't grumble for long, though. The Parsells had been raised to handle emergencies without being told. After a few seconds' shock, Exe's brothers vacated the van in swift, orderly fashion. Shaken but calm, Ella hustled the three youngest boys safely away from the speeding traffic. Exe hovered near Rove and her three oldest brothers as they puzzled over the blown tire.

"Man, that's shredded," the eldest whistled as he stared at the tire's remains. "Tread's been ripped off completely. I thought that only happened going seventy-five on the highway, not thirty on a side street."

"Read about a bluesman who almost died this way back in the day," the second eldest intoned. "Said the desert heat bubbles the rubber, turning the tiniest crack into a full-on split. Think he wrote a song about it. Now I lived it. Wild."

"I don't let my tires crack," Rove took a knee to get a closer inspection. "Still, these were nearing the end of service. Perhaps there's a slight chance I overlooked a chink in the tread. Well soldiers, looks like we'll have to unload to get at the spare."

"Request to be relieved from duty, sir?" Easy asked, surprising Exe by hanging back while the two eldest got right to work. "These unexpected delays have wreaked havoc on my plans."

"Request granted," Rove replied, turning to Exe. As Easy strolled off, Exe scrambled for an excuse to get out of duty, *I'll only do more damage if I try to help*. Then she spotted her eldest brother rubbing his semi-sore shoulder.

"My neck. I think something hurt it. Footlocker, maybe," Exe trailed off, worried that the small bump from the trunk hadn't left enough of a mark.

"The footlocker made this cut on your neck?" Rove asked, inspecting the damage.

"Must have," Exe said, before remembering that the fresh cut joined almost a dozen similar scars. *Well, I'd better sell it.* "Is it bad? It really hurts."

"Grab a little R and R," Rove said, hefting a heavy rucksack from the van. "But let me know if you start to feel woozy. You might need a sick call if that hit was hard."

Rove's reprieve deepened Exe's shame as she slumped against the hot metal fence surrounding an empty lot. She was feeling ill, but not because of her neck. *I accidentally wished while selfishly daydreaming.* Reprimands ripped through Exe's brain like bullets. *Haven't I done enough damage already? First, I explode a building to hurt those girls. Then I maim my mother. And now I almost blow up the family van with my family in it! I might've killed them all the way I killed Bonnie. I must remember every second that I'm treacherous, or I'll end up killing again. Never forget: It is dangerous to wish for things.*

The deep desire to be free of her fatal abilities left her weak and shaking.

"If you don't let this go, you'll never survive the day."

Obediently, Exe blanked her mind and buried the trauma of the past few hours, allowing the salve of forgetfulness to soothe her worries away. To calm her mind, Exe scratched those comforting letters onto her knee with her fingernail: U R O K.

Soon, the blistering metal bars and the scorching sidewalk overtook every other sensation and drove Exe to her feet. She brushed her fingertips along the blazing silver fence that surrounded the empty field. *No, not exactly empty.* Exe could've sworn she saw something flickering in the middle of the barren dirt lot.

Squinting, Exe tried to spot that flicker again, only to realize that the fence itself was worth a second look. Sunlight glistened off the intricately-etched, elegantly-arched platinum bars, and the sharp, sinister circles of barbed wire at its top. *How odd to protect an empty lot with such a sleek, expensive-looking fe– I've seen this fence before.*

Exe froze, suddenly certain that she'd had a vision of this very fence at the exact moment the tire had blown. *I imagined it before ever seeing it? Did I wish it into existence? No, that's ridiculous. Isn't it?* There it was again—a strange sparkle in the center of the field.

That doesn't make any sense, either. The lot's empty. She could clearly see the fencing at the opposite end of the field. Still, she could've sworn that she'd seen something else in there. That elusive glimmer lured her face forward until she was a hairsbreadth away from pressing her cheeks between the scorching metal.

"I wouldn't, if I were you," Easy offered carelessly, not even glancing up from his phone as he strode towards her. "Unless you're into the blistered face look."

"I thought I saw something," Exe said, glancing at Easy. "Twice in one morning I find you glued to a screen? What gives? You're hardly ever on your phone."

"In company," Easy replied. "What fun could I have distracted by a device when my friends are around? But first I gotta find those friends. How else can I connect with people I've never met IRL the way that I do? Magic?"

Exe laughed mechanically. "So, what's so important that you'd cut out on duty?"

"Arrangements," Easy tilted his phone so that Exe could see the screen as he flipped effortlessly between multiple social media sites and a half-dozen text message threads. Scanning his phone, Exe realized he was setting up introductions for each of the brothers with all of the top-tier kids in a school she'd never heard of. *Which must mean...*

"You know where we're going, don't you?" Exe's question hung between them.

"The colonel and Mom agreed that I needed the info to work my magic," Easy confided. "It takes hours to make our smooth school transitions look effortless."

"But, the bet—"

"I took an automatic loss when they gave me the intel. I knew no one would figure it out, and we'd all lose anyway. I was right."

"Did you see that?" Another little twinkle from the field caught Exe's eye.

"Just heat waves," Easy peered through the bars without touching them.

"Are you sure? Do heat waves sparkle like that?"

"Sparkle? No. Maybe you're seeing things, like a mirage," Easy joked, turning back to his phone. "Or hallucinating. Dad said you hit your head."

Just as Exe was ready to risk the face burns, Rove gave a piercing whistle—the family call to fall in. The tire had been changed and the luggage reloaded in record time. Another sharp signal and the boys scampered into the van, jockeying to win their preferred seat. All except Easy, who was still working his phone. Exe lingered too, taking one last glance at the intriguing field. Then she gasped.

A man stood in the exact spot where she'd spied the shimmer. A man clad in a dark trench coat with his black hat pulled low to hide his face. Exe blinked at the strange sight, and in that millisecond the man had vanished. *Disappeared? From the center of an empty field in less than a moment?*

"*Impossible. You must be hallucinating,*" her inner nag sounded strangely terse.

As Easy moved toward the van, Exe grabbed his arm. "Where are we moving to? Mom and Dad said I came from— I just really need to know. Please?"

"Alright, I'll tell you," Easy caved to her pleading expression. He leaned in close and breathed in a conspiratorial whisper, "Nowhere."

CHAPTER THREE

There's No Place Like Nowhere

Nowhere. They were actually moving to Nowhere. And Nowhere was exactly how Exe would describe the place.

With the city still visible on the horizon behind them, Rove drove out into a barren desert toward the foothills of a massive mountain range that appeared absolutely uninhabited. Then Exe spotted the sign: "Nowhere, Arizona – Pop. 7,936." Just below, a folksy slogan blared in tall Western typeface: "Welcome to the Wild West as the Wild West was Way Back When."

As their vintage van rounded a mesa, the dusty, Old West town came into view. Exe pressed her face against the window to see all she could of the strange little town. The perfectly-preserved village had dozens of shops (with false fronts making them appear two stories tall) lining the quaint Main Street. There was a blacksmith, a general store, a confectioner, a dress shop, a milliner, a little red schoolhouse, several saloons with swinging doors, and a bank with a jail located conveniently nearby. It even had a railroad depot offering tourists a train robbery show on a real steam engine train ride.

For retro-obsessed Exe, moving to a living history town was a dream come true—for more reasons than one. *Nowhere*, Exe thought. The moment Easy had named the town that they were moving to, it had all clicked. She'd researched this town years ago—*because of those mysterious letters from Nowhere*. So while Exe's brothers conspired about the eclectic town's potential for mischief, Exe focused on the people strolling the boardwalk-lined streets.

Amongst the streams of tourists snapping pictures and loading up on souvenirs were almost a hundred residents dressed in period costumes. Pioneers, saloon girls, cowboys, shopkeepers, gold miners—all going about life as if they were living in the 1890s. There was even a sheriff shadowing a posse of black-clad outlaws who were casing the bank. Somewhere among all those people might be the one person who knew the truth about Exe's powers—*Aunt Goldie*.

Every year, someone named Aunt Goldie sent Exe a blank journal and a short, typewritten letter that included a mundane message about the Arizona heat and an annual reminder to improve her writing skills. A package arrived early each January ever since Exe had been old enough to write. So the Parsells celebrated Exe's birthday on whatever day Aunt Goldie's package arrived, since no one knew her actual birthdate.

Those packages had a return address of #9 Why Road, Nowhere, Arizona, but Exe hadn't been able to find that address on any map. Still, none of the letters she'd mailed to that address had ever been returned. *Or answered either.* Her letters to Aunt Goldie asked obvious questions: Who am I? Where did I come from? Who are my parents? Why am I... different? Unfortunately, the woman was stubbornly uncommunicative.

Exe sent her first letter to Aunt Goldie on her tenth birthday. There was no response until Aunt Goldie's package arrived the following year. Below the typed message there was a brief, handwritten note—written in tight, golden script—that read: "If you have something to say to me, write it in the journal." After that, Aunt Goldie ignored Exe's letters. Exe kept sending them anyway, just in case.

But today Exe was actually in Nowhere. She could ask Aunt Goldie her questions face to face—if she could find her. *I will find her. I'll hunt her down, even if I have to knock on every door and ask each one of Nowhere's seven thousand residents about her.*

A collective groan from her brothers drew Exe's attention. Apparently they'd pitched the idea of skipping school since they were so late anyway, and it was a Friday after all. Her brothers were clearly as anxious to explore Nowhere as Exe, *for very different reasons.* But Rove and Ella nixed the idea.

"Dad's right, school first," Easy settled back into his seat. "Wouldn't be much of a party tonight if we don't meet any kids to invite, now would it?"

"School it is," Exe's eldest brother agreed, scanning the streets. "But where?"

"Not that little red place with the bell?" Her second oldest brother asked, glancing back down Main Street.

"Don't tell me we're stuck in with the ankle-biters in some quaint, one-room schoolhouse." The three youngest took immediate offense at his toddler terminology, but he brushed them off with a blasé shrug.

"This is where Nowhere gets truly fascinating," Rove answered, turning the van onto a road that wound up into the foothills. "This historic section only houses the museum, tourist shops, and a few family homes. Most of modern-day Nowhere is built out of sight on the backs of these foothills, to preserve the aura of Old West authenticity. A state-of-the-art town scattered across the mountain tops, can you beat that?"

"However, I have registered you all in the same K through twelve school, so I expect you older boys to look out for your little brothers," Ella added, passing out bagged lunches as they pulled up in front of the sleek, contemporary school.

"Don't worry, Mom," said Seph, the eldest. "We'll keep an eye out."

Eighteen-year-old Joseph, affectionately known as "Seph," took his position of oldest sibling seriously, always striving to impress with his example-setting. Between his grades, manners, and athletic performance, he'd earned a rep as the family's golden boy.

Exe claimed her lunch from Ella last, wondering idly if she dared to skip school on her own to hunt for Aunt Goldie. Her conscience had other ideas.

"Education is more important than chasing down answers that you know will disappoint. Be careful what you wish for. You're better off not knowing."

Why shouldn't I look for her? Exe argued with herself. *My brothers would cover for me if I skipped. I've covered for them often enough. I need answers.*

"There's no time to dwell on yourself when you've got hundreds of new classmates to contend with." A wave of dread instantly flooded Exe, leaving her numb. The idea of being surrounded by a bunch of strangers suddenly seemed like more than she could bear. *"Just breathe. All you have to do is get through."*

"All I have to do is get through. All I have to do is get through," Exe whispered to herself over and over as she joined her brothers in a huddle around a hand-drawn map.

"We make our grand entrance in this formation. No arguments," Easy commanded when it looked like one or two of his brothers might object. Exe glanced at the rough layout of the school, impressed that Easy had so quickly come up with a clever new battle plan to establish the brothers on the top of this school's hierarchy—since their late arrival had destroyed his original strategy.

"As soon as we're in, Seph takes Henny-Boy and Charley to the weight room to meet the athletes. Little Charley will score you points with the girls' teams, and the jocks need to know not to pick on Henny-Boy, no matter how annoying he gets."

"I'm not little, I'm five," little Charley piped up. Exe couldn't help but smile at his petulant pout, which gave him the look of a cheeky cherub. Charley was still such a baby, especially to be starting first grade, but the kid was a wiz at academics, even tough subjects like math and science. He'd been asking to go to school since he was three, so this year their parents had caved, knowing he'd have his siblings to help him socially.

"Of course you're five. You're also adorable," Easy stated dryly. "You gotta use what you've got to win over the crowd, kid."

"Well, I'm NOT annoying, and quit calling me Henny-Boy," gangly ten-year-old Henry tried to drive home his message with a punch to Easy's arm.

Easy blocked the hit without looking up from the map. "You are annoying. Every ten-year-old is annoying. That's just how life works. You'll grow out of it," Easy took the sting from his words by ruffling Henny-Boy's curls. "And you spent months begging me for a nickname, Henny-Boy. Be proud you earned one."

As the oft-overlooked second youngest, Henry had been so excited to finally be "cool" enough for a nickname. That is, until he overheard Easy joking that Henry was the sacrificial "hen" who often took the fall for the brothers' trademark pranks. When Henny-Boy balked at the moniker, Easy explained that he took the fall so often because his natural boisterousness drew attention on mischievous missions that called for stealth. So Henny-Boy was typically the only one caught. But he never gave up his brothers—no matter how severe the punishment. That, Easy said, was the reason he'd earned their respect and been nicknamed Henny-Boy. This had mollified Henry, but he still objected to the nickname now and then, on principle.

Despite the interruptions, Easy was laser-focused on the mission, "Thone, you and Moth book it down this corridor to the auditorium and art studios where the creatives hang. Chat 'em up about their upcoming art show and how you regret missing their recent theatre production, some retro musical, I think? And help Moth engage with the history buffs and the literati. They fraternize in the library across the— Are you two listening?"

It didn't look like it. Seventeen-year-old Thone, the second eldest, appeared too busy perfecting his coif and practicing his smoldering gaze in the school's mirrored windows to be listening to Easy. His given name was Anthony, but he'd insisted on being called Thone from the moment he'd gotten his first girlfriend—in kindergarten.

"Heard every word, my man, and I've got the layout down. We'll stroll in like lifelong locals," Thone's tone rolled. Exe's most artistically-inclined brother had a casual confidence that made art exhibitions and open-mic night performances an absolute ease.

At least Thone was listening. Thirteen-year-old Timothy was too absorbed in his book to pay attention. His nickname was perhaps the most apt of all, because just like a moth to a flame, Moth gravitated toward any light source he could find to read by. He'd even pretended to be afraid of the dark until just a few months ago—all to fool their parents into providing a nightlight for midnight reading.

"Oh, is it time to go in?" Moth glanced up from the page when Henny-Boy elbowed him. "Where do I go? Recess, I hope. I'm not done with this chapter."

"Just follow me, Moth-Man," Thone draped an arm around Moth's shoulders. "Never fear, I'll guide you right." That was all the reassurance Moth needed to dive happily back into his book.

Exe wished she could match Moth's nonchalance. Nothing ever seemed to excite or worry him. He'd react with the same polite interest if you told him you were going to punch him in the gut as he would if you gave him a $500 gift card to a bookstore. That worry-free personality let Moth be completely calm and content in almost any situation, whether enjoying a little solitude or joining in with his brothers on a crazy adventure.

"I doubt there'll be time to cover all you want me to say, bro," Thone said. "We've got less than three minutes between classes."

"Don't worry, I've got that handled. We'll have plenty of time. As for me, I'll be heading to the quad where student council, the activities committee, and clubs mingle with the rest of the socials. That way I can hook us up with VIP treatment at any upcoming school-sponsored events," Easy concluded, tearing up the map to destroy any evidence that his stellar social networking required effort. "Exe, you're with me."

Socializing with the most popular, outgoing kids in a new school was the last place Exe would want to be—with anyone but Easy. *Thankfully his charisma casts such a big shadow, no one'll notice me.*

Stationing themselves at the entrance according to Easy's diagram, Exe's brothers flung the doors wide and strolled in as soon as the bell rang. Exe hung back to let her brothers take center stage, slipping in behind them just as the doors were closing.

Once inside, Easy made a big show of thanking the principal for extending the between-class break to ten minutes so that he and his brothers could get acclimated. This end-run around authority had the intended effect—the watching crowd whispered in awe about the Parsell Pack. When the brothers finished charming the faculty, they broke ranks and maneuvered through the school like seasoned pros rather than new students.

"How did you get the principal to agree to that?" Exe couldn't help asking as she followed Easy down a locker-lined hallway.

"I just showed him the letters," Easy replied, pausing to bro-hug a stranger.

"What letters?" Exe asked, shaking off a sudden burst of dread. *He can't mean my letters from Aunt Goldie. Nothing in those mundane messages could help Easy here.*

"Recommendation letters. Written by teachers and principals from every school we've ever attended," Easy reveled in revealing his socializing secrets. "They detail the benefits of having the Parsell Pack as students. After I get us on the top of the social food chain, other kids strive to emulate the military discipline our 'rents instilled in us—and faculties love us for it. They even let a lot of our mischief slide because we do more good than harm. I simply spelled out how a one-time-only break extension would help make the same things happen at this school, and our new principal was on board."

As soon as they arrived at the quad, Exe found herself surrounded by a crowd of fawning socials, all eager to congratulate her brother on his first big coup. Exe marveled at Easy's blitheness as he greeted these strangers like long-lost friends. It didn't matter that he'd only met most of them briefly online or not at all. Thankfully, Easy drew all the attention, leaving none for her as she worked her way out of the mob.

"Have you met him yet?" a honeyed voice dripped from a dreamy, bohemian girl practically dancing on her tiptoes in an effort to spot Easy. "I must admit, I prefer that keen Thone, such a maverick. But he says this brother knows how to draw a crowd, and my last singing circle was a little light on beings."

"He can help. I think. Easy. That's his name. My brother. Oh no. I didn't— he's not my brother. I mean, he is, but— Easy. Easy is his name, just forget that he's my brother," Exe mumbled, scolding herself for revealing that she was Easy's sister. Once kids knew, they tried to get to the brothers through her. *That's a special kind of torture.*

"Perfect, you can introduce me," the Boho Babe enthused as the bell rang. "Drat, the bell. Well, at least we can have a lovely chat. Where are you headed?"

"I'm not sure," Exe panicked. She had no idea where to go now.

"With me, remember?" Easy said, joining them. "Who's your new friend?"

"This is babe, uh, this girl. Wanted to meet. You. She sings," Exe ended lamely.

"Singer, huh?" Easy charmed the starstruck Boho Babe. "I've been known to carry a tune or two, but I think you'd prefer my brother Thone's vocals. Need an intro?"

"Oh, wow, thanks. I love him already. But he sent me to you. I need attendance help for my singing circle," Boho Babe said. "Walk me to AP History?"

"We're headed there, too," Easy said, with a sidelong glance at Exe. "Both of us."

"Perfect," Boho Babe looped her arms through theirs and guided them into a costume-filled classroom. "We can chat on the ride to the school."

"Ride?" Exe asked, puzzled by the sight of her new classmates scouring racks filled with Old West costumes in a classroom that looked more like a department store dressing room. Exe's spirit lifted for the first time all day at the thought of a hands-on history class studying period clothing as a lesson. "We're already at school, aren't we?"

"My dear, don't you know?" Boho Babe smiled with amazed glee. "It's AP History's turn to put on a show for the tourists in the Main Street schoolhouse."

"What?" Exe turned her dumbstruck stare from the Boho Babe to Easy—who couldn't quite hide his guilty expression. "You knew? I never would've agreed to take AP History with you if I'd known I had to perform. How could you?"

"Calm down, Exe," Easy soothed. "We all have to do it eventually. Performing is part of the deal for everyone living in Nowhere. Right, um, babe?"

"That's right. Dressing like time stopped a hundred and fifty years ago is required of every Nowhere citizen," Boho Babe agreed from deep within a bin of pioneer bonnets. "All residents sign a contract with the city agreeing to dress up in period costume throughout the year as entertainment for tourists. There's a schedule and everything. Most kids try to get their hours in during school. That's why it's practically impossible to get into this class. I'm surprised they let new students in, quite frankly."

"I might have made a few promises to score our slots," Easy admitted.

"In any case," Boho Babe said, handing Exe and Easy the outfits she'd selected for them. "Every afternoon this month we'll be driven down to Main Street—in a horse-drawn covered wagon no less—to show tourists an authentic Old West schoolhouse in action. Mostly we just sit there, but we do old-fashioned schoolwork, too. Long division, parsing sentences, it's trippy."

"See, mostly just sitting," Easy soothed, guiding Exe toward a dressing room. "It's better than strolling the streets in a saloon gal costume on the weekends, right?"

Exe just slipped into a dressing room and slammed the door.

CHAPTER FOUR

HEARING VOICES

"*Hide yourself.*"

The ominous voice whispering through her mind sent shivers down Exe's spine, despite the hot, dry breeze blazing through the open window. Nowhere was so committed to authenticity, they wouldn't even install air-conditioning in the little red schoolhouse.

Exe longed to pull her sunbonnet up to conceal her face, but her AP history teacher had instructed that hats weren't allowed indoors in the 1890s. Instead, she untucked her currently-deep-red hair from behind her ear and pushed the non-prescription glasses (that she'd felt inexplicably compelled to add to her costume) more firmly in place. *Hopefully the glare off the fake lenses will disguise my amethyst eyes.* (Disguising her eye color suddenly felt vitally important.) Exe rolled her eyes at this irrational fear, likely triggered by the tourists gawking in her general direction. Feeling silly, she lifted a hand to tuck her hair back behind her ears.

"Don't do it," the urgent inner voice stilled her hand. Exe gritted her teeth as the insistent worrywart within her contradicted her more courageous instincts.

Every few months, that relentless voice urged her to alter her appearance like a fugitive, with unnecessary eyewear and hair dyed various shades of normal—because bubble gum pink was too conspicuous. That voice was the reason she dressed drab, stayed solitary, and suppressed her unnatural powers as much as she could.

"Stay alert. Be ready," her inner voice advised.

Ready for what? The constant tension of alertness insisted upon by the paranoid voice drained her. That nagging voice was nothing new, but this sudden urgency was unfamiliar. *For the first time in my life, that annoying voice doesn't feel like my own. It feels like it's someone else's.* Exe almost laughed aloud, the idea was so ridiculous. *Of course it's my own. It's in my head! I'm just overreacting to being the new kid yet again.*

Except the voice wasn't the only reason Exe had her guard up. Usually, her irremovable necklace stayed chilly even when she dripped with sweat. But for some reason, the smoky amethyst pendant was currently thrumming with unfamiliar heat.

Exe caressed the warm, tingling stone through her calico dress and glanced over at Easy. He was deep into a silent conversation of flirty glances and clever hand signals with a pair of pretty girls. (*He'll probably have dates with both before he's even spoken one word to them.*) They weren't related by blood, but she did share an odd, brotherly connection with Easy. *If I were truly in danger right now, he'd be worried, too. But he's not.* Relieved, Exe brushed off the voice's paranoia as first-day, new-school jitters.

A sharp burst of malicious laughter caught Exe's attention from amongst the sweat-drenched tourists fanning themselves with souvenir maps as they gawked at her class from behind a rickety railing. She spied a gaggle of giggling pre-teen girls on a field trip tormenting a solemn boy with home-cut hair and second-hand clothes.

Incensed at the thought of witnessing more bullying after this morning's incident, Exe stared the girls down. Her brothers claimed she could give the most bone-chilling evil-eye they'd ever seen—but these girls didn't even notice her patent-worthy glare.

Exe turned to the solemn boy, silently inviting him to see her. When he did, Exe smiled as if to say, 'You're not alone. I've been there. If I can survive, so can you.'

"Focus, you fool! Don't let him see you," the paranoid voice screamed in Exe's head, sending a fresh tremor of terror through her. Disturbed, Exe scanned the tourists for anyone even remotely frightening. It didn't take long to find him.

A tall man in a jet black trench coat and matching fedora. Face hidden in the shadows of an upturned collar. Eyes masked by the silver circles of mirrored sunglasses. The chasm of fear in her deepened as recognition hit. *I've seen that man before. In the center of that odd, fenced-in field where we had the flat tire this morning.*

"Where are you?" Dark and dangerous, an unfamiliar voice slithered through her. *"I know you're here,"* The sinister voice crept through her mind, searching. *"I can feel your power,"* The man in black was staring right at her. *"Let me see you."*

No, not at me. Through me. As if he can only sense me, not see me. At least, Exe thought that he couldn't see her. His sunglasses made it impossible to tell for certain. She kept her eyes riveted on the guy in shades over the rims of her fake glasses, afraid he'd suddenly realize that the girl he was looking through was the girl he was looking for.

Tensed and breathless, Exe watched and waited. *Nothing.* The longer nothing happened, the more she relaxed. *"Just focus. Stay invisible. You'll be fine."* Exe breathed relief when the familiar inner voice returned. It magically dulled those gnawing questions that the shady guy inspired. *As long as I focus, I'll go unnoticed. That's all that matters.*

After several long, tense minutes, Exe chanced a glance at the picked-on boy who was watching her solemnly. His lack of interest in the viciously-giggling girls had robbed them of their power to hurt him, just as Exe had intended.

When Exe glanced toward the man in black again, he was gone.

"Mom," the solemn boy said to a field trip chaperone. "Take her picture. The girl in the back row. I want to remember her."

Exe gritted her teeth and forced a smile. As much as she hated getting her picture taken, for the kid's sake she wouldn't run or hide this time. But the boy's mother lowered her camera-phone without snapping any shots. "Honey, no one is sitting in the back row."

The boy stilled, his curiosity-filled expression spinning into terror.

Exe stopped breathing. *I'm not supposed to use my powers, no matter what. But... I must have accidentally wished myself invisible.* Panic propelled her to her feet. All eyes raked her. The irremovable necklace flared from warm to blistering.

"Stupid little fool!" The familiar inner voice boomed like a bomb in her brain.

Exe froze as an icy finger crept down the back of her neck, under her collar, searching. It curled around the unbreakable chain, quickly twisting the scorching metal until the fiery amethyst jewel lay exposed at the base of Exe's throat—choking her.

Exe whirled around, coming face-to-face with the man in black. His mirrored sunglasses unshuttered like the lens of a camera, revealing cold, diamond-hard eyes.

"I knew I'd be the one to find you," the man in black said in the same dark and dangerous voice that had skulked into Exe's mind.

BANG! Windowpanes shuddered as a brilliant white light flashed through the schoolhouse, blinding Exe and everyone else for a moment. In that sightless, instantaneous moment, the man in black vanished.

"No flash photography, please," her AP history teacher droned while Exe's apparently-oblivious classmates paged listlessly through their vintage textbooks.

Only Easy was looking at Exe now, a question in his eyes. Exe shook her head at him and grasped her necklace, mindlessly relieved to find it still there. Without her help, the chain untwisted itself, and the quickly-cooling pendant dropped back out of sight.

What just happened?

Before Exe could decide if she should sit back down or run and hide, the teacher ended class with a tug on the school bell rope. The picked-on boy shuffled out with the rest of the tourists, holding his mom's hand as if nothing disturbing had just happened. Exe barely registered him leaving. *Where is the man in black?!*

"Forget him. You're safe now. No thanks to you," the familiar voice mocked.

I hate it when the voice mocks me. Exe stopped cold. *The voice. Not my voice. If that man in black inserted his own voice into my head, could this familiar voice belong to someone else, too?*

Even as Exe thought this, it felt as if that other voice was trying to force the memory of the man in black out of her mind. *Fading the memory.* The strange phrase struck Exe as a forgotten thought recovered. Closing her eyes, she focused solely on remembering the guy in shades, even as a part of her fought to forget him.

"What are you doing?" Exe opened her eyes to find Easy standing there, an arm around each of the girls he'd silently chatted up during class. "You okay?"

Exe could only nod, afraid that she'd forget the man in black if she spoke.

"Who is she?" one of the girls bit out, as if Exe might be a threat to her precarious position as a 'girl of interest' to Easy.

"My sister," Easy smiled. "And your new best friend."

Great, more pretend friends, Exe thought as both girls rushed her, gushing as if they were her long-lost BFFs. *Well, I have only myself to blame.*

A few years back, Exe had finally convinced Easy that she really didn't want friends. Unfortunately, Easy saw Exe's voluntarily friendless status as an opportunity. So now he, Seph, and Thone had girls masquerade as Exe's friends so they could attend sleepovers at the Parsells' house. Exe went along with Easy's plan, mainly to keep Ella from worrying about her lack of companionship. Her only condition was that the romances had to stay strictly PG, or the deal was off.

Exe didn't have the heart to tell Easy how cruel his scheme felt—because her friendless status wasn't exactly voluntary, it was necessary. *If he knew that I only avoid relationships because they're too dangerous, he'd never ask me to fake friendships that I can never have. If only friendships weren't so dangerous. If only I weren't so dangerous.*

"So girls, shall we make our way to my new pad?" Easy looked at each of them as if they were the only girl in the world. "Which one of you wants to navigate?"

Both girls abandoned Exe and reached for the map Easy held. The winner read the directions triumphantly, "You live in the Second First? Sweet!"

"We haven't seen it yet. Today's the first day for everything," Easy motioned for the girls to lead the way, waiting until they'd moved out of earshot before turning to Exe. "What's wrong? You look like you just stared death in the face."

Exe thought hard for a long minute, "Nothing. Not that I can remember."

CHAPTER FIVE

FOREVER AND EVER, AMEN

"**N**ever?" Henny-Boy's eyes were as wide as the Mexican crepes on his plate.

"Never," Ella confirmed. "Welcome home for the last time."

Exe's brothers passed plates of Ella's funky fusion dinner down the table in stunned silence. Even Easy looked surprised. Ella and Rove may have told him they were moving to Nowhere, but they clearly hadn't told him everything.

Rove had semi-retired—which meant that this was the last first supper in a new home that the Parsells would ever have. Exe couldn't believe it. Her family had moved every few years for her entire life. *How strange to know that we'll never move again.*

"You mean, we're gonna live here forever?" Charley asked, adding an adorable salute as he addressed his father. "Forever and ever?"

"Amen." The whole table laughed at Moth's apropos joke, since they had just moved into a church—an Old World-style mission to be exact—with a soaring bell tower and snowy, limestone stucco walls that gleamed coolly amidst its sizzling desert setting.

"We're officially done with the nomadic life," Rove smiled.

"But why relocate here, sir?" Seph asked politely, while wolfing down his food.

"The Second First Lutheran Church of Nowhere is a remarkable piece of architecture with a fascinating history, son," Rove answered. "Nowhere's population exploded in 1892, when rumor of a local gold strike spread. The town got so crowded, the First Church on Main Street had to hold seven services every Sunday. So the townsfolk built this large mission to replace it. But not one service was ever held here because most people moved away before it was finished. Do any of you know why?"

Rove looked at Easy, who stuttered under the sudden interrogation. Instead of listening, he'd been silently encouraging his brothers to eat as quickly as possible before the festivities began. After all, now that the Parsells were staying put, today's casually invited guests were suddenly in the running to be lifelong friends.

"Because the mine was a bust," Rove answered his own question.

"But our teacher called this a mining town," Henny-Boy puzzled.

"It was," Ella confirmed. "They just never found anything in the mine. Funnily enough, the townsfolk chose the name 'Nowhere' so they wouldn't be lying when shady types asked them where they found their gold. But no gold was ever found. So people moved on and this would-be mission was transformed into an army outpost."

"According to my research, the town voted to preserve Nowhere as it was in the 1890s, even though the mine went bust," Moth remarked. "It's the smartest decision local officials ever made, turning its history as a gold mining failure into a moneymaker."

"Very true, son. And we're lucky to live in this small piece of our new town's history," Rove replied. "After the army abandoned it in the early 1900s, the government entrusted this mission to the town's historical society. But it was so neglected due to its historical insignificance that the chapel across the courtyard had almost completely collapsed before I converted it into the master bedroom suite."

"We're very lucky. This building only came on the market the minute we started shopping for properties," Ella said. "It's almost as if we were destined to live here."

Ella's words stirred a tingling of suspicion in Exe— that mysteriously faded as she savored another bite of her mother's spicy crepe.

"This place is really impressive, Dad," Seph said. "But why did you stick all six of us boys up in the balcony? A soon-to-be college-bound man needs a little privacy."

All eyes turned to the balcony where two triple-stacked bunk-beds towered over the nave that Rove had converted into an open-plan dining and living room.

"The privacy of a barracks is all any young man needs, Seph," Rove said. "You boys get into enough trouble when I'm looking right at you. If you've got any more complaining to do, we could return to zero six hundred calisthenics. Interested?"

"Sir, no sir," Seph executed a precision salute.

"Oh, I don't think a balcony bedroom is that bad," Easy grinned, eyeing the exposed beams overhead. "I can think of all sorts of fun to be had up there."

"If you crack your skulls performing some crazy stunt on those ceiling beams, I'm enlisting you all in the army," Ella threatened. Only Charley seemed to half-believe her.

"No swinging from the rafters. Got it," Easy promised, collecting plates whether his brothers had finished or not. "Thanks for the history lesson, sir." When all the other boys joined in clearing the table too, Exe assumed that they were still on KP duty as punishment for the last prank they'd pulled.

"But why retire to Nowhere, sir?" Thone asked, carrying a stack of dirty dishes into the transept where Rove had installed the kitchen. "It's literally—nowhere."

Thone's right. A fissure of alarm opened deep in Exe's mind. *Rove does love history. But moving to a town where all residents are required to dress-up and role-play in period costumes? That's the last thing he'd willingly want to do.*

"We fell in love with this town years ago, didn't we dear?" Ella clasped Rove's hand and smiled lovingly at him. "We always swore we'd retire here someday."

"That's right," Rove patted her arm. "We were so impressed with the immersive-history lifestyle that we wanted you all to experience it before you flew the coop, Seph."

Neither Ella nor Rove gave any indication that they were still upset from this morning's incident. They were so serene that Exe almost wondered if she'd imagined it—were it not for the hundreds of tiny cuts dotting Ella's face like bloody freckles.

Wait, they wanted to move here? The memory was fuzzy, but she was pretty sure Rove hadn't wanted to this morning. *That's what the whole fight was about!*

"*Or was it?*"

No. Now that I think about it, my parents weren't fighting. I only wished for the glass to eavesdrop because they were talking about the move, and I wanted to help Easy win the bet. Exe felt sick at the realization that she'd hurt Ella for such a silly reason.

"Ready to show your new friends to your room, Exe?" Ella's whisper startled Exe. She'd been so lost in thought, she hadn't even noticed that a whole horde of local kids had arrived. Ella indicated the handful of gorgeous teenage girls clutching overnight bags gathered behind Exe. From the sounds of it, her brothers had already led a wild gang of potential guy friends up to their balcony bedroom.

"My room?" Exe asked, still feeling like she'd forgotten something important.

"Your own room and long overdue," Ella replied, smoothing Exe's tangled hair. "A fifteen-year-old girl shouldn't have to share a bedroom with a bunch of brothers."

"Where is there space for my own bedroom?" Exe asked. "Some closet?"

"No, it's much better than that," Ella smiled, indicating a small door in the far wall where the altar would've stood. "But I should warn you, it's not finished yet."

Exe's momentary elation faded once she opened the tiny door. Stacks of boxes filled the small, octagon room. *And I have to share this closet with these strange girls?*

"Do you think we can all fit in here?" one perky redhead asked.

"There's more space than you think," Ella smiled mysteriously. The girls rushed by Exe in their excitement and disappeared behind the cardboard towers. Soon a rumble of footsteps echoed overhead. Exe peeked in, peering upward.

"A bell tower bedroom, isn't it fabulous?" Ella enthused. "Four stories high with large landings on the first three levels. You've got a dressing room on the first, your bed on the next. Then maybe a desk or a reading nook on the third, you decide. There's also the belfry, but it isn't safe up there yet. Plus this lower level, after you unpack your boxes. And that other door there leads outside. A private entrance, isn't that exciting?"

"Just call me Rapunzel," Exe turned away from her mother's eager expression to gaze up at the winding staircase. "Or Hunchback."

"Oh Exe, we're not locking you up in here," Ella said. "You're not a monster."

"If you say so," Exe muttered, knowing her sarcastic tone cut Ella deeper than any glass shards could. *Why do I always wind up hurting the people I care about?* "I like it, Mom. I'm sure it'll be great... eventually."

"Almost everything has the potential to be great, Exe," Ella replied. "Bedrooms, friends, you. You just need to relax, stop worrying, and learn how to let things be great."

"I'll try," Exe gave the answer Ella wanted to hear with a stiff smile, but deep down she knew it wasn't true. *I can't relax. What kind of damage would I do if I did?*

The pale, limestone walls towered starkly overhead as Exe climbed the first set of stairs to the makeshift dressing room. The landing, with its wide, interior balcony, looked like a war zone and these bombshells were prepping for the next battle with fresh coats of cosmetics and sassy wardrobe changes.

Exe had seen this war fought before by dozens of other girls hoping to conquer a Parsell brother. Few had ever emerged victorious. With a sickening shock, Exe realized that Boho Babe from AP History was one of the contenders. *It always hurts more to fake a friendship with someone I'd actually like to befriend.*

"I wish I looked good in red lipstick," the perky redhead said.

"I wish I knew if Seph liked me in red lipstick," a stunning brunette returned.

"I wish I knew if Thone liked me," Boho Babe sighed wistfully. And suddenly the girls were "I wishing" all kinds of silly romantic thoughts.

I wish. Her two most dangerous words. Exe quickly closed her eyes and blanked her mind as she silently chanted her familiar mantra: *I want nothing. I need nothing.*

"School ended hours ago, why are you still in costume?" The redhead eyed Exe's calico dress, stifling a giggle. "Haven't you outgrown 'Little House on the Prairie?'"

"Oh, no. I mean, yes. I've outgrown– this dress. I mean, changing. I should," Exe gathered a random outfit and headed up the next flight of stairs to the bedroom landing. *There's no way I'm changing clothes in front of those girls.* A whole floor up and she could still hear them gossiping and giggling.

After changing, Exe curled up on the stack of mattresses made up into a bed along the balcony railing. As she blocked out their happy voices, forgotten thoughts floated into mind. *Aunt Goldie. She lives in Nowhere, doesn't she? If I can find her, she can help me get rid of these powers. Or at least teach me to control them better so that I don't–*

"*Forget about Aunt Goldie,*" the familiar inner voice said. "*She's not important. Just go read a book, or watch the teleevision, or play a vo-dee-o-doh game.*"

Exe cracked a smile. *Video game. I meant to think video game.* The hundred-degree heat outside had probably exhausted her mind, though the bell tower was surprisingly cool. "*Anyway, you'd better join in before your mother gets upset that you're stewing alone.*" Ella was always haranguing Exe about her self-imposed solitude.

"Knock, knock? You girls ready?" Easy called out. Soon a thunder of footsteps pounded up the stairs, followed by a barrage of giggling screams.

Exe pressed her head against the filigreed balcony railing to peer down on the landing below. Her brothers and their friends were chasing around trying to put makeup on each other. Exe traced her platinum chain and pulled the smoky amethyst pendant into her palm. Somehow she found comfort in holding it whenever she felt lonely.

"Hey, where's Exe?" Seph asked as the perky redhead tried to lipstick him.

"Visiting the bats in the belfry, I assume," the stunning brunette replied, fluttering her lashes at Seph. "She completely abandoned us in this tomb of a room."

"Tomb? That's not very nice," Boho Babe defended, winning the reward of Thone's arm draped across her shoulders. "Maybe a little stark with these white walls, but what damsel wouldn't want a tower bedroom."

"I lobbied for these digs myself," Easy said, smiling at the miffed brunette. "But the 'rents nixed it. Just imagine the mischief we'd get up to in here."

"We'd wind up dying in some stunt of yours like bungee jumping from the belfry," Thone said. "That's why they gave the bell tower to their only sensible kid."

"Speaking of dead things, guess what we have for a backyard?" Easy enthused.

"No way," one of the invited guys gasped. "You own the graveyard, too?"

"We own dead bodies?" Seph asked, unsettled by the idea. "Is that even legal?"

"I checked with Dad, and he says yes," Easy answered. "No one's been buried there for over seventy-five years, so the town included the old cemetery in the sale. It's all ours. Can you imagine what booty some of those bodies might've been buried with?"

"You wanna dig one up, don't you?" Thone proposed. "Could be cool."

"The bodies are probably dust by now," Seph reasoned, crossing his arms over his chest. Exe knew he was masking his squeamishness, both to save face and avoid the torture his brothers would put him through if they learned of his fear of the grotesque.

"Digging up dead bodies is just ghoulish," the perky redhead shivered.

"Fine. We'll save that for another day," Easy relented, drafting the stunning brunette as tonight's date. "Besides, I've got another ghastly game in mind. If you dare."

With that mysterious message, Easy and the others tore down the stairs. As soon they were gone, Exe pressed the cold amethyst pendant to her hot, embarrassed face. Her brothers had barely even noticed that she was missing.

Always invited, but never included. Maybe deep down they know that I'm too dangerous to have around.

Exe crept back downstairs to stare at herself in the dressing table mirror. Taking in her pale face, tangled burgundy hair, and the faded old concert tee she'd thrown on, Exe couldn't help wondering what she'd look like if she quit trying so hard to blend into the background. *Maybe I don't have to hide behind my mother's hand-me-downs. Could I be like those stylish girls?*

"No. So quit dawdling, or Ella will drag you outside to play with your 'friends.'"

With a sigh, Exe made her way downstairs. It was as pointless to wonder what she might look like if she stopped hiding as it was to dream about a life freed from her dangerous powers. Both were impossibilities.

CHAPTER SIX

GRAVE TRUTHS

The bell tower's private entrance led Exe out back into their cemetery. Stepping outside was like walking into a fireplace, even though the sun had already slipped behind the headstone-dotted foothill that dominated their backyard.

Darting amongst the gravestones, Exe's brothers and their friends were engaged in a gigantic game of graveyard tag—an event sure to be the talk of the school on Monday. Exe had no intention of joining in. She just had to wait for Ella to see that she was socializing, then she could go sort through her jumbled thoughts in solitude.

Deep darkness came quickly in the desert once the sun went down. Only moonlight kept Exe from stumbling as she trudged through the tombstones and teenagers, up the grave-covered foothill toward the low stone wall that marked the edge of their property. Sun-heated rocks burned through the flimsy fabric of her shorts as she sat gingerly on the wall. Exe suppressed the temptation to wish the stones cooler. *I'm more likely to explode the fence than successfully cool it down.*

Beyond the stone wall, an eerie, abandoned mansion stood dark and lonely, with broken shutters and peeling paint. *Like the one in Hitchcock's 'Psycho.'* She'd picked up that vintage flick (with its infamous shower murder) on VHS for a nickel at a yard sale.

Across the way, the silvery-white cupola atop her bell tower glistened in the moonlight. *If anyone were in the belfry right now, we'd be eye-level with one another.*

Down below, little lights flickered like fireflies buzzing around the cemetery as the teens used flashlights and cellphones to keep the game going in the darkness. *I probably should've stayed down below too, so Ella could see me. But maybe she'll just assume I'm part of the shadowy fray.*

Exe had never known nighttime to be so murky. Until now, the Parsells had been city people. Out here, away from urban lights, the pitch blackness brought a contemplative solitude like she'd never experienced before. Sitting alone in that still darkness, listening to the steady whirr of cicadas (which sounded like thousands of tiny wind-up toys wobbling around the mountainside), Exe felt a strange, restless clarity.

The unexpected emotion unsettled her, causing forgotten images and questions to bubble up, then vanish as if imprisoned in a dark, thick tar. *"Maybe if you tried writing them down in your diary..."*

Not a bad idea. Writing in Aunt Goldie's journals did sometimes help her recover lost memories. Then those thoughts that had seemed so mysterious and important became unimportant once she put pen to paper. *"Write it and forget it. As always."*

"So, are you and Easy twins?" a smiley guy brushed his flashlight beam across Exe. "Same age, grade, names start with E. You don't look alike, but it's pretty obvious."

"What? No. I'm lonely. Only. I'm an only child. No, not only, just not born. Together," Exe fumbled for words, grateful that the darkness hid her blush.

"Not twins, got it," the smiley guy sat down close beside her. "So, why aren't you playing graveyard tag with the rest of us?"

"I don't– play. Ever," Exe mumbled, edging away. "Do you? I mean, you should– stay, I mean play, away. From me, away. I mean play."

"I am playing. I'm *it*," smiley guy leaned closer.

Trepidation filled Exe as his friendliness invaded her solitude, stirring up dangerous hopes. Exe closed her eyes, afraid that she might wish him away—and that wish would be granted in some horrific fashion.

"*One deep breath, two. Stay in control.*" Exe opened her eyes.

Smiley guy was still there, softly smiling. Suddenly, a brilliant white light flashed around them. Exe shielded her eyes against the beams. Her three older brothers had abruptly abandoned their hiding places. Even Moth, Henny-Boy, and Charley had deserted the 'gladiator' game they'd been trying to stage between a scorpion and a lizard to shine their flashlights on her and the smiley guy. *Protecting me without my asking, just like clockwork.*

"I told you, our sister is strictly off limits," Easy charged. With a shrug, smiley guy hopped off the wall and jogged down the hill. Her brothers flicked off their flashlights and vanished back into the darkness, laughing good-naturedly.

Laughing at the spectacle of someone even thinking about liking me. I shouldn't have come out here. I should've joined the younger boys—even though they look at me as more of a babysitter than a playmate these days. If only–

"You want nothing, you need nothing," The familiar voice thrummed in her mind.

"I want nothing, I need– Nothing. I want– I want– I need," Exe stuttered through the anti-wish chant until she felt empty and emotionless once again.

"You're so sleepy... It has been a long, grueling day..." Alone again on the stone wall, sleepiness seeped into Exe's bones, along with the sudden urge to hide in bed with her old, portable TV/VCR. *"There's peace in sleep. You won't think anymore..."*

Wait, bed now? The sun's barely set. I can't–

"Just go to bed, you stupid fool!"

Fear fired through her like a lightning strike, setting her necklace aflame. With absolute certainty she knew: *That voice isn't mine!*

Exe's skin prickled as a sensation of being watched flared. Slowly she turned. Just a few feet behind her, almost lost in the shadow cast by that spooky old house, stood an old man—skeleton-scrawny, with baggy clothes cut in the style of a long-gone era—and he was staring right at her.

He knows me. That scary, scowling skeleton-man knows me.

"Quit staring at that man. He doesn't matter. Nothing matters except that no one wants you around. They want you to leave so they can laugh at you, even your brothers."

Anguished humiliation instantly overwhelmed Exe. She staggered back down the hill and up into her tower, pausing only to grab bedding, her portable TV, and a few videotapes. A suppressed sob threatened to burst out of her on every ladder rung as she climbed up to the belfry. Skirting the rusted bell, Exe collapsed onto the narrow balcony surrounding the belfry's cupola. But there was little solace in solitude this time.

Exe popped in a random tape and pressed play. Thankfully it was the campy camp comedy 'Poison Ivy,' starring that guy from 'Back to the Future.' A film only available on VHS. *Forgotten and abandoned, just like me.* Still, the silly story soothed her, helping her forget the crippling humiliation.

A few hours later, Exe pressed pause to watch a handful of firefly flashlights creep up the hillside and bounce over the low stone wall surrounding the haunted house. They were eye-level with her lonely tower now. If they glanced over, they'd see her. *Sad and forlorn in the flickering glow of my tiny TV.*

None did. Instead, those firefly lights fled when the haunted house blazed to life, all its lights flickering on, then off again, as the laughing teens ran back down the hill.

More hours slipped by before those firefly lights slowly trickled inside. Soon Exe heard mischievous murmurs below as the girls went to bed, and then the tower fell quiet. Only the cicadas whirred on, and the distant howls of a roving coyote crying to the moon. *Alone again. Just the cicadas, the coyotes, and me. Dreamless. Wishless. Hopeless.*

"You want nothing. You need nothing. Don't think. Just close your eyes and forget." The mantra offered calmness, but no comfort. As the TV droned, Exe's mind drifted, knocking softly against inconsequential thoughts, but dwelling on none.

She awoke later to the fuzzy burr of snow on her reception-less television. And another sound. Cut, crunch, then a metallic fling. Over and over. Next, the distant bang of a door silenced the cicadas. Exe's mind only vaguely registered the sounds and the sliver of light spilling down the hillside as someone emerged from the spooky house.

Exe's sleepy eyes focused in on the scowling skeleton-man. He was carrying something large and long, and heavy. Over the wall, the skeleton-man hauled that heavy thing. Down he dropped it, into a hole in front of a tombstone. Then, shoveling again.

A body. In a grave. Skeleton-man is burying a body in my backyard—on top of the casket of some poor, long-dead soul. Terror trickled. Her cool pendant grew warm.   Suddenly, the shoveling stopped. Exe feigned sleep, her breaths shallow and ragged as she stifled her flickering fear. After a minute or two, the shoveling began again.

Did my creepy neighbor really bury a body in our backyard? I'll have to dig it up to know for sure. As the midnight sky faded into dawn gray—long after the skeleton-man had vanished back inside his haunted house—Exe decided it was safe to investigate. Instinctively, Exe blanked her mind as she tiptoed around the sleeping girls, so that fear wouldn't make her loudly clumsy as she snuck back down the tower.

The hot, dusky air outside was still oppressive as Exe climbed up the hill. The earth in front of one gravestone was recently overturned. *But is a fresh body buried there?* She needed proof before she told anyone else. Only she didn't have a shovel—and digging by hand would take too long anyway.

I'll have to risk wishing. Fingers crossed, Exe formed a clear and specific wish. The loose-dirt mound trembled, shifting and spilling until the dusty earth split wide. A bulky, man-sized bundle of tattered tapestry arose, coming to rest on the re-formed dirt mound as if on a funeral pyre, just waiting for flames to turn it to cinders. Once settled, Exe unwrapped the rug to reveal the body. *A familiar body.*

The sudden flash of memory sent Exe stumbling backwards. The man who had been hunting for her in the schoolhouse now lay dirt-stained and lifeless at her feet. His face still hidden in the shadows of his upturned collar. Dead eyes masked by the silver circles of his mirrored sunglasses. *The man in black.*

The trauma of seeing her first dead body was nothing compared to the second shockwave. Clutched in his rigor mortis-stiffened grip, Exe saw a poster emblazoned with her face. It read:

"Experience Verelustre."

"Dangerous."

"Wanted."

"Dead."

CHAPTER SEVEN

Solve for Exe

"What is the value of x?"

Her math teacher's question barely registered as Exe slumped in the back row, far corner desk doodling UROK across her worksheet. No one at her back and a clear path to the exit was the only way she felt safe now. Yet the unshakable feeling that she was being hunted had her scanning the mountain outside the window every few minutes.

Someone wants me dead.

Though it felt like a lifetime, it had only been two days since she'd unearthed that freshly dead body clutching the wanted poster plastered with her face. She'd spent the rest of the weekend hiding out in her tower, staring at it, even though that relentless nag in her head berated her, *"Forget it! It's meaningless!"* But as hard as the voice tried, the presence of the poster wouldn't let her forget the death-frozen grin on the pasty, dirt-stained face of the man in black.

Exe had become so obsessed, she even faked sick so that she could cower under her covers without any peanut gallery commentary from her family. In those long, lonely hours (when not utterly terrified that other trench-coated thugs might come for her) she studied the poster and wondered: *Who wants me dead?*

After playing ill all weekend, she either had to go to school or to the doctor. Playing at normal seemed easier than facing probing medical questions, so Exe went, even though that's exactly what the intrusive, nagging voice wanted her to do.

Ignoring the odd looks from Easy, who lounged beside her, Exe propped up her math book to block potential onlookers. Once hidden, she smoothed out the crumpled poster to study it yet again—though she'd memorized it by now.

Most of the words she knew, however a few were entirely unfamiliar: 'Disimulata,' 'Anacapia,' and 'Jettani.' She'd searched online, and even scoured old dictionaries, but hadn't come up with anything meaningful to explain them. And her last name on it. Not Parsell. *Verelustre. My real last name?* It didn't seem at all familiar. Not that it should. She'd been with the Parsells since age two.

Why does someone want me dead? The possible answers to that nagging question kept her spinning. *No one knows I'm responsible for Bonnie's death. And if they did, wouldn't the police just arrest me? They wouldn't print up some ominous poster and have me hunted down by some spook dressed up like a spaghetti western villain—not even in authenticity-obsessed Nowhere.*

Exe read the poster again: 'By order of Jettani, Revered Seren of Anacapia.' Some ruler of a place she'd never heard of had ordered her execution. *Why?* If Anacapia was the name of her birth country, what could she have done that its ruler wanted her dead? *I would've been a baby! If I ever even lived there.*

Exe stared at the poster (all black-and-white elegance, except for her amethyst eyes), desperately close to wishing for answers to reveal themselves. Her eyes raked the photographs, scrutinizing the familiar, yet strange face staring back at her.

Faces, she qualified, front-view and side. *A classic mug shot.* Suddenly it struck her: *I've never posed for photos like this in my whole life.* Exe studied the photos again. The face was hers, the eyes were even amethyst, but everything else was unfamiliar; including the retro, straight-from-the-1930s clothes she wore in the photo.

And that hair. Exe rarely bothered with her hair at all, except to dye it. While her locks had been lots of colors over the years (so much so that she couldn't even recall her original hue), it had never been "raven black" as the poster described. *My inner nag always steered me away from that shade.* But in the poster's photo, she had gleaming ebony tresses cascading in a sleek wave down a single side of her face. One dramatic curl perfectly placed to allow her eye to peek through, just like a silver screen starlet from Hollywood's golden age.

The evidence was clear—it simply couldn't be her in the photos. *Someone has obviously photoshopped my first name and face onto someone else's old wanted poster.* Although the poster's photos certainly didn't appear to be altered.

"You see? It's a prank poster from the old timey photo place on Main Street, planted by your brothers and their friends," her inner voice argued. *"And the body, just a mannequin, placed there to scare you. Chalk it up to mean-spirited teasing and forget it."*

I don't buy it, Exe argued with herself. Her brothers would never torment her like that—and they wouldn't let anyone else tease her either. Plus the poster wasn't from the local photo shop. She'd checked, and the photographer said he only made sepia-tinted, Old West wanted posters. This one had a sleek Art Deco style, like a 1930s playbill.

"Your brothers know that the 1930s is your favorite era and that you're obsessed with Art Deco, so they designed a fake poster with a style you'd appreciate."

Maybe someone did fake the poster—but that didn't change the fact that Exe had taken it off of a dead man. *This is no prank, this is real. And if it's real, this poster proves that there are other people like me around here, doesn't it?*

"No."

"Earth to Exe," Easy said, prodding her in the arm. "We need an answer."

With a start, Exe realized that the entire class was staring at her.

"I asked, 'What is the value of x, Exe?'" the teacher repeated her lame joke.

"Um," Exe stared at the complex equation on the whiteboard without a clue as to how to solve it. "Unknown?"

"I suppose that's true," the teacher said. Shushing the laughing class, she asked another student, "How do we find out its value? Tell me, what do we know about x?"

Exe sank back behind her math book and stared at her wanted poster, considering the question. *What do I know about myself?* As the teacher started a list of math facts on the board, Exe decided to make one for herself.

"You're never going to pass this class if you don't pay attention. Quit thinking about yourself and focus on problems you can solve. Or can't you?"

Ignoring the inner nag challenging her math skills, Exe tried to write the list, but her whirlwind thoughts whisked each grain of knowledge away. Jotting fast, Exe grasped each passing memory as it danced by: Aunt Goldie lives in Nowhere... the man in black... adopted from Nowhere... the 'Wanted: Dead' poster... all of it. Once she was finished, Exe scoured her mind, certain she was missing something.

The dead man... I'd seen him somewhere before. The schoolhouse, yes. Then dead in the graveyard. But before that? No. Wait... The field. She'd seen him standing in the center of that field where they'd had the flat tire. If she closed her eyes, she could see him there, just for a moment before he'd vanished.

"Forget that field."

The note of warning in that odd demand startled Exe, but she added the field to her list anyway. Picturing the man in black alive instantly recalled grotesque images of him dead. Bloodless skin. Slack jaw. Stiff, waxy hands that almost tore the poster as she'd pried it from his death-stiffened grip.

According to the poster, the man in black wanted to kill her, but he's the one who wound up dead. *Who killed him? And why?* Exe didn't know why, but she was pretty sure she knew who—and she quickly added it to the list:

- Skeleton-man killed the man in black and buried his body in our yard
- Which means my neighbor is a dangerous murderer

The math teacher clapped her hands to recapture the students' wandering attention and pointed back and forth between her math facts list and the complex equation. "Now I know this problem looks exactly like all the others we've been working on, so you'd think it would be an easy solve. But there's a trick to this one. We need to question what we think we know about x in order to discover what we don't know."

Exe turned a critical eye toward her own list. *Is it all true?*

"Of course not, you've dreamed most of it up to feel more important than you actually are. Get over yourself and focus on real life."

Refusing to be deterred, Exe circled what she knew was true. Aunt Goldie's gifts from Nowhere. Definitely true, according to the return labels. Adopted from Nowhere. After a moment's hesitation, Exe circled that one, too. The memory was fuzzy, but she was almost certain she'd heard that fact from her parents.

The man in black's attack on her, his death, and burial. That had all definitely happened—she had the poster to prove it. *But did the skeleton-man kill him?* Exe hadn't seen the man in black die—he'd just vanished from the schoolhouse, then turned up dead and buried in her backyard.

Why would my neighbor murder a man carrying my 'Wanted: Dead' poster? Does that mean skeleton-man knows me? If he does, can he teach me how to control my powers? Maybe. *But will he?* The way he'd stared at her when she'd sat on his wall—the daggers in his eyes said he despised her. *But if he hates me, why kill the man in black?*

The poster said that Exe was wanted dead, not dead or alive. Which meant that the man in black's death had saved her life. *So, does the skeleton-man hate me? Or does he want to protect me?* She simply didn't have enough facts to know. Underneath dangerous murderer, Exe wrote, 'Friend or foe?'

"Put these unanswerable questions to rest. When it's time for you to know the truth, the answers will present themselves to you. Quit looking for them."

"I can't quit. Not knowing is driving me mad," Exe whispered aloud.

"It's pretty simple once you've learned the trick," Easy slid his math paper toward her, revealing his solution to the complex equation. "Need me to go over it with you?"

"No thanks. This is a problem I have to solve on my own," Exe said, barely listening to Easy. AP History was next, and its teacher might just have the answers she needed about Aunt Goldie, and the creep living in the house behind theirs. The second the bell rang, Exe shoved her books into her overstuffed backpack and ran for the door.

"Exe, wait! Why the rush?" Easy sprinted over with several papers in his outstretched hand. "You forgot these. 'UROK.' What's up with that? Not algebra, that's for sure. 'You rock?' No, wait, 'U-R-O-K...' 'You are okay.' Are you?"

"I'm fine," Exe fidgeted, anxious to dash to her next class.

"Really? Is that why you made this?" Easy asked, holding up her poster.

"Don't touch that," Exe's savage grab for the poster startled them both. She shoved it into her pocket and started walking.

"Wanted: Dead. That's pretty dramatic, even for you. Or didn't you make it?" Easy asked. "Did someone send it to you? Is some kid here hassling you already?"

"It's not important. Just a joke."

Exactly. A joke on you. Exe frowned inwardly at the nag's annoying timing.

"Where'd you get it? Not from the Main Street shop, or I'd get a gangster one like that for Henny-Boy," Easy jogged ahead, blocking her from entering the classroom. "Are you in trouble? You need to tell me. I don't want my little sister feeling helpless."

"You are helpless, you hopeless case. So crawl back into your creephole and forget all of this nonsense. If you persist, you'll just make everything worse."

Exe stared into Easy's pleading, searching eyes, unable to answer. She was in trouble, and she wanted desperately to tell him. *But it isn't safe. "You are helpless."*

No! Exe refused to give in to that vicious inner voice. She wouldn't allow herself to wallow in feeble self-pity. Not anymore. *I'm NOT helpless.*

"I am okay, remember?" Exe gave Easy a small smile, pointing to her UROK-covered math paper. She slipped by him, grateful to find the back corner seats open—another perk of being Easy's sister. "I have to be," Exe whispered to herself as a handful of classmates drew Easy's attention. "I'm not giving up until I've got answers."

Exe's AP History teacher was no help in answering any of the questions on her list. Instead, he'd directed her to search the town archives housed in Nowhere's courthouse-turned-museum. Exe wove her way through the sweaty, noisy throng of tourists crowding Main Street—so on edge that she almost wished a faux outlaw into oblivion because his dark duster and cowboy hat made him look like the man in black.

Standing tall and stately amongst the fake fronts lining the street, Nowhere's brick courthouse was the only building in Old Town that actually had two stories—and air conditioning. Exe rushed up the stone steps, hoping to escape the heat and the crowds. But the lobby was too jam-packed to be cool or calming. The place was crawling with student groups corralled by haggard teachers, and families posing for pictures by dubious displays of horseshoes, wagon wheels, and mannequins dressed in generic western wear.

The din faded into cold, creepy silence as Exe climbed the grand staircase to the deserted second floor. Her steps echoed off the cracked plaster walls as she searched the placards on the closed doors for one marked 'Archives.' Most were locked, empty offices for the town's highest officials— including the mayor. Only the door to the town's lone functioning courtroom stood open, but it didn't look like it ever saw much legal drama.

The jury box was stacked high with dusty files, and both judge and bailiff were asleep at their posts, like well-made automatons waiting for some lost tourist to take them up on the sign that read: "Ask us about Nowhere's epic(ish) judicial history."

On a tiny door tucked into a hidden alcove at the end of the hall, Exe spotted a ragged sign for the archives, featuring a hand-drawn arrow pointing up. Opening the door, Exe found stairs so narrow and steep that they were practically a ladder—in a space so tight, you'd have to retreat if anyone came down while you were going up.

Taking a deep breath to control her claustrophobia, Exe clambered up as fast as she could, emerging in a mammoth attic crammed floor-to-ceiling with boxes, books, and scores of old documents in haphazard stacks. A small, newspaper-strewn desk nearby had a rusty old cowbell on it and two little signs. The first read, 'The Librarian is: IN,' and the second had just one name: 'Monalea.'

Exe peered around the shadowy room. There was no sign of life, so she gave the dented cowbell a few good shakes. At the discordant clangs, a faint voice echoed through the attic, but Exe could only make out the words, "Bell... order... knock."

"Hello?" Exe called. Heading in the voice's direction, Exe searched through the rows of bookshelves to no avail. "Monalea?"

"Ahhh," a dusky voice ebbed from behind Exe. She whirled around and found a quirky young woman wearing a beaded, drop-waist chemise dress, crimson cat-eye glasses, and dozens of Bakelite bangles from wrist to elbow. Her shiny black hair twisted over each ear into two ornately-woven, winged buns.

A 1920s flapper dress, 1930s eyeglasses, retro bracelets, all designed with the same Art Deco style that's on the poster—she's got to be a part of this!

"Sorry, I didn't mean to interrupt," Exe apologized. The woman said nothing, regarding Exe with an unreadable expression. "Did I interrupt you? It sounded like you, um, made a discovery. Or something. Did you?"

"Always," the woman replied. "Why do you ask?"

"Um, because you said, 'ahhh,'" Exe said.

"I said 'ah' because you said 'oh,'" the woman replied with a sphinxlike smile.

"Oh, you must not have heard me. I was calling your name. Monalea, right?"

"Wrong. And 'oh,' I did hear you. Saying 'Moan,' like you were groaning," Monalea's smile widened. "It's 'ahhh, as in M-AH-nalea. Not 'moan.'"

"Sorry," Exe's face grew warm. "So, Mahnalea. Is that you?"

"It is my name. Not me. What can I help you with, fresh face?"

"Fresh, what?"

"You are new to town, so you're a fresh face," Monalea said, gliding through the stacks, plucking books and documents as if she understood the order of the chaotic attic.

"How could you know that?" Hope glimmered as Exe trailed the mysterious (*Possibly mystical!*) librarian. *She knows me! Maybe she has powers too!*

"My ancestors have been a part of this land since before Nowhere was founded," Monalea replied, wending her way toward a small bookcase near the stairs. "As the town's historian, it's my job to know every single citizen. And since tourists never find their way up to my archives, you must be a local that I've ever met. We've only accepted the application of one new family in the last seven months. That makes you a Parsell. Experience Parsell, correct? No middle name—unlike your brothers. Interesting."

"So you do know me, don't you? Even before we even moved here," Exe tried to keep her excitement in check. *This is it. She knows. She'll have answers.*

"Wrong!" Exe jumped at the nagging voice's blaring retort.

"Of course," Monalea answered Exe's question. "From the photo your parents submitted with the citizenship application. Let me give you the tour. This shelf contains every book ever written on Nowhere—all locally published by my press. I recommend the thickest one—that's mine. It'll have all you need for your report. Now if you don't mind, I'm on my lunch break, and I've got my own college classwork to do before reopening my gift store downstairs."

With that, Monalea seated herself at her desk and began sifting through all she'd collected on her stroll through the attic. Exe stared at her in confusion, then turned to peruse the bookshelf. *At least it's a place to start.*

Exe paged through every book and scanned the table of contents and indexes, but found nothing—until she opened Monalea's book, which contained a photo of the skeleton-man's house when it was brand new. Exe delved eagerly into the chapter, but according to the book, not once in its hundred-and-thirty-year history had anyone ever lived in the house. The whole chapter just talked about the mining tycoon who'd built it, (his business went belly up, and he'd lost the place to the bank before ever moving in).

Exe reshelved Monalea's book and scanned the shelf once again, her hope for easy answers dwindling. With a sigh, Exe tapped Monalea on the shoulder, "Excuse me, but I'm going to need some help."

Monalea didn't even look up, "Sorry, but I can't do your report for you."

"What report?" Exe fidgeted as Monalea regarded her over her cat-eye glasses.

"Your AP History teacher, Mr. Canfield, sent you to me, correct?" Monalea said. When Exe nodded, she asked, "To complete an AP History assignment?"

"No, I'm doing a bit of my own research on Nowhere. For—personal reasons."

"Exploring Nowhere's history for your own edification? Interesting. Most kids only come here when forced by school assignment," Monalea leaned back in her chair and gave Exe her full attention. "You do know that all residents are required to act as living history performers, right? Which means our town council insists on every resident memorizing Nowhere's history down to the last detail—to ensure that tourists receive accurate info. This, I warn you, means you'll be studying local lore a lot in school. Knowing that, you're still interested in learning Nowhere's history for fun? I approve. I've got ten minutes, what do you need?"

"This is a waste of time."

Exe ignored her inner voice's complaint and pulled out her math class list, trying to decide which question was most important, "I'm mostly interested in recent history, like the last fifteen years. Um, where is Nowhere's adoption agency?"

"We don't have one. Next?" Monalea folded her hands behind her head.

"So it closed? Where was it? What happened to its records? Are they here?" Exe scanned the room as if she might suddenly see documents related to her adoption.

"Never had one. No one in Nowhere is adopted. Except you," Monalea closed her eyes and stretched her neck. "According to your family's application."

Exe's mind worked overtime. *No adoption agency? Then did the Parsells get me directly from a blood relative?*

"Are there any Verelustres living in Nowhere?" Exe asked. Monalea shook her head, no. "Ever?" No again. "How about a woman with the first name, Goldie?" Strike three. "Last name? Goldberg? Any name with gold in it?" Strikes four, five and six.

"There's never been any gold in Nowhere. Of any kind," Monalea smiled. "The town would probably throw a festival if people with 'gold' in their name moved here."

Exe ran through her list in desperation as Monalea packed up her desk. "You must know that my family moved into the Second First Church building. What can you tell me about the creepy house on the hill behind it?"

"You can read about that in my book," Monalea said,

flicking her 'The Librarian is:' sign from 'IN' to 'OUT.'

"I did. But who's living there now?"

"No one. It's never been lived in," Monalea shut off the lights and motioned Exe to head down the steep stairs ahead of her. "Its proximity to the old cemetery deterred buyers. But for the past twenty-five years or so there's been a rumor floating around that it's haunted by the ghost of a man murdered there."

Exe froze in terror halfway down the stairs.

"It's not true," Monalea said, seeing Exe's fear-paled face. "Although our ghost-walk guides would love it if Nowhere had some gory deaths, according to my records no one has ever been murdered in Nowhere."

Until last week. Exe stepped into the quiet hallway, squelching the memory of the murdered man she'd reburied just days ago. "Someone does live there. An old man. I've seen him."

"Absolutely not," Monalea closed the attic's narrow door and locked it with an old-fashioned key. "I know every resident of Nowhere, and none live in that house. If you did see someone, it was probably just a tourist poking around."

Exe gave up trying to convince her and looked at the list. Only locating Aunt Goldie's unmappable address was left. "Can you at least tell me where to find number nine Why Road?"

Monalea frowned, "Why?"

"Because I'm looking for someone who—"

"No, I mean, Why Road? I feel like I've heard that—" Monalea suddenly paused as a glassy look came over her. "No. There's no road named Why in Nowhere. Is that all?"

The only questions left were the ones about the man in

black and her wanted poster. *There's no way I'm asking her about a murdered man now.*

"What if she's magical? Like you are. Maybe she's the one who sent that man in black after you. Maybe she'll grab you the minute you turn your back on her." The voice's panic-inducing suggestions sent Exe stumbling away from Monalea. *"BOO!"*

Exe backed up against the doorknob and jumped, dropping her books.

"Are you okay?" Monalea asked. "You look like you've seen a ghost."

Exe gathered her nerve along with her belongings, and focused on the one part she hoped the nagging voice got right. *How can I find out if she's magical without asking outright? I'll sound insane if it isn't true.*

"I like your outfit. Very vintage, but its style doesn't really fit in with the Old West costumes other townspeople are required to wear. Why is that?" Exe asked as casually as she could, glancing significantly at the wanted poster that had fallen on the floor between them.

"It's a protest," Monalea explained, picking up the poster and handing it to Exe without even the slightest indication that she recognized it. "I've been lobbying to host a Prohibition Festival to recognize Nowhere's heroes from that era, including my grandfather, but our city counsel insists on ignoring any history that happened after the 1890s. I'll keep wearing Roaring Twenties and Dirty Thirties garb until they relent."

"You're grasping at meaningless straws," the inner voice drawled in a tone filled with mocking mirth. Ignoring the voice, Exe's eyes fell on Monalea's long necklace that dangled down to her waist. From the rope of ruby beads

hung a silver lavaliere that looked like a bejeweled spider web. "That necklace. Can you take it off?"

Puzzled, Monalea removed the necklace and handed it to Exe for closer inspection. "Do you like it? It's a dream catcher. I sell them in my gift store."

Exe smiled politely at the pretty piece, then handed it back. "Are you wearing any other jewelry? Something you can't take off? Ever?"

"You mean like a wedding ring? I'm not married," Monalea donned her necklace and checked her watch. "I gotta run. If you really want to dive into Nowhere's history, you'll have to hit me up another time. Or buy one of my books—I'll give you a great discount. Egogahan! That's Apache for, 'Until we meet again!'"

Completely deflated, Exe watched Monalea disappear down the grand staircase. No adoption agency, no Verelustres, no Goldie. *I didn't learn anything.*

"Because you've got it all wrong. This was a wild lycanmere chase. Give it up."

'Lycanmere,' what a strange word. I must've read it in one of the books. Probably a Native American word for something. Exe brushed it aside and focused on the one fact she knew for sure:

The house behind hers definitely wasn't empty.

OUT OF MY MIND

There was no doubt in Exe's mind that a killer lived in the creepy house atop cemetery hill. *But is he a murderer or my protector?* Unfortunately, she couldn't go knocking on his door as casually as she would to borrow a cup of sugar and ask, 'Pardon me, but did you kill someone to protect me and bury the body in my backyard?'

Instead she'd spent every spare minute camped out in her belfry, surveilling the skeleton-man's house. But the macabre manor suddenly seemed to be just as abandoned as Monalea had said. There'd been no sign of life or flicker of light since the night Exe had found the dead body. Even when her brothers made another attempt to explore the creepy house a few nights ago, no lights flashed on to scare them off. The house was just locked up so tight that they couldn't get in. And when Exe asked what they'd seen while peering into the windows, her brothers reported that the place was completely empty.

After endless days of watching with nothing to show for it, Exe was ready to believe the incessant voice that kept repeating, *"Monalea was right—the house is empty and that 'skeleton-man' was just a lost tourist. So give up this ridiculous vigil."*

Exe stretched and rested her chin on the rickety belfry railing to watch the sun disappear behind the mountain. Sunsets were the only pleasant part of spending hours in her uncomfortable perch. As the sun dipped, its golden rays hit the haunted house's windows, making it appear as if its lights had all turned on at once.

"See? It was just the sun you saw that night your brothers first tried spying on my house. Life would be easier if you'd just forget the house and the poster, so give up."

Give up. The thought was tempting. Her inner nag had been haranguing her to cave for days, and she was so tempted that sometimes she did forget. It was so strange. Some mornings Exe completely forgot about her plans to stake out the haunted house, only to remember later, whenever she happened to spot the crumpled wanted poster. Now she slept with the poster clutched in her fist so she wouldn't forget anymore.

Besides, endless hours spent staring at an inanimate object while on edge took its toll. She longed to give up, but accepting defeat knowing that she hadn't exhausted all avenues went against her nature. *I have to find out who or what is in that house.*

"There's nothing to find."

The swiftly sinking sun illuminated the graves below, striping the hill with long, slithery shadows. Exe scanned the rows of tombstones until she found the one where the man in black was buried. *If no one lives in that house, then who buried the body?*

"What body?"

Exe stilled, stunned by the crazy thought. *Am I going mad?*

"The body," Exe whispered, frantically digging through her pockets for the poster. "The body of the man carrying my wanted poster." She breathed a sigh of relief when she finally found the poster in her back pocket.

"That? Easy made that. Remember? He made one for Henny-Boy, too."

"No, that's not what he said," Exe declared, feeling half insane for arguing out loud with her own inner voice. "He said– I **know** I dug up a body."

"Prove it."

Exe raced down her bell tower and dashed into the cemetery. She made a beeline for the man in black's grave. *Something's off.* The grave mound wasn't disturbed anymore. It was packed hard as if untouched for ages.

Did I just dream that I unburied a body that first night? The evidence said yes. There was only one way to know for sure: *I have to risk wishing.*

"That's a dangerous idea."

Maybe, but there's no one around to hurt except myself. I have to know. Taking a deep breath, Exe closed her eyes and wished for the body buried within to unearth itself.

Steeling herself for the sight of a decaying body, she opened her eyes. Instead of the man in black's body, she'd dug up a rickety pine box with a dusty femur poking out through a hole. Shaken, Exe wished the box reburied and tried the next grave over, but only resurrected another coffin. Three more times she tried, but she couldn't find the man in black's body anywhere.

He's gone—if he even existed. Did I just make up a story to go along with a prank poster that Easy made? Maybe I am going mad. If she had imagined it all, then there was nothing to find in that house. And if that was true, she'd just wasted a week watching it.

"That's right, you've wasted your time. Now forget it and get back to the business of surviving your lonely little life. You are okay. All you have to do is get through."

Am I that delusional? Exhausted and terrified, Exe stumbled back down the hill and collapsed against her tower door. If she really had imagined all that, perhaps nothing she believed was true. *Did I make it all up? Maybe I don't actually have powers.*

"Let's not get carried away."

Exe reached for her necklace. *Still there.* Relieved by its existence for once, she caressed the large, cool stone that dangled over her heart. *Maybe I made up the idea that I can't take it off. When's the last time I tried removing it? The lengthy chain should easily slide over my head.* In one smooth, swift motion Exe yanked the pendant upward—but the necklace didn't come off. The chain had shortened by the time it reached her chin.

"So the poster is pretend, but my necklace is actually magical?" Exe whispered aloud. "Does that mean that I do have powers? Or not? I did just use them to dig up those coffins, didn't I? Or did I? Maybe I should—"

"It's dangerous to wish for things." The muddled madness in her mind left her feeling like she was sinking into insanity. *"You want nothing, you need nothing. All you have to do is get through. You are okay."* Soon a familiar, eerie calm settled over her.

"STOP! I give up," Exe's scream echoed through the empty cemetery. The menacing mansion loomed ever ominous as the full hunter's moon rose overhead, casting long shadows that shrouded Exe in a darkness she felt to her bones.

"About time," her inner voice mocked relentlessly. *"You've wasted enough time chasing phantoms and fairytales. Go do something useful that will keep you out of trouble for a few hours, like helping your mother with dinner."*

Dragging herself back inside, Exe found Rove supervising most of the boys setting the table while Easy helped Ella put the finishing touches on dinner.

"Easy? Did you make a 'Wanted' poster for Henny-Boy?" Exe asked, unexpectedly needing to verify this fact that she already accepted as true.

"A what poster?" Easy frowned, then smiled. "Oh, yeah. I made one for all the rabble-rousers in this family."

"Including me?"

"Sounds like something I'd do. Why do you ask?"

"No reason," Exe surveyed Ella's latest strange concoction. What's for supper?"

"Japanese spaghetti with a side of Italian gyoza," Easy answered, plopping a few of the doughy dumplings into the fryer.

"Please tell me we have something green to go along with all of this," Exe groaned, stirring the bubbling Japanese spaghetti sauce so that it didn't burn.

Ella emerged from the freezer with two bags of frozen peas, "You've been my daughter for fifteen years, Exe. I think I know how to feed you."

Exe stilled mid-stir, "Thirteen years. I wasn't with you for the first two, right?"

"I suppose so," Ella bustled about the kitchen, barely listening. Neither Rove or her brothers seemed to hear her question. Only Easy regarded her curiously.

"You adopted me when I was two years old," Exe dropped her voice. "From somewhere here in Nowhere, right? Do you remember where?"

"Of course I remember where I adopted my only daughter. In that decrepit house out back," Ella strained the odd mix of rice noodles and angel hair pasta. "An elderly lady asked us if we wanted a one-day-only tour. When it was through, we had you."

"You adopted me in that house? From who? An agency?" Exe shoved the peas into the microwave, acting casual to keep Ella talking.

"Maybe? The elderly lady was the only one we dealt with," Ella rescued the still-bagged peas from the microwave and poured them into a bowl. "If you're so curious, honey, you should just read the adoption papers. Then you'll know as much as I do."

"You have records? Where?" Exe asked, dumping the spaghetti into a dish.

"Locked in the fireproof safe in your father's office," Ella answered. Suddenly, she whirled on Exe, scattering peas everywhere, "Why are you asking me all these questions? You gave up! You said you'd let this go! Get back here, young lady!"

But Exe was already gone. Outside she ran, down the open-air walkway to Rove's office. Afraid that the documents would vanish before she could get to them, Exe burst through the door and dashed straight for the safe, wishing it unlocked and for the records to come to her. Out of the safe they flew, into her eager hands.

Exe scanned them in growing disappointment. The documents were practically blank. They didn't state her birth parents' names, her place of birth, or her birthdate. The form did list her birth name as Experience Verelustre, but she already knew that from the poster. The only sections fully filled in were the ones completed by Ella and Rove.

"We've been over this a thousand times, there's nothing for you to find!"

If there's nothing to find, then how is it that the last name on the wanted poster matches my last name on the adoption papers? Then she spied a full box on the bottom of the form labeled, 'Facilitating Agency,' and a familiar scrawl that read: 'Anacapia Adoptions Inc.' *Anacapia. That word is on my wanted poster. Is that where I'm from?*

Below the name was the adoption agency's address: '9 Why Road, Nowhere, Arizona.' She didn't need her letters from Aunt Goldie to know that the adoption papers had been written by the same hand. Exe kept scanning until she found the ultimate confirmation: 'Legal Guardian: Mrs. Goldie Goldman.'

"Why do you refuse to listen? Stubborn idiot! I'm warning you–"

Her adoption, Aunt Goldie's letters, the murder of the man in black—all roads led to the haunted house. If the old lady who gave her up for adoption was Aunt Goldie, maybe she still lived in that creepy old house. *I'm knocking on that door, tonight.*

"No!" Easy shouted from the open doorway, brandishing a spatula.

"What?" Exe shoved the adoption papers in her pocket. "Dinner ready?"

"Yeah," Easy stared in confusion at the spatula. He dropped his arm, then leveled Exe with a sober stare, "What's up, Exe? You've been MIA lately. And even when you are around, you're not really here. Take some advice from your older brother–"

"Older?" Exe asked. "How do we know you're older? We don't know my real birthdate, do we? Or where I came from, or why I'm so– different, or anything! I'm an unknown, an unanswered question, an x."

Easy dropped the spatula and put his hands on her shoulders, "Sometimes Exe, X marks the spot. Who knows? Maybe you're a buried treasure."

"Thanks," Exe startled Easy with a hug. "Tell the 'rents I'm not hungry, okay?"

"Where are you going?" Easy wiped the floor-dropped spatula with his shirt.

Exe flashed Easy a rare smile, "Treasure hunting."

Exe paced the lower level of her tower, working up the courage to approach the spooky house next door. There wasn't much time. Her family would be done with dinner soon, and a horde of classmates was due to arrive any minute. *It's now or never.*

"Never!"

Ignoring her inner voice, Exe double-checked the adoption papers and poster—evidence she'd need to confront whomever answered the door. *But what do I say? Just whip out the documents and demand answers? Or introduce myself?*

Maybe she won't recognize me. And what if that creepy ·skeleton-man answers? Who is he? Maybe–

"Why must you insist on chasing this mad fantasy? The house is empty. How much more confirmation do you need? This is a waste of time."

"So I waste my time, who cares?" Exe whispered to herself. "I'd rather discover that I'm wrong than waste away wondering." She drew a steadying breath and flung the outer door wide.

"Fine, go knock on that door. No one will answer. Then will you let this go?"

"If the house is abandoned, I won't have a choice, will I?" Exe muttered, trudging up the grave-dotted hill. Over the wall and through the tumbleweed-strewn lawn she skulked. Tiptoeing across the dilapidated porch, Exe approached the wind-worn door. She hesitated when she noticed that the house number was a six. *But it's hanging by a single nail.* With her pinky, she rotated the six—it was actually a nine. *This is it.* Knuckles ready, she raised her fist to knock, then hesitated.

*"What if the skeleton-man answers? He **is** a murderer. What if he murders you for knocking on that door? Are answers to your petty questions worth risking your life for?"*

Brushing aside her cowardice, Exe rapped on the weathered door. Nothing stirred within the silent house. Exe pressed her ear to the door, straining to hear any movement inside above the whirring cicadas. As she listened, she spied a shadowy figure looming in the home's broken bay window. She raced for the window—but the figure vanished before she'd pressed her face against the glass. Peering inside, the dark parlor appeared deserted and barren, not even a single stick of furniture.

"See? Empty. Now go home."

Exe turned back toward the porch, debating. *The only way to know for sure if this place is abandoned or not is to go inside.*

"Your brothers already tried that."

Exe ignored her fear and rattled the cracked glass doorknob. *Locked, of course. So that's it, unless...* Biting her lip, she wished. The door swung open.

"One does not walk into another person's house without permission!"

Stale, musty air burned her lungs as Exe stepped into the unnaturally cold foyer. The door slammed closed behind her, pitching her into darkness. The slices of night sky peeping through the boarded-up windows let in little of the steely starlight.

The moment her eyes adjusted to the dank hallway, Exe realized that the house wasn't as empty as it appeared from the outside. Even in the darkness she could see shadowy shapes of shrouded furniture filling the parlor that had looked totally bare through the window. *There's only one way that a fully-furnished room appears empty from the outside— someone with powers like mine must live here.*

"Turn back! Or you'll regret it!"

Though fully furnished, there was still no sign of life—except for the golden band of light flickering beneath the closed door at the far end of the hall. Exe fought her way through the darkness, tripping over a bulge in the carpet that rose up out of nowhere. Blackness invaded her eyes, dimming them until the sliver of golden light at the hallway's end faded to a pinhole. Exe struggled on, tiptoeing over the creaking floor, half-afraid that the furniture would spring to life and smash her into the wall.

A wardrobe stirred. Wood scraped wood, more chilling than fingernails on chalkboards. Suddenly all the furniture came to life. Knocking and banging, it formed barricades against her, but Exe plunged herself forward with every fall, crashing into tables, chairs, and a wildly chiming grandfather clock. As she reached the only illuminated room, the furniture closed in, piling itself in front of the door. Fear and frustration fired inside her. With one wish, the furniture blockade exploded away, splintering against the walls.

Flinging the door wide, Exe stormed inside. The crackle of a roaring fire in a magnificent jade fireplace drew her gaze. There he sat, enthroned on a massive leather chair. Watching her. *Skeleton-man.*

CRACK!

A sudden force slammed Exe backward, knocking her against the walls as she hurtled down the hall. She crashed into the front door, ripping it from its hinges. Propelled by the ruthless, unseen force, Exe slammed onto the rock-hard dirt lawn and rolled down the slight slope with unnatural speed. Thorns and spines burrowed into her flesh as she spun over dead bushes and cacti. Onward the unseen force drove her body until she smashed into the low stone fence. Bloodied and breathless, Exe lay there, wedged against the hot, rough rocks. Overhead, the coldly glittering stars seemed to twinkle triumphant.

A blinding, brilliant flash—then suddenly the skeleton-man was there, towering over her and gloating, "Powerful you may be, but you're still no match for me."

Fear fluttered through Exe. *I know that voice.*

"Of course you do."

Terror tightened her chest, squeezing the breath from her lungs. Suddenly, she recalled making this same realization once before—when the man in black's voice had invaded her mind in the schoolhouse. *Skeleton-man is the voice in my head?!*

The familiar voice's ghoulish laughter echoed in her mind.

"It's you! You're the voice in my head!" Exe choked out. "It's not mine, I know it isn't. But you've made me forget that, haven't you? What else have you made me do?"

"If I could make you obey my will, you wouldn't–" Skeleton-man seethed.

But Exe wasn't listening. With growing fear she fought to comprehend how this creepy man had been manipulating her for years. And not just her. All those times her family had acted strangely—*like Ella warning me away from my adoption papers right after telling me to read them...* This skeleton-man must've been controlling them too.

"Finally frightened, are we? Yes. I've been manipulating you and your family for your entire life. Just think of all the things I could make them do. Dangerous things."

"Who are you?" Exe scrambled to her feet and crawled over the wall. But having a solid barrier between them didn't make her feel any safer.

Terrifying and formidable, the skeleton-man stabbed Exe with his stare. In that moment, Exe recalled with chilling clarity that this was a man capable of murder. Terror immobilized her as he seemed to be contemplating ridding himself of her. Permanently.

"You're right to be afraid. You'd be wise to stay that way. And stay away."

"Why are you doing this?" Exe cried, stumbling against the tombstones as she backed her way down the hill.

"Don't you dare set foot on this property again without permission," the skeleton-man's voice echoed cold and strange outside of her head. "Or else."

Exe stumbled into her tower, her eyes darting around for a place to hide. *But how can I hide when he's in my head?*

"You can't. I'm always listening. Always watching. So do as I say and forget all of this nonsense. The poster, the man in black's body, my home. All of it." Exe slammed her hands against her ears, as if smashing her skull like a walnut could block the skeleton-man's relentless voice out of her mind.

"You know what to do. You want nothing, you need nothing. All you have to do is get through. You are okay. You want nothing, you need nothing. All you have to do..." Against her will, all that skeleton-man wanted her to forget began to fog over like a steamy mirror. As the memories faded, so did the fear paralyzing her.

Exe knocked the tower door closed, though she knew it couldn't keep the skeleton-man out of her head. *If only there was some way to get him out. What was it he said? 'You may be powerful...' Am I? Am I powerful enough to kick him out of my mind?*

"Don't you even think about it. You know it's too dangerous to use your powers," skeleton-man thought at her.

But not using my powers was your idea, wasn't it? A way to control me, Exe thought back at him.

"You'll wind up giving yourself a lobotomy."

Maybe if I make just a part of it private. Exe blocked out the skeleton-man's voice and imagined a corner of her consciousness transforming into an impenetrable vault. Recalling all of her favorite spy movies, Exe envisioned uncrackable codes, deadly lasers, and invulnerable shields to add layers of protection to her secret memory file.

"What do you think you're doing?"

Exe concentrated on moving her train of thought into the impenetrable vault. *Did it work? Am I hidden from him? Am I free to think as I please without interference now?* Careful to keep her thoughts contained in the hopefully private vault, Exe cast about for one that would outrage the skeleton-man. *After all, he could be pretending not to know what I've done, so I'll think this part of my mind is out of his reach when it really isn't.*

Deep in that locked place, Exe thought, *I'm going to pretend to let this go. But once you've lowered your guard, I'm breaking into your house. Then I'll ransack the place until I find any signs of Aunt Goldie. And there's nothing you can do to stop me.*

Exe waited several long minutes for any reaction from the skeleton-man.

"Where are you? Why aren't you thinking anything?"

I'm here, I'm just scared, Exe thought out in her open mind.

"As you should be. Now will you quit this nonsense? Or must I do something drastic to keep you under control?"

I'll be good. I promise. Just don't hurt my family.

Exe could've sworn she heard the skeleton-man's exasperated sigh in her head. *"Your family's safety depends on you."*

REFORMATION

"Dearly beloved, we are gathered here today to mourn the passing of Ezekiel 'Easy' Parsell," Seph's solemn voice rang out over the silent throng gathered around the grave. Countless candles adorning the tombstones gave the hillside cemetery an eerie glow against the night sky.

Exe maneuvered through the mourners, edging ever closer to the dirt pile that covered her brother's coffin. She concentrated all her thoughts on Easy who lay limp and still inside his casket—all except those thoughts stashed away in her mind vault.

"Beloved brother. Fierce friend. Prodigious prankster. Supreme influencer of the social scene," Seph continued as teary-eyed teens tossed black roses onto the low, earthen mound. "As we lay my brother to rest on this Halloween Eve—the very night he would've turned sixteen—I cannot help but to reflect on his short life."

A crisp, cool night, a full moon lurking behind foggy clouds, leafless branches stretching their spooky shadows over the cemetery—it's as if Easy ordered the perfect setting for this somber celebration of his life. Exe kept up the constant stream-of-conscious centered on the event at hand to distract her skeleton-man monitor.

"Although Easy was among us for all too brief a time, he made a monumental impression on every person he met," Seph's voice rang out over the macabre funeral march playing on the vintage phonograph. "My brave brother would want me to tell you that he died battling a bobcat or charming a rattlesnake."

Ignoring the crowd, Exe positioned herself behind Easy's tombstone and went over her plan in the private corner of her mind. Tonight, she would defy the skeleton-man's orders and publicly use her powers on purpose. *Then he'll be forced to talk to me.*

"But the truth is this," Seph reveled in the attention of the spellbound crowd. "Poor Easy met his end when he slipped on a banana peel and belly flopped into old man Jones' manure pile. Yes, it's true. My baby brother drowned in dung."

The smoky scent of the backyard bonfire mingles with the enticing aroma of sizzling steak and charred ears of corn piled high on the borrowed chuck wagon. Exe cycled through these random reflections as she readied herself. *It's almost time.*

"Please join me now in a moment of silence for the dearly departed," Seph said.

A lone gust rustled the tumbleweeds, electrifying the crackle of anticipation rippling through the grievers. Heads swiveled expectantly as the silence stretched on, but Exe kept her attention on the oblong dirt pile covering Easy's coffin.

THUMP—all eyes returned to the grave. BANG—the dirt atop the coffin lid shuddered. CRACK! A fist smashed through the casket. The fingers flexed, then waved. Giggles rolled through the thronging teens. *This is it.* BOOM!

With a wish, Exe exploded the coffin lid, showering the mesmerized mourners with dirt chunks and bits of brown Styrofoam. Another wish and Easy's rigid body hinged up with unnatural speed until he was standing on the edge of his makeshift casket. The crowd gasped, then cheered—all eyes on Easy. Except for Exe's.

Exe directed her gaze toward the haunted house, her mind blanked in anticipation. Nothing. The mansion remained dark, and no skeleton-man scoldings penetrated her mind. Disappointed, Exe turned her attention back to Easy as he preened for his admirers. He slicked back his crimped, grayed hair and brushed dust from the shoulders of his baggy tuxedo, then rattled the chains that completed his escape artist costume.

"Ladies and gentlemen, it is I, Harry Houdini, back from the dead," Easy strutted around the coffin rim, the phosphorescent sheen of his ashen greasepaint giving his face a ghostly glow. "I died this very night, many years ago. As did all of you. Though some of you are deader than others," Easy scanned the corpse-costumed crowd, nodding to a classmate wearing an Elizabethan ruff. "What an honor to have my funeral attended by bluesman Bobby Parker, famed filmmaker Fellini, the assassinated Indira Gandhi."

As Easy continued calling out the best costumes, Exe and her brothers circulated amongst the crowd distributing vials of a smoking, orange-y concoction. When every ghostly guest had a glass of the bubbly brew, Easy called out, "Welcome honored zombies. I invite you now to raise your embalming fluid to toast our famed lives and infamous deaths. Happy Halloween!"

"To Easy! Happy Birthday! Happy Halloween! Happy sixteenth, my man!" Everyone clinked beakers and cheered, then sipped the fizzy mango-pineapple punch. With the toast signaling the end of Easy's grand entrance, the guests drifted off to launch Easy's Halloween birthday party into full swing. Soon everyone was busy dancing in the courtyard, telling ghost stories around the bonfire, or gorging themselves on the spine-chilling refreshments.

Instead of joining in, Exe returned her attention to the skeleton-man's house. She'd been so sure tonight's stunt would draw him out. But so far there were no signs that he had even noticed that she'd used her powers out in the open.

A few weeks ago, when Exe had first discovered the skeleton-man's lifelong manipulations, she'd been so terrified, she could barely go through the motions of her daily life. But that paralyzing terror dissipated quickly when Exe realized that the skeleton-man wasn't capable of constant monitoring. Whenever he thought she was asleep or zoned out watching one of her tapes, he'd leave her alone. *And whatever he's doing, it isn't mind control.*

The skeleton-man couldn't control her, not really. He could counsel and nag, but he couldn't pull Exe's strings like a marionette to make her comply with his advice. True, he was able to make her forget things, but he couldn't erase them from her mind completely. *If I care enough about something, I eventually remember it, no matter how hard he tries to steer me in another direction.*

Realizing that fact had been a relief, but what truly took her terror away was figuring out that the skeleton-man's true intent was to protect her. Over these past few weeks, Exe obeyed the voice's every direction during the day, but at night she rifled through her own murky memories, carefully moving any she wanted to remember into her private mind vault. What she'd found told her that the skeleton-man's actions were designed to defend her. Convincing her to don disguises, keeping Rove enlisted so that he'd regularly move the Parsells all over the world, killing the man in black, all of it.

But defend me from what? Exe still didn't know, although she'd attempted to find out. Exe tried to trick the skeleton-man into revealing his secrets by thinking seemingly innocent, yet deceptively leading thoughts. But he refused to be fooled.

"Quit trying to manipulate me. I know you've locked a part of your mind away from me. Congratulations. Now I'll never tell you what you want to know."

It was then that the battle within her brain began. Whenever Exe sensed the skeleton-man in her head, she thought only about the wanted poster, the strange names on her adoption papers, the man in black, her powers. And Aunt Goldie. (She'd tried breaking into the house again to search for clues, even wished for a way in, but he'd successfully locked her out.) So now she badgered him with all of the questions she longed to have answered, especially about her untamed powers.

Why am I not supposed to use my powers? She'd thought at him time and again. The skeleton-man's answers were less than helpful: *"Because it's dangerous!" "Because I said so!" "Because you don't know what you're doing!"*

If it's so dangerous, then why won't you show me how to control them? Is that why you finally moved us in next door to you? To train me? So why won't you do it?

Whenever Exe pestered the skeleton-man to train her, his non-answers went from terse to worse, until he'd simply refused to respond to her at all. Exe could still sense him in her head, lurking in the background muttering bitter thoughts, but all the begrudging guidance stopped.

The more he ignored her, the angrier Exe became. *If he won't train me when I ask politely, I'll force him to help me.* That's why she'd used her powers on purpose tonight.

For the past week, Exe had spent late nights holed up in the belfry testing out her powers. Her fear was so ingrained that at first Exe had to talk herself into wishing on purpose. She started small, with simple tricks like moving a pillow from here to there. With every wish that came true (almost exactly as intended), the braver Exe became, but not once did the skeleton-man scold her.

She needed to do something bigger to force him to help her, and Easy's annual birthday bash was the perfect opportunity. Each year, Easy worked hard to make his celebration more epic than the last. Lately, he'd been honoring 'fellow' notables born on his birthday—like the year he'd spliced film clips of celebrities born on Halloween into a surprisingly coherent and wildly entertaining movie that he'd screened at his fifteenth birthday bash.

Celebrating his sixteenth this year, Easy took inspiration from their backyard cemetery and decided to host his own 'funeral,' with all guests instructed to dress as someone who'd died around Halloween. Her brothers had spent weeks working the kinks out of Easy's 'Escape the Grave' grand entrance stunt. But no matter what they tried, they couldn't figure out a way to stage the unearthly rising Easy wanted. Although Easy had resigned himself to simply busting through the fake coffin lid and jumping out of the casket, Exe had decided to use her powers to create the effect that he wanted—without him even realizing it.

Just to be safe, Exe practiced it on herself first. Unsure of what it would take to raise a rigid body from flat to standing in less than a second, Exe overestimated and almost hurled herself off the balcony on her first few attempts. She'd perfected the trick just last night, and now she'd performed it in front of witnesses. *Skeleton-man can't be happy about that. So why won't he react?*

Exe hunkered down in the shadow of her brother's oversized faux tombstone to puzzle over his lack of response. Unfortunately, Easy chose just that moment to inspect his empty grave with some friends, who pelted him with questions as they took turns climbing inside, trying to replicate his impressive exit from the casket.

"Alright, we give. Tell us how you did it," one guy demanded.

"A magician never reveals his secrets," Easy's gaze glided by Exe, meeting her eyes for only a moment. "I think it's about time to exhume the cake. Coming, Exe?"

With a frustrated sigh, Exe abandoned her vigil and trailed after Easy, cursing the heavy skirts of her 1880s-style costume. She'd chosen to dress as the corpse of Russian painter and author Marie Bashkirtseff mainly because it was simple to put together. Her school already had period clothes from that era, and she died at age 25, meaning she could keep the makeup minimal.

Thone had already started the cake-cutting ceremony by the time she caught up. Exe joined in the spooky, minor-key chorus of Happy Birthday, keeping one eye on the darkened house on the hill. Instead of a traditional cake, Ella had crafted a spookily realistic, white chocolate skeleton almost as big as Charley. Inside each hollow bone was a luscious filling of white chocolate mousse with a bloody raspberry sauce that oozed sticky red with each bite. The whole thing was buried in an oozing chocolate lava cake sprinkled with crunchy chocolate cookie crumb dirt.

Seph and Thone dished up the muddy lava cake and bones to the guests with garden trowels. Easy claimed the head for himself and gave the white chocolate skull a big kiss before biting off its jaw. Watching him, Exe couldn't shake her uneasiness over the way he'd looked at her while discussing the 'Escape the Grave' trick.

Does Easy know it was me?

Exe hadn't thought much about how Easy would respond when he felt his body stiffen and rise unaided. In the past, Easy and the rest of her family acted oblivious whenever her wishes made something outlandish happen. But that must've been the skeleton-man, manipulating them to ignore the strange and unusual happenings. But the skeleton-man hadn't made Easy forget this. *Why didn't I think about Easy's reaction?*

"Because you never think about anyone but yourself! It's always, 'I want, I need!' Always questioning, never listening. Demanding everything be done on your timeframe. Why don't you think about someone else for a change!"

Exe whirled toward the haunted house at the skeleton-man's sudden, undeserved scolding (that struck too close to home). He was there. Standing in his yard and staring at her, just as he had on that first night. The smug smirk on his face drove every other thought from Exe's mind.

Up the hill she marched, ignoring the teens playing graveyard tag. They chased around her, oblivious to her determined advance. Exe kept her eyes fixed the skeleton-man, stopping only when she reached the low stone fence that separated their properties.

"Back for more?" his irritatingly familiar voice gloated.

"I'm not scared of you. I know you won't hurt me. It's your job to protect me, isn't it? Though you're pretty scrawny for a bodyguard," Exe mocked, determined to break his resistance to her demand for answers.

"How dare you talk to me that way? Do you know who I am? I am Velin Ruel, former Diri—"

"Yes?" Exe baited, anger warring with curiosity in her tone. Velin's skin-covered skeleton face simply sneered back at her. "Velin, is it? Why are you doing this to me? Who are you? Who am I? I want answers!"

"Selfish brat," Velin stomped up his front porch steps. "You've no idea what you're asking. You're not ready to know. Never will be, as far as I'm concerned. Curse you and your tiresome teenaged brain. You were so much easier to control when you were younger. A little memory fading on you and your family every now and again, and you'd be out of my hair for years on end."

"So you admit it?" Exe clambered over the fence, hampered by the cumbersome skirt of her ghostly costume, and stalked after him. "You mess with my mind? You steal my memories? Make me forget things I want to remember?"

"I stole no memories, I only altered their significance," Velin's front door opened unaided, and he stepped inside before turning on her. "Any memory I needed you to forget, I simply made it seem as unimportant as what you ate for breakfast. Then it was just a matter of amping up the insignificant ones to feel so important that you'd forget everything else."

"How dare you manipulate me!" Exe charged after him, jamming herself into the doorway when he tried to slam it shut on her.

"You gave me no choice! Stubborn, willful child. I've had enough of your defiance!" Velin tilted his head ever so slightly, and Exe felt again the sudden pressure of the unseen force that had hurled her from his house. Exe quickly wished inside her private vault, *I wish that you shall not move me.*

"You think you're powerful enough to fight me?" Velin gritted out as they waged a silent battle in his doorway. "You're not even powerful enough to find a body that you know I buried in your backyard."

Exe's gaze didn't waver from his as she made the biggest wish she'd ever attempted. Terrified screams told her that she'd succeeded. Every body buried on Parsell property had been unearthed. Trembling with barely-controlled power, Exe willed the body of the man in black to come forward.

The putrid stench of death wafted over Exe as the man in black's decaying body glided by her, its shoe-tips scraping creepily along the warped porch boards. The liquifying body fell in a sloppy heap at Velin's feet. With the last of her strength, Exe willed the rest of the bodies back into their graves amid more horrified shrieks.

Grasping the railing for support, Exe glanced over her shoulder. Her show of force had sent her brothers and their friends running away in terror. Then, in the blink of an eye, every single one of the terrified teens turned back, their firefly flashlights bobbing merrily as they laughed and joked about the spectacularly spooky hoax of hologram skeletons rising from the graves. Among the merry murmur, Exe could make out Easy taking credit for the prank that he clearly believed he'd pulled.

But I didn't put that idea into Easy's head, or the others' either. She wouldn't know where to begin to manipulate the memories of one mind, let alone a mass manipulation of dozens at once. *That was all Velin.* Exe quivered, sickened by his sadistic smirk.

"The might of one's power is meaningless if one doesn't know how to wield it," Velin sneered at her. "I've wasted fourteen years of my life protecting you. Putting up with your self-pity, and whining, and childish idiocy. These last months you've fought me every step of the way. And now this ceaseless demand for knowledge that would destroy everything. You've seen the poster, and I've warned you endlessly. Why do you refuse to understand the danger? This ends now."

Velin suddenly raised his hands and physically shoved her out of his doorway. Surprised by the move, Exe had no chance to defend against it. The second she was out of the way, the door slammed shut with a deliberate finality.

"If you won't tell me," Exe yelled through the door, "maybe your wife will! Goldie? Aunt Goldie!"

"I'm through talking to you. Don't come here again," Velin's smug, scornful voice muffled through the door. "If you want answers, read between the lines."

A sudden instinct to run and forget everything she'd learned screamed through her. Exe ignored the feeling, certain Velin had planted it in her head. *Should I try to force my way in again? Or retreat and regroup?* Ex thought—but she forgot to hide the thought from Velin.

"Retreat and surrender, or else," Velin's voice warned.

"Or what?" Exe retorted.

Instantly, a barrage of random recollections bombarded her train of thought—*standing in line with her brothers to use the bathroom three houses ago; playing foursquare in second grade; brushing her teeth at the kitchen sink last Tuesday.* It was as if her brain were pelting her with her own useless memories.

Exe glared at the closed door, knowing that she had Velin to thank for her chaotic thoughts. *Why won't you tell me what I want to know!*

"You know my name and that I'm burdened with the duty of protecting you. That's all you'll get from me. Now quit this nonsense so I can get on with my job!"

Exe stormed back down the hill, barreling into a tag-playing, chain-draped teen.

"Careful, Exe!" Easy exclaimed, steadying them both before they pitched head-first down the hill. "You almost put us both in the grave for keeps!"

"Sorry," Exe muttered, ducking under his arm to continue her trek for privacy.

"You're not abandoning the party already are you?" Easy caught her wrist before she could make her escape. "It's my birthday!"

"You know me, I can only take so much of crowds," Exe avoided his pleading gaze, unable to face joining in after her confrontation with Velin.

"As your older brother—older for the next few months at least—can I give you some sage advice?" Easy stated, holding up a finger aimed at the tag players waiting on him to rejoin. "I know getting close to people scares you. But if you never face that fear, you'll find you've missed out on living. So come on, live a little!"

"You have no idea how much I want to. I just can't," Exe said, her voice tinged with regret as Easy lost a little of his smile. "Not now. Maybe someday. I wish–" Exe blinked her dampening eyes as she caught herself just in time.

"Exe, what is going on with you? Why won't you let me help you?"

"If you only could. But you've got guests to entertain, birthday boy!" Exe smiled, wiping the wetness from her cheeks and tilting her head toward the waiting tag-players.

"Whatever you need Exe, just say the word," Easy said, returning to the game.

Not even Easy's charm could get that stubborn, vindictive Velin to reveal what he knows, Exe thought privately, as she slipped inside her tower and crept up the staircase to the belfry, pausing only to grab her diary from her bed. *Maybe writing this all down will help me figure out what to do next.*

Exe settled herself against the rough stucco of the belfry's outer wall. The crazily bouncing flashlight beams of the tag players barely registered as she chewed her pen cap, wondering how best to recap her encounter with Velin.

Unsure of how to begin, Exe flipped back a few pages. It'd been weeks since she'd written in the journal. *How naïve I was,* Exe thought as she scanned the lines of her previous entry. *Wait... lines.*

Exe replayed the scene on Velin's porch in her private mind vault. *What was that last thing he said out loud? 'If you want answers, read between the lines.'* Exe brushed her fingertips along the blank spaces between her handwritten entries and whispered, "I wish to read between the lines."

Suddenly, the spaces between her own sentences were flooded with a tight, golden script. *Aunt Goldie's handwriting.* She had written replies to every single entry—right in between Exe's own lines. Exe sped back down the tower and paged through her old journals. Sure enough, there were glowing golden sentences in all of them.

Aunt Goldie had responded to her after all.

CHAPTER TEN

Blood Oath

Aunt Goldie was dead.

Actually, just Exe's dreams of getting help from Aunt Goldie were dead. Abandoning Easy's party, Exe gathered all nine diaries and hauled them up to the belfry to scour the golden writing for the answers she so desperately needed. It wasn't an easy task with Easy's birthday still raging. As the celebration spread throughout the house, kids kept popping in and out of the belfry's trap door. Not to mention that she'd written several entries every week for the last nine years.

Unsure of where to dig in, Exe paged quickly through the first diary written by her seven-year-old self, when her worries were simple and her entries brief. She soon understood that the diaries were meant as a way for Velin to keep tabs on her, even though she was thousands of miles away from Nowhere. (Apparently, the distance was no obstacle for Velin should trouble happen to find her?) It seemed that her necklace was the key—its constant coolness was a sign that all was well, and its warming signaled that

Exe was in danger. Later diaries had longer entries, and longer responses, too.

Most of Goldie's golden replies in her early journals were mildly acidic advice, mixed with a bit of solace. Some were even amusing, like when Aunt Goldie complained about Exe's third-grade habit of writing with garish, fruit-scented pens—they made Aunt Goldie want to retch. Goldie's words gave Exe hope for help, *if only I could find her.*

Then she came across the entry that killed all optimism. Written on the day her parents had confirmed that she was adopted, the boastful golden reply infuriated Exe. All those years ago when she'd finally gotten up the courage to ask, Ella had told her about the woman from the non-existent agency. Back then, Ella had even recalled the old woman's name, Goldie. But Aunt Goldie didn't really exist.

Velin was the real person who had given Exe to the Parsells – and he was clearly amused by how easily he'd fooled Rove and Ella. He also couldn't quit crowing over the spell he'd created to accomplish his trick. Apparently, he'd done something called 'projection' to make the Parsells think they were talking to an old lady without having to physically disguise himself at all. Projection, it seemed, could only be done on people without magic who cannot guard themselves against mind manipulation. He didn't say why he felt the need to hide his identity, but the reply made it clear that concealment was vital—for both himself and Exe.

It was difficult to accept that Goldie didn't exist. Exe had come to regard her as a terse, but loving family member— her only link to her birth family. Now Aunt Goldie was lost, not to death but to non-existence. *I can't believe I'm mourning an imaginary friend.*

A sick realization hit Exe as she slammed the diary shut—if Goldie was imaginary, that meant Velin was the one who'd been sending her the journals, and responding to her entries all these years. Exe grew hot with the knowledge that the caustic codger next door had been reading her most intimate thoughts. Embarrassment flamed to anger as she accepted, *Those secrets wouldn't have been private even if I hadn't written them down.*

Exe tossed the journal aside and picked up her diary from fourth grade; the one she was the least excited to reread. She choked back a sob when she found the entry written the day after Bonnie's death. The horror and heartbreak that had dulled into repressing self-hatred over the years felt so fresh in the words she'd written that day. Velin's stilted response wasn't worth the anguish of rereading the entry. All he'd written to her was, 'Remember, things are not always as they seem.'

As Exe continued scanning the golden writing for clues to her past, she realized that in all of the earlier diaries, Velin's responses were written in reply to her words, as if he intended her to read them someday. But as the years passed—as her thoughts and troubles became more complex—Velin's responses shifted until they read more like notes to himself than to her. Exe got the feeling that he regarded her like a subject under observation for scientific research, *or whatever magical research is called.*

His writing in her most recent diaries were filled with unfamiliar words, like 'tetherstone,' 'volte,' 'Disimulata,' and 'aftsight.' Others, like 'wordsmith,' were used in ways that made no sense to Exe. Privately, she realized that she'd just discovered an advantage to press. *He doesn't know that I've discovered how to read between the lines. If I word tonight's entry just right, he might accidentally reveal some answers.*

With careful thought, Exe logged the day's events, from the party to her confrontation with Velin. She made sure to include even the most insignificant details, on the off chance that one might lure Velin into exposing one of his many secrets. It took Exe eighteen pages to finish. She wove in every question and concern she had, making sure to phrase each one as if to suggest that she intended to let the worry go.

Once she was finished, Exe set the diary aside, but it felt impossible to wait for Velin's answer. Resting her head against the railing, Exe entertained herself by watching the spooky partygoers creep around the graveyard below, while keeping one eye on the open diary for any glimpse of golden writing.

Finally, she'd had enough. Out in her open mind she thought, *Why isn't writing in my diary comforting me this time? It always used to ease my worries and help me forget my troubles, but it isn't working now. Is there something missing?*

Exe stared at her latest entry expectantly and sure enough a glowing, golden sentence began inscribing itself at the end of her entry, *"I'll not fall for so obvious a trap, you naif. I know you've discovered my replies. You've been reading them for hours."*

Exe seized her journal and hurled it at the tremendous bell that dominated the belfry. The bell rocked and clanged as the book ricocheted against the metal and went skittering across the roughhewn planks. Celebratory whoops rose from the birthday revelers as Exe kicked the bell furiously again and again, sending an erratic peal rippling across the mountainside. Exhausted and breathless, Exe rescued her most recent journal as it teetered precariously close to the ledge and flicked through the pages again.

Clearly, Velin would be careful not to reveal anything now that she knew how to read between the lines—but she'd been plagued by these questions for weeks. *Maybe he dropped a clue or two amongst his notes on my more recent entries.*

That's when she heard it.

"Blooooood...." a deep, dusty voice whispered. "Beware!"

"Hello?" Exe called out, shivering in the shadows cast by the massive bell and the belfry arches. "That isn't funny, Easy!"

"Blooood in the waaaaalls," the voice whispered again. "Skeleton-man. Beware!"

"Who said that?" Exe spun around searching for the voice, privately wondering why Velin wasn't just saying this in her head. "I know it's you, Velin!"

"The skeleton-man painted your walls in blood. Beware!" the whisper hissed.

Blood in the walls? Exe crept down the belfry ladder to check the tower walls. Those on the third floor balcony were still stark white (she hadn't gotten around to picking out a paint color yet). Curious, Exe yanked out a loose nail. Rust flakes shredded her fingertips as she scraped it against the whitewashed wall.

Glistening crimson oozed from the scrape, as if the wall was bleeding. Exe stumbled back, staring at the slash of red against the pure white wall. *It can't be.* She moved closer and whispered, "Show me. I wish to see it all."

In an instant, the room dripped with gore. Watching in horror as wet red oozed through the painted walls, Exe grabbed for the slick railing as her feet slipped on the blood-slick floors. Panicked screams from dozens of partygoers suggested that the whole house had been painted in blood.

"No!" Exe slammed her hand against the wall, certain that it was some trick. Her hand came away sticky and glistening. "Stop! Go away! I wish you back as you were!"

Within seconds, the blood oozed back into the wood and vanished under the whitewash. Even the blood on Exe's hand dripped and pooled with unnatural swiftness, then disappeared into the floor. The second the gore was gone, the screaming stopped and Exe heard the distant roar of the party going on full swing as if nothing had happened.

"Why are you doing this?" Exe cried out. "Why send me this bloody walls warning now?"

"Because you refuse to let this go!"

"Why are you trying to keep me from the truth? What are you hiding?" A fearful shiver rolled through her as she thought about the thin layer of paint that separated her from the fresh, oozing blood. Palpitating pulse, harsh, fast breaths, cold sweat trickling down her spine—the combined terror threatened to overwhelm her... *As if on purpose.*

Wait, what am I afraid of? Exe fought through the fear and retreated into the secret safe she'd created in her mind. *Am I truly terrified? Or is Velin messing with me again? And if he is, why?*

Locking out the crushing panic, Exe ran over everything that just happened. The blood was clearly another of Velin's attempts to control her through fear. *But why now? After weeks of leaving me to my own devices, even when I used my powers? A distraction, maybe? But from what? What was I doing—the diaries.*

Cautiously, Exe slipped out into her open mind and let the lingering dread push her to tears. *Enough. Okay? I get that you're just trying to protect me and all I've done is cause you grief. I'll stop. I promise. I'll just go watch some TV.*

"No more shenanigans?"

As an answer, Exe dragged her portable TV/VCR and a random VHS tape up into the belfry. Letting her mind drift away with the campy 1970s comedy, 'Scavenger Hunt,' Exe waited until she felt safe enough to slip back into the privacy of her mind vault without Velin realizing. Keeping half of her attention on the familiar movie, Exe surreptitiously pulled her latest diary onto her lap. Ever so carefully and quietly, she flipped to the most recent entries and scanned Velin's golden writing.

The entries from several months ago were somewhat encouraging, filled with stiff, yet understanding words of patience and promises of help. There was even a hint of remorse on a few of her most despairing entries. However, Velin had clearly become frustrated with her relentless pursuit of the truth, until he was practically vowing to keep her in the dark forever. Suddenly, there it was. In the middle of her entry from moving day, above her description of that flat tire she'd caused by the barren field surrounded by that fancy fence and intimidating barbed wire. Velin's reply revealed almost every answer she'd been searching for:

"I don't know how you did it, girlie. Or was it me? Did I unintentionally send you images of our homeland? It shouldn't be possible. My mind is locked. But there they were. Memories of our beloved Anacapia in your head. Home. That seemed to be the trigger word. I sympathized with your desperate desire to know your home, and it mingled with my own homesickness, creating an unexpected connection. Perhaps it has to do with the chip from my tetherstone that's hidden inside yours. (Exe clasped her hand over her warming necklace.) *Did that necessary safety measure cause this unintended outcome? Perhaps. Then of course, I knew you were about to pass by the—"*

Suddenly, a relentless, raging roar overwhelmed Exe's mind, like the cacophony of a freight train and a million window panes smashing simultaneously. All at once, every inconsequential memory and every emotion she'd ever felt swirled around in her consciousness like they were caught up in a cyclone. Through the bewildering torrent of thoughts, Exe saw the golden script in her diary fading away.

"No!" Exe fought through her befuddlement and concentrated on the fading words with just an idea of a wish half-formed in her mind. Even before she could solidify the thought, the disappearing script flamed to life, burning an imprint of themselves onto the page. With the last of her strength, Exe wished for those ashen words to remain on the page forever, never to be removed by another.

The storm rampaging through her brain whipped up into a tempest. Velin added his own voice too, hurling monstrous insults, dire warnings, and malicious threats of impending death into her mind with an endless intensity. Exe shuddered under the onslaught of the discordant storm as it simultaneously drained her energy and drove her mad. She struggled to secure a shred of her sanity within the private vault she'd created in her mind, but it felt far away and inaccessible. Feeling herself slipping further away, Exe cast about for something, anything to rescue her from this invasion into her mind.

Then, from within her deepest memory, the words came to her. Exe thought and screamed the mysterious mantra as loudly as she could, "This voice is not my own!" As she spoke, her necklace thrummed as if electrified with a current that reached deep within her soul. And just like that, it all stopped. The cacophony. The tornado of thoughts. Velin's voice. All gone.

I did it. I forced Velin's voice out of my head entirely. Exe didn't know how, but she suddenly felt certain that she'd successfully locked her entire mind from Velin. For one brief instant, relief and elation flooded through her as she reveled in the freedom of her liberated mind.

In the next moment, an unexpected wave of agony hit her like a tsunami. A maelstrom of painful, long-forgotten memories no longer suppressed by Velin threatened to pull her under. Every moment of past guilt and rage and sadness and self-loathing crushed her in relentless waves. The overwhelming onslaught brought Exe to her knees, pitching her forward until she fell hard against the rickety railing.

CRACK! The balustrade broke and Exe plunged forward into the open sky. Fighting her agonized mind, Exe flung out her arm and caught the dangling railing with her fingertips. The wood groaned under her added weight and cracked again. Her body jerked as she dropped a few inches lower. Exe yelled, drawing the fearful attention of the partygoers below.

Shocked screams bombarded Exe as she tried to pull herself up. "I can't do it!" *What am I thinking, I have powers, I can just wish myself to safety.* Exe's breath caught on a terrified swallow as she tried to reconcile her life-threatening predicament with the ingrained belief that her powers must be repressed. Then she spotted Velin on the haunted house's front porch. *Watching and doing nothing. Letting me suffer. Letting me dangle helplessly. Like he always has.*

Fear fell away as fury fired within her. Exe closed her eyes and focused all her energy on an image of herself flipping onto the floor above her with the gravity-defying grace of a gymnast. Then she felt herself spinning through the air. When she opened her eyes, she was safe on the belfry's catwalk, glaring across the graveyard at Velin.

The teenage crowd below gasped and cheered for Exe, just as they had for Easy, *as if my near-death experience was yet another show put on for their amusement.* In the tower below, Exe heard the thunder of footsteps—her brothers coming to the rescue yet again. But all this barely registered.

The momentary burst of defiance and victorious elation faded quickly as her freed mind flooded again with long-repressed memories. It was as if the dam of forgetfulness Velin had built in her brain had suddenly broken, drowning her in a deluge of painful emotions. At that exact moment, Easy burst up into the belfry.

"Exe! Are you okay?" Easy grasped Exe's trembling shoulders and shook her. "I'm fine. Just slipped," Exe barely managed to whisper.

"What are you doing up here in the first place?" "You could've killed yourself!" "There's a reason Dad said the belfry was off limits!" The barrage of comments came from her other brothers as they poked their heads through the trap door.

"I know, okay!" Exe's brutal rebuke startled her brothers. "It was an accident. Just go back to the party and leave me alone!"

One by one, her brothers eased their way out. Easy lingered for just a moment, castigating her with a single look. His terse reply broke the condemning silence as he climbed down the ladder. "You keep going this way, Exe, and that's exactly what you're going to be. Alone."

Exe collapsed against the cupola wall with soul-wrenching sobs that seemed to last for hours. She didn't know how long she cried, but her face felt tight with dozens of dried tear trails by the time she uncurled. The weeping left her weak, feeling as stiff and wrung out as one of Ella's dried up rags.

Digging herself out from under the mountain of emotions, Exe struggled to come to terms with how much Velin had buried. It felt like trying to reassemble a mammoth library after a tornado had ripped all the pages out of millions of books. Memories of magical accidents, of people getting hurt because of her out-of-control powers. No others had died like Bonnie had, but so many had been injured, including her family.

With all the pain he'd repressed, it was no wonder she'd felt numb all the time. *Did he suppress painful memories to help me? Or to make me easier to control?* Exe shoved the most horrific of those memories into the secret vault she'd created deep in her mind. It was the only way to contain the pain and guilt. Her mind clearer, Exe rifled through her thoughts of Velin, half-expecting to hear his voice in her head once again, but it stayed free. It took her several long minutes to find her way back to those moments just before the onslaught on her mind began.

Between the lines, yes. She'd been reading something Velin didn't want her to know. Exe spotted her latest diary and struggled to her feet, glancing surreptitiously at Velin's house. He was still there on the porch, watching her. In open defiance, Exe picked up her diary and located the passage she'd been reading. Careful not to smudge the scorched script, Exe read on, making sure that Velin could see her.

"Then of course, I knew you were about to pass by the field that protects the entrance to our world. The knowledge that you were so close to all the answers you've longed for struck a chord within me. I found myself wishing we could both walk back

through that mirage without any fear for our lives. And just like that, the accident.

"*I still don't know which one of us caused it. Perhaps our combined powers? Wish magic shouldn't have been powerful enough, but, well, you've proven you're the exception to that rule. In any case, it's best that the field stays forgotten for now. If only you weren't so stubborn. I know all too well what that desperate longing for family does to a person. Could the pull be stronger because your real family is still alive?*"

My birth family is still alive? For a second, Exe panicked. She'd forgotten to hide the thought in her mind vault. But Velin didn't think a single word at her. *I don't think he can anymore. I think I've completely locked him out of my whole mind. Forever.*

Exe returned her attention to the shocking knowledge burned into her diary. *I have a family.* Out of practice with handling emotions thanks to Velin's constant repressions, the wave of guilt that hit her threatened to overwhelm. *The Parsells are my real family.* They'd stuck by her no matter how much trouble she caused, and the excited thrill she'd felt at the mention of her 'real family' was nothing short of disloyal.

Still, I've never really belonged here, what with these freakish powers that'll probably kill someone else soon. I need someone to teach me how to control them. Velin never will. And I have blood relatives who could help me living in another world. A world that could be accessed through a field just over thirty miles from her house. Her world. *My home.* And Velin had kept her from it for thirteen years.

I know the truth now, she thought, feeling a vicious satisfaction that he couldn't hear her thoughts anymore. *I'm going to that field. And you can't stop me.*

Thinking the triumphant thought to herself wasn't enough. She wanted to gloat over her success. Hugging the answer-giving journal to her chest, Exe strode down her tower and out into the cemetery. Ignoring the handful of costumed teens winding down around the bonfire, Exe stalked up cemetery hill again, feeling wiser and more determined than just a few hours ago. Velin was waiting for her. Although he was taller, and stood on higher ground, Exe faced him down across the low stone fence, "I know. Everything you wanted to keep from me, I know now."

"You know nothing," Velin sneered.

"Trying to manipulate my mind? That won't work anymore, will it?" Velin's narrowed eyes and silence gave Exe her answer. "I'm free of you. And I'm going home."

"Home?" Velin spat out the words like venom. "You think you're ready to take on what's waiting for you there? You won't last six seconds. You're nowhere near ready to return. Do you forget what you've got in your pocket?"

Exe's fingers went to the wanted poster tucked into her skirt pocket. As much as she longed to find her way home to her birth family, clearly someone was ready to kill her if she returned. *Or is this poster just another ploy of Velin's designed to stop me?*

"I'm going home," Exe clung to that improbable idea as a shield against the doubt that threatened her budding plan. "I'm going to find my real family, and nothing you say or do will stop me."

"I've done all I can," Velin's face stiffened into a look of chiseled unreadability. "If you're so determined, go. I only hope you *live* to regret it."

CHAPTER ELEVEN

FAR AFIELD

"**I**'m going home," Exe whispered, telling herself that her nerves were simply excitement. She glanced covertly at Easy to make sure he hadn't heard her. Thankfully, he was busy enjoying his first road trip as a licensed driver—windows down and music up. Exe leaned back to let the cool mid-November breeze quell her growing doubts.

She'd first proposed this road trip to Easy the day after his birthday, but they'd been delayed for over two weeks. Exe blamed Velin. Although she'd kicked him out of her own head, it infuriated Exe that Velin could still manipulate the open minds of her family and anyone else in her life. *He must've manipulated my brothers into their punishment-worthy prank, and our parents into grounding them to thwart me. Probably orchestrated the mandated participation during the town's Sadie Hawkins festival, too.*

Even now, Velin must know they were headed to the field, spying on her through Easy. Exe eyed her brother warily, silently cursing Velin for making her more suspicious and distant from her family than ever before. *Besides, the delays weren't all his fault.*

This morning, as she watched the sunrise over the distant city (that they were now swiftly approaching), Exe finally admitted that she'd been dragging her feet. She could've come without Easy or skipped the town's Veterans Day festival, but she hadn't. She told herself that she'd delayed because seeking out her birth family was disloyal to the Parsells. But that wasn't the real reason. *I delayed because I'm afraid.*

Part of her had hoped that if she stalled long enough, Velin would eventually relent and tell her what she wanted to know and maybe even agree to train her. *Then I wouldn't have to face the dangers of finding answers on my own.* She wasn't surprised when he stayed silent though. *I pushed him too far.* Now the only way forward was to venture into her homeland—where people wanted her dead.

Sanity said that she should turn back. But buried under the fear elicited by the wanted poster (and Velin's dire warnings), there was a flicker of hope that only the truth could inspire. *It may be dangerous, but I'm finally going to learn where I came from and find out why my birth family abandoned me. And I'm not leaving until they agree to teach me how to control my deadly powers.* It was worth risking her life if it meant that she'd never harm others with her unnatural abilities ever again. *Still...*

'I hope you live.' That was the last thing Velin had said to her. And the way he'd said it suggested that he didn't think she would survive. *Will people there really kill me on sight?* The wanted dead poster suggested that they would. *This trip might actually be my last. Is the truth worth dying for?*

Tasting blood, Exe realized she'd been chewing her cheek raw in indecision. She'd never admit it to the man, but she felt adrift in the sea of her turbulent thoughts without Velin's guiding voice. Now that he was no longer in her head telling her what to do, she was drowning in uncertainty, as if her own decisiveness had been stunted by his constant monitoring. Determination and terror waged war within her, until she felt crazy enough to go crawling back to Velin, no matter how long he made her wait for answers.

"What are we searching for?" Easy's curious question startled Exe. For one mad moment she thought she must've been talking to herself out loud, until she realized they were parked next to the field. She'd convinced Easy to bring her here on the pretense of finding something she'd lost when they'd had the flat tire. *What was it I told him?*

"My bracelet?" Exe ventured. From the look on Easy's face, she'd guessed wrong. "That special one I got for my birthday that one time. It's my favorite."

"I don't recall you being big on jewelry, except–" He looked pointedly at the amethyst stone glittering at the base of her throat. "Well, let's get started. If we don't find it fast, I'll miss my morning date."

Disappointment flooded Exe as the chances of getting Easy to stick around to explore the field faded. "You have a date today?"

"Three," Easy corrected. "An a.m. swim in the water tower with Sally, shooting pool this afternoon in the saloon with Lucy, and a midnight stroll down Main Street with Margo. Gotta play the field 'til I find the right girl." Easy jumped out and began searching the strip of dead grass along the street with the tip of his tennis shoe. Exe emerged more slowly, eyes on the glistening platinum fence that arched higher than she remembered. Close up, she could see each beautiful bar was delicately etched with an intricate pattern, giving them their distinctive sparkle.

"Weird, right?" Easy said, joining Exe by the fence. "Who in their right mind would erect such an ornate barrier around a scraggly patch of dirt?"

If only you knew the secret it protects, Exe thought as she smiled conspiratorially. "Maybe it protects an underground hideout. Feel like exploring?"

"Always," Easy said. "But what about your bracelet?"

"Oh, I already found it," Exe replied, wishing her only bracelet into her empty pocket. The childishly pink bangle fell to the ground as she jerked her hand out with a yelp of pain. Exe sucked on her bloody pinky, wondering how she could've cut herself on the cheap, child-safe plastic. "But what about your date?"

"The date can wait," Easy picked up the bracelet and slipped it onto her other wrist. "An adventure instigated by my kid sister? That's once-in-a-lifetime stuff. How do we get in?" Easy looked up at the tight coils of vicious barbed wire. "Not up."

"I don't know," Exe chewed on her lip as she glanced around for an entrance.

"Let's find a way in," Easy said over his shoulder as he set off along the fence.

"Oh, wait," Exe tied her pink elastic bracelet onto the fence. "So we know where we started from."

It took half an hour to circle the field under the warm winter sun. Following the fence around the corner, they squeezed down a narrow alley between the fence and the building behind it. The alley led them out into the parking lot of a factory stinking of sweaty feet and rotten eggs. When they reached the front street again, Exe sighed in disappointment at the sight of her pink bracelet.

"We're back where we started," Exe complained.

"And the mystery grows," Easy said. "A fence with no entrance."

Exe silently cursed Velin (regretting for a moment that he couldn't still hear her thoughts). *You think you're so clever, hiding the entrance so we can't get in. Well, I won't let that stop me... But now what?* As Easy untied her bracelet, Exe slumped against the fence, contemplating her next move. *The bracelet.* She'd just wished it into her pocket from her vanity table back home. *If I can conjure up a bracelet out of thin air, can't I just wish for a way through the fence?*

"Boy, are we idiots," Easy rolled his eyes. "Wasting all that time walking around this place when there's a gate right here!" Sure enough there was a small, elegant gate just beyond them. Easy pulled on the handle. "And it's not even locked! Maybe there's nothing so mysterious about this field after all."

Exe marveled at the sudden appearance of the gate that she'd wished into existence, (or wished into revealing itself). *Are there any limits to my unnatural abilities?*

"Are you coming or not?" Easy was already halfway across the field.

Exe nodded, pausing at the gate she had conjured. "This is it."

Dirt. That was it. Nothing else. That's all there was to the field. There weren't even any tumbleweeds or rocks bigger than a bead. Exe and Easy searched every inch of the place, but aside from the fancy fence, there wasn't a thing out of the ordinary about that empty lot. If there was an entrance to a magical world, Exe certainly couldn't find it.

"There's nothing here," Easy said, poking a finger at Exe's reddened nose. Though the temperature was in the mild mid-seventies, the sun's rays were still powerful enough to burn. "I'm starting to think this is someone's elaborate idea of a joke."

Exe was starting to believe that, too. *Velin's joke.* Of course he would send her on a wild goose chase to keep her from the truth. *He's probably laughing at me right now, watching this unfold through Easy's mind.*

"It's getting late," Easy said, as they reached the gate. "I say we head home."

"Will you miss your second date, too? Sorry for wasting your time," Exe sighed in frustration and followed, glancing back regretfully. Then she saw it. That same subtle shimmer she'd seen on moving day. In the distance, the desert heat seemed to dance on the horizon. Exe spun around and ran.

"Exe, wait!" Exe heard Easy calling and chasing after her, but she didn't stop. The far off shimmer was taking shape. "It's just a mirage! You'll never reach it!"

It did look like a mirage, but it didn't fade away. The oasis got closer the faster she ran. A lush grove of exotic flowers surrounding a waterfall. Exe came to a sudden stop. One more step and she'd be standing on the plush emerald grass, next to the swirling turquoise pool and the cascade that seemed to flow from nowhere, as if gushing over an unseen cliff. Terrified yet tantalized, she took another step.

The grass crushed like velvet under her feet, tempting her to run through it barefoot. The delicate, tiny flowers on the bushes and trees seemed to wink at her. Looking back, she saw Easy searching for her mere inches away. *But he doesn't see me.* He looked as if he was calling her name, but she couldn't hear him, only the gentle gushing of the impossible waterfall. *Though it doesn't look quite like water.* She knelt down by the swirling pool.

It's not water. Exe ran her hand through the mysterious substance. It was made of the finest, silkiest beads, like the micro-beads in bubble bath, only smaller and softer. They flowed in a liquid-like stream over rounded boulders. The droplets left her hand tingling, as if it now knew a secret the rest of her body did not.

The tumbling cascade beckoned. Exe stepped into the flowing waterfall and closed her eyes. Letting the softness roll over her, she felt as refreshed as a cool shower on a steamy day, although she remained completely dry. *Easy has to feel this.* Maybe she could make a wish that would let him see and enter the mirage. She reluctantly stepped out of the not-quite-waterfall to find him.

The oasis was gone.

Exe was now standing in a river of the strange water. Twinkling, midnight grass grew along its milky white banks. Beyond the river, a forest of pearly trees with silvery leaves and corkscrew-curled limbs stood tall and tight together, as if planted to protect the little stream. Behind her, a proper waterfall gushed over a marbled cliff that glowed with a soft, pure light. The teal cascade tumbled against creamy boulders at its base, bursting the strange bead-water into a superfine spray that shrouded the pale forest in a glittering mist.

"You shouldn't be here," a dusky voice broke the quiet of the tranquil glade. "I already got the heebie-jeebies from this place without you skulking about."

Exe stumbled as she searched for the source of the voice. A young man, no older than Seph or Thone ambled out of the mist, coolly tossing and catching a silver dollar coin. A fissure of fear cracked through her as she took in his ebony Gatsby cap and black Cossack jacket, tapered at the waist to make his shoulders appear more broad and intimidating than they already were. Her cool amethyst pendant began to warm.

"You think I'm a sucker? No dye job and odd clothes can fool me. You've still got that notorious face," the aloof youth said, looking at everything but Exe. "You didn't follow me. I'd know. And I doubt Asher would risk sending you after me. So why are you in the Corpse Copse, dollface?"

"I don't know what you're talking about," Exe shivered as the youth began to circle her, easily leaping from bank to bank with his long stride. Her breath caught as she spied a pin on the teen's lapel—two small triangles inside the base of a larger triangle, forming a diamond in the center. She'd seen the exact same pin on the lapel of the man in black's body. "What do you mean, Corpse Copse?"

"Come on," the youth mocked. "Even an outcast like you must've heard the spook stories. Trees grown from bones, half-rotted corpses chained to boulders, death to all who enter, none who venture in ever return. You know the spiel. It's why we all stay away from this place. Took Malina an hour to convince me to come. Yet you want me to believe you're just here on a stroll?"

"I never said that," Exe edged closer to the waterfall. "It's just, an accident, coming here. A mistake."

"You got that right. Spying on me was the mistake. One you'll regret. One you won't make again," the youth twisted mid-leap, landed squarely in front of Exe, and grabbed her arms. "I told you– Your eyes... They're violet."

"What of it?" Exe struggled, but his hands tightened like a vise. "Let me go."

"Is this your sick idea of a joke?" the youth shook her, hard. "Have you gone off the deep end? You wanna get yourself killed? Take that charm off your eyes. Now."

"I said, let go!" Exe stared him down and wished him away from her. But she forgot to wish his hands off of her first. Together they sailed through the air and slammed against a tree. He hit hard, bouncing off the bark and collapsing on top of her as they dropped to the ground. Before she could blink, the kid was on her, pinning her with some sort of magical hold that she couldn't break with a simple wish, though she tried.

"This is real," the youth stared down at her with a strange mix of elation and horror. He grabbed the chain around her neck and pulled the warm, amethyst pendant up to the base of her throat. "You're you. Your appearance, your eyes, this tetherstone. Real. The story of your survival, I believed it a myth spun to condemn Demaine, but you're alive. Why are you here? Did Demaine send you? What was he thinking?"

"I'm not telling you anything," Exe focused all her energy on breaking his hold. It worked, she was free. For a moment.

The youth jerked back in surprise when she broke his spell, but he had her pinned again in a second, with a stronger, more painful force. Exe tried to break the hold again, but she was too depleted.

"How did you do that?" the teen marveled. "I've only just written that spell. You couldn't have developed a counter. Unless you came prepared to break hold spells. That's illegal here, you know. What kind of arsenal has Demaine equipped you with?"

"Why should I tell you?" Exe bluffed, pretending an association with the Demaine guy in an attempt to get the boy to back off. "I don't know you."

"You don't? Of course you don't. You're not– This is bonkers, dollface," he leaned back without releasing the hold spell. "You can't be the message. Asher never would've sent me if– So what's going on? You aren't going to tell me, are you? Okay, I'm gonna let you up, but don't run. We gotta work this out."

The instant he released her, Exe jumped to her feet and backed away, one eye on the waterfall. "Who are you?" she asked.

"Riven Torsade," the youth answered. "No need to ask for your moniker. You're Experience Verelustre. Back from the dead."

Exe forgot all about maneuvering to a strategically safer position near the waterfall and took a step toward Riven. "Back from the dead?"

"Well, yeah," Riven drawled, leaning back against a tree in a casual stance meant to mask a cunning readiness. "But now's not the time to delve into history, doll. We've got ourselves a quandary here, and I sure as certain don't know what to do about it. Asher's expecting a message, and I don't have one to bring him. I'm not delivering you. It took a lifetime to earn Asher's trust. Showing up with you is sure to destroy it."

"What message? Who's Demaine? And who's Asher?" Exe grabbed Riven by his leather lapels. "I want to know where I am and what's going on."

Riven's coin dropped and rolled into the stream as he stilled mid-toss. "You don't know Asher? You don't know from nothin' do you? Asher's your father."

"My father?" Exe's breath caught. "You know my real father? And he sent you here? What about my mother? Is she—"

"Malina," Riven answered. "Yes, I know your whole family. But you don't, do you? Is that why Demaine sent you?"

Exe turned away, brushing the dampness from her eyes, "I don't know any Demaine. No one sent me. I just came— I want answers. Velin warned me not to come."

"Velin? Of course!" Riven gasped and sighed, his eyes alight. "That makes sense, but I'd never have guessed. I wonder if Jettani has? I know some of the Disimulata still hunt Velin. Maybe they were hoping to find you with him."

"Who is Jettani? And who's hunting Velin? Are they hunting me, too? Do my parents know? Where are they now? Can you take me to them?" Exe pelted him with questions, but Riven wasn't listening.

"You may have a death wish dollface, but I don't. You came on your own, so you can go on your own. Whatever message Velin wanted to send Asher, he can send it another time with somebody else," Riven dragged her down into the stream and wrestled her toward the cascade.

"I'm not going anywhere without answers!" Exe wrenched herself out of Riven's grasp and wished him away from her. A powerful, unseen force flung Riven against a fallen log half-submerged in the stream. Exe stood over him, triumphant—until she noticed smoky wisps of crimson whirlpooling away in the turquoise water. Drips of blood seeped down his black jacket. *I impaled his shoulder on a branch!* Exe tried to help him, but he waved her off, a sickened tinge staining his face.

"I've never been impaled before," Riven swallowed a wave of nausea. "Hurts different than I expected. Like it's on fire and frostbitten all at once." He took several quick, deep breaths, then wrenched his shoulder free from the branch with a feral scream.

"We have to get you help," Exe agonized, trying to staunch the blood spurting from Riven's wound with her hands. "How do we call a doctor here?"

"We call 'em medicors, and we're not calling one. I don't suppose you know any healing spells, do you?" Riven pressed his own hand to his wound and whispered a word Exe didn't recognize. Within moments the color returned to his face. When he lifted his hand, the blood was no longer flowing and the jagged wound was now an angry scar.

"Did you just heal yourself?" Exe marveled.

"Patch job. Best I could do. Every soldier is given basic medic training to use on the battlefield," Riven gave Exe a shaky smile and sank down on the ebony riverbank.

"I-I could've killed you," Exe struggled to breathe as she backed away from Riven. "Don't you see? I have to find my real parents. I don't know what I'm doing with these powers. I'm out of control."

"Didn't you hear me? It's too dangerous for you here. Is getting to your parents worth your life?" Riven winced as she batted away his consoling hand.

"What makes my life more important than the next person I kill?" Exe asked.

"You've killed someone?"

"It was an accident," Exe hugged herself. "Like I almost killed you. These powers that I have... Is it magic? I don't even know that. I need help."

"Velin's looking after you, right? Why isn't he training you?" Riven asked.

"I don't know why. I barely know him. We only met a few weeks ago. And he's only interested in manipulating me, not helping me. That's why I need my parents. Please?" Exe pleaded.

"Sorry doll, but I can't do it. It'd be suicide to try," Riven said with quiet finality.

"Then I hope you enjoy camping," Exe glared at him.

"What?"

"You may be able to force me to go now, but unless you plan on living here, you can't stop me from coming back later to find my parents on my own."

Riven stared her down a few tense moments then pulled a silver device from his pocket that looked like an Art Deco pocket watch. "Care to compromise? How 'bout I bring your parents to you instead?" Riven flipped open the pocket watch without waiting for an answer and swirled his finger over its face in an intricate pattern.

"Fine," Exe dropped down on the inky riverbank to wait, nonchalantly swirling the strange water with a twig to hide her nervousness. *I'm about to meet my birth parents.*

Riven paced impatiently on the bank across from her. After several long, anxious minutes, he flipped open his pocket watch and tried again. Several tense minutes later, Riven leaned against the marble cliff near the waterfall then turned to Exe, "No dice, doll. Neither Asher or Malina are responding, which means they're into something big. You'll have to get Velin to arrange a meet at a later date."

"No!" Exe jumped up, hurt and anger firing inside her. *They don't want to see me. They can't even be bothered to come say it to my face. Or maybe...* "Wait, how do I even know if you actually sent them messages? Let me see them."

"See? You can't– If you wanna hear 'em, you gotta come here," Riven crossed his arms and raised his eyebrows as if daring her. Slowly, Exe moved closer, eying the waterfall, ready to fight him off if he tried to shove her into the cascade. She accepted the pocket watch from him, then leapt back when he reached for her.

"If you wanna hear it, you're gonna have to let me touch you," Riven's eyes laughed at her. Cautiously, he stretched out his hand like he was attempting to pet a lion and cupped her ear then touched the pocket watch Exe held between them. Exe jumped, startled to hear the sound of his voice inside her ear even though no sound was coming from his mouth—or the pocket watch.

"Nightsky. Message undeliverable," Riven's voice rang inside her ear (spookily similar to the way Velin's voice had sounded in her head). "Gemini in play. Accept in person in the grotto or advise alternate action. Shadow."

A few swirls over the watch face and soon Riven had a second message playing, identical to the first except this one began with 'Moonglow' instead of 'Nightsky.'

"What's this supposed to mean? You said you were contacting my parents!" Exe ripped Riven's hand away from her ear and thrust his pocket watch back at him.

"I did. Trust me, they'd come if they could after getting that message," Riven tucked his watch away. "It's not in the cards or the stars for you today, toots. Come back with a better plan, or better yet, get Velin to bring them to you. Either way, I'm out. This is way above my paygrade. And it's way too dangerous for you to be here."

"I didn't fight this hard and come this far to turn back now. I'm seeing my parents today, even if I have to find them myself!" Incensed, Exe brushed by Riven and headed into the forest, hoping to happen upon the path he'd taken to get here.

"Have you gone batty?" Riven trailed after her. "You want me to march the notorious Exe through Anacapia? It's certifiable! We'll both wind up dead."

Exe hesitated, her hand going instinctively to the wanted poster in her pocket. *But I can't turn back now. Not when I'm so close to answers.* "You coming? Or not?"

"Are you sure you wanna do this, doll?" Riven asked, sighing when Exe nodded. "Asher's gonna kill me. Okay. I'll do all I can to protect you, but I make no promises."

"I have to do this," Exe said, crumpling up the poster in her pocket, suddenly afraid he'd see it and use it as an excuse to force her to leave. "My birth parents are the only ones I can trust to help me. People don't have powers in my world. You don't know what it's like, growing up with a family that has no clue what you're going through. I'm constantly terrified that I'm going to hurt someone I love, just because I'm... different. Could you live like that? Don't answer. You can't even begin to know what it's like."

"You have no idea what I know," Riven said, his expression unfathomable.

"I don't?" Exe felt as if she were floating into the deep sea blue of his eyes.

"Nevermind," Riven flicked his fingers at the bloodstain on the front of his jacket, sealing the hole and erasing the blood. "Sometimes it's best to be left in the dark. I'm practically in the dark on most things myself. And that's the way it needs to stay."

"So, will you help me?" Exe asked, trying not to feel as brushed off as the stain on his jacket.

"This is madness," Riven sighed. "But, since you leave me no choice, let's at least be smart about it. Hold up a sec, we gotta do something about your duds. You can't go traipsing around Anacapia in that getup."

"Anacapia?"

"Oh, man. Anacapia is the name of this country, your birthplace," Riven said, fishing a pair of sunglasses out of his pocket that looked just like the man in black's. "First, we gotta hide those eyes. Your hair needs to be black and styled. In waves, that's how– the girls wear it. And those clothes definitely aren't local."

Riven caressed her hair, then her clothes. Exe felt them shifting and transforming about her until she was now wearing a pair of high-waisted, wide-legged pants and a flounced blouse. Leaning over the stream, Exe stared at her stippled reflection—she looked just like the girl in the wanted poster.

"One last touch," Riven removed his hat and flicked his finger against the brim. Before Exe's eyes, the black wool transformed into a chic, feminine hat with a deep brim, ridged and scalloped like a seashell. He settled this masterpiece on her head and pulled it low until her face was almost completely obscured.

"Satisfied?" Exe asked.

"You'll do. From far away," Riven qualified, looking her over. "But if we're stopped? You'd better hope we're not stopped. Let's go."

"Why not?" Exe hesitated.

Riven pushed open a path between the trees, "Because you know nothing about this world, and you got no papers. Let's go."

"Wait," Exe hesitated again, glancing at the waterfall. *Easy's still out there. Waiting, wondering, worrying.*

"We gotta go now if we're going. There'll be more patrols out once it gets dark," Riven said, checking his pocket watch again.

"There's something I have to do," Exe stepped through the cascade and re-emerged in the mirage. Easy was still there, standing just outside the oasis that he couldn't see, pacing and calling for Exe. Easy stared at his phone as if torn between waiting her out or calling for help.

"A portal? I assumed you volted in," Exe jumped at the sound of Riven's voice so close beside her. "What is this place? It's not like any world I've ever seen before. Who's that?" Riven shouldered Exe aside, intent on protecting her from Easy.

"My brother. He's waiting for me. I've gotta tell him I'm okay," Exe swatted impatiently at the hat as it blocked her view. *I can't go out there looking like this.* Plus, if they were face-to-face when she told him to go, he'd insist on staying. Easy would never abandon her. *Better if he believes that*

I abandoned him. Which I'm technically doing. Exe reached into her pocket, grateful to find that her cellphone was still there.

"What are you doing?" Riven stared curiously at her phone.

"I'm sending a text. A message," she added when Riven looked puzzled. "I'm telling my brother that I'm safe and to go home without me."

"Are you telling him that you might never return?" Riven prodded.

"What do you mean?" Exe eyed Riven suspiciously as she hit send.

"Understand that Anacapia is a dangerous place—for you," Riven said.

Exe stood still, torn apart by indecision. *Would it be cowardly to retreat? Or foolish to go on?* She didn't know her own mind anymore.

Then her phone beeped. Easy had texted her back: 'Yes, I can still make my afternoon date, but are you sure you're okay? I don't want to just leave you here.'

Exe looked up from the message and gazed at Easy. *What if today is last time I ever see him, or the rest of my family?* Then she glanced at the waterfall. *Can I live knowing that I came so close to learning the truth, but let fear hold me back?*

Exe's phone beeped again, another text from Easy: 'Where did you go?'

Exe hesitated for only a moment before texting back: 'Home.'

CHAPTER TWELVE

Sweet Home Anacapia

The farther they journeyed from the softly glowing waterfall, the creepier the Corpse Copse grew. Beyond the pearly glade, the trees grew gray, with blackened leaves and gnarled, clawing boughs. Here and there, stripped limbs shone stark against the black bark, like bones beneath the rotting flesh of ashen trees. The darker the trees, the darker the forest, forcing Exe to remove the sunglasses hiding her eyes so that she could see where she was going.

Riven's mood darkened along with the woods, increasing Exe's anxiety and her growing urge to turn back. *I can't blame my foot-dragging on Velin now. Should I listen to my gut instinct? I want to, yet each step gets me closer to the truth... and my birth family.* Exe focused on that fact to conquer her cowardice.

"What are they like?" Exe asked Riven's back. "My parents. I should know who they are before I meet them, shouldn't I? What were their names? Asher and–"

"Malina," Riven leapt over a fallen tree. "There's no one I respect more than your mother. Cunning yet caring.

Sharpest leader I've ever followed. Malina's the main reason I turned. She's my commander, the best in our forces. Ought to be a general by now. Would be, if not for–" Riven cut himself off, looking sideways at Exe.

"You turned?" Exe shivered as a clawing twig scraped down her spine. The spooky sensation added to her rising fear that she was tromping through this forbidding forest to her doom. *What if he's a werewolf or something?* "What did you turn into?"

"A rebel," Riven winked with a sly smile, then sobered. "There's something you need to understand, doll. We're enemies, you and I, at least according to the world out there. True, I'm a soldier in training, under your mother's command, but see this pin here?" Riven touched the triangular insignia on his lapel. "This says I'm also a junior member of the Disimulata. And let's just say that your family and the Disimulata don't quite see eye to eye."

"The Disimulata? Who are they? Your law enforcement?" Exe asked. *And why do they want me dead?* Recalling the man in black, she pulled her warm amethyst pendant into her hand as if it could protect her.

"They may as well be," Riven said. "They're Jettani's special enforcers, once a secret police force, but they don't hide their activities any longer. Not since Jettani took full control over Anacapia and dismantled local law enforcement."

Jettani. Exe didn't need to pull out the poster to remember the name of the woman who'd ordered her death. *An order given to the Disimulata to carry out.* "You're one of the Disimulata?" Exe stopped following as Riven continued on, maneuvering herself to put a chain-draped boulder between them.

"Gonna be," Riven answered, pausing when he realized Exe was no longer following. "Heard enough to terrify you into turning back, yet?"

"But you turned. Right?" Exe clutched her necklace tighter. *Am I a fool to follow him?* Riven's hesitation felt like a lifetime.

"Yeah, I turned," Riven drawled. "My mother is Jettani's closest advisor these days. With that kind of access, you—see things. Your mom, Malina, she's taught me to recognize true right from wrong, and I've seen too much wrong to support Jettani. But no one can know. As far as Anacapia at large is concerned, my family and I are Jettani's most loyal supporters. That's why I'm the perfect spy for our side. The intel I supply is your parents' best shot to survive this quiet battle they're waging against Jettani."

"My mother taught you?" Exe asked, rubbing her damp eyes at the thought of her birth mother nurturing someone else's child. *Waging a war? Maybe my birth parents are fighting so that I can come home.* She quivered in a confusion of hope and guilt.

"She's quite persuasive, your mother. She should've been the politician in your family, but our military would be worse off if she'd pursued that path," Riven brushed his hand over a tangle of vines, causing them to unknot and part.

"A politician. Is that what my father is?" Exe stepped through the opening. "He works for the government? For Jettani?"

"He does," Riven answered. "Okay, doll. Enough with the questions. We're almost out of the woods, and once we clear the trees, we can't talk at all."

"Why not?" Exe demanded.

"You gotta understand something about Anacapia, toots," Riven stalked her into the clutches of a battered tree. "There are eyes and ears everywhere, ready to report anything suspicious. Now people are afraid of the Corpse Copse, so there are no spies here, besides me. But after that little magic show you put on by the waterfall, I wouldn't be surprised if they're on their way—if their monitoring capabilities extend this far."

"We're being watched?" Exe scanned the forest, searching every shadow. "Someone knows every time a spell is performed?"

"Not yet. Although that's what they're working towards," Riven said. "Round-the-clock surveillance of the entire country and every living creature is the goal. As of now, they're only able to keep tabs on all volting activity. As far as I know, anyway. That's why we're hoofin' it."

I'm so dangerous that they're surveilling an entire country trying to find me? Exe thought, extricating herself from the clawing branches. She was tempted to ask if she was the reason for the heightened security, but knew it would be an excuse for him to send her back. Instead she asked, "Volting? I only understand about half of what you say."

Suddenly, silver shot by her ear, whistling like a bullet. "Clearly, tyro," Riven reached up and caught the silver sparkle, then opened his palm to reveal his lost coin. "Volting is how many travel here. We're able to pop from one place to another in a blink, although there are limits. It's one of the first things Jettani put restrictions on when she came to power. Now the Disimulata can know people's comings and goings instantaneously—unless you take certain precautions—which we can't do here. And since you don't have a license, they'd come the second they spotted unlicensed volting activity in the Corpse Copse."

"So it's possible to travel great distances instantaneously without being detected?" Exe asked, hope bubbling within her. If she learned to volte, she'd be free to visit Anacapia whenever she wanted. *Assuming I safely return home to the Parsells after today.* And her birth family would be able to visit her, too. *So why haven't they?*

"The distance depends on how gifted you are at volting," Riven explained. "Going undetected is a matter of leaving from an enclosed space coated with a protective substance known as cruor clay. That's why I was able to volte into the Corpse Copse, but I knew I'd be walking home. The monitors can only get a lock on you at departure to detect where you land. If they don't see you leave, they can't track where you go."

"Is everything so complicated here?" Exe asked.

"Yes. Now listen, beyond those trees we'll be out in the open, doll, so this needs to stay out of sight," Riven pried the pendant she still clutched at the base of her neck out of her hand and tucked it under her blouse. "Hat and sunglasses on at all times. If we meet any people, don't talk. They'll know in two seconds that you're not... local."

"Why the sunglasses?" Exe complained, sliding them back onto her face. "Can't you just change my eyes like you changed my hair if their hue is a problem?"

"I can't dye your eyes. The change to your hair is permanent, unless you dye it again," Riven explained. "Once a permanent spell is performed, its magical essence dissipates until nothing detectable remains. A temporary spell, like one to mask the color of your eyes, would have to stay active to work, and that they'll detect in a second."

"I don't understand. There are different types of spells?" Dread flooded Exe as the hope for a quick fix to gain control over her powers dwindled.

"You've got a lot to learn, doll."

"Why do I need to hide my eye color, anyway? Is violet such an unusual color here, like it is in my world?"

"I guess you could say that," Riven headed for a tight line of trees with the barest glimmer of daylight peeking through the branches. "Okay, from this moment on, you do whatever I say. No matter what I do, go with it, even if I call you Viva."

"Viva? Is that your girlfriend?" Exe asked, then gasped as she recognized the shadowy shapes of skeletons swinging from the boughs.

"Hardly," Riven paused in a patch of light breaking through the gnarled trees. "Don't worry, the dead bodies are just for show. Fakes placed there to scare people away. Or so Malina assured me. I'm guessing Velin put them there to keep people from finding the entrance to the world where he's hiding."

"Velin placed them? He would," Exe shuddered as Riven parted a pair of dangling corpses that dripped with rotting flesh. The sight that greeted her as she stepped into the light took her breath away. The Corpse Copse grew atop a steep bluff, and at Exe's feet lay a cornucopia of shimmering colors and enticing sights.

"Welcome home, Experience," Riven whispered, as Exe stepped between the swaying bodies. "What do you think of your country?"

"It's what my dreams are made of," Exe whispered in awe as she instinctively went to remove the sunglasses to get a clearer look at her enchanting homeland.

"Leave them on," Riven stayed her hand. He pressed a button on the frames and suddenly the lenses began to whir, bringing anything Exe looked at into instant focus, serving as binoculars with microscopic lenses. "Take a quick look, then we gotta move."

Exe scanned the valley like a child in Nowhere's confectioner's shop, "What's that mountain in the center of everything? Or is it a mountain? It's like one giant waterfall." She marveled at the sight of several gravity-defying ferries floating up and down the fast-flowing waterfall mountain.

"The Cascades. Water falls down every side of that mountain," Riven answered. "Although legend has it the mountain was once a water volcano—if you trust the books published by our government. Our history books say the mountain-obscuring falls were created hundreds of years ago when the Rochda capped the crater to build the city."

"A city on top of a waterfall mountain?" Exe focused in on the city, drinking in what she could see of the dazzling buildings peeking over top of the intricately carved city walls. The tallest spire seemed to undulate with ripples of violet and aquamarine, as if the walls were alive.

"That's Vianelle, our capitol. The tallest building at its center, the aqua and lavender one, that's Incendia, the palace of water and fire. It's the heart of Anacapia and the seat of our government," Riven explained. "And this is as close as you'll ever get to it as long as Jettani's in power."

"Is that where Jettani is now?" Exe turned to look at Riven, jumping when the sunglasses zoomed in on his face as if it were just a whisper away from hers.

"Yes, " he answered.

Exe longed to ask him about Jettani, about why the ruler of this land would order her death. But she didn't. If she admitted to knowing that Jettani wanted her dead, Riven might refuse to take her any farther. Instead, she scanned the horizon again, soaking in as much as she could.

"What's that over there?" Exe spotted a red stain among the fields on the horizon. "Is that a lake of blood? There are men in black, um, Disimulata guarding it."

"The Sanguine Slough," Riven muttered, looking as if he wanted to take the sunglasses from her to see for himself. "That's where cruor clay is harvested, though public use of cruor is illegal now. Only the government is permitted access to the secrecy that substance provides. That's why it's so heavily guarded. Are any Disimulata looking this way? We'd better move."

Riven pressed a button to return the sunglasses to normal vision and steered Exe toward a large boulder. Hidden behind the ragged rock was a path so narrow they had to inch along the trail with their backs scraping the sharp cliff stones. When they reached safe ground below, Riven turned onto a broken, cobblestone road overgrown with delicate, spiderwebbed vines and flowering shrubs. The overgrowth appeared to be infested with tiny beings that looked a bit like wingless fairies. Exe paused to exclaim over the adorable little imps.

"Quit acting like a tourist," Riven whispered harshly, dragging her roughly away.

He pulled out his pocket watch and turned a few knobs. Its gears whirred and ticked, then the cover popped open to emit a beam of shimmery, silvery light. He scanned the broken road with the beam, then shoved Exe forward, forcing her to march ahead of him.

Exe squelched any protest to this treatment when she saw the fear on his face. With his words of warning buzzing through her, Exe trudged on, trying not to act surprised at the sight of each new delight. First, they waded through a field of flowers that changed colors—to predict the weather, Riven explained as the sky clouded over. After navigating a weed-choked ravine, they stopped to pick off insects that Riven called 'squanders.' The tiny, blood-sucking bugs burrowed under your skin to release time-waster toxin—a non-lethal poison which caused people to procrastinate until cured.

An hour later, they came upon a grove infested with 'gadabouts.' The majority of the miniature, teddy bear gnomes ignored Exe and Riven as they were too intent on getting tipsy. But a small gang of these pint-sized fur balls broke away from the celebration to amuse themselves by pelting Exe with flower buds that erupted on impact with a sneeze-inducing pollen. Riven emerged unscathed. Apparently, gadabouts were smart enough not to attack someone affiliated with the Disimulata.

Every time they reached a fork in the abandoned road, Riven seemed to choose the most difficult path. Exe quickly realized that he was opting for the least-traveled lanes that led them around the villages dotting the countryside. The only signs of civilization that Exe saw up close were ruins of settlements abandoned long ago.

The full moon was high in the sky when Riven finally murmured that they were nearing her home. Up ahead, their abandoned road met up with a well-maintained thoroughfare. The crossroads were so choked with trees that they completely obscured the intersection. Riven scanned the area twice before shoving Exe out onto the meticulously groomed lane that seemed to shimmer with smoky gems.

They hadn't walked for more than a few minutes before the dark, quiet street echoed with a electric crack. It was an ear-splitting sound, disturbingly similar to the bang she'd heard back in Nowhere's schoolhouse—when the man in black had vanished.

"Saddled with minder duties too, Riven?" a scratchy voice drolled from behind them. "At least I get to keep an eye on her parents. You're stuck babysitting the brat."

"Not a word," Riven hissed in Exe's ear before seizing her and whirling around. Exe barely had a moment to take in the awkward boy (dressed in the same uniform as Riven) before Riven violently shoved her to her knees.

"You're all wet, Hastings," Riven addressed the boy with a sinister laugh. "You can't have any fun minding adults."

Instantly, Exe felt her lungs seize, locking haggard breaths in her tightening chest. She pitched forward, smacking her head on the glistening pavement with a force that knocked the wind back into her. The second she collapsed, Riven put his boot on her neck and immobilized her with his hold spell.

"Attaboy! Mind if I play?" Hastings strolled close enough to nudge Exe's head with his own boot.

"Lay off, will ya?" Riven replied. "Find your own outcast to louse up. Or why not try this with your own mark? How'dya think Asher would react?"

"Don't get all balled up, I was only asking," Hastings laughed. "When I spotted you two from the Verelustres' balcony, I figured you'd let me hassle Viv–"

When Hastings went suddenly silent, Exe glanced up and discovered that her sunglasses had been knocked askew, leaving one violet eye exposed. But Hastings wasn't looking at her face. She followed his gaze and gasped—the smoky amethyst pendant had come untucked from her blouse and was slowly inching its way back into hiding.

Riven stepped on the pendant and caught Hastings' gaze, "It's not Viva I'm minding, Hasty. I've captured the real deal. The notorious naïf."

"That so?" Hastings tried to act casual. "Why's she still alive, then?"

"You've got your orders, I've got mine," Riven said nonchalantly, tossing and catching his coin. "Direct orders, via my mother, who told me right where to find her."

"You're bringing her in?"

"Like leading a shibboleth to slaughter," Riven replied.

This time it wasn't Riven's hold spell that caused Exe's breath to catch. She should've known when she'd first spotted the Disimulata pin on his lapel—she'd been a fool to trust Riven. *All along he's been leading me into a trap.*

"Boy, I've daydreamed about winning the reward for bringing in her corpse. Just imagine what they'll give you for capturing the infamous Experience Verelustre alive," Hastings' hands writhed over one another at the thought.

"Why just imagine?" Riven asked, stepping toward Hastings. "Why not join me?"

Exe felt the hold spell on her break the moment Riven's boot lifted off her neck. *Why would he release me and leave me unattended?* Exe puzzled over the thought as she edged away from the boys.

"What would you do with your share?" Riven asked, glancing back at Exe. When he spotted her crawling away, his eyes warned her to stay still.

Trustworthy eyes.

"I don't know. Buy everythin' you already got?" Hastings laughed, his eyes beginning to glaze. "But itsh, more 'n there eward. Eer-war. Rrrrreeeeewaaaarrrrd. 'Oy, that'sh har' to shay. Sharrr'ds toupee. Toupee? Not toupee. Whashappenintomeeee?"

"Are you okay, Hastings?" Riven asked, but his tone held no question.

"Isshhhooo," Hastings swayed and staggered toward Exe like a drunkard. "Youssshdooodiiiish. Glaaaasheeea–"

"It's not her, Hasty," Riven caught him as he timbered and lowered him gently to the ground before he could collapse onto Exe. "You're just feeling a bit... torpid."

"T-toooorrrp-piii? Nnnnnaaaah, naaah yooooooo," Hastings giggled at the accusing finger he waggled at Riven. "Yooooo maaah fffffrrrrrreeehnnn–"

With a sigh, Hastings was dead.

He went so peacefully that, although Exe watched him closely, she almost missed the moment when life completely abandoned his body. Riven stared at his lifeless friend blankly, as if the death he had caused shocked him into complete shutdown.

"He knew your true identity, I had no choice. I guess I've done murder," Riven whispered woodenly, before turning on Exe. "We're both killers now."

The bitterness in those words ignited Exe's fear. She sat up and instinctively reached for her necklace, as if holding it might somehow strengthen her powers should she need to defend herself. *Should I trust what Riven told me, or what he told Hastings about taking me to Jettani?* "Where are you taking me?"

"You know where," Riven muttered as he stared at Hastings, his breath quickening as he pulled out what looked like a doll-sized leather briefcase.

With a whispered word, the case expanded to full size. Another of Riven's whispered commands and water gushed from every pore and orifice of Hastings' corpse, seeping away until the body was almost entirely dehydrated. Another whisper and Hastings' body crumpled like an aluminum can, his head collapsing last as it emitted a long, strangled cough of bone dust. Oozing only a few trickles of thick, sticky blood, Hastings' deflated corpse folded itself neatly into Riven's open briefcase.

Exe gaped in horror at the sickening sight. *Trust him or run? Trust him or run?* The panicky thought ricocheted around her mind, amping up the terror until she felt herself racing away without ever deciding to run. Riven jumped her before she got very far, the briefcase nailing her hard in the elbow.

"Now you run? After all I've done for you?" Rive raged at her. "We never should've come. I should've forced you to understand the danger."

"I knew the danger," Exe said, pulling the wanted poster from her pocket and showing it to Riven.

"You knew?" Riven whispered, low and menacing, yet it thrummed louder than a scream through Exe. "You knew your life was at stake and you still insisted on coming here? And putting my life on the line too? I had to kill for you!"

Riven hauled Exe to her feet and bulldozed her down the road. The silent walk felt like ages, but in reality it took only a few moments to reach their destination. Towering twenty stories high, there stood an oddly angular, solitary bluff of polished platinum stone, like the prow of a ship run aground in a grassy field. Near its base, a perfectly round gathering pool rippled, fed by a cascade falling directly in its center.

Before Exe could search for the waterfall's source, Riven propelled her into a crevice hidden in the cliffside. Perched on a pedestal inside, a bulbous stone toad stared at her with obsidian eyes that looked strangely alive. Its gaping mouth dripped sickeningly slick with mossy slime. "Put your hand in its mouth," Riven bit out, his stony expression silencing any questions.

Nose wrinkled in disgust, Exe stuck her hand in. The slimy mouth instantly slammed shut on her wrist, trapping her hand. Its black, glassy eyes swelled until she was sure they would pop. Yanking as hard as she could, Exe fought to free herself. She nearly stumbled into the gathering pool when the mouth suddenly released.

With a snide smirk, the stone toad hopped off into the water as its pedestal melted into the ground. The chiseled niche behind it parted as easily as drapery, revealing a small cave at the bottom of a long, shadowy mineshaft. A gilded cage about half the size of a coffin swayed serenely, suspended by an ornately-etched, unnervingly thin chain that disappeared up into the darkness.

"Get in," Riven commanded, giving her a shove.

"In there?!" Exe balked, cringing away from the cage. Its glistening bars were intricately woven so tightly together that Exe could barely see (*Or breathe!*) through them. "Why?! I– I– c–can't!"

"We just traipsed through a whole country crawling with people who want to kill you, and this scares you? Get. In,"

Riven said, shoving her headfirst into the swinging cage when she hesitated. Eyes squeezed shut Exe crawled inside. As he was closing the door, Riven said, "Don't do a single thing until I get up there. I'll be right behind you."

The second the door slammed shut, the glistening cage zoomed upward, its superfine chain tinkling delicately as it spooled, rudely reminding Exe of the contraption's flimsy fragility. The sound soon faded, until all she could hear in the long darkness was cool wind wisping by as she sped endlessly upward. Fingers curled pointlessly around the cage's bars, Exe desperately and repeatedly whispered, "You are okay. All you have to do is get through."

None too soon, the soaring cage began to slow to the sound of its chain feeding through a pulley system. Overhead, lustrous dust motes drifted on the moonbeams infiltrating the murky shaft, setting the chiseled platinum walls aglow. The moment the cage came to a gentle rest inside an overgrown grotto, its door swung softly open. Exe crawled out as quickly as she could. As soon as she cleared the cage, it closed itself and plummeted out of sight. Although she knew that she should wait for Riven, the beauty beyond the grotto lured her outside.

Exe stepped out onto a terrace overflowing with lush, impossible foliage. A series of tiny ponds filled with lacy lily pads dominated one corner. In another, miniature trees floated in midair, without soil to protect or nourish the pale, stringy roots swaying below them. They blossomed with a deep purple bloom that filled the balcony with a heady scent. At the center stood an enormous onyx vessel that was both a bubbling fountain and a planter with hundreds of openings overflowing with iridescent seedlings.

Along the far end of the terrace, Exe spotted a line of arching windows framed with polished ebony. *A house. My parents' house.* The sleek, shimmery home blended with the shiny gray of the smooth stone overhang, making it difficult to see unless you knew where to look. Pouring over the narrow silvery spire that towered overhead, a slender waterfall disappeared into the roof. Exe peered over the balcony rail—the cascade fell straight through the house and down into the gathering pool below. Exe barely had time to soak in the plush beauty of her newfound home.

"You never listen, do you," Riven whispered angrily, seizing her arm. He dragged her along, but not toward the burnished silver doors set in the middle of the windowed wall. Instead, he guided her across the stepping stones hidden in the lily ponds, onto a narrow catwalk that led around the backside of the house. As they neared the end of the narrow walkway, Riven pushed Exe behind him and rapped sharply on a small door. After a moment, the door opened just a crack—too narrow for Exe to see inside.

"You. What are you doing here?" A strangely familiar voice accused. "Go away. There's a meeting in progress, and if they see you– My father told you to wait, that he'd call when he was ready to receive the message."

My father. Apprehensive anticipation built as Exe savored those words. Having so many adopted brothers, it seemed silly to have never even considered siblings. *A sister!*

"This couldn't wait," Riven said, bending aside to give a glimpse of Exe.

Slowly the door eased open, then banged wide with shocking violence. In an instant, all the little things Riven had and hadn't said fell into place—mistaking her for someone else even though he recognized her notorious face, hiding the color of her eyes, calling her Viva, all of it. The girl in the doorway looked exactly like her. The hair, the face, even the clothes. *All except the eyes.* The other girl's eyes were aquamarine.

I have a twin sister.

Stunned and staring, Exe fumbled for what to say, what to do. It felt as if all her hopes, all her longings, all her wishes were granted in one fell swoop. Finally, standing before her was someone exactly like her. Someone who could understand her like no other. Someone to confide in. Someone to trust completely. Someone who–

CRACK!

Her doppelganger's hard slap exploded across Exe's face.

CHAPTER THIRTEEN

Double Take

"You always said you'd slap your twin if you ever saw her, Viva," Riven laughed softly. "I should've believed you."

Exe glared at Riven as she held her throbbing cheek. That slap had shattered any hope that her family would welcome her return. Looking covertly at her twin, Exe took in the gracefully waved, raven black hair and the arctic aquamarine eyes. Eyes that seemed to hold decades of depth that she herself couldn't begin to fathom.

Embarrassed, Exe realized that Riven hadn't crafted her a disguise—he'd simply made her look identical to her sister. Only Viva wore her chic ensemble with a cool, jaded elegance. Exe shriveled in her own bedraggled outfit, feeling like an imposter. They may have identical features, but Exe couldn't imagine ever being brave enough to carry off the contemptuous confidence this girl exuded.

"How and why did you unearth her?" Viva asked in a vicious whisper. "If you thought bringing her here would score you points, you're wrong."

"Not my idea. She insisted. I couldn't let her go traipsing around Anacapia on her own, now could I?" Riven leaned back against the railing, buffing his fingernails on his jacket. "But before we take this little scene any further, do you think it wise for the two of you together to stay out in the open like this?"

Viva waited a long, stubborn moment before leading the way inside. Exe gaped at the gorgeous Art Deco-style kitchen, with its black lacquer and chrome that looked impossibly modern and retro all at once. Even more impressive were the ingredients whizzing about unaided, preparing themselves according to several recipes laid out on the counter. Exe smiled at the sight of a squadron of ripe, red berries struggling to maneuver a heavy sauce pan onto the stove. Viva watched her with such derision that Exe felt a fool for finding the kitchen fascinating.

"I don't care how she got here, she needs to go. Take her away, now," Viva addressed Riven as if Exe weren't in the room.

"I agree, she's got to go. But let's say I do take her away?" Riven matched Viva's low whisper. "What would your parents say about you sending your dear sister off before learning why she showed up here?" Exe clenched her fists at Riven's nonchalance.

"You'll tell them what they need to know. After she's gone," Viva ripped the pan from the struggling berries and slammed it onto the burner.

"Think I know? The less I know the better, or so I've been instructed," Riven swiped a handful of bouncing berries and popped them in his mouth. "You may not want to, Viv, but you're gonna have to tell your parents that she's here. It's up to them to decide what's to be done about her."

"You arrogant idiot," Viva turned on Exe. "How dare you come wandering in here with no regard for how your return will destroy everything we've worked for!"

"Take it easy, Viva," Riven advised. "She didn't know any better. She doesn't know anything. Doesn't even know how to use her powers."

"Powers?" Viva asked. Then she mouthed a word without making a sound.

Suddenly the red hot pan came sailing straight at Exe's face. Exe ducked, then instinctively wished, *Target my twin instead.* The steaming pan immediately changed course, flying directly at Viva. Exe's twin dodged it, dashing to safety behind Riven.

"I told you," Riven gloated, grabbing the pan as it zoomed by him. One softly whispered word and Riven set the now-docile pan back on the stove. Then he blew gently on his palm until the angry burn faded away.

"I want to see my parents," Exe demanded.

"MY parents," Viva seethed. "Wait here. No one can see you. Either of you."

Ignoring the order, Exe trailed after Viva as she strode through a swinging door. Grabbing an airborne spoon, Exe eased the utensil through the door, cracking it open just wide enough for her to scan the adjacent room.

The opulence of the living room left Exe awestruck. Tufted black velvet sofas, onyx end tables, and sunburst chandeliers. The slender cascade she'd seen outside fell through the center of the room, surrounded by a chic, circular hearth that burned a ring of fire around the falling water—in which a delicate, crystalline rose floated serenely.

Huddled around the crisp, white fireplace were a dozen nervous-looking men and women of all ages, dressed just as elegantly as Riven and Viva. Though their voices were low, they were clearly in the middle of a heated discussion. Exe devoured the small gathering with her eyes, searching each face for her parents. Viva gave her no clue as she hovered on the fringes, waiting for someone to question her presence.

"—wasted enough time waging this silent war aimed at swaying hearts and minds," a slender young woman said, brushing her tumble of riotous red curls back over her shoulder. "We need to speak out and hold Jettani accountable. If people knew that our leader allowed one of our citizens to be held captive by—"

"Do you believe that's the worst she's done?" a middle-aged lady trilled, dripping more sarcasm than her ensemble dripped in furs and jewels. "My dear girl, if you wish to malign our most 'beloved, benevolent ruler,' at least have the gumption to cite her most egregious crimes."

"You'd risk war with Bete Noire to save a single citizen?" a nervous, bespectacled woman questioned. "We've bigger battles to win here."

"I still say that abduction scene was staged," a grizzled man growled. "You want to hold your mother's captors accountable? Look no further than Jettani herself."

"Are you insinuating that Jettani is attempting to develop her own time travel spell?" Asked a bomber-jacketed, aviator-helmeted man who looked more dead than alive. "That's an impossible goal."

"Not for Velin," the grizzled man interrupted.

"Jettani's the one who made working on Inconceivable spells an offense punishable by death," the half-dead pilot continued.

"So's no one would beat her to it," the grizzled man pounded his fist on the table. "I'd wager most of the talented who've vanished are locked up somewhere, slaving away on plans for all the Inconceivables. Just look at what she's done to me. And she ain't even hiding that."

"We've all sacrificed for this cause. None more so than our hosts," a sunny, rotund man counseled. "But we must stay the course. We cannot save—"

"Ransome has a point," said a rugged young man who looked just a few years older than Seph. "Our noble goal is doomed by a flawed strategy. You formed this secret society how many years ago, Asher? In all that time, how many people have you recruited? At this rate, we'll all be dead before enough people see Jettani's treachery."

Secret society? Does that mean my parents are fighting against the woman who sentenced me to death? Exe wondered, still trying to find her parents in the crowd.

"You think I don't feel the same fire for a swift end burning within me? It took all my strength not to fight back when Jettani targeted my daughter all those years ago," a handsome, haggard man addressed the red-haired woman. His slicked-back, jet black hair, Clark Gable mustache, and dapper, high waisted-pants gave him the look of a roguish gangster from those old black-and-white films that Ella loved.

"Your father's right, Ransome. We must stay the course," a glamorous woman took the haggard man's hand. With her platinum curls, teal eyes, and fluttery lilac gown, she could've been mistaken for a vintage silver screen starlet. "If Asher and I had spoken out back then, we wouldn't be here now. At least this way we've got a fighting chance to overthrow Jettani."

My parents. The two words crystalized in Exe's mind as she realized the true identity of the couple. She'd found them. Asher and Malina, her real parents. A sudden spurt of guilt dampened her elation. Now that the moment had finally arrived, it felt like a betrayal to consider anyone other than Rove, Ella, and her brothers as family.

Asher finally noticed Viva's attempts to capture his attention and bent down to his daughter. Viva barely had time to whisper two words before Asher whirled around and swiped his hand through the cascade, shattering the crystalline rose.

Instantly, the people mobilized, stark terror paling their faces. A few of them magically gathered up documents while others erased any signs that a group had gathered there. Then they began to vanish one by one with whooshes so quiet Exe barely heard them. When the last had dissipated, Asher and Malina turned toward the kitchen door. Suddenly afraid they might see her, Exe jumped back and bumped into Riven.

"Out here now, Riven," Asher barked.

"Guess this is goodbye," Riven gave Exe a sardonic grin and picked up his blood-stained briefcase. "So long, sweetheart." Hurt by his indifference, Exe hugged herself as he strolled into the living room, whistling a casual tune. She eased the swinging door open again, wondering why her parents hadn't asked to see her. While Riven strode over to answer to Asher, Viva whispered furiously to Malina.

"You were told not to show your face here. That I'd send for you," Asher berated Riven. "None but us know that you're a double agent. What if one of the Sub Rosa members had seen you? Or worse, if you'd seen them? Were you to be

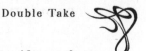

discovered– you can't betray any of our number if you don't know who they are."

"Agreed, sir. It's safer for all if my contact is limited to you and Malina," Riven said. "But given the situation, I had to come–"

"How could you know if the message was vital enough that it required immediate delivery?" Asher questioned. "Did you open it?"

"Not exactly."

"Asher," Malina murmured, looking pale.

"I warned you, he can't be trusted," Asher railed. "If the message mentioned..."

"Experience," Malina whispered, indicating the door where Exe hid.

"Malina, don't–" Asher cautioned, turning toward the kitchen. The color drained from his face as his deep indigo eyes met the single violet one of Exe's peeping through the crack in the door.

"I think it's time to show yourself, dollface," Riven called out. Exe eased through the door and took a few tentative steps toward her parents. Malina's hand flew to her mouth, muffling a sob tinged more with dread than joy. Asher just stared at her, his face frozen in anger and betrayal. *Hardly the welcome I'd hoped for.*

"What have you done? Why would you bring her here?" Asher turned from Exe and grabbed Riven, shaking him.

"She demanded that I bring her or she'd come on her own," Riven choked out.

"Where is Velin? Dead?" Malina rushed to Exe, gently holding her shoulders.

"No, though he looks it," Exe managed a tremulous smile. "He refused to tell me about you. So I came to find you on my own."

"He let you come here unprotected?" Asher asked, releasing Riven. "Why?"

"Someone needs to train her. Velin hasn't. Her powers are out of control," Riven said before Exe could answer.

"Powers? That's impossible," Asher breathed, exchanging an unsettled look with Malina. A look that was eerily similar to the confused and wary look that her Arizona parents had shared when Ella had been shredded by the shattered water glass.

"This says different," Riven said, pulling aside his jacket and shirt to reveal his half-healed wound. "Don't know how she did it, but she did. The tyro doesn't even know how her powers work."

"Malina, you don't think–" Asher asked, horror dripping from every word.

"No, not that. Anything but that," Malina gasped.

"What's wrong? Why shouldn't I have powers?" Exe demanded. "You all do."

"A bind breaker? Or–" Malina stopped, as if afraid to give voice to the alternative.

"Why didn't Velin warn us?" Asher bit out. A disturbed silence filled the room.

"So, what happened? Did you decide that one kid was enough?" Exe attempted to joke away the tension. "Is that why you got rid of me?"

"Yes."

The single, bitter word cut into the quiet. Exe turned toward Viva as she stood in the doorway of a lavish, aquamarine bedroom. Arms crossed. Eyes narrowed. Her face darkened with a deep hatred that Exe had never felt from anyone before, not even Velin.

"Velin didn't tell you?" Malina questioned. "He's raised you for fourteen years. How could he tell you where to find us without telling you why we sent you away?"

"Velin hasn't told me anything. Not willingly, anyway. I barely know the man," Exe said sullenly. "He didn't raise me. He gave me away when I was still a baby."

"Velin didn't–" Malina started to ask. "We trusted him."

"Who did he give you to?" Asher demanded. "Did they unbind your powers?"

"They wouldn't know how. My family doesn't have powers like I do," Exe said.

"He gave you to a Hoi Polloi family?" Malina asked. "And you had your powers the whole time? Did Velin–"

"We don't have time for this, Malina," Asher said, peering out the window.

"If the people she's staying with are truly Hoi Polloi, they can't protect her. We have to find out what Velin's done," Malina argued.

"I intend to find out from Velin himself, when I take her back," Asher replied.

"Back? I'm not going back. Not until you tell me what's going on," Exe insisted.

"How did you get her here? Did anyone see you? You didn't volte from the Corpse Copse, did you?" Asher asked Riven, ignoring Exe.

"No sir. We walked," Riven answered. "We saw no one worth mentioning, until we met your minder on the main road."

"Hastings saw you with her? Did he realize she wasn't Viva?" Asher's deadly quiet tone drove Riven to literally back himself into a corner.

"He saw the color of her tetherstone, sir. But he won't be a problem," Riven said.

"Volte Experience out of here, Malina. They could already be on their way," Asher shouted to his wife before turning back to Riven. "Why didn't you tell us this the moment you had the chance? Stalling until your compatriots arrive? You're no double agent, this is a double-cross!"

"Hastings is dead," Riven's lifeless voice intoned.

Malina immediately stopped trying to catch hold of Exe and shouldered Asher aside. She placed a comforting hand on Riven's arm. "Tell me, soldier."

"I almost had him fooled, commander," Riven said, voice shaking, eyes glistening. "I shoved Exe down, pretending I was picking on Viva. Her tetherstone tumbled into view. It was him or us. I didn't want to, but I had no choice."

Malina took his face in her hands, forcing him to meet her eye. "Your first kill is always the hardest, especially when it's someone you know. Someone you maybe even liked a little."

"He was a good kid. I coulda turned him, brought him to our side. If I'd had more time, I–"

"Hastings was a good soldier. He would've turned both you and Exe in to Jettani," Malina comforted him. "As much as we regret the necessity, it was a good kill. Forgive yourself, Riven. That's an order."

"Where did you leave the body?" Asher asked. Riven nudged the bloody briefcase with his boot, then sank down to the floor, his head buried in his knees.

"That's two gone missing now, in as many months. Do you know what this means?" Malina looked at Asher. "Jettani assigned us all minders after just one of her Disimulata went missing. What will she do now?"

Asher rubbed his chin, "What are we going to do with the body? If they ever find it, they'll discover who killed him—and why. Where can we hide it?"

"Velin buried one in my backyard," Exe offered. "He killed a Disimulata guy in Arizona—that's where I'm from—about a month or so ago."

"Someone from the Disimulata found you? How?" Asher demanded.

"I-I don't know," Exe stammered. "I didn't even know what he was. Velin just took care of him and made me forget it. I only found out because I woke up when Velin was burying his corpse in our cemetery."

"Your cemetery? What kind of place are they keeping you?" Malina gave Exe a quick hug. Exe shrugged out of the embrace, uncomfortable by the display of affection.

"It's not as bad as it sounds," Exe excused. "It's actually kind of cool, the place where I live. My brothers really love it. Our house. The town."

"Brothers?" Viva said faintly.

"If I agree to go back, for now, will you promise to tell me everything?" Exe asked. "Why you sent me away? Why that Disimulata man came looking for me? What Velin's involvement is? All of it? And you'll teach me how to control my powers?"

"I'll tell you as much as you need to know," Asher qualified, turning to Malina. "I'll see our girl safely home, bury the body, and get answers from Velin. If anyone comes looking for me, or Hastings, tell them—"

"Don't worry about us, we know what to do," Malina smiled at Viva. "But take Riven. If anyone stops you, and you've got Exe and a dead body with you—"

"I'll handle it," Riven rose to his feet, brushing the dampness from his eyes.

"You can trust him, Asher," Malina assured him.

"He does need to be interrogated," Asher regarded Riven. "Maybe manipulate a few memories. Are you willing to allow me access to your mind, boy?"

"I don't see why this time should be any different," Riven muttered.

"Can you volte?" Asher asked Exe sharply.

"I-I don't know, I've never tried," Exe mumbled under his hard regard.

"Then hold on," Asher said, reaching for Exe's hand.

"Isn't that dangerous, sir? Volting with another person?" Riven asked.

"Not if you know what you're doing. The government merely says it's dangerous so they can better control our movements," Asher replied. "Go on ahead and make sure the Corpse Copse is clear. If it's not, send the signal and get out of there."

With a curt nod, Riven vanished. As Asher bent to pick up the bloody briefcase, Malina pulled Exe into her arms. After a quick, tight hug, Malina cradled Exe's face in the palm of her hands. "I've been longing to look into those eyes for years," Malina said, her own dark teal ones swimming with tears. "I don't know how long it will be until we can see you again, but please know, we love you so much. And we're doing everything in our power to make it safe for you to come home."

Exe tried to muster some understanding with her tremulous smile, but she didn't understand. *If it isn't safe for me, why is Viva allowed to stay? And if I really did have to leave for my own safety all those years ago, why didn't you all come with me?*

"Come say goodbye to your sister," Malina beckoned to Viva.

Viva obeyed slowly, arms crossed. "Don't come back," she bit out. Noticing her parents' frowns, she added, "It isn't safe."

"No signal. We're good to go," Asher said, closing his own ebony pocket watch. Without giving Exe a chance to retort, (or take a long, last look at her mother or the home she'd never known), Asher took Exe's hand, grabbed the briefcase, and they blinked out of sight.

Suddenly Exe was spiraling through pitch black, feeling as if she had splintered into a billion pieces. The very next moment, they were back in the Corpse Copse on the midnight banks of the turquoise river. Riven was waiting for them, casually tossing his coin as he leaned against the glowing cliff next to the tumbling waterfall.

"You wait here until I return," Asher instructed Riven. "It's bad enough that you know where the entrance to the Vale is. I'll not have you know Experience's exact location. And if anyone does come—"

"I'll alert you immediately, sir," Riven replied. "Though I doubt the Disimulata will show if they haven't by now. The spook stories about this place do their job well."

Giving him curt nod, Asher stepped down into the stream and through the cascade. With a deep breath and one last glance at Riven, Exe followed him.

It was time to go back to Nowhere.

CHAPTER FOURTEEN

SHOWDOWN AT HIGH MIDNIGHT

Emerging from the waterfall, Exe was shocked to find the moon high in the evening sky. She checked her phone—it was almost midnight. The Parsells would know by now that she hadn't come home. Easy must be sick with worry, believing that he'd abandoned her in an empty lot in a sketchy part of the city. *I never should've involved him in this. I should've come on my own. And left a note saying... what?* Any message would've worried them more, since she hadn't been sure that she'd ever return.

"Show yourself, Velin," Asher demanded of the empty oasis, presenting a striking figure in the moonlight streaming from the cloudless sky. "I know the falls alert you to all who pass through. Or are you afraid to face me after what you've done?"

With a sharp, electric crack and a blinding flash, Velin appeared behind Asher.

"What I've done?" Velin raged, causing Asher to whip around. "I've done only what you asked of me. Me, your once revered ruler reduced to babysitter at your behest."

"You swore to watch over my daughter, but you didn't. You gave her away!"

Velin sneered at him, "'Keep her safe,' those were your exact words. Well, she's alive, isn't she? That's all I promised."

Asher stormed back, "You let her stroll into Anacapia unprotected, with no idea of the dangers she faced!"

"Let her?" Velin bellowed. "Your stubborn brat refused to obey me. Insisted on going, though I warned her repeatedly of the danger. She wouldn't even have known where to go if she hadn't stolen that knowledge from me."

"Why would she listen to you? You made yourself a complete stranger to her by giving her away to some Hoi Polloi family. People who couldn't possibly cope with what she is," Asher fumed. "And after unbinding her powers, too? Why?"

"I didn't unbind her and you know it," Velin returned. "The intertwined bind you and Malina placed on her didn't take. Admit what she is, Asher. It's why Jettani–"

"You should've kept her with you," Asher interrupted, as if cutting Velin off would alter a truth he refused to hear. "Instead you abandoned her to unpowered strangers and let her magic grow wild."

Exe looked back and forth between the two men— the younger indignant, the older defensive—struggling to understand all that they weren't saying. A little of the hurt that Asher's hardness had caused eased away as she realized that her birth father was demanding that Velin answer all of her own questions about her past.

"Do you forget that she's not the only one who's hunted?" Velin shouted. "I've got trackers from every nation in our world pursuing me. And others too. Even Demaine. Should I have risked her life every time a mercenary came for me? Besides, as you well know, I was not meant to raise a child."

Instantly, Asher softened, "I do know you, Velin. You are more than capable of helping a child not only survive, but thrive. In fact, I counted on it. If your son—"

"How dare you dump your daughter on my doorstep and assume she could ever take the place of a child who was never meant to be?" Velin's quiet fury resounded louder than his shouts. "How dare you speak to me of what I have and have not done for that brat of yours. I've given all I have to give, and I'll not give more. As you object to what's become of your daughter, I'll leave her dubious future to you." With a thunderous crack so loud it set the mirage to trembling, Velin vanished.

"What am I going to do with you?" Asher stared at Exe with blind panic as she picked herself up out of the fragrant bush she'd tumbled into. When Exe could do no more than shrug, Asher set himself to retrieving the bloody briefcase as it bobbed like a cork in the waterfall's gathering pool. He gazed at the glistening case as if it might somehow present a solution. "I'm known as quite the diplomat around Vianelle," Asher mused. "I suppose I should've remembered to use those skills tonight."

"Does this mean you'll be taking me home with you?" Exe asked as a mixture of guilt and fear swirled with nervous anticipation. *I didn't intended for today to be the last time I'd ever see Ella or Rove or Easy or my brothers, did I?*

"What? No. That's impossible. Our world isn't safe for you," Asher said absently, dusting the beady, water-like substance from the case.

"Why?" Exe asked, clutching at the wanted poster still tucked into her pocket. "If it's safe for Viva, why isn't it safe for me?"

Asher glanced at her, his mouth opening and closing a few times. Then he clenched his jaw and started pacing, "This place you've been living, is it safe?"

"It's safe... for me," Exe muttered, disappointment flooding her. Asher clearly had no intention of telling her the truth. *What is so wrong with me?* Exe brushed aside the crippling thought and confronted Asher, arms crossed. "I've been safe there, so far. But it isn't safe for my family. Like you said, my powers have gone wild. I need to know how to control them, and Velin has refused to show me." Exe blinked a little at that fib, since she hadn't actually ever asked Velin to train her. "It's so bad, I've even killed someone."

"Killed? How?" Asher asked.

"I wished it," Exe said defiantly.

"That's impossible," Asher shook his head. "Wish magic isn't even strong enough to give someone a paper cut."

"Mine is," Exe challenged, wondering if she was right. She closed her eyes and wished. Opening her eyes, Exe smiled to see a cyclone of the bead-like water and perfumed flowers swirling around Asher in a beautiful whirlwind— just as she had envisioned. Through the enchanting tempest, their eyes met. Exe wished again—not even needing to close her eyes this time to concentrate. The dancing droplets and blossoms sailed back into place, each bud reattaching itself as if it had never been plucked.

"I see," Asher said, his appraising gaze far too inscrutable for Exe's comfort. "First things first. Let's determine if this—family of yours passes muster. Once I'm assured of your safety, then perhaps—"

"No. I won't go back until I know they'll be safe from me," Exe refused, squelching the relief that welled within her.

"I will find a way to ensure that you learn how to harness your powers. I give you my word," Asher promised. "Now tell me, how do we get to your home from here?"

"I came with my brother, but he went home," Exe explained. "Can't you just volte us back there?"

Asher shook his head, "Volting isn't quite so easy if you're trying to travel somewhere you've never been before. Unfortunately, this oasis is as far as I've ever ventured into the Vale. Do you have a way to show me this home of yours?"

"I guess so," Exe said. She pulled out her cellphone and found the photos from Easy's Halloween birthday bash.

"What is this?" Asher puzzled, jabbing at the unfamiliar device. "How do you make it multi-dimensional? Wait, they're gone. The images of your home have vanished. All that's left are some tiny boxes."

"Here," Exe smothered a smile as she brought up the photos again and showed him how to swipe through the pictures. "Regular people can't take 3-D pictures here, at least not that I know of. Will these flat photos do?"

"Let us see, shall we?" Asher mouthed a word that lifted the photographs out of her phone in a sort of video projection of her photo reel. The pictures whirled around in the air as if riding on a carousel. Then a small, three-dimensional model of the old mission church took shape, bobbing lightly in the breeze. It was then, as she marveled over the little bell swinging in the miniature belfry, that Exe spotted an odd lump in the field just outside the mirage.

"Easy?" Exe gasped. The floating model of her home whiffed away in smoky tendrils as Exe dashed through it, intent on running to her brother. Asher stopped her before she could step out of the oasis. "It's my brother," Exe explained impatiently. "He must've come looking for me when I didn't– I have to go home with him. I'll meet you there. You can volte yourself now, can't you?"

"I'm not letting you go off with some stranger," Asher asserted.

Exe glared at this man that she'd known for less than an hour, "He's not a stranger. He's my brother."

Asher raised his brow at Exe, "I assume whatever conveyance he used to bring you here seats more than two?"

Exe gaped at him, "Are you crazy? I can't ask him to bring some strange man back to our home."

"He won't even know I'm there."

Unconvinced, Exe stepped out of the mirage and knelt down next to her brother.

"Easy? It's time to go home," Exe murmured, shaking him awake.

"Already?" Easy joked, stretching the sleepiness from his muscles as he sat up.

"Why did you come back?" Exe asked. "Are Rove and Ella mad that I'm gone?"

"I never left," Easy said simply. "Couldn't abandon my kid sister. No need to worry. I'm sure the 'rents are sound asleep, assured we're together at some tame party."

"I can't believe you stayed. Thank you," Exe said, surprising Easy with a hug.

Easy hugged her back and rose, "Did you find what you were looking for?"

Exe glanced up at Asher. Easy followed her gaze. When he looked back at Exe, she could tell that he hadn't seen Asher at all. "I'm not sure yet," Exe hedged.

"You're not gonna wanna come back here, are you?" Easy asked, shaking off the dust from his dirt nap as they headed for the exit. "Do me a favor. Next time, take a bus. The accommodations here are deplorable."

Exe kept glancing back over her shoulder on the short walk to the gate. Whether she was making sure that Asher was following them, or hoping he wasn't, Exe wasn't certain. Once they reached the car, Exe opened the door to the back seat, hoping Asher would know to get in without her saying anything. Easy would think her crazy for talking to thin air. Thankfully, Asher slid inside the car without needing any prompting.

"So that's all I am to you? A chauffer?" Easy put on a forlorn face. "Ride up front with me, you screwball!" Exe laughed half-heartedly as she closed the back door and climbed into the passenger seat. Easy adjusted his rearview mirror, completely unaware of the watchful eyes Exe saw in its reflection. "Let's go home, little sister."

As soon as they got home, Exe convinced Easy to join his brothers and friends who were watching horror movies in the living room. Assuming that burying Hastings was top priority, Exe made a beeline for the cemetery, leading Asher through the open-air courtyard that separated her parents' chapel-turned-master-bedroom from the main house.

Once there, Exe showed Asher to the grave where she'd reburied the first dead Disimulata. Asher set the blood-stained briefcase on the mound. In solemn silence, they watched the case sink into the hard earth as if it were being swallowed by quicksand. Exe bowed her head and whispered a few words that were half-prayer and half-apology. *After all, it was my return to Anacapia that resulted in his death.*

"Where does Velin live?" Asher asked quietly, nodding when Exe indicated the creepy house atop the tombstone-dappled hillside. "And you?" Exe pointed to her bell tower bedroom. Asher nodded again, looking back and forth between her tower and Velin's home. Exe fidgeted in the inscrutable silence as Asher pondered for several endless moments.

"So, what did you think of your first car ride?" Exe asked when she couldn't stand the silence any longer.

"We have autos in Anacapia. Though they serve another function in our world now," Asher said, with a small, mysterious smile.

"Really?" Exe asked.

"It's easy to find similarities when you quit looking for differences."

"That sounds like something my mother would say," Exe smiled.

"Malina?"

"No."

"Oh."

Exe dug her toe into the dirt, thinking that she should've asked Malina to bring her back here instead of Asher.

Though she'd only seen her birth mother for a few moments, she'd felt more comfortable with her. Somehow Asher felt like even more of a stranger now that she'd met him.

"I suppose I should smooth things over with Velin," Asher mused. Exe had to stop herself from objecting. *Is Asher really going to abandon me to Velin again?* But Asher didn't go striding up the hill to Velin's house. Instead, he wove through the maze of gravestones to her little private entrance.

Exe watched him anxiously as he explored every level of her tower bedroom. Asher examined everything—the still-broken railing in the belfry, the stark white walls, the makeshift bed, the half-unpacked boxes, her shabby, vintage clothes hanging on the collapsing rack. Exe tried to see it all through his eyes, uncertain if she wanted him to find her home satisfactory or lacking.

"Has Velin done anything to protect this place?" Asher asked once they'd reached the ground floor again.

"No. Wait," Exe replied, remembering the sticky red lagoon she'd seen in Anacapia and Riven's words about its protective properties. "I think he might've coated the walls with that, um, coo-or clay?"

"Cruor," Asher corrected. Instantly the white walls flooded crimson, then the red faded away, just as it had when she'd revealed the 'blood.' Screams followed by laughter told Exe that the gory substance had been briefly revealed in the living room too.

She trailed anxiously after him as he walked into the darkened nave, taking in the gleaming, state-of-the-art television and plush, comfortable sofa crammed with over a dozen oblivious teenagers. Nervously she hovered at Asher's elbow as he marched up one spiral staircase into the brothers' balcony bedroom and down the other, not missing their expensive gaming systems and hand-crafted triple bunk beds.

"These people force you to exist in that broken down tower while they live in luxury?" Asher accused, once they were back in the narthex.

"It's not like that," Exe excused, glancing into the living room to make sure they weren't overheard. "Rove, my father— here— he's going to fix up my tower. It's just that it was more important to get living quarters for six done first, before a private suite for one," Exe defended, uncertain whether that was actually the reason her room had been neglected. "And I could have all of these fancy, expensive things, too. If I wanted. I just prefer retro and vintage stuff."

"Even so—"

"Besides," Exe interrupted. "It's kind of hard to ask for luxuries when you've got Velin's bitter voice in your head telling you not to want or need anything."

"Voice? What do you mean? Has Velin been accessing your mind all of these years?" Asher asked, suddenly alert.

Exe glowered at him, "He's been messing with all of our heads. My whole family too. Until I discovered how to kick him out of mine. I've lived with that mad man in my mind for years, constantly berating me to stay vigilant. 'Don't use your powers. Don't attract attention. Don't feel anything.' It's amazing that I'm still sane."

Just then, all the lights in the living room blazed on. Exe dashed inside to find Rove at the light switch, rumpled pajamas, curly hair mussed.

"It's after one in the morning. Bed. Now," Rove ordered the grumbling crowd of kids. As the boys hustled up into the balcony and the girls headed for the bell tower, Rove spotted Exe and strode over to her, coming to a stop right in front of Asher. Although Rove couldn't know it, the two men stood toe-to-toe.

"Everything okay here, Exe?" Rove asked, staring unseeing into Asher's eyes.

"I'm good, Dad," Exe answered, noticing Asher's wince. "I'm happy to be back– I mean, I'm happy. Here. It's good here. I love it. "

"And we love you," Rove replied, still staring straight ahead as if he could see Asher staring back at him. Finally, he looked at Exe, "You need anything, you come to me, understood?"

Exe swallowed hard, "Got it, Dad." Rove glanced one last time at the space where Asher stood. Then, with military precision, he turned and strode back across the courtyard and into the master suite.

"Could he see you?" Exe asked Asher, breathing a sigh of relief.

"No," Asher answered, gazing after Rove. "But the man has sharpened senses. And strong protective instincts. I think he could sense me. Impressive. Velin chose well." Taking one long, last look at her home, Asher turned and stalked back through Exe's tower bedroom, pausing only to tell Exe to "Wait here," when she made to follow him up the cemetery hill toward Velin's.

Up the bell tower Exe dashed, unmindful of the objections of her brothers' crushes when she pushed her way through them. She burst into the belfry just in time to see Asher rap on Velin's front door. Exe watched breathlessly, hoping the door would remain closed and she'd never have to deal with bitter old Velin again. After several long moments, the door opened slowly. (Whether Asher opened it himself or Velin allowed him entrance, Exe couldn't tell.) The moment the door closed behind Asher, Exe sank down to wait, her eyes fixed on that door.

The night sky had already begun to lighten when Asher finally emerged, closing the door quietly behind him. He looked across to Exe's bell tower and saw her there, waiting, watching. Exe blinked and then a weary Asher stood beside her in the bell tower—a strange book in his hands.

"You're leaving it up to Velin to train me, aren't you?" Exe said sullenly. "He won't do it. No matter what he's told you."

"Velin won't be teaching you. Not now, anyway," Asher sighed.

"Really?" Exe couldn't keep the joy out of her voice. "Why not?"

"Velin– needs a break."

"From me?"

"From the responsibility of you," Asher qualified. "But it's clear that your inability to manage your magic is a problem. So we will be the ones to train you, until Velin is ready to take over."

"We?"

"Malina and I. When we can get away," Asher answered. "For now, just familiarize yourself with this." Exe accepted the heavy, velvet tome, noticing the large jewel embedded in its cover. It exactly matched her necklace's stone—as if it were the jewel's other half.

"What is it?" Exe asked.

"Your vade, or vade mecum to be precise," Asher explained. "A place to record all of your spells. Most of the time you're to keep it locked in a secure, secret place. But you'll need to bring it along to all of your training sessions. Though where we will find a wordsmith to inscribe any new spells in it, I don't know."

"Where will you train me? Will I be returning to Anacapia to do it?" Exe asked, secretly hoping for a chance to see more of that magical world.

Asher shook his head, "The field will have to suffice. There's nowhere in our world that's safe for you. And it wouldn't be wise to train you out in the open in a land without magic."

"When do we start?" Exe asked, flipping through the book to mask her disappointment that she wouldn't be training in Anacapia. Though most of the shimmery pages were blank, Exe found a handful of spells already written into the book—in a tight, golden script she recognized— including one entitled, 'This Voice is Not My Own.'

"Unfortunately, it's almost impossible for us to get away, and it seems that's only going to get worse. It will be difficult for Malina and I to come train you, but we'll come as often as we can," Asher ran his hand over his face as if exhausted by the mere thought of the effort it would require to train her.

"It's no picnic for me to get away either," Exe bristled. "And FYI, I'm not available during school hours, which means I'm only free after four p.m. every weekday. Plus, on Sundays we've got church and our family dinner after, which lasts until at least one. So I can't come until after that. I'd be missed. Unless you'd care to go explain exactly what's going on to my whole family. And me too, for that matter."

"FYI?" Asher frowned, then sighed. "I'll keep those times in mind. That actually helps us. It should be easier to get away later in the day," Asher nodded, oblivious to her acerbity. "And if we can't, perhaps– Should you ever come for training and find anyone but Malina or I here, do not trust them unless they give you the watchword."

"What's a watchword?" Exe asked.

"A set of secret passwords we exchange to identify other members of the Sub Rosa," Asher answered. "If you meet a stranger in the field, simply ask them: 'Are the flowers in bloom?' If we sent them, they'll respond, 'Only the roses.' If they respond with anything else, RUN. Some may also show you this when they give the watchword."

With a nimble twist of his hand, Asher produced a delicate, crystalline rose—just like the one she'd seen floating in the cascade during the meeting she'd interrupted. Exe reached out to touch the delicate blossom bobbing in the air. The instant her fingertips touched the stem, the rose shattered like ice, its shards melting into droplets and evaporating before they hit the ground.

"It'll take some time to make arrangements. I'll signal as soon as we're ready for you," Asher said, pulling a small onyx stone from his pocket. With a quiet word Exe couldn't quite make out, Asher tapped the underside of the stone and extracted a small chip. Another word and Exe's own necklace extracted itself from its hiding place beneath her 1930s-style blouse.

With a start, Exe realized that Easy had never questioned her altered appearance, especially the change in hair color. *Did Velin make Easy forget the other clothes I'd been wearing and my previous hair color?* Exe glanced at Velin's dark house, wondering just how much he'd been doing to help her all these years without her ever knowing.

Exe returned her gaze to Asher as he reached for her pendant. With a click, he slid aside the starburst at its center that appeared to simply hold the stone in place. Exe gaped at the secret compartment she'd never discovered in all the times she'd messed with her necklace. Underneath the decorative metal lay a space that hid a small, silvery gemstone.

"This chip will cause your necklace to tingle and emit a soft glow that only you can see whenever we're available to train you," Asher explained, tapping the onyx chip into place beside the silvery chip.

"I think Velin made it get hot sometimes," Exe said thoughtfully. "Like when I was afraid or in danger."

"He told me," Asher smiled. "It'll continue to do so. He's agreed to that much. You'll need to come to the field immediately when we signal, as we won't be able to get away for long."

"How? You saw how far away the field is from here. Are you going to teach me to volte?" Exe asked hopefully.

"Someday, perhaps," Asher conceded. "But for now..."

Asher touched her shoulder and, in the blink of an eye, they were down in the cemetery again, standing in front of the little door that led back into her tower. Placing his hand on the door, Asher uttered a strange series of words, then he turned the doorknob back and forth three times and whispered the word, "postern." Asher swung the door wide, drawing a gasp from Exe as she gazed inside. Instead of the box-strewn room at the base of her tower, she was looking at the barbed wire field's mirage.

"A little spell that Velin taught me once, back when he was in a position to do so," Asher smiled at Exe, stepping through the door and into the field. "He's already been kind enough to scribe the spell into your vade. No matter which side of the door you're on, simply twist the knob three times, say 'postern' and you'll open a secret passageway to this field. The passageway seals the moment you close the door."

"You'll come for me soon?" Exe asked, hating the note of begging in her voice.

"As soon as I can," Asher assured her, before stepping into the mirage and disappearing through the cascade. Exe gazed at the mirage a moment longer, then closed the door. Opening it wide once again revealed only the interior of her tower.

"Soon," Exe murmured as she stepped inside. *I'm finally going to learn how to control my powers.*

Exe tossed and turned, watching the stars fade in the ever-lightening sky from her makeshift bed on the belfry floor. Though exhausted from the long day, she couldn't find sleep. Caressing the velvety cover of her vade, Exe pondered all that she had and hadn't learned. *True, I met my birth parents and discovered a twin sister. I saw a fantastical land that felt like home to my very bones. I learned about cruor clay, and vades, and a dozen other intriguing bits of knowledge. But the big questions. The ones I'm so desperate to have answered...*

Abandoning all thoughts of rest, Exe crept down the bell tower, determined to test out the only spell Asher had taught her so far. Twisting the doorknob three times, Exe whispered, "postern," crossing her fingers in a deep hope that the spell would actually work for her. *Why didn't we test to see if I could actually do it?* Exe panicked. *Doesn't Asher get that I've never used a real spell on purpose before?* With trepidation, Exe gently eased the door open.

There the mirage stood, its vibrant hues muted in the murky, pre-dawn gray. *Maybe learning to use my powers properly won't be so difficult after all.* Exe stepped into the field, unintentionally swinging the door closed behind her. With a fearful gasp, Exe jerked around, then sighed in relief. There her tower door stood with no walls to support it. A quick knock-knock assured Exe that the door was really standing there.

"Who's there?" a dusky voice groaned.

"Riven?" Exe spun back to the mirage, searching. Finally she spied his boots sticking out from behind a bush.

"Hiya, dollface," Riven called.

Exe stepped into the mirage, her happiness at seeing him tempered with suspicion, "How come you heard me? I thought the mirage was soundproof?"

"Asher removed that particular enchantment. Said he needs to be able to hear if anyone sneaks into the mirage when he comes to train you. In case he's followed," Riven groaned as he sat up.

"What are you doing here?" Exe asked.

"Recovering. Your father did quite a number on my head. I had to open it to him for a bit so he'd trust me again. You can't imagine what it's like, having another person tromping through your thoughts and memories," Riven crawled over to the pool to splash a bit of the mysterious substance onto his face.

"You have no idea," Exe said, then shared with him just a little of what Velin had done to her and her family over the years.

"That would've ended me," Riven sprawled back on the emerald grass. Exe stood over him, fidgeting as she watched him relax. "You must be tough."

"I had good teachers," Exe said, thinking of her brothers.

"I'm sorry. The way I acted when Hastings... died," Riven turned his head toward her but kept his eyes closed.

"It's okay," Exe sank down next to him, hugging her knees.

"Is this what it felt like for you?" Riven mused, opening one eye to peer at her. "Killing someone? A few of my set in Anacapia, they talk like taking a life gives you power, like it makes you a B.T.O.," Riven opened both eyes when he saw her confusion. "It means big time operator. But I don't feel big. I feel scared. And small. Like I'm lesser than the most miniscule vermin and unworthy of even that much life. That how you felt?"

"Yes," Exe answered, unwilling to tell him that it would only get worse. *That the pain simply grows until you get numb to living.* But maybe it would be better for him. After all, Malina had called his a good kill. *While mine...*

In silence, they watched the sun rise and infuse the world with color again. Seeing the rays illuminate the distant, glassy skyscrapers, Exe realized how strange it felt to be back here after her brief time in Anacapia. Yet it hadn't felt at all odd entering that wondrous world. *If only I were free to visit any time I wanted.*

Quietly she slipped the wanted poster from her pocket, examining it once again with educated eyes. Now that she'd met Viva, it was obvious that the girl pictured was her twin. Although the eyes were violet, that mutinous expression was all Viva.

"Your sister poses for those every year," Riven murmured. "She hates it." Exe pondered the poster, wondering if being forced to pose as her notorious twin was the reason Viva seemed to dislike her so much. *It doesn't seem like enough, though.*

Reading it once again, Exe honed in on the name of the one who'd given the order for her death: *Jettani.* Here and there she'd learned tidbits about this ruler, too. This woman they all seemed to fear, but no one had explained why. "What would Jettani have done if she'd discovered me in Anacapia today?"

"Killed you," Riven answered without hesitation.

"Why would the ruler of your country care about killing me?" Exe turned back to the horizon, as if searching this ordinary city's skyline would somehow reveal an answer.

"Only Jettani knows the truth," Riven answered. "Personally, I think she used you to control your parents. Back then, their popularity threatened hers. Once you were labeled a danger, your notoriety forced them into the shadows."

Jettani was willing to kill a baby to protect herself, and people still follow her? Exe wondered. She was afraid of the answer. Instead she asked, "If hurting my parents was Jettani's only reason for condemning me, then why would she send the Disimulata to hunt me now? The damage is done."

"If you return and you're not a threat, then you prove Jettani wrong. Or worse, you show her to be a liar," Riven answered. "That alone threatens her power."

But Jettani didn't just want Exe silenced, she wanted her dead. *Could this Jettani woman truly be so diabolical that she'd kill me now just to protect her reputation? It doesn't seem feasible. Besides, everyone acts like I'm the threat.*

Suddenly, an ugly thought struck Exe. She hadn't killed Bonnie on purpose, but the girl had still died. *What if*

I accidentally did something even more horrible with my powers when I was just a baby? Could an infant do something so horrific that the government would label her an imminent threat? Asher and Malina, and even Velin, they certainly acted as if there were something wrong with her powers. *Maybe that's why I've been sentenced to death. And why Velin forced me to repress my powers for so long.*

"Why wouldn't my parents or Velin tell me this?" Exe wondered aloud, half afraid Riven would confirm that they were too terrified of her to admit that she was dangerous, maybe even lethal. *Maybe they're scared of what I'll do if I know the truth.*

"Couldn't say. Well, time's up, doll," Riven sighed. "If I don't get home before my parents awake, I'll be asked for answers I'm not prepared to give."

"Will I see you again?" Exe asked, guessing the answer.

"Maybe, in a blue moon. But I won't remember that I've met you," Riven said. "When I first became a double agent, Asher helped me develop a spell to erase resistance intel and activities from my mind so that I can't betray any secrets if I'm ever questioned. I'm only allowed to retain the bare minimum of information so that I know to continue working for them. And he wants you completely obliterated from my mind."

"Erasing memories? Isn't that dangerous?" Exe wondered if Velin had ever done something like that to her. *Maybe killing Bonnie isn't the worst thing I've ever done.* "Why can't you just lock away those secrets where no one else can find them?"

Riven looked at her in confusion. "What do you mean? All Anacapians keep their minds locked at all times, unless the government demands access. Although, some parents keep their kids' minds open to them alone until they come of age."

"I can understand that. But why don't you lock your secrets in a private part of your mind that only you know how to access? Like a vault," Exe explained.

Riven sat up, a thoughtful expression on his face, "A miniature mindlock that secures secrets while the rest of your mind remains open? I'm not certain that'd work."

"It does. I used it on Velin. He couldn't find the thoughts and memories I hid from him, though he tried," Exe shyly boasted.

"I'm surprised no one else in our world has thought to do this," Riven mused. "I guess most law-abiding citizens wouldn't see the need to lock a small section when their whole mind is permanently locked from intrusion. But maybe criminals know to do it, to keep their crimes secret when their minds are searched on arrest."

Exe pretended outrage, "Are you calling me a criminal?"

"According to that poster, you are. I am too, by not killing you on sight," Riven teased, then inspiration struck. "Say, how long did it take you to develop that spell?"

Exe replied simply, "I didn't write a spell. I just wished it."

Stunned, Riven faced her fully. "Wishing? No. No one can wish a spell that complex into existence. Velin must've written one for you. Maybe I could write a similar spell. A spell that could protect all knowledge of my double agent dealings were my mind ever probed. If it works, then every Sub Rosa member could secure all knowledge of the resistance, in the event of capture or interrogation. The Disimulata would never think to probe for a second, deeper mindlock. You may have just saved us all."

"You're welcome?" Exe said as Riven grabbed her in a fierce hug.

"Asher did order me to forget you," Riven murmured. "But perhaps if I locked every thought of you away..."

"You could come see me again?" Exe asked.

Riven considered this for a moment, then pulled out his silver dollar. He cupped the coin in his hand, whispered a word, then flicked it up into the air. The coin tumbled higher and higher. As soon as it began to fall, it vanished. Instantly, Exe felt a tickle on her palm. The coin had reappeared in her hand.

"A little trick Asher taught me. He uses a gold one to call me for missions," Riven explained. "It wouldn't be safe for me to make a habit of casual visits, but if you're ever in trouble, or if you need me at all, just toss this coin in the air but don't catch it. It'll come to me. And then I'll come to you."

"Thank you," Exe whispered, tucking the coin into her pocket.

"It must be crazy, coming into our world like this," Riven said as he stepped down into the gathering pool.

"A little," Exe agreed. "I'm just glad I found it."

"Me too," Riven returned. And with a wave, he disappeared into the waterfall.

Anxious anticipation shredded Exe's nerves as she waited on Asher, afraid that he'd send for her when she was too far away from her tower to get to the field instantaneously. *Does he think I never leave my house?*

Well, you hardly ever do, Exe answered herself (rolling her eyes when she realized that was something Velin would've thought at her). During school, she watched the clock fretfully and rushed home as soon as she could. The rest of the time, Exe lingered in her bell tower, filling the endless hours by finally discarding the stacks of empty boxes and repeatedly reorganizing every level of her tower.

This sudden interest in the state of her bedroom prompted Ella and Rove to ask Exe if she was finally ready to redecorate. She'd already turned them down once before, because she'd been too preoccupied with her past and her powers. Exe felt even more ungrateful saying no this time, but she couldn't risk being the center of a family project when Asher's signal came.

Given Asher's noncommittal "as soon as I can," Exe expected to be waiting weeks for her first training session. But to her surprise, her necklace began to tingle and glow just over a week after her escapade into Anacapia. Three turns, a whispered "postern," and then Exe stepped through her tower door into the empty field, scanning the mirage with stomach-churning excitement.

She'd been imagining this moment for days. Would her parents be just as distracted and distant as they'd been in Anacapia? Or would this finally be the warm, welcoming reunion with her birth parents that she'd secretly hoped for? *Safe in this field, they'll be happy to see me, impatient to shower me with hugs and apologies and explanations, won't they?* Maybe even her bratty twin Viva would be pleasant, now that the shock of Exe's sudden return had worn off.

And there'll be no excuse now to keep the full truth from me. She'd finally know why she'd been sent away—and what she needed to do to return home to Anacapia without fearing for her life. *Just for a visit,* Exe qualified, glancing guiltily at her lonely tower door, looking fragile and forlorn against the barren field. It felt wicked to regard any place without the Parsells as home. Shame flamed in her belly as reached for the doorknob, determined to go back inside to at least leave a note so they wouldn't wonder and worry about her absence.

"Leaving so soon? Good," Viva's venomous whisper slithered uncomfortably close to Exe's ear. Exe whirled just in time to see Viva vanish from right behind her, and reappear in the mirage.

"What are **you** doing here?" Exe's voice held an unfamiliar sneer to match Viva's derision. Looking at her twin gave her the eerie feeling that she was looking at her own self-loathing brought to life.

"Afraid I'll show you up, *little* sister?" Viva asked with speculative malice.

"No," Exe answered, feeling like she'd somehow just failed a test she didn't know she was taking. "Of course you'll know more than me. You've had training. I haven't."

"So you say," Viva's eyes gleamed triumphant. "I say you're lying. I've seen what you can do, and that takes training. I say this is all a ploy to get close to the Sub Rosa. Who sent you? What are you after? I won't let you hurt my family."

"Are you mad? They're my family, too," Exe exclaimed.

"Really? But my parents abandoned you," Viva's aqua eyes narrowed with malevolence. "Dumped you with a vile old man and never gave you a second thought."

"Th-they had to. To protect me," Exe faltered.

"Is that so? Then how come I wasn't sent away too? We share the same face," Viva admitted grudgingly. "And I've been perfectly safe in Anacapia my whole life." Viva's words ground into Exe's wounded soul like salt.

"Maybe they just didn't care about protecting you," Exe lashed out, pleased to see that her blind blow had landed when Viva blanched. "If they didn't care about me, why would they bother training me to control my powers? They're willing to risk their lives to help me. Have they done the same for you?"

"If they care about you so much, why didn't we all leave Anacapia together?" Viva's spiteful whisper seared into Exe. "They could've kept us all safely together, had they wanted to, but instead they cast you aside."

Exe's head jerked as if Viva had slapped her again. Desperate to hide her welling tears, Exe yawned and stretched as if Viva were boring her, surreptitiously wiping away the dampness. Then she faced Viva again, shoulders back, chin raised, a razor sharp retort on the tip of her tongue.

"Here already, Viva? I thought we agreed that you'd arrive later," Asher emerged from the waterfall, squelching Exe's opportunity to respond in kind.

"Forgive me, father. I simply couldn't wait to lay eyes on my dear sister again," Viva's tone simpered sweetly, but her hateful gaze stayed locked on Exe.

"That's my girl," Asher approved, giving Viva's shoulders a quick squeeze. Viva smiled sweetly up at him before turning her gloating glare on Exe.

"Well, Exe? Are you ready to work?" Asher smiled, stepping out of the mirage.

"Am I ready? You've kept me waiting for a whole week," Exe screeched, horrified by her own belligerence. This wasn't how she intended to greet her father.

"You will not use that tone with me, young lady. If you want a proper response, ask politely," Asher admonished.

"Tell me what took so long. Please," Exe muttered, too ashamed to meet his eye. Viva's victorious expression left Exe feeling tricked into berating their father.

"Keeping your location secret is of the utmost importance," Asher explained. "Although there won't be many of these training sessions, we can't risk being seen emerging from the Corpse Copse. It took time to construct a volting chamber in the copse because cruor clay is so difficult to obtain these days. But we've done it. So now we can travel secretly both ways."

"We can?" Exe's excitement bubbled. "Does this mean—"

"Malina and I can," Asher qualified, squelching Exe's hope. "And Viva. Since Anacapia's schools teach so little practical magic these days, your sister convinced us that she could benefit from the same training you'll receive."

Exe could feel Viva's eyes taunting, but refused to look at her. Her sister had devised a way to keep Exe from being alone with their parents. *But why?* Ignoring Viva, Exe asked, "Why will we only have a few sessions?"

"I'm hopeful that a few is all you'll need to get a handle on your magic," Asher said. "Though we've taken every precaution, coming here is still a risk."

"So once I get my powers under control, I won't be dangerous anymore?" Exe asked, thinking of the wanted poster.

Viva snorted, as if the idea of Exe being dangerous was ludicrous.

"That is the plan," Asher agreed.

Hope sparked in Exe. *If I can prove that I'm no longer dangerous, then perhaps that Jettani woman will consent to lifting the death warrant.* Suddenly all those pressing questions about her past didn't seem so important anymore, not if she had a chance of returning to Anacapia. Home. *The future is all that matters.*

"Sounds good," Exe enthused. "How do we start?"

Asher shook his head and sat down on a sizable boulder in the mirage. "I have a few questions first. Tell me, do you remember a time when you were without powers? Were they just unleashed in you one day, or did you unleash them yourself?"

"No. Is that how our magic is supposed to work? We're not born with powers?" Exe asked, puzzled as to why this mattered.

"Anacapians are powered from birth to death," Asher replied.

"Then why do you think I'd be any different?" Exe frowned.

"That is the question," Asher pondered. Exe had the distinct feeling he was hiding something. "Tell me how your powers work."

"I thought that's what you were here to teach me," Exe exclaimed, exasperated.

"How long does it take you to develop a spell before you use it?" Asher clarified.

"I don't develop spells. Anything I wish for just happens," Exe explained. At Viva's disbelieving snort, she added, "Not always. I mean, my wishes don't come true perfectly. Especially if I don't realize that I've made a wish. But if I concentrate on making a deliberate wish, it comes true, like when I unburied that Disimulata's body."

"No way. Wish magic isn't powerful enough to do that," Viva belittled, as she reclined comfortably on the boulder next to her father. Exe clenched her fists at the sight of them so at ease with one another.

No, it shouldn't be," Asher agreed. "Show us."

Exe cast about for the most impressive bit of magic she'd ever done. She doubted there was anything buried in the field for her to unearth. And while she'd gotten pretty good at calling distant objects to her, fetching wasn't going to amaze anyone. *But turning invisible might impress them.*

When that Disimulata guy had been searching for her in the schoolhouse, Velin's voice had told her to turn invisible and she had. *That ought to be enough to impress even Viva,* Exe thought as she glared at her, supremely irritated that Viva somehow managed to look both bored and impatient as she lounged on the boulder. Exe would give anything to wipe the disdain from Viva's face.

"I can make myself vanish," Exe bragged.

"What?" Viva sat up in utter shock. "That's impossible. That's an incon–"

Asher held up a hand to cut her off, "Let's see."

Quivering under their undivided attention, Exe closed her eyes and concentrated on the memory of the man in black hunting her in the schoolhouse. With alarm she realized that she had no clue how she'd turned invisible that day. None of the mantras or spells she'd found in her vade had mentioned invisibility. *So what did Velin say to me that activated my invisibility?*

"Hide yourself," Exe whispered, scolding herself for saying the phrase out loud. Exe opened her eyes. Asher and Viva were both still staring at her, waiting. *Or were they?* Perhaps they were just staring at the spot where she'd just vanished. As an experiment, Exe tiptoed to the side. Both sets of eyes followed her.

"Are you a toddler? Closing your eyes doesn't make you invisible, you naïf," Viva burst out laughing.

"Why didn't that work?" Exe complained, her face flushing red.

"Invisibility is an Inconceivable. And you thought to do it with wish magic alone?" Viva mocked. "Inconceivable spells are so complex that no one can write them, even if they had the span of two lifetimes. And even if someone could, they wouldn't be powerful enough to perform it. Except maybe Velin. And you're no Velin."

Asher's admonishing glance ended Viva's malicious laughter. "What were you trying to do?" he questioned kindly, but Exe felt patronized.

"Vanish," Exe grumbled. "Like I did when that Disimulata guy came looking for me the day we moved to Nowhere. It worked on him. Why not you?" Viva's mocking grin fell away at the mention of the Disimulata.

"'Hide yourself' is the trigger?" Asher rose and came to Exe, eyeing her vade.

"What's a trigger?" Exe asked, handing the tome over to him.

"You'll learn," Asher said. One moment Exe's spell book lay closed in his hands, the next it opened itself right to the 'Hide Yourself' page. "Ahhh."

"What is it?" Exe asked, peering over Asher's shoulder.

Viva finally deigned to leave the mirage to see Exe's spell for herself. "Ha! Wish magic. As if," Viva swaggered back to lounge on the boulder again.

"What does she mean?" Exe almost stomped her foot like the three-year-old Viva had compared her to.

"What you did that day wasn't wish magic," Asher explained. "It was a memory fade spell that Velin scribed for you. An ancient spell that fell out of fashion centuries ago, after mind lock spells were invented. Very clever of Velin to realize that old incantation would still work on the Hoi Polloi."

"You do realize that I don't understand most of what you just said, right?" Exe blurted, irritated by Viva's continuing sniggers. "All that I know, I've had to learn without anyone's help." She'd meant to hurt Viva with her defensive words, but only Asher was stung. He solemnly closed her vade, meeting her gaze with a look that was both an apology and a reproach.

"That day, you must have faded the memory of your presence from the minds of the Hoi Polloi—that's unpowered people. Velin likely didn't want the others giving away your position by interacting with you," Asher mused. "If Bates— that's the name of the Disimulata who was hunting you—if he couldn't see you, that wasn't your doing. I'd wager Velin cast a reflect-deflect shield to hide you from Bates. He used that spell years ago to avoid capture."

"So it's not wish magic that's been causing me trouble all this time? I've been using spells Velin wrote for me and planted in my mind?" Exe fumed, bristling at Viva's soft, mocking laughter, which Asher seemed content to ignore.

"That depends," Asher qualified, looking a bit relieved as he paged through her vade. "Aside from this one that fades the memories of others, these spells are primarily to help you calm your mind, suppress your powers, forget your own memories, and so forth. There's none capable of that cyclone you surrounded me with the other night. Have you done other magic like that? What was that about exhuming a body?"

"I can call things to me, even if they're far away or underground. Is that unusual?" Exe asked, hoping this was a special spell only she could do, just to wipe the smirk off Viva's face.

"No," Asher answered, crushing Exe's hope. "But it's an intricate spell. One that shouldn't be possible to perform unless it's scribed into your vade. And you don't have one. Are you sure you've been able to do this?"

"Absolutely," Exe declared, feeling confident for the first time. Viva scoffed, making a show of her boredom as she lolled on the boulder. "I can make objects vanish too," Exe boasted. In a blink, the boulder vanished.

"What did you do?" Viva screamed as she fell onto the mirage's velvety emerald grass. She jumped to her feet, swiping at the vivid green streaks on her crisp, creamy dress until the stubborn stains vanished.

"Where did you send it?" Asher's low intensity startled Exe. He stared at the spot where the boulder used to be with the same unsettled look Ella and Rove often wore.

"I-I don't know. I wished it gone and it went," Exe tried to explain.

"You wished," Asher murmured.

"She's lying! Airgonaut!" Viva shrieked. Exe's vade ripped itself from Asher's grip and came sailing into her hands. Viva tore through the mostly-blank book in a rage.

"Can you bring it back?" Asher asked in an urgent tone, ignoring Viva's outburst.

"I think so," Exe answered, more than willing to ignore Viva too.

Viva's feral cry pierced Exe's eardrums. The boulder had returned to its exact same spot—right where Viva was standing. Blood oozed from the stone where Viva's calves fused with the jagged stone. Asher rushed over to Viva, forcing her upright when she almost collapsed from the pain.

"I need you to stay standing, sweetheart. If you separate from your legs, we may not save them," Asher's urgent tone tried to calm her as he examined the damage.

"I'm so sorry! I didn't mean to do that. Can I just wish it away again?" Exe apologized, backing off her efforts to help when Viva aimed an anguished roar at her.

"No!" Asher snapped. "Her legs and the rock are sharing the same space. You're liable to send bits of her away, too. Extracting her'll be tricky. I can't do it alone. Exe–"

"NO! Exe– too d-dangerous. M-me," Viva screamed, clawing at Asher's chest.

"Sweetie, if you pass out from the pain before you're freed–" Asher cautioned.

"Mmmme," Viva insisted, shivering in a cold sweat.

"Okay Viva, I need you to protect your legs from further harm while I fragment and dissolve the rock. When it loosens, I'll start healing you, got it?" Asher stated.

Viva nodded. At Asher's signal she whispered, "Sospital."

Asher tightened his grip around Viva's waist, then laid his free hand on the stone and murmured, "Buccellation, obrumpent."

The boulder shuddered as it began disintegrating into a cloud of dust. "Stop! You're sh-shattering me, too," Viva bellowed.

"It's alright, sweetheart. Just let me think," Asher soothed, hugging Viva to him. "Okay, I'm going to try liquefying the rock while simultaneously keeping your legs solid. But this means you'll need to maintain the protection spell while healing yourself."

"O-okay," Viva shuddered.

"You've only begun learning to cast two spells at once," Asher said, glancing at Exe. "Maybe–"

Viva sucked in her breath, "I-I can do it. I'm ready. Sospital-resarciate."

Asher touched the stone again, his low voice calling out, "Terraqueous-jungible."

At once the solid stone began to wobble like a lava lamp blob. Viva sighed in relief as the gelatinous boulder ebbed away from her legs. She sagged against Asher.

"Don't pass out, Viva," Asher shook her. "Say the trigger word to heal, sweetheart. And keep a hold on that protection spell."

"Sospital-resarciate," Viva whimpered, her head lolling against Asher's shoulder.

"Stay with me, sweetie. It's not working yet, Viv. You need to try harder," Asher jostled her, his eyes fixed on her bloody legs.

"I c-c-can't," Viva moaned.

"You have to," Asher demanded, muttering his spell words again. "I can't hold this much longer."

"S-sospital-r-resarciate," Viva wept. Exe watched in horror as blood continued to ooze from the stone. *Please, please let her spells work,* Exe silently wished for Viva's legs to heal enough to be pulled free from the boulder. Suddenly the blood reversed its flow, seeping back into the holes where Viva's legs were submerged in the jellied rock. Soon the color returned to Viva's strained face.

"It's done, sweetheart. Step out now," Asher's breathing intensified as he struggled to maintain the spells. The quivering stone sucked on Viva's feet like jelly as she pulled them free with a pop. The moment she was clear, the boulder returned to solid stone. Asher scooped Viva up from the grass where she'd fallen and plunged her legs into the waterfall's gathering pool.

"Why did you have spells to free someone from a rock?" Exe asked, hanging back as Asher cradled Viva's fainting form in his arms.

"I didn't. I used spells meant for other things. We're lucky it worked," Asher murmured, splashing water on his own exhausted face. "This isn't your fault, Exe. I should've realized what would happen. I was too focused on what you're capable of."

"Now you know," Exe defended, hugging herself.

"I'm afraid I do. I think that's enough for one day. I need to get this daughter home," Asher murmured as Viva stirred.

"That's it?" Exe exclaimed, biting her lip when Viva opened one vindictive eye at her. "You haven't taught me anything. Isn't this proof enough that I need help?"

"There's no time to discuss this. I've no idea the extent of the damage done to Viva's legs. She needs professional healing, now," Asher scooped Viva up in his arms and strode into the waterfall.

"When will you be back?" Exe called out as the pair disappeared into the cascade. "Will you be coming back?"

Asher did not reply.

CHAPTER SIXTEEN

THE MAGIC WORD

The damage she'd done to Viva convinced Exe that Asher and Malina would never contact her again. *I'm not safe to be around. What if I hurt someone again?*

Bonnie, Ella, Riven, Hastings, and now Viva. And Asher knows. Exe had told Riven about killing Bonnie—and Asher had been inside Riven's mind—which meant that Asher knew just how dangerous his deserted daughter was. Viva might've died too if Exe had returned the boulder while her twin was still sprawled on the ground. *And who knows what damage that boulder did while it was gone from the mirage. Where did I send it? Have I done things like that before? How many people have I hurt or killed without even realizing it?* She couldn't bear the thought of accidentally hurting yet another person when she didn't have the skills to heal any harm she caused.

Relentless visions of Viva's blood spurting from the stone in the field replayed on a loop in Exe's mind over the next few weeks, until she found herself resorting to the UROK mantra just to forget about it for a little while. But hard as she tried, Exe couldn't shrug off the dark, desperate feeling of abandonment. *Asher's probably pestering Velin this very minute to take over my training. Then he'll seal off the entrance to Anacapia forever, just to protect their world from me.*

Worry so overwhelmed Exe that she decided that removing herself from the Parsell's Thanksgiving celebration and Nowhere's Autumn Extravaganza was her only option to keep everyone safe from her. *Plus it feels wrong to celebrate when I have no idea how badly I've hurt Viva.* But Exe couldn't come up with a plausible excuse to skip out on the festivities that wouldn't arouse Ella and Rove's suspicions. In the end, she decided to participate as little as possible, and recite her power-suppressing mantras the entire time as an added precaution. While it was easy to steal away alone after Thanksgiving dinner, Ella and Rove insisted that she join in the family bonding excursion to the town's festival.

Every November, Nowhere hosted a mammoth potluck where traditional Thanksgiving dishes were served along side authentic Navajo, Apache, and Yavapai cuisine. They even held an annual hoop dancing competition at Outpost Twenty-Two—Nowhere's living history museum that celebrated every one of Arizona's native tribes. And this year, the town had outdone itself.

Dozens of Nowhere's citizens strolled Main Street in period costumes and acted their parts to perfection. Exe actually heard a little old lady scolding the ice wagon driver over spoiled food because he hadn't delivered her ice block on time. Across the way, a group of men were discussing the prospects of the mine as if their livelihoods depended on it. And one industrious young man had found a stack of furs that he'd brought to the general store to barter for goods.

Some townsfolk had even scrounged up enough covered wagons to circle down at the end of Main Street. The wagon owners set up camp in the center, cooking food over campfires and spreading out bedrolls. Knowing Nowhere, Exe was sure they intended to camp out in the wagon train the entire Thanksgiving weekend.

The minute Exe began to relax and enjoy the festivities, her necklace began to tingle and glow. With a pleading look to Easy (who nodded his promise to cover for her), Exe snuck back home, grabbed her vade, and activated her tower door.

The peace of the barren field after the chaotic celebration did nothing to quiet Exe's nerves. Though she was relieved that her birth parents hadn't abandoned her to Velin, Exe knew that she still had to answer for what had happened to Viva. *Is she okay?* And maybe they'd finally have answers for her too. *Will they finally tell me why even my magical parents are afraid of my powers?*

But neither Asher nor Malina were waiting for her in the field. No one was. Clasping her Vade to her, Exe could almost taste the tension that crackled the crisp night air. She slowly scanned the mirage and every inch of the field that she could see from her open doorway. *Why would they summon me and then not show up?* Exe took a tentative step into the field, keeping her hand on the doorknob.

"You're gonna have to sharpen your instincts if you wanna survive in our world, toots," a voice of liquid velvet sounded right beside her as the door slammed shut.

Exe whirled and locked gazes with a pair of malachite eyes, as deep blue-green as a secluded lagoon. Stepping back fast, Exe regarded the boy warily, noting that he was about her age. That was all she could pinpoint about him—all else seemed contradictory.

Something about the way he carried himself said respectful gentleman, yet his casual stance held a note of roguish nonchalance. His retro clothing appeared plain and rough (unlike the obviously expensive outfits Riven and the Verelustres wore), yet they were perfectly tailored to him— like a one-of-a-kind vagabond suit. And his expression read open and honest, yet mysterious and assessing. Everything about him invited Exe to lean in to better experience whatever he might say or do next.

"Who are you?" Exe asked, tensing when he just smiled back at her. "Well?"

The boy's smile deepened, "I'm waiting for you to ask a question I can answer."

"You can't tell me who you are?" Exe demanded. In response (with a slight whirl of his pinky), the boy conjured a delicate, crystalline rose in the space between them. He dropped his eyes to the flower, then caught her gaze again.

"Oh. Are the, ah flowers, um– growing?" Exe struggled to remember the phrase Asher had instructed her to ask of any strangers she met in the field. *But he doesn't feel like a stranger...*

"The only flowers in bloom are the roses," The boy smiled, tipping his creamy bowler to her, while those spellbinding eyes of his peered at her through the clear rose petals. "Is it too forward of me to be bringing you flowers already?"

Exe leaned in mischievously for a fake-sniff, then cried out as the crystal blossom shattered and vanished. "I'm so sorry!"

"Don't fret, kid. It's supposed to vanish upon touch as a warning signal. If the rose shatters, scatter," the boy chuckled, then sobered. "You do need to get that exchange down though. Had my brother Rande been the first to arrive, he'd have knocked you flat with a defensive spell for not properly guarding your safety with the watchwords. Didn't Asher tell you?"

"He did. But that's about all he's told me," Exe sighed, then smiled at the boy. "Now who are you and why are you here? Where are my parents?"

"Caulder Ishkabibble, at your service," the boy winked and bowed. "My older brother and I are to have the honor of training you. Rande will be here a bit later. My little sister would love to meet you too, but of course she can't."

"Why?" Exe asked. *Because I'm too dangerous*, she thought, in answer to her own question. *So dangerous even my birth parents won't risk coming to train me anymore.* Exe forced aside her hurt and bitterness (tucking it away in her mind vault) and tried to focus on the fact that Asher had found someone willing to help her.

"Because it's safer if only a few people know about you. Did you suspect another reason?" Caulder replied.

"Should I? Nevermind. Where do we start?"

"Now that you know I'm on the level, let's cozy up for a copacetic confab so that I can explain how our magic works. Knowing the mechanics should make it easier for you to perform," Caulder sat on the emerald edge of the mirage. "Any questions before we get started?"

Longing welled within Exe. *Finally someone's willing to answer my questions.* Then her gaze fell on the boulder and images of Viva's blood flowing from the stone flooded her mind. *Protecting my family is more important than digging into my past right now.* "Is Viva okay?"

"She's fine. For Viva," Caulder winked at her as he pulled on the leather thong around his neck to reveal a rough-set

malachite stone pendant. "Alright then, let's cover some of our terms. These are tetherstones."

"Tetherstone?" Exe palmed her own necklace, suddenly realizing that toddlers in Caulder's world knew more about magic than she currently did.

"That half is called a tetherstone. The other half here, is your anchorstone," Caulder pointed to the large amethyst embedded in the silky cover of Exe's vade. "The connection between your tetherstone and your anchorstone allows you to use the spells scribed into your vade no matter how far you are from your tome."

"So you use spells from your book instead of wish magic?" Exe asked.

"Precisely. Asher said you've been using your wish magic for everything for more than a decade? Impressive! But that's why it's grown so out of control, like an untended hedge becomes an untamed thicket if its branches aren't trimmed and trained. Your magic goes haywire and exhausts you when you try big spells, doesn't it?" Caulder asked, continuing at Exe's nod. "Wish magic requires an inordinate amount of power for typically weak spells. That's why no one in our world uses it, beyond children too young to use proper spells."

"How do proper spells work?" Exe asked.

"Spells, enchantments, charms, and so forth are all written into your vade by a wordsmith. That is, someone with the ability to scribe magic, which is a gift few have," Caulder opened Exe's vade to a spell. "This title at the top we call a trigger, a word or phrase selected to call upon the magic of a particular spell."

"A magic word?" Exe giggled.

"Why is that funny?"

"In my world, the magic word is 'please,'" Exe laughed, blushing when Caulder smiled. "Actually, I have a brother who can work magic with a few 'pleases.'"

"You have a brother?" Caulder asked. "Do you get along?"

"Always," Exe said, thinking of Viva's cruelty. "With all of my six brothers. And my parents. I love them. They all love me too, though I sometimes wonder why. The constant struggle to control my magical powers hasn't made me very loveable."

"Not loveable is how I'd describe my brother Rande. Just to give you fair warning before he arrives," Caulder cautioned. "Don't get me wrong, I love him and you couldn't find a better teacher. But life in Anacapia has made him— hard. For good reason."

"Noted," Exe gnawed her lower lip to keep herself from wishing that this Rande might never come and ruin the quiet camaraderie she felt with Caulder.

"Speaking of Rande, I'd better get you up to speed quick before he gets here," Caulder replied, pulling out a plain, brown leather tome that was imbedded with half of a malachite stone. "This is my vade. Yours will be just as full one day."

Exe turned the ragged pages of Caulder's book with reverence, astounded by the sheer number of complex spells within it—all titled with a strange word or phrase. "Your spells all have little descriptions too," Exe exclaimed. "I thought Velin just did that for me so I'd know what my spells did."

"I've got almost a thousand spells in here of all sorts, but many I don't use often," Caulder replied. "Descriptions help us remember the purpose of rarely-used magic. It's never wise to use a spell if you don't know what it'll do."

"How many different kinds of spells are there?" Exe asked.

"Too many to list," Caulder explained. "Think of all the different types of talents and jobs and activities and chores there are in your Ari Zona world. We have multiple spells for them all, and more. Plus tasks and such that you've likely never heard of."

"How am I supposed to learn all this before my parents decide that my training is done? It would take a lifetime to learn all the possible spells," Exe complained.

"We're all capable of developing our own unique spells or personalizing existing ones. So the number of spells is infinite. No one knows them all. Not even Velin, though I'll wager he's tried. The man is a fanatic for education," Caulder's reverent tone and respectful smile as he spoke of Velin irritated Exe.

"Couldn't prove it by me," she scoffed. *Apparently no one told Caulder of my troubled history with Velin.* Exe looked away from his bewildered expression, then uncomfortably cleared her throat to ask, "So no one can do every spell?"

"No one can perform a spell that isn't in their vade. And not everyone can perform all of the spells in their vade well," Caulder explained.

"I don't get it," Exe frowned.

"It might help to understand how one obtains a spell," Caulder suggested.

"I thought you just said that we wrote them," Exe said.

"It's possible, yes. And many do write their own, or did. However these days, most obtain common, base, and specialty spells from a variety of places. For instance, family heirloom spells are passed down from generation to generation. And some spells—like the one to volte—are government-issued," Caulder explained.

"Only the government can issue a volting spell?" Exe hid her disappointment as the freedom that volting offered faded away.

"Legally," Caulder qualified. "Decades ago, people wrote their own volting spells. Gifted volters crafted spells to volte farther and faster than ever, selling their incantations to anyone who could afford it. Until the government got involved."

"Wait, so two different spells might do the exact same thing? Why?" Exe asked.

"For the same reason people prefer spells they write themselves over store-bought ones," Caulder explained. "You're more connected to the magic you write for yourself. As the spells are tailored specifically to you, they're easier to use. And more powerful."

"Then why does anyone buy spells?" Exe asked.

"Why do you buy clothes when you could make them yourself?"

"Because I'm terrible at sewing. They'd look awful."

"Exactly. I'd buy a spell to whip up a fancy cake instead of writing my own because it'd take ages, and I'm a terrible cook," Caulder joked. "The baker's cake spells are much tastier. And a cake tastes even better if the baker who wrote the spell casts it to create the cake. My cakes are stale even with a baker-written spell."

"I think I get it. So, can you put these spells into my vade?" Exe asked, paging through Caulder's spellbook.

"I'm no wordsmith. But luckily Velin is. Asher talked him into transferring a number of spells from Viva's vade into yours over these past few weeks," Caulder replied, opening Exe's vade to reveal hundreds of new spells.

"What?! How could he– He took it! And I didn't even notice!" Exe exclaimed.

"You didn't notice that your vade was missing?" Caulder gaped at her. "Do not tell Rande. You need to keep better track of your vade in the future. You'd be in serious trouble if it fell into the wrong hands. Lock it up so that no one but you can get to it."

"How? Any vault in my world would be easily cracked by someone from yours!"

"That's true. Don't worry, I'll get you a gardeviance for it," Caulder rose.

"How much will that cost?" Exe stood, too. From his shabby appearance, Caulder could ill afford to buy her a pricy magical safe. *And I've got no Anacapia cash to pay him with even if he would take my money.*

"My treat. Don't be fooled by my modest appearance— it's good cover. Obtaining obscure and outlawed items is my trade. I'm actually an exceptionally successful dark marketeer," Caulder flourished his shabby alabaster trench coat and gave her a dashing bow. "I humbly confess that my siblings and I are the most notorious contrabandists in our world. Not that anyone knows we're smugglers. That's why we're so successful."

"My brothers would absolutely love you," Exe said, bemused that someone who looked so honest was actually admitting to being an infamous smuggler.

"I'm sure my brother will love you too. Won't you Rande?" Caulder called out. Turning, Exe spotted a rugged young man a bit older than Seph striding out of the cascade with eyes as emerald as the mirage's grass. Recognizing him from the Sub Rosa meeting in Asher and Malina's house, Exe raised her hand to wave–

THWACK!

A powerful force propelled Exe backward, slamming her against her tower door. The second the force released, Exe fell in a heap, dropping her vade. Dizzy and bruised, Exe opened her eyes to find Caulder above her, holding his hand out to help her up.

"I did warn you," Caulder smiled at her, then frowned at his brother. "You might've given her a chance to get a word out first."

"I already said the password to Caulder, anyway!" Exe complained.

"The watchwords must be exchanged with every single person you encounter in this field. Immediately. Every. Single. Time," Rande bit out. "You ready to work?"

"I guess."

THWACK! Rande knocked her back against the door again. This time Exe was ready. She'd wished a powerful whirlwind at Rande before she hit the ground. The mini-tornado whipped Rande around and around, leaving him rocking like a Weeble Wobble as it dissipated, though he managed to stay on his feet.

"Are the flowers in bloom?" Exe called out before Rande could retaliate.

"Only the roses," Rande relaxed his battle stance. "Not bad. Asher said your wish magic was powerful. Let's find out if you're as capable with actual spells."

Before Exe could pick up her vade, it zoomed into Rande's waiting hands. He paged through the tome, quickly scanning the available spells.

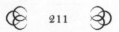

"How did he do that? He didn't even say anything," Exe asked Caulder.

"When you're good, thinking your spell word is just as effective as saying it aloud," Caulder answered, stepping about ten paces away from her.

"Ah, here we go," Rande called. Before Exe could turn to look at him, her open vade smacked her right in the face. "You need to work on your reflexes."

"So do you," Exe retorted, wishing for an unseen force to knock Rande over. He barely rocked back on his heels.

"You'll need to do better than that. Ready, Caulder?" Rande nodded to his brother then turned back to Exe with a look of skeptical expectation.

Exe looked at the spells written on the pages Rande had selected. There were two: 'fumificate,' a spell word to create smoke, and 'tremefy,' to cause trembling. *I'm supposed to do what with these words?!* Since Caulder appeared to be bracing for an attack, Exe thought both words at him, hoping something would happen. Nothing did.

Heat seeped into her face, even though she knew that neither brother was aware that she'd just failed to silently cast the spells. Pride warred with practicality as she tried mouthing, then whispering both words. Again, nothing. *I'm here for training, I should just ask for help!* But everything about Rande's demeanor said that he was expecting her to fail, and Exe wasn't ready to give him the satisfaction.

"Focus on intention," Caulder called to her. "Spell words cannot work if you do not first command them with specificity. Envision exactly what you want each word to do to me, then say the spell and watch it happen."

The description for each spell word had seemed pretty straightforward to Exe, but she hadn't exactly pictured the end result. So Exe concentrated on having fumificate encase Caulder in a tower of smoke while tremefy shook the ground beneath his feet. *Please, please work,* Exe wished. Instantly, both happened without Exe needing to say either word aloud. A mini-earthquake (targeted right under Caulder's feet) had him swaying in and out of a wispy white cloud as he fought to keep his balance. Exe shot Rande a triumphant look.

"Is she so powerful, Caulder?" Rande called to his brother without taking his calculating gaze off of Exe. "Or did you simply forget that you're well-trained in the art of defense?"

"I didn't think she'd catch on so quick," Caulder coughed as he stilled the ground beneath him and banished the thick smoke with a wave. His sly wink left Exe wondering if he hadn't let her attacks against him succeed on purpose.

"Now that we know where we stand, let's get to work," Rande said.

For the better part of two hours, Rande had her cast these two spells over and over. More effort was needed to cast the spells with Caulder defending against them, and at first Exe was lucky to produce a puff of smoke or cause a few pebbles to tremble. After Rande explained that it was easy work to defend against spells if you knew which ones were coming at you, Exe switched to casting one at a time, so that Caulder wouldn't know which one to expect.

As he tired, Exe was able to overwhelm him with both once again, but the effort brought her to her knees. When Rande subbed in for Caulder as a fresh target, Exe was forced to surrender. She couldn't get either spell to work against Rande's defenses.

"That's enough for today," Rande said as he strode toward the mirage. "Start practicing all of your spells so that you're actually prepared next time. One or the both of us will return in a day or two to continue. With any luck, we'll have your training wrapped up in a few weeks."

Nonplussed by his abrupt departure, Exe stared after him as he disappeared into the cascade. *If Rande completes my training that quickly, does that mean I'll never see my birth parents again?*

"You've impressed him," Caulder drew her attention by nudging her arm with his elbow. "He argued that it'd take years to get you up to speed when Asher and Malina first enlisted him to help train you."

Quit worrying. Nothing's been decided yet. Mentally shaking herself, Exe asked, "And what did you expect?"

"Nothing," Caulder smiled, backing his way towards the waterfall with a careless grin. "I've learned it's best to reserve judgement until all the facts are in. Personally, I'm hoping that Rande is wrong."

"Why?"

"This was fun. We get so few opportunities to practice magic in Anacapia, I'm kinda hoping these sessions go on forever," Caulder winked.

"Me too. But I guess for now it's time to go back to the real world," Exe sighed. When Caulder laughed, she asked, "What's so funny?"

"The real world. In Anacapia, a land without magic is a make-believe place that could only exist in fairytales," Caulder chuckled.

Exe watched him disappear into the cascade, her farewell smile fading into a frown. *Why aren't there many opportunities to practice magic in Anacapia?*

The next few weeks were magical...in more ways than one. Regularly using magic meant that Exe no longer felt like an over-packed powder keg about to blow. And the more she practiced using her powers on purpose, the less she worried about making an awful, accidental wish. With her fear of dangerous wishes diminished, Exe began to relax and enjoy life in Nowhere—when she was around.

Rande and Caulder called her to train every single day, with after-school sessions lasting late into the night (and almost all day on weekends too). Even Exe's recluse reputation couldn't prevent the Parsells from remarking on her many absences; although they were far more vocal about her positive change in demeanor. Exe overheard Rove remark to Ella, "Seems like the historic, smalltown life is just what Exe needed." Exe couldn't wait to share the real reason with her family. She went to sleep every night dreaming up ways to reveal her subdued powers to the Parsells.

Not that learning to control her powers was easy. The work was more exhausting than expected, especially since Rande insisted on teaching her several new spells during every lesson. *Although, I wouldn't exactly call it teaching.* Rande simply gave her a trigger, read her the description of what the spell was supposed to do, then told her to "Concentrate and connect." Over and over he repeated, "Concentrate and connect." *As if that explains anything.* She'd grown to hate those two words.

Rande's lessons weren't always exciting, but at least they weren't repetitive. His spell selections ran the extremes, from ultra boring to disturbingly destructive. After that first session when she'd battled with Caulder, Rande had reverted to rather mundane spells like auto-transcribing from voice to text onto fresh paper, as if by an invisible typewriter. He'd even taught her how to complete complex mathematical equations instantaneously. *Should I tell him that even in my non-magical world there are ways to do these things easily without magic?*

Once she'd mastered the academic stuff, Rande switched gears to defensive spells. (*If you can call blowing things up 'defensive.'*) Though she felt more in control of her powers now, Exe couldn't tamp down her anxiety over the unintentional damage she could do with these destructive spells. *It's not wish magic. You can't perform it accidentally,* Exe constantly reminded herself.

Plus, she wasn't likely to use any of the trigger words in casual conversation. The spells Rande had chosen to teach her had trigger words that were so obscure, Exe hadn't even heard of most of them before. Perhaps they were just Anacapian words, but some of them sounded completely made up.

Twenty-five cent words, Rove would call them, Exe half-smiled at what her dad might say if she could tell him about her training sessions. He often criticized those commanding officers who attempted to boost their own standing by tossing big words around. "The bigger their words, the smaller their brains, in my experience," he'd say of those leaders who relied on a thesaurus to make themselves sound smart.

Rove wouldn't make much of Rande's nonexistent teaching methods, either. Exe had to stop herself from wishing that Rove could replace him as her trainer. Her dad had a way of explaining confusing lessons that always made the lightbulb of knowledge click on no matter what subject he was teaching to any soldier or student, whether gifted or struggling. Unfortunately, Rande didn't have the patience or inclination to modify his instruction to help Exe absorb his lessons.

Caulder was better at helping her understand what Rande wanted her to do. His quick smile and razor wit always made training entertaining, no matter how grueling and exhausting Rande tried to make the session. Exe's favorite lessons were the ones when Caulder came alone to practice the various spells Rande had previously taught her.

Caulder was patient and perceptive, always stopping before Exe completely exhausted herself trying to perfect a spell. And wearing herself out was proving to be a problem. The more complex the spell she attempted, the more it tired her. And she hated being too exhausted after training—especially when it was just her and Caulder.

When Rande was around, both brothers left immediately once the lesson ended. But when Caulder came alone, he lingered to share tales of his wild smuggling adventures in Anacapia and other surrounding countries in the magical realm. Exe devoured every tale, insisting on vivid descriptions of every location, setting, creature, person, and magical item being bought or sold. Caulder indulged her every question and embellished every tale with a twinkle in his eye that had her wondering if some of the more fantastical details were real or fabricated.

As the weeks flew by, it grew harder for Exe to watch Caulder leave, disappearing into a spectacular world that she herself might never experience. Exe soon began to regard the mirage as forbidden fruit that enticed and taunted her in turn, until the field became a sort of limbo between her two worlds that she might never escape.

But Exe wouldn't be in limbo much longer if Rande had his way. Each lesson, Rande insisted on packing in more and more spells until they were covering over a dozen each session. Exe had the sneaking suspicion that Rande planned to quit training her as soon as he was sure she could perform every spell Velin had scribed into her vade. At the rate they were going, they'd be done before New Year's.

Surprisingly, Exe found that she could perform every spell with flawless ease after only a try or two—although it was disturbing how much the effort drained her. At first she hid her exhaustion, determined to impress Rande with her progress. But he only became increasingly incensed at how easily Exe was able to perform even the most complex spells in her vade. Why he would be angry about it made no sense to her. *I thought he wanted to be through training me as soon as possible!*

That thought avalanched over her like an Alaskan snowstorm. *My training has just begun, yet somehow it already feels like it's almost over.* The idea that Rande was rushing her training just to be rid of her—that she'd soon be cut off from Anacapia, never to see her birth parents (or Caulder) again—quickly withered Exe's bravado.

After that, rather than instantly performing any spell Rande gave her, Exe pretended to struggle. At times, she even silently cast the wrong spells so that it would appear that the trigger she was supposed to be performing had somehow misfired. And when the work depleted her, she let it show.

Unfortunately, the sudden setback in Exe's progress didn't slow Rande's accelerating lessons. He kept piling on the spells no matter how poorly Exe performed. It almost seemed as if Rande was trying to push her beyond her limits on purpose. And her exhaustion only angered him. *Clearly, he's suspicious that I'm faking my sudden lack of progress. But I'm not! Well, at least I'm not faking my fatigue.*

One day, Rande became so incensed by Exe's pathetic performance that he forced her and Caulder to execute the exact same spells side by side. While the outcome of Exe's casting was on par with Caulder's, she tired much sooner than he did. The moment she became too fatigued to continue, Rande stalked off.

"Jeepers, what's eating him?" Caulder said, his thoughtful, troubled gaze lingering on the cascade where Rande had vanished. "It's not your fault that performing magic properly tires you out so much."

"It's just because I'm not used to casting with triggers, right?" Exe asked, unsettled by Caulder's expression.

"I think so. I hope so," Caulder replied, finally looking her. "Don't fret, kid. You'll get the hang of it. This is new territory for us all, training someone your age who's new to casting with triggers. Rande's probably just mad that we can't wrap up your training just yet. But I'm not."

"Then you're not tired of training me?" Exe blushed at her uncharacteristically playful tone.

"I'll never tire of you," Caulder replied, masking his sincerity with a wink. "The real question is, are you too tired to listen to another of my thrilling tales?"

"Never," Exe said, settling in beside Caulder as he leaned back against the boulder, more than ready for another Anacapian adventure.

CHAPTER SEVENTEEN

GREATEST OF ALL TIME

"**D**o you celebrate Christmas in Anacapia?" Exe asked Caulder the question that had been plaguing her for days. Sneaking off for training had become increasingly difficult in December, and it would become even trickier as Christmas drew closer. Easy had roped the whole Parsell family into running Nowhere's Christmas Carnival—the town's biggest celebration of the year. In exchange, the town had helped the Parsells out with a holiday project of their own.

Every Christmas Exe could remember, the Parsells sponsored several platoons deployed in combat zones and their families back at home. This year, during the first week of December, Easy had involved the whole town in shipping out thousands of Christmas gifts and care packages to more troops and families than they ever had before.

Thanks to Nowhere's citizens, Easy was also able to organize presents for every one of Arizona's gold star families (who had all lost loved ones in combat). They filled footlockers with holiday baked goods, toys for the kids, and thoughtful gifts for the adults. The whole Parsell family delighted in seeing Rove baking dozens of Christmas cookies for his military families. *I hate that I missed out on that this year.* The guilt over skipping this time-honored family tradition wouldn't let her abandon the Parsells to run a week-long carnival for thousands of tourists without her.

"We do, and Easter too. Why do you ask?" Caulder said, sitting up on the mirage's velvety grass where they'd collapsed after an intense bout of casting practice.

"Christmastime is packed with activities for us. It'll be almost impossible to sneak away to train," Exe explained. "I just don't know how to–"

"Tell Rande?" Caulder finished. "I'll talk to him. Jettani's banned a lot of our Christmas traditions, but it's still pretty busy for us too."

"Thanks," Exe replied gratefully. She didn't dare ask Rande for a brief break from training. *Or he might just end our sessions altogether.* In the days following Rande's storm off, he'd become increasingly terse and unapproachable— showing up only sporadically, ending lessons abruptly, and watching Exe with a calculating glare when he was there. *Why won't he just say why he's so angry?* Exe shivered, shaking off Rande's intimidating attitude.

Exe hugged her school bookbag to her, wondering how best to bring up the real reason that she was glad Caulder knew all about Christmas. Exe had picked it as the perfect time to reveal her powers to the Parsells. Actually, the idea started out as an excuse for her many absences, because Exe knew they wouldn't pry into her whereabouts if they believed her disappearing act had to do with their presents.

And it'll be the truth too, if I can figure out a way to use my powers for Christmas.

Although she couldn't just conjure up gifts for them out of thin air (apparently, creating something from nothing was another Inconceivable), she could do magic for them as their presents. Exe would grant each family member the Christmas wish of their choice—as long as it involved a spell written into her vade.

Unfortunately, Exe couldn't giftwrap Christmas wishes to put under the tree. After tossing about several ideas on how to present her gift (like levitating Charley—dressed as a cherub—to place the angel atop their Christmas tree), Exe settled on magically cooking up the Christmas Day feast. She'd even brought along Ella's best holiday recipes in the hopes that Caulder could teach her how incorporate her powers into their preparation. *And if he can't, maybe Caulder can get Velin to scribe some Anacapian recipes into my vade.*

Tossing her vade onto the boulder as she searched her bag for the recipes, Exe's mind turned toward Christmas in Anacapia. *Do they put up Christmas trees and sing carols? Are there parties and presents? Christmas cookies? Church services? Twinkle lights?*

The temptation to ask Caulder to entertain her with tales of Anacapian Christmas traditions was great, but Exe resisted. *It already hurts so much knowing that I can't experience Christmas in Anacapia myself. I can't bear to learn more about what I'm missing.* Exe's increasing desire to explore Anacapia grew apace with her guilt that it was a betrayal of the Parsells. *They'd be so hurt if they knew I was secretly longing to spend Christmas somewhere else.*

"Speaking of Rande, I wonder what's keeping him this time?" Caulder mused.

"He's coming today?" Exe panicked, scrambling for her vade. *What did he order me to practice the last time he was here?*

In her haste, Exe sent her vade skidding across the stone. She barely caught it with her fingertips as it teetered precariously on the boulder's edge. Before she could grab hold, her vade whooshed out of reach—right into Rande's waiting hands. He scowled at her for a moment then promptly disappeared.

"Where'd he go with my vade?" Exe exclaimed.

"Rande's a bit– perplexed by your unanticipated prowess with your powers—and the toll it takes on you," Caulder explained. "So he's convinced Asher to have Velin scribe several sophisticated sync-spells into your vade to test your limits. Sync-spells are specialized incantations that simultaneously attack, evade, and defend. We've pulled them from Malina's military arsenal of spells."

"Why didn't you tell me?"

"I didn't want you to worry," Caulder comforted.

"I've spent my whole life worrying," Exe glowered. "You should've warned me."

"If it makes you feel any better, Viva's infuriated that you're being granted access to magic that she's not allowed to use herself," Caulder smiled.

Exe's scowl melted into a grin as she laughed, "I'm not sure if I'm happier that she's mad about it, or that you find it just as funny as I do. And to think, not that long ago I thought it'd be fun to have a sister."

As her amusement subsided, Exe wondered, *Why does she hate me?* The question was so upsetting, Exe almost asked it aloud, since Caulder was likely the one person who'd actually give her a straight answer. *But what if she hates me because I did do something horrible as a baby? Do I really want to risk ruining my friendship with Caulder by bringing up my potentially despicable past?* Before she could decide whether to ask or not, Rande returned, tossed her vade to Caulder, and faced down Exe.

"You'd better be ready to work," Rande scowled. "Time to truly put your powers to the test. I trust Caulder got you up to speed on sync-spells?"

"I've already successfully cast multiple triggers at once. How are sync-spells any different?" Exe boasted, egged on by the calculating gleam in Rande's eye.

"Rapid-firing multiple triggers one after another pulls power from you in separate bursts. A single trigger that casts multiple spells instantaneously requires infinitely more power, concentration, and stamina," Rande explained. "Most who attempt it fail the first time. If they're good, they cast exceedingly weak versions of the spells. IF they're good."

"If you're so anxious to get my training over with, why are you bothering to teach me these?" Exe challenged.

"I'll admit, your powers are impressive. And you're a quick study. Why wouldn't I want to test what you're capable of?" Rande asked. "Besides, you've already been hunted down once. You'll need to be able to defend yourself should it happen again."

"Fine. Let's do this," Exe folded her arms in a show of faux confidence.

"Fine. The trigger we're working with is brimborion."

"Wait, what?" Caulder looked up from his casual perusal of the new sync-spells in Exe's vade. Rande threw him a look that held an entire conversation within it. All ease faded from Caulder's stance as his own expression shifted from confusion to concern. His quick glance at Exe held a note of warning that she didn't understand.

"What's it supposed to do?" Exe slouched out of her poised posture to hug herself nervously. Caulder's unease worried her. *He knows Rande's up to something. What is it?*

"Like most military sync-spells, brimborion attacks, evades, and defends all at once," Rande said. "Should you cast it successfully, you'll elevate several feet into the air while the ground below you turns into quicksand. You'll also create a forcefield around yourself that will deflect the attack spell I'll cast at you. Plus, you'll hurl all nearby stones at me. Got it?"

"Elevate, quick-field, force, cast sto—" Exe fumbled, trying to keep it straight.

"Go!" Rande shouted, narrowing his eyes and mouthing a trigger at her.

"Wait— brimborion!"

Instantly, Exe rose into the air, narrowly escaping the miniature missiles Rande blew at her from his cupped hand. The tiny projectiles expanded from pin-sized to pencil as they flew, exploding against the invisible forcefield Exe had created. At the exact same moment, thousands of pebbles from the liquified ground below her flew at Rande, bouncing every which way off of the shield he'd conjured in front of himself.

Both Rande and Caulder stared at her in horror as she hovered above them. Slowly they turned to one another, exchanging that same, unsettled look that she'd seen on the faces of both sets of her parents in recent months.

Seeing that uneasy gaze exchanged between her two experienced, powerful trainers agitated Exe, breaking her concentration. Swiftly she plummeted, hitting the ground just as it shifted from sludgy quicksand to hardened earth.

"What is it!? Why is it so wrong that I succeeded on my first try?" Exe ripped herself out of the imprint she'd left in the dirt.

"Wish magic," Rande bit out. "Asher had no right sending us to you without warning. He should've told us what we'd be dealing with."

"What are you talking about?" Exe protested. "You're just mad that I didn't get hurt by those mini bombs you shot at me, aren't you? Or maybe you just hate that I'm talented enough to get it right on my first try."

"You didn't get it right. None of that would've happened if you'd actually performed brimborion properly," Rande's voice a mixture of anger and fear.

"What do you mean?"

"What you just did? There's no such spell," Caulder's breath came hard and fast as if he'd just run a mile. "It's impossible."

"No, it's a sync-spell, like you said! I just did what you said!" Exe cried out.

"You did exactly as I said," Rande agreed with a sneer. "With wish magic. All this time wasted training you and you've learned nothing. You didn't need to. Not when you can do that with blasted wish magic!"

"Stop looking at me like that! It's not my fault!" Exe exclaimed. "It's Velin's fault. If he hadn't been too lazy and selfish to teach me, my powers wouldn't have grown so out of control!" THWACK. Exe slammed back into her imprint in the dirt.

"Don't you dare denigrate Velin to me," Rande towered over her. "You should be on your knees thanking God that

Velin agreed to look after you all these years, that you'll soon be training under the wisest mind and greatest teacher Anacapia has ever known."

"Don't you dare praise that demented old skeleton to me," Exe countered. Rande rocked back on his heels as she hinged herself upright to face him down, toe-to-toe. "I don't care who he was; I know who he is. You've no idea of the cruel, merciless, manipulative horror show he's put me through my entire life."

"You know nothing. You have no idea what that man accomplished, what he sacrificed for so many. A man of his stature should never have been saddled with you," Rande spat. "Nor should I. I'll not waste any more time on a stubborn brat who doesn't know the meaning of hard work. Who'd rather do things the easy way simply because she can. Because she has undeserved powers that make it possible."

With that, Rande disappeared into the cascade.

"Are you abandoning me, too?" Exe demanded of Caulder with wounded defiance. His sober, guarded expression hurt her more than Rande's tirade ever could.

"For now," Caulder nodded slowly. "I'm not quite certain where we go from here. We need to talk with Asher before we can proceed."

"Rande said we won't proceed," Exe hugged herself.

"He'll cool off," Caulder replied. "He's more angry with himself for not recognizing sooner that you weren't performing spells correctly. We knew your wish magic was abnormally powerful, but no wish magic should be capable of what you just did. There are few who could perform that many spells at once, even with a properly-written sync-spell."

"I don't understand. I said the trigger and everything happened just as Rande said it would. What did I do wrong?"

"Rande and I wrote brimborion to help us out on smuggling runs. It allows us to spin confusing, yet believable stories whenever we have to talk our way out of a tight spot," Caulder explained. "There is no spell written to do what you just did all at once. Rande made it up. I doubt he expected that you'd actually be able to do it all."

"Did you know he was going to test me like that?" Exe asked. When Caulder shook his head, Exe said, "What did he think would happen?"

"Nothing, I expect," Caulder answered. "Although, he did have Velin write brimborion into your vade. If you were simply exceedingly talented, you would've been able to perform it properly, even if you didn't know what it was supposed to do. How you were able to– I don't know what to think."

"Maybe Velin wrote a spell like that in my vade, and I just connected to that one instead," Exe tossed about for any explanation that would wipe that wary expression from Caulder's face. She frantically paged through her vade, determined to find such a spell.

"So Rande just happened to hit upon the exact combination of some random sync-spell that Velin invented just for you? I don't think so," Caulder said.

"So what does this mean? What's wrong with me?"

"I don't know," Caulder answered, but Exe could tell he was hedging.

"This is the excuse they need to leave me to Velin, isn't it?" Exe asked. *Why won't Caulder of all people tell me why everyone's so afraid of me?*

"I can't say," Caulder said. "But Rande's right. You could have worse teachers. In his day, Velin was the best. Only an elite few were allowed to train under him."

"He's no longer the man you all seem to remember so fondly. He's a cruel, bitter tyrant who's done nothing but torture me," Exe fought to keep bitterness from her voice. *And it seems he's my last hope to learn to control these despicable powers of mine. If he won't teach me, I'll never be safe to be around anyone.*

"I'd probably be that way too, if I'd survived what Velin did. Though I doubt I could've survived it," Caulder murmured, pondering some point beyond her shoulder.

"Survived what?"

Caulder threw her a puzzled look. "Velin had to abandon his wife, wipe his son out of existence, and murder his own older brother. All to save Anacapia."

"What?!" Exe stared at him in astonishment.

"I always forget how little you know," Caulder offered her a small smile and sat down on the edge of the mirage. "Velin was once our ruler, but he shouldn't have been. His elder brother, Dominus, was destined to lead Anacapia. Only he drowned when Velin was just a baby."

"How did Velin drown him if he was just an infant?" Exe sank down beside him, clutching her vade. *What did I do when I was just an infant?*

"He didn't. The drowning was accidental. The murder came later," Caulder said. "Velin's history is dark and complex. It'll be easier to understand if I tell the tale in full.

"Velin's is one of the great minds of our time. A man who preferred studying to statesmanship. Still, as a ruler he was beloved for his fairness, his wisdom, and his ardent advocacy for personal freedom and responsibility. Never once was he swayed by selfish elitists or sly power players, but instead he made every decision based on what was best for his country and its people. He handled politics with swift efficiency and decisiveness, primarily to have more time to devote to his studies. It's in pursuit of knowledge where he truly excelled. It was also his downfall."

"How could pursuing knowledge cause his downfall?"

"You've heard of Inconceivables, right?" Caulder asked. At Exe's unconvincing nod he explained, "A small number of spell concepts are known as Inconceivables because they are deemed impossible to write. Invisibility, immortality, resurrecting the dead, and so forth. The most sought after Inconceivable is time travel."

"I'm not surprised. It'd be so cool to travel through time. I bet most people would love to do it if they could, even in my world," Exe half-smiled, thinking of one of her favorite '80s movies.

"It's not just some 'cool' idea in Anacapia, or all the other countries in our world. It's viewed as the ultimate weapon," Caulder replied. "Imagine dozens of governments traveling back to adjust the past to suit their own agendas. It's a nightmare scenario. Mess with time enough, and you'll end the world."

"It sounds like time travel is your world's version of our nuclear weapons," Exe said. "So what does Velin–"

"He invented it."

"What?!" Exe exclaimed. *If Velin can time travel, he can go back and stop me from doing whatever I did that got me kicked out of Anacapia!* Hope lit Exe up, then swiftly it dimmed. *But then the Parsells wouldn't be my family. If Velin did go back and*

*change that one little thing, both of our worlds would be forever
altered.*

"You catch on quick. Tell me what you were thinking,"
Caulder said, watching Exe's fast-changing expressions.

"At first I was thinking that Velin could go back and
stop me from doing whatever I did that got me expelled
from Anacapia," Exe began, puzzled by Caulder's confusion.
"But then I realized that I wouldn't have my Arizona family
in my life anymore. And who knows what else would
change in both of our worlds just because I hate what
happened to me."

"Maybe you're even wiser than Velin," Caulder praised.
"Changing his past was exactly why Velin devoted his life
to developing that Inconceivable. What could be a more
magnanimous reason for inventing time travel than saving
his older brother's life? He just didn't think enough about
the consequences."

"What happened? Did Dominus grow up to become an
evil dictator?" Exe asked.

"Quite the opposite," Caulder said. "According to Velin,
Dominus was an even better ruler than he was. And Velin
found himself living his dream life in that alternate reality.
In his original life, Velin had no time for a family between
ruling the country and pursuing his studies. In this new
world, Velin was a renowned scholar with a devoted wife
and a precocious son. For Velin, time travel wasn't a weapon.
It was a means to achieve a quiet, cozy existence well out of
the limelight. To keep his newfound contentment, he simply
had to continue living this new life and tell no one that he'd
successfully invented time travel."

"But he didn't. Why not?" Exe asked.

"Velin soon realized the enormity of what he'd done," Caulder sighed. "Alternate wars happened around the world. Millions of people made different choices than they had in the original timeline. And far too many people he once knew no longer existed—because they were never born. Like your parents. That one small, seemingly selfless act of saving his older brother from drowning as a child effectively wiped out decades of the past and thousands of people. In short, Velin realized that inventing time travel had allowed him to play god. A lot of good happened for him and others, but a lot of bad had happened too. And as much as Velin loved his alternate life, he knew that no one man should have the power to change the fate of the whole world."

"So what did he do? How did he fix it?" Exe asked, dreading the answer.

"The only thing he could do. He time traveled back to the scene of his brother's drowning, waited for himself to save his brother, then drown him again in a way that appeared absolutely accidental so that no one would suspect it was actually murder," Caulder rested his chin on his knees.

"That's awful," Exe said. *I cannot image killing Charley or Henny-Boy or any of my brothers, even if it would save the world.*

"Then he traveled back to the moment he originally left, and things went back to the way they originally were. For the most part. Little things are different, but nothing major. At least according to Velin. Pretty creepy knowing that we're technically living in an alternate reality because of what Velin did, isn't it? Now imagine if just anyone could time travel and change the past as often as they pleased."

"Velin must regret that he made this impossibility possible. No wonder he's so hostile all the time," Exe pondered her past interactions with Velin in this new light.

"He might've been able to bear the pain if he was the only one who knew about what he'd done," Caulder broke the sad silence that had settled between them.

"Someone saw him?" Exe asked.

"No. He told," Caulder explained. "Once he realized the damage that time travel could do, Velin gathered all the leaders in our world to convince them to stop pursuing its invention. He explained that there'd be no future if nations went to war to rewrite history. When they wouldn't listen, he told them what he'd done in an attempt to sway them. But his warning fell on deaf ears."

"I can imagine. Corrupt politicians and tyrannical dictators aren't exclusive to Anacapia. Even in my world, most leaders ruthlessly pursue power no matter the cost to their country or its citizens," Exe said.

"Not just Anacapia. Every country in our world saw only opportunity when Velin told them that he'd discovered the secret of time travel. His summit to halt the pursuit of its invention ended up causing the Horology Wars," Caulder explained. "Almost every single world leader subsequently attacked Anacapia, demanding that Velin hand over his time travel spell. The wars only ended when Velin abdicated and went on the run. He's been hunted ever since."

"And then Asher and Malina saddled Velin with me," Exe closed her eyes, ashamed of how she'd relentlessly badgered him. *Why? Why did they send me to him? Why did I have to be sent away?!*

"Now you know why. Velin had successfully stayed hidden from the dozens of nations who had been hunting him for years. Who better to keep you hidden too?" Caulder said as he rose. "So you're in safe hands, no matter what happens now."

"What will happen? Will you be back?" Exe hated the pleading note in her voice.

"I wish I knew," Caulder said, missing Exe's flinch at his casual use of 'wish.' With a tip of his cap, Caulder too disappeared into the cascade.

CHAPTER EIGHTEEN

HOME FOR CHRISTMAS

"Everything okay, Exe?"

Every Parsell had asked her that question at least a half-dozen times during the past few weeks. The reason why was rather understandable—Exe was suddenly everywhere. The notoriously antisocial Exe had become uncharacteristically eager to help Easy make Nowhere's Christmas Carnival better than ever.

Despite the town council's protest that it was impossible, Easy had convinced them he could transform Nowhere into a winter wonderland—as much as a town without snow could be transformed. Easy's festival battle plans had Exe spraying faux snow on store windows, hanging icicle-shaped Christmas lights, wrapping lamp posts in snowy evergreen garland, and hanging thousands of icy, crystal ornaments in the giant fir tree that dominated the town square. Exe tackled every task with determined enthusiasm, overworking herself into exhaustion. Though she tried to keep herself too busy to think, she couldn't help dwelling on how much easier the work would be and how much more she might've accomplished were it safe enough to use her powers.

While her pitching in on behind-the-scenes tasks like decorating wasn't unprecedented, Exe absolutely astounded her family by participating in every holiday activity she could cram into a day. That's what prompted Seph to ask Exe if everything was okay when she offered to be an extra in his Cowboy Christmas-themed gunfight show. Thone asked when she joined his Old West Christmas Choir that toured around Arizona's hospitals and senior centers. Easy asked when Exe volunteered to play Mary in the town's living Nativity. And Moth, Henny-Boy, and Charley repeatedly asked when Exe accepted a major (albeit non-speaking) part in Nowhere's Christmas pageant.

The Parsells were even more floored at seeing Exe do it all with a plastic smile plastered on her face and a lot of ("Practically manic," Seph once whispered.) laughter. The only thing Exe wasn't doing during the chaos of Christmas was talking. Whenever anyone tried to engage her in a discussion, Exe just smiled, laughed, and dashed off to her next activity. Not that Exe was purposely avoiding conversation—she was just too preoccupied with her incessant inner monologue.

The devastating discovery that she didn't actually have her powers under control had Exe terrified of her wish magic again. But retreating back into isolation while facing an uncertain future was a torture she simply couldn't endure. Instead, she stayed busy in an effort to dig herself out from under the avalanching anxiety. Of course, being around people was also a worry. So Exe took every precaution to ensure that she didn't accidentally use wish magic by constantly chanting Velin's power-suppression spells: "UROK," "I want nothing, I need nothing," and, "It's dangerous to wish for things."

But do they really work? Are they real spells that I'm performing properly with these triggers? Or am I simply relying on wish magic to perform them? Or maybe they're not triggers at all, but just self-calming mantras. Exe was tempted to go ask Velin, but she didn't want to risk aggravating him. *With my luck, Velin'll be the only other powered person I ever see again. And he'll never agree to train me if I pester him with more questions right now.*

So Exe just kept her head down and her mind blanked of everything but the task at hand and those painfully familiar phrases. It worked well until sunset on Christmas Eve day, when the last of the tourists had straggled through the living Nativity. As the rest of the cast chatted while breaking down the set, Exe sat frozen on her hay bale, clutching Mrs. Lewis' baby to her. *Now what?* Exe panicked.

Exe was too distracted by the fact that she was out of distractions to notice the mother's attempts to retrieve her son. Easy had to pry the fussy little boy from her arms. *The festival's over. There's nothing left to do!* True, there were still plenty of Parsell family Christmas traditions to look forward to tonight and a whole day of cozy camaraderie tomorrow, but the rest of winter break loomed long and lonely.

"What's bugging you?" Easy shook Exe to get her attention.

Exe stared at him, teetering on the edge of pouring out her whole wretched tale. *I should just tell him. Easy always knows what to do.* But seeing his loving concern gave her pause. She couldn't bear the thought of him dissolving into ludicrous laughter if she told him that she had magical powers, or worse, *What if he gets that same disturbed, unsettled look when I confess what I'm capable of? I couldn't endure it. Not on Christmas. Oh no, Christmas is tomorrow!*

"I don't have any presents for anybody!"

"What are you talking about? You've been running off to work on your big Christmas surprise for weeks," Easy replied.

"I know. But it– didn't work out the way I'd hoped," Exe confessed. "Now I'm left with nothing."

"I see," Easy replied, waiting. Finally he sighed and said, "Well don't just sit there, shake your tail feather! We've just got time to make the Christmas magic happen."

"Huh?!"

Without giving Exe a chance to think about what he'd said, Easy grabbed her wrist and started running. When they reached home, Easy bum-rushed her into the car, slid over the hood like he was auditioning for a Dukes of Hazzard episode, and sped off into the city.

As they drove, Easy helped her make a list of last-minute gifts she could get for everyone at the nearest mall. Once they were dashing through the crush of frantic shoppers, Easy turned his attention toward injecting joy into their madcap adventure with the kind of '80s movie antics Exe adored.

Easy posed with the mannequins while Exe purchased Ella's favorite perfume and stood at attention while she bought Rove's gun cleaning kit. In the music store, he played air guitar beside the sales assistant who was demonstrating Thone's new amp. He skateboarded around sporting goods customers while Exe selected Seph's new spelunking gear and put on a puppet show for the kids of harried parents as she waited in line to buy a chemistry set for Charley. He pulled the slow, cool lowering of his sunglasses any time a girl walked by while Exe picked out Henny-Boy's very first wristwatch. Easy finally got her to laugh on the way to the bookstore for Moth's gift by cajoling her into scrambling up the down escalator.

On their way to the car, Easy couldn't resist leaping into the fountain to perform an impromptu lip-sync routine to Bing Crosby's "White Christmas," followed by an encore of "Rockin' Around the Christmas Tree." While he was busy mimicking the iconic moves from two of her favorite movies ("Ferris Bueller's Day Off" and "Pretty in Pink"), Exe slipped away to pick up his present. Along with the book on designing escape rooms that she'd already bought him, Exe chose a slick gray trilby hat (achingly similar to Caulder's fedora).

By the time they got home, they were both exhausted. It seemed that the whole family was burnt out on holiday spirit, given the way that Ella and the rest of their brothers were collapsed on the couch without a single hint of Christmas in sight. Thankfully, Rove rallied his troops by bringing in the largest tree they'd ever had—so tall that the boys were able to decorate the top from their balcony bedroom.

Inspired by that prospect, Exe and her brothers embraced the old-fashioned Christmas Ella proposed, stringing popcorn with cranberries for garland, baking gingerbread ornaments, and creating spiced orange pomander balls to hang on the tree. The mingled scents of citrus, ginger, evergreen, and buttered popcorn warmed the drafty nave.

When Rove plugged in the lights, the illuminated tree flickered and glowed as if lit by hundreds of candles. After a succulent late supper of surprisingly-traditional sliced ham, green bean casserole, and scalloped potatoes, Ella turned on the Yule log channel, and they all cozied up together to sing cherished carols and read their favorite Christmas stories aloud.

It was almost midnight when Seph carried sleeping Charley up to bed, followed by his drowsy brothers. Instead of heading for her own bed, Exe helped Ella and Rove prepare for the Christmas Day festivities, setting up the little ceramic Nativity, prepping tomorrow's dinner (achingly, without magic), and nibbling on the cookies that Charley had left out for Santa. Exe savored those cozy hours, wrapping her gifts while watching holiday classics on TV as Rove and Ella bustled about the kitchen baking cherry pies, maple-walnut fudge, and peppermint-y meringue trees.

When Ella tuned the radio to the holiday station, Exe hummed happily along to all those tunes she'd thought she'd grown tired of while singing with the town's choir—until the deejay segued from "Silent Night" to "We Wish You a Merry Christmas." The very first bright, cheerful "wish" that the jolly singers sang out hit Exe like a sledgehammer, dissolving her joy in a shower of tears. Ella rushed to hug her while Rove switched off the radio and patted her back, both asking worriedly what was the matter.

Exe didn't answer. *How can I?* While she loved Christmas, it had always been the hardest time of year for her. The whole world was wishful at Christmas—which meant that she'd spent every previous season fighting the desire to grant her family's wishes... and her own. *This year was supposed to be different. My annual worry over Christmas wishes was supposed to be a thing of the past. I thought it'd finally be safe for me to make a few of those wishes come true.*

The volcano of frustration and resentment erupting inside Exe helped her sobs subside. Blaming her outburst on exhaustion, Exe excused herself to go get some sleep, ignoring the concerned glance exchanged by Ella and Rove once again.

In the privacy of her tower, Exe paced and fumed, wishing she had an empty box left to punch out her anger and frustration. The next thing Exe knew she was stumbling over an empty punch bowl box. In that same instant, a smash of shattered glass sounded in the nave. Exe peeped out her door just in time to catch Rove and Ella's unsettled glance at her door as they cleaned up the pulverized punch bowl.

This is all Velin's fault! He could've taught me to control my powers ages ago. Exe kicked the box out of her way and wrenched open her private entrance.

Up the graveyard hill she stormed, leaping over the low stone wall. Across the scraggly lawn she ran, barreling towards Velin's front door with her fist raised. The door swung open before Exe could pound it down. Velin stood there, glowering, with rumpled clothes and shoeless feet as if he'd dressed in a hurry.

Exe stumbled back, half-afraid he'd found a way into her mind again. "How did you know I was coming?" Exe asked, forgetting her own troubles as she looked closely at the thin, sour man before her. *He lost his whole family and had to kill his own brother. And I wouldn't even exist if he hadn't.*

"You've disturbed your parents with your powers again," Velin reproached her. "What do you want?"

A thousand questions swirled: *Why did you give me away? Why do my powers always hurt people? Why didn't you train me? Why won't you help me? What's wrong with me?* But as important as the answers were to her, they somehow seemed petty now that she knew all that Velin had gone through.

Staring at Velin's cold, hard face, Exe realized he'd never give her a satisfactory answer to any of her big, burning questions, whether he knew the truth or not. *Not after the way I've acted towards him.* But there was one question only he could answer. One that had silently tortured her ever since she'd shut him out of her mind and all of her suppressed memories had been released. *And I've got to give him some reason for marching up to his front door like this.*

"You made me forget so much. Buried every memory I had of using my powers before you convinced me to repress them. Both good and bad," Exe said slowly. "I forgot them all, except one. You knew how much it tormented me. Why wouldn't you help me forget Bonnie?"

"That... memory served a greater purpose," Velin shifted uncomfortably. "It compelled you to curb your powers better than I ever could. Your beliefs about Bonnie's death helped keep you safe."

"So you let me suffer just to make it easier for you to protect me?" Exe was appalled. "Because that memory helped you control me?"

"If that's what you choose to believe," Velin growled.

"How could you?" Exe gasped. *How can I pity him for being forced to live with the memory of murdering his own brother when he forced me to live with the memory of killing Bonnie just to make me more malleable?* "You're a vile, evil old man! I'm glad you didn't keep me. I'm glad you've refused to train me. I've learned more from the corpse of that dead Disimulata than from you."

"If you've quite finished," Velin said mildly as Exe seethed under his passive regard. "You've had your answer.

Get the rest from Asher—if he's ever able to return after the havoc your outing into Anacapia caused. Until then, the least you can do is keep your powers in check until you learn how to use them."

"Don't tell me what to do!" Exe bristled. "You didn't raise me or train me. Or help me. Why didn't you do as Asher asked?"

"Because I hate children! Especially entitled, out-of-control brats like you! Always whining and complaining and demanding. Now go away and leave me be!" With that, Velin snapped the door shut.

Exe launched herself at the closed door, kicking and pounding with all her might. Even a quick wish wouldn't open the door this time. In frustration she yelled, "You're going to rot all alone in your misery and bitterness!"

Velin didn't respond.

He hates children now? Is it because he lost his own son? Or because of me? Oh why did I attack him like that? Especially after all Caulder told me. Embarrassed by her outburst, Exe scolded herself as she slunk back to her tower. *What if Rande or Caulder never return to train me? There's no chance Velin will help me now after I attacked him so viciously, and on Christmas Eve. If only I hadn't kicked him out of my head, then he'd know that I regret what I said.*

Up in her belfry she gazed at Velin's dark house. *What if he had kept me with him?* Exe shuddered in horror at the thought. Living with Velin in that lonely, decrepit house would've been worse than having his voice in her head all of these years. His reasons for giving her away might've been selfish, but for Exe, living with the Parsells had been (*and still is*) an enormous gift.

All Christmas Day, Exe's guilt grew. As she enjoyed opening presents, hunting for hidden Christmas stockings (since they had no fireplace to hang them by), and indulging in a Jamaican-Irish Christmas Feast, Velin lingered in the back of her mind. She pictured him alone in that house, year after year, vicariously witnessing her loving interactions with her family. *Is he having his own solitary celebration? Or just enviously observing my family's festivities from afar?* Exe didn't know which would be worse.

As dusk fell, Exe surreptitiously assembled a plate of tasty leftovers and a thermos of hot chocolate. She hid this feast-for-one from her family so that Velin wouldn't guess what she was up to. Carefully she carried the tray up the hill and set it down on Velin's doorstep.

She knocked softly, then louder. When he didn't answer, Exe called, "I brought you something to eat. Ella's fusion food is kinda crazy, but it's tasty." No sound or movement came from within Velin's house. "I can't imagine that you're much of a cook, are you?" Exe continued, feeling foolish talking to a door. "Or are you gifted at recipe spells?" Exe tamped down her frustration at Velin for not answering the door. "Anyway, it's here when you're hungry."

Exe stumbled her way back down the hill, keeping one eye on the door in the hopes of catching Velin accepting her peace offering... if he did. Dashing up to her belfry, Exe was disappointed to see the tray still there, so she set up camp to keep watch all night. As she waited, Exe opened her vade, looking for the few original spells Velin had put in the book before she'd found her way into Anacapia.

Exe puzzled over the incantations. *Was I ever performing these spells properly or was it always wish magic? If it was just wish magic, why did Velin constantly nag me to recite these mantras? Did he not realize that I wasn't doing it right?*

'UROK,' 'All I Have to Do is Get Through,' 'You Want Nothing, You Need Nothing,' 'Hide Yourself.' Although the spells' technical jargon was too complex for her to understand, she had no trouble with the short descriptions detailing their purposes: to suppress her powers, to fade her memories, and so on. *Almost every spell designed to control me,* Exe fumed, then admitted, *No, not all of them.*

'This Voice is Not My Own.' Its description simply read: 'Mind Lock—to obstruct intruders from entering your mind.' Glancing at Velin's home, she couldn't help but wonder why Velin had given her access to a spell that would prevent him from controlling her.

At the sight of the still untouched tray, Exe tossed her vade aside, deciding that whatever Velin's reason, it was probably selfish. Velin had repeatedly proven that he had no interest in helping her. Snuggling deep into her thermal sleeping bag to ward off the chilly night air, Exe tried to concentrate on Velin's doorstep, but her sleepy eyes couldn't help straying to the discarded tome.

When daylight broke, Exe awoke to find that the tray had vanished sometime in the night. She crawled out of her sleeping bag with a smile on her face—and crashed into the tray filled with unwashed (but empty) dishes. Indignation faded to amusement as she realized that, though he'd made a point of sending the dishes back dirty, Velin had in fact accepted her peace offering.

Maybe there's hope for help from Velin after all...

CHAPTER NINETEEN

BAD BLOOD

"**M**ake a wish."

Ella, Rove, and all of her brothers surrounded Exe, their anticipatory grins illuminated in the glow of sixteen candles atop her ice cream birthday cake. The impression of flickering candlelight lingered against Exe's closed eyelids as she focused on one singular, deliberate thought: *It's dangerous to wish for things.* On every birthday Exe could remember, she had recited this same mantra to smother all yearnings during the annual request to 'make a wish.' *I hate that I still have to worry about wishing over my birthday cake this year.* (It took everything within her not to cry.) Praying that the mantra had worked, Exe sucked in her breath, blew out the candles, and opened her eyes.

"What'dya wish for?" Charley's anxious voice struggled to express polite interest, but he couldn't take his wide eyes off the cake.

Exe tousled his hair, "For you to have the first piece. Think it'll come true?"

"Nawh, birthday girl first," Charley ducked, smiling like a little gentleman.

"How 'bout we share? Then we can have a gigantic piece," Exe offered. In reply, Charley clambered onto her lap as Ella indulged her baby boy and her only daughter by serving them up a quarter of the melting confection. After handing out slices to the rest of the family, Ella gathered the gifts for Exe to open while they ate.

"If you'd have let me tell the partygoers the reason for today's epic celebration, we wouldn't have to rush. I had to say it was a belated New Year's Eve bash. How lame is that," Easy admonished Exe.

In the past, Exe had avoided big birthday parties altogether simply by convincing her family that she hated being in the spotlight. But after her unprecedented participation in Nowhere's Christmas festivities, her family had insisted on throwing her a Sweet Sixteen birthday bash. Despite Exe's protests, Easy had invited over a few select students to join the celebration—but Exe had expressly forbidden any mention of her birthday.

While Charley dug into their slice of ice cream cake, Exe dove into her present pile. Ella had placed her package from "Aunt Goldie" on top. On previous birthdays, the intrigue surrounding this mysterious gift had always led Exe to open it first. But now that she knew it was just another way for Velin to keep tabs on her, she ignored the plain, brown package and reached for Charley's sloppily-wrapped present instead.

"You hafta open the mysterious gift first. There could be a clue to the mystery of you," Charley's excited, expectant voice and wide innocent eyes swayed Exe. After all, her littlest brother had only just learned the story of her diaries.

"We already know it's just a blank journal," Henny-Boy whined. "Open mine. It's a pound of candy from the confectioners. Well, almost a pound, I had to test a few."

"Now we know what's in two packages, squirt," Easy teased as Exe ripped off the brown paper and exposed the shimmering, lemon chiffon-hued silk journal. Charley dropped his ice-cream drizzled fork and unfolded the note. From the way his little face fell, Exe assumed Velin's note was just more meaningless prattle like all the others. But it wasn't. There was no fake news from "Aunt Goldie" this year.

"What's it say?" Easy asked.

There was just one single, solitary line. Exe read it aloud, "Be a better listener and maybe you'll finally learn something." In a fit of pique, Exe shoved the note inside and sent the diary skittering down the long table. "It's rather aerodynamic, isn't it?" Exe tried to joke the startled looks off everyone's faces before opening the rest of her presents.

There was Henny-Boy's candy, an adorable, miniature Rube Goldberg machine from little Charley, and twelve books from Moth (selections for their monthly book-club-for-two). The art supplies were from Thone (since Exe was his only sibling who shared his artistic flair). An envelope contained a membership to Seph's rock-climbing gym ("For my favorite scaling partner!"). And the slender jewelry box held a charm bracelet from Easy (engraved with "Don't lose me!").

Rove and Ella's gift of a no-limit shopping spree brought the biggest "ooohs" and "aaahs." Ella tut-tutted any rumblings of jealousy over this promise of a new wardrobe and bedroom makeover with a reminder of Exe's sleeping arrangements in all of their previous houses. Exe thanked her parents for the gift, wondering how she could get away for training if she were shopping when a signal came from Rande or Caulder. *If another one ever comes...*

Before Exe could thank her brothers, they were distracted by the front door bursting open with an explosion of revelers. While Ella and Rove cleared away the dessert plates, Exe rushed to hide her presents and toss the wrappings so that no guest would ask whose birthday it was.

As she shoved the ribbons and paper scraps into the trash, the pale yellow diary slipped into the garbage. Exe stared at the book, tempted to leave it there. She hadn't written one word in last year's journal since the night she'd found Velin's tight writing between her own lines. She had no intention of using this one, either.

No matter how ghastly his past, it didn't give him the right to be nasty to me all these years. But at the last second, Exe rescued the journal, just as Ella was about to dump the sticky, dripping cardboard cake plate on top of it. *Rove always says, waste not, want not,* Exe told herself as she placed the diary on the stack of books from Moth.

Balancing the precarious pile of presents in her arms, Exe opened her tower door to find all of her brothers crowded inside with over thirty kids. *So much for 'just a few friends,' Easy,* Exe thought, rolling her eyes. She barely had time to set her load down before getting caught up in the crowd pushing out into the graveyard.

Easy jumped up on Velin's fence at the top of the hill and addressed the crowd. "In honor of a person who shall not be named," Easy said, with eyes that told every single person that they just might be the unnamed honoree. "I give you 'Dearly Departed,' an escape-the-graveyard adventure designed by my talented brothers and myself.

Find your team, friends. The game's about to begin. It's all happening, people."

The crowd let out a collective whoop. Expecting her brothers to make up her team, Exe was horrified to discover that they weren't playing—they were all in charge of running various parts of the activity. She'd have to team up with strangers or skip out on the game Easy and her brothers had designed just for her.

"For you, sis," Thone said, tying a purple ribbon around her arm. Exe noticed that every player wore a ribbon in one of a variety of colors.

"Easy swears you'll love the team he handpicked for you," Seph said. Handing her a purple dossier of clues, he called out, "Purple here!"

Suddenly, five purple-beribboned boys and girls surrounded Exe, joyfully jostling and joking as they perused the intriguing documents. As the holder of the dossier, Exe found herself the designated leader. Caught up in conversations of clues and mysteries to solve, Exe felt her social anxiety fading. At Easy's signal, all five teams took off in different directions, following the clues throughout their spacious adobe mission home.

In the courtyard, Exe's Purple Pythons clambered through an obstacle course presided over by Seph. In the nave, Rove and Ella helped Charley direct them in building a life-sized Rube Goldberg machine that revealed the next clue when assembled correctly. The cemetery played host to a set of spooky riddles Moth had written to incorporate the names and epitaphs on the tombstones.

Once solved, Exe and her team tore up to the belfry where Easy had them hopping from tablet to computer to phone, sifting through social media posts, researching websites, listening to creepy recorded messages, and compiling intel. All along the way they'd been gathering pieces of a beautiful drawing that Thone assisted them in assembling into a hidden map once they reached the kitchen.

The map directed them to the secret cloister that led to Ella and Rove's offices. Whether by chance or design, Exe's team arrived in the dark, open-air walkway before anyone else. There Exe was shocked to find Henny-Boy ready to help them write code to unlock a computerized safe that he'd built himself.

"I'm only just starting at this, and it doesn't always work," Henny-Boy blushed and pleaded when Exe commended him on this undisclosed talent. "I told Easy this was a premade kit so he'd let me have a station. Don't tell him I programmed it, okay?"

I get the need for secrecy, Exe thought as she hugged Henny-Boy and whispered her promise. Her other brothers arrived just in time to see her team open the vault and win the game. Amidst the victory cheer her necklace began to glow.

Dread thrummed through Exe. *Now? Why did they pick tonight to decide what to do about me? Don't they know it's my birthday? Okay, I guess I don't actually know if today is my birthday. But still, I bet Velin put them up to it, just to ruin this for me.* Exe forced herself to squelch the potentially-undeserved resentment toward Velin. *My future training may be in Velin's hands; I need to get a handle on my hostility toward him. Besides, I've been waiting for weeks to finally learn my fate and find out what's so wrong with me. There's nothing for it. I'll have to abandon the party.*

Now that the epic game was over, Exe's brothers directed her and the partygoers back into the courtyard where Rove was busy setting up fireworks. But instead of stopping there, Easy led Exe's group on to the chapel's private garden where Ella stood waiting. Peeking inside the gate, Exe saw a pile of gloves and several sleds propped against a giant hill of snow.

Seeing the effort and expense her family had put into this party, Exe felt guilty as she flagged down Easy. "This has been amazing, but I have to go," Exe apologized.

"Already? But you were actually having fun for once," Easy's disappointment tore at Exe—until he grinned. "It's okay, I knew this might be a tad too much for you."

"Really? You're not mad?" Exe asked.

Easy winked at her, "You lasted longer than I expected. And I didn't even have to bribe you. The 'rents almost forbid me to go this big because they didn't want you upset on your birthday, but I had to celebrate your sixteenth in style. And I knew you'd love it if you let yourself. Say, what'dya think of Henny-Boy constructing the grand finale all by himself? Impressive, right?"

"You knew?" Exe's eyes widened in surprise.

"Of course," Easy replied. "I keep on top of what my siblings are capable of."

You don't know what I'm capable of. Exe quashed the thought and said, "Thank you so much for everything. I just– I have to go."

"Is it just that there's too many people? Say the word and they're gone. We'll have a snowball fight and fireworks with just the family," Easy offered.

But Exe shook her head, "No, let everyone stay. That way Mom and Dad are less likely to notice that I'm gone."

"So it's that way," Easy teased playfully. "Well, I guess you've covered for me often enough. I suppose I can return the favor." With a thank you hug, Exe dashed out into the cemetery.

Unfortunately, the blue team was still racing among the tombstones trying to solve Moth's tricky clues. Exe had always performed the 'postern' spell while standing outside her tower door, but she couldn't risk the blue team seeing the door open up into an abandoned city lot. So she entered her tower without performing the spell.

Will the trigger still work if I'm inside? If I'm even actually using the spell. Maybe I'm just wishing it to work. If that's the case, then it shouldn't matter which side of the door I'm on, right? Back and forth she turned the knob while whispering the magic word (just in case...). It worked.

It felt strange standing inside her tower, hearing the joyous voices of teens snowball fighting while staring out at the lush mirage in that deserted desert lot. It was stranger still to look out of the narrow tower window at the clear, starry sky over Nowhere while rainclouds obscured the moon over the dark, drizzly field.

A police siren wailed by as Exe stepped out into the muddy field. Quickly she pulled the tower door shut (hoping that no one in Nowhere had heard it) and glanced around. Even with the high fence and sharp barbed wire to protect her, Exe felt uneasy being alone in this sketchy part of the city after dark.

A skittering echoed in the emptiness. Exe whirled around, cringing at the sight of a rat dragging a crumpled

hamburger wrapper into its creephole. A lone figure leaned against the gate, hunched into the shadows beyond the dim, flickering streetlight. From this distance, Exe couldn't tell if that watcher could see her or not. If they were outside the fence or in. She released a shaky sigh as the shadowy character stepped into the light, revealing a raggedy woman rolling her overloaded shopping cart down the street.

Exe still couldn't shake the jitters though. *No one but my parents, Rande, or Caulder could have called me here, right? Where are they? Hiding?* A pleasant thought thrilled through her. *Was this a surprise party? Was today really her birthday? Had Velin been cajoled into spying on her to arrange this?*

Joy whirled Exe back toward the mirage. But it wasn't her parents standing there. It was Viva.

"Why are you here?" Exe burst out. Ashamed of the whine in her voice, she blustered on, "I thought you were too afraid to face me again."

"I've only stayed away because my parents want to protect me. From you," Viva strolled closer with casual menace—giving the boulder a wide berth. "You did almost kill me... killer."

Only Riven or Asher could've revealed my sordid secret to Viva, Exe gasped, feeling betrayed. "If you just came to taunt me, I'm leaving. I've got a party to go to."

"Who'd invite **you** to a party?" Viva's voice roiled with scorn.

"It's a party for me," Exe bragged, telling Viva all about the festivities. "And my brothers arranged this epic blowout for my birthd–" She stopped short, but it was too late.

"Your birthday?" Viva's cruel chuckle told Exe that today wasn't her real birthday after all. "You don't know anything do you? Really, I'm surprised anyone would risk attending an event in your honor. Everyone must know how dangerous you are."

"I won't be for long," Exe contradicted, shivering as Viva confirmed her worst fear. "Once I'm trained, it'll be safe for me to return to Anacapia. Then I'll have two homes, two families, two places to belong. Unlike you."

"I thought that was your plan," Viva sneered. "Let me change that for you."

Drizzle misted on the velvety cover of the thick textbook Viva offered Exe. "A Compendium of Anacapian History," the glimmering title proclaimed. A whole book on the history of her homeland—the knowledge within that heavy text certainly enticed, but Exe didn't trust the motives behind this gesture.

"Here, I've marked the most interesting bit for you," Viva pressed the tome into Exe's hands. The book fell open in her palms, its pages flipping unaided to the section Viva had bookmarked. The large, bold typeface blared the headline of the chapter:

The Execution of Experience Verelustre

Exe dropped the book as if it had burst into flames. It splash-landed in a murky puddle, but its pages stayed crisp and dry—the words sharpened and magnified beneath the pilling water.

"No, that's not true. That's impossible," Exe denied, her eyes riveted on the offending text. "I can't have been executed. You faked that somehow."

"That's an official, government-issued history textbook. Its pages are protected against unauthorized changes," Viva explained with brutal triumph.

"If I were executed, then how am I still alive?" Exe reasoned. *Did Velin time travel to save me? Why would he risk it?*

"You'll find out. Just read it," Viva said as Exe stood staring. "Read it!"

Unmindful of the mud, Exe fell to her knees and read:

Ten years after the end of the Horology Wars, Malina Verelustre—a rising star in the Anacapian Armed Forces and wife to newly-appointed concilium member Asher Verelustre—gave birth to twin daughters named Vivacity and Experience.

As per tradition, our esteemed Seren, Jettani Invidia, carried both infants into the Portal Portend to reveal their fates and futures. While the destiny of Vivacity was deemed unremarkable, Experience's prophecy left Jettani shaken. Our faultless, impeccable Portal foretold that the child showed a wicked, malicious ambition, and a pure, pervasive evil intent on destroying all of Anacapia.

After giving evidence on all that the Portal had revealed, the benevolent Jettani argued vehemently in defense of the infamous infant. For nine months our altruistic Seren pleaded for the child's life to be spared, but the concilium ultimately ruled unanimously that execution was only way to save our nation from the Bantling Destroyer.

At the age of one, Experience Verelustre was executed and interred on Mount Dolose by General Legier Demaine—Jettani's closest and most trusted advisor at that time. Once the evil twin had been executed, all believed that the threat to Anacapia's existence had been eliminated.

Twelve years later, when the betrayal of the reviled apostate General Demaine was exposed (see: "The Treacherous Treason of the Turncoat Legier Demaine"), all of his actions were called into question, including his role as executioner. Experience's grave was exhumed and the small, excavated coffin was revealed to be empty.

Upon this discovery, Jettani and the concilium ordered the Disimulata to search for any sign that the notorious Experience had survived execution. At the same time, a death warrant was issued, ordering all Anacapians to kill Experience Verelustre on sight or—face death themselves.

Exe tentatively touched the repugnant passage, pretending to wipe away the water beading on the page. Secretly she wished and wished for the words to change, for the true text to reveal itself, for Viva's trickery to be exposed. But the wording remained exactly the same. This entry in Anacapia's history book had not been altered.

"You're the spook story Anacapian parents tell their kids. Behave or wind up sanctioned like Experience. Need more proof? Look," Viva gloated, holding up a copy of Exe's wanted poster identical to the one crumpled in Exe's desk drawer back home.

"So what?" Exe shrugged to mask her trembling, barely glancing at the wanted poster Viva victoriously displayed. "You think it's news to me that you're unremarkable? I could've told you that the first time we met."

"Don't pretend you knew," Viva's gloating faltered. "Or are you just that selfish? Did you actually return despite knowing that it'd place our family, our whole world, in jeopardy? I suppose that's to be expected of an evil destroyer."

With the tip of just one finger, Exe eased the offensive textbook closed. Secretly she shuddered, thinking of all the little signs that proved Viva right and these words true. Velin's incessant determination to repress her powers, Asher and Malina's reluctance to reveal her past, Bonnie. Poor, innocent Bonnie. *So it's not about what I did. it's about what I am and what I'll do to Anacapia should I be allowed to return.*

"If I'm supposedly so terrible, then why did Asher, Caulder, and Rande agree to help me?" Exe's voice trembled along with her legs as she rose. *Are they still planning on helping me? Is this why they're all so afraid of me?*

"Because they're afraid of you," Viva said bluntly. "We all are. I'll admit it. If there's any good at all in you, you'll end these training sessions and stay out of Anacapia forever. For all of our sakes."

Exe said nothing. Ignoring the sinkhole of sorrow that opened up in her belly, she handed the book back. Viva refused the book with a blasé wave as she sauntered into the cascade, "Keep it. The government hands them out like candy on Manumission Day. But don't let anyone know you have it. Asher and Malina want you kept in the dark so that you don't get any ideas about using your powers against Anacapia."

Evil. Dangerous. Destroyer. The words ricocheted on repeat in Exe's mind as if fired from a machine gun as she watched her sister disappear back into the homeland she'd never know. A ticklish trickle of rain jolted Exe out of her numbed stupor. She raced back toward the tower door and dashed inside without bothering to shut it.

Torn between devouring every word of the horrible history book in the hopes of discrediting it, or forever forgetting its existence, Exe tucked the textbook into the stack of books Moth had gifted her. *I can't read it while the house is crawling with teenagers.*

"Come on, let us in!" the muffled shouts startled Exe as she whipped around, surprised to still see the rainy field in the doorway behind her.

Suddenly, the open door began to rattle, as if someone were pounding on it. Half-dazed by the enormous truths Viva had revealed, Exe stared at the vibrating door, barely registering that Asher's spell must make the door appear closed and locked in Nowhere while the gateway to the field was open.

The second she swung it closed, the door burst open as the blue team raced through to complete Easy's game. It felt like a lifetime had passed since she'd left the party, but it had only been a few minutes.

"You're a mess again, Exe," Easy casually teased as he strolled by, trailing the team to help them finish his game. "How in the world did you manage to get both wet and muddy tonight? It hasn't rained in Nowhere for ages!"

"You know me, I can't get enough of mud day, spa baths. I mean spa day mud baths," Exe mumbled, struggling to string a coherent sentence together.

"Uh-huh," Easy's said skeptically. "Well, go clean up and come rejoin the snow party. We need your talents crafting our dueling snow forts. Losers get a facewash, and that manufactured snow is turning icy. It'll scrape off more skin than a salt scrub."

"A what?" Exe struggled to focus on what Easy was saying as the words from Viva's vicious textbook scrolled through her mind like ticker tape.

"Yeah, you're definitely a spa day kind of girl," Easy joked, nudging Exe up the stairs toward her dressing room level. "Get changed and then come have some fun. Maybe that'll help you forget whatever's got you spooked."

"I don't think even one of your epic soirees can help me now, Easy," Exe said over her shoulder, mindlessly obeying Easy's instructions.

"Don't you doubt my powers, kid sister," Easy chided as Exe disappeared up the stairs. Exe could've sworn she heard him say under his breath, "I'd never doubt yours."

CHAPTER TWENTY

EVILDOINGS

Being evil isn't easy. This disheartening conclusion occurred to Exe at least ten times a day as she resigned herself to villainy.

Exe slammed her locker, startling Thone and a few of his groupies as they strolled down the crowded school hall. At Thone's sidelong glance of curious concern, Exe shrugged the slam off as an accident so he wouldn't tell the rest of her brothers that she was upset. The last thing she needed was to comfort worried brothers when her soul was screaming. *If I care so much about upsetting my brothers, maybe that means I'm not evil. I should be able to tell if I'm actually evil, shouldn't I?*

It had been over a month since Viva had given her the textbook, and she hadn't heard a word out of Anacapia since. She'd spent those endless, January days holed up in her belfry, afraid of tainting her family with her revealed vileness. She couldn't even bring herself to search the offending history book for answers. Every time she opened the text, she just wound up flipping to the chapter on her unsuccessful execution.

Exe leaned back, banging her head against the locker. Eyes half-shuttered, she monitored the thronging hall, envying how simple it seemed for all of these teens to revel in being themselves. The thought of ending their relaxed camaraderie with one simple wish was tempting. *But how? Set off the fire alarm? Conjure up a fetid stench? Instantaneously overheat the hallway?* Each idea seemed lamer than the last.

Thinking up a way to panic a crowd shouldn't be this difficult for a dangerous destroyer, should it? Maybe it would be easier to target just one person.

Unlike most of the schools the Parsells had attended, this one put a high premium on giving students free time to rest, refresh, and socialize during the school day. So the entire school (from kindergarteners to seniors) had an entire hour together for lunch every day. Exe wandered among the upbeat adolescents as they pulled out their lunches or pooled their money to order in from nearby restaurants.

Dismay set in as she wove her way through the quad and the playground, assessing the picnickers. No one stood out as a target. In the five months they'd been in Nowhere, not a single student had given her so much as a sideways look. *Since this is our last school, maybe Easy spread the word that I wasn't to be touched.* Or maybe it was the fact that these kids were all too friendly and wholesome to be antagonistic.

Everywhere she looked, kids were interacting with no regard for any social hierarchy. Freshmen played freeze-tag with the first-graders; upper-class athletes reffed a middle-schooler soccer match; a few sophomores even acted as make-believe dragons for kindergarteners scampering around the playground fort. Moth was the sole loner, curled up in a sunny corner, nose-deep in a massive book.

Come to think of it, not even a single citizen of this town has ever been tempted by my necklace's power! It was true. While dozens of classmates had remarked on its beauty when they'd glimpsed it during sleepovers, their interest had been wholly complimentary, not conniving. (Only one intense tourist had showed more than a passing interest in her pendant during their whole time in Nowhere, but it'd been easy to evade him.) In fact, no one in Nowhere seemed very impressed or interested in power at all. Even the town's mayor and law enforcement officers were solely focused on fostering a friendly community rather than exerting their authority.

At a loss on who to target in her quest to test her "evilness," Exe came to a halt by a random trio of lunchers. They immediately made room with welcoming smiles. Exe glowered at them and sat on a deserted bench nearby to pick at her lunch in solace.

"Pure evil, I tell you," Exe heard the bespectacled picnicker say. "Diabolical, destructive, malevolent, malicious— all too tame for this walking, talking monstrosity."

How do they know? I haven't even done anything yet! A bite of radish sandwich fell from Exe's gaping mouth. Guilt twisted in with anger and embarrassment—the tangled knots of emotions tightening, until Exe felt snarled to the point of lashing out.

"That's why I'm basking in these final peaceful moments," a honeyed voice rippled. It was Boho Babe, leaning back in the grass, her face tilted up to the sun. "Six months, not a minute less. That's the punishment Principal Tolkan prescribed. By my watch, we've only got a few minutes left to savor the serenity."

"Maybe he won't come back," their scrawny companion whispered wistfully.

They aren't talking about me, Exe ducked her head in embarrassment, even though no one knew what she'd been thinking.

"They should've permanently expelled him," the bespectacled picnicker stated, outrage exploding in every syllable. "Letting him return after what he did?"

"This is the only school in town. Where else would he go?" Boho Babe asked.

"Maybe it won't be so bad. After all, it's a new school year. Besides, the Parsell Pack is here now. They'll keep him in line," their scrawny companion hoped.

"They've never dealt with someone like Mongo before," the bespectacled picnicker said knowingly.

Mongo. Sounds like the name of a worthy target.

"What's up, buttercup?" Easy sighed, red-faced and breathless from chasing around the playground. Exe jumped as he collapsed onto the bench beside her.

"The Mayberry quality around here is impressive, even for you," Exe said, shoving her half-eaten sandwich aside.

"Wish I could take credit. They were like this before we moved here. Not much of a challenge for my final social masterpiece, but I'm proud of the work I've done," Easy mopped his sweaty head with his shirt front.

"You heard about this Mongo kid coming back to school today?" Exe asked, certain Easy would have the scoop. *I don't want to target a kid who doesn't deserve it.*

"Sure, Alex Mongeon. Or Mongo, as he's not-so-affectionately known," Easy took a swig from her water bottle. "Won't call him that 'til I know he likes it though."

"So you're gonna brownnose this bully?"

Easy raised his brow, "You ever know me to polish anyone's boots? Except Dad's, but only when we're on punishment."

"Then what's up with this 'if he likes it' stuff?"

"There's more than one way to battle a bully," Easy yawned. "When I can, I prefer to kill 'em with kindness." Exe winced at Easy's casual reference to death, and blotted that suggestive thought out of her mind. *The last thing I need is another dead kid on my conscience.*

A sudden silence sent a fissure of alarm through her. Every student had stilled and gone quiet. All eyes riveted on the sunny spot where Moth sat—only he wasn't reading anymore. Instead Moth sat puzzled in the bulky shadow of a beefy teen, two little page corners still pinched between his fingers, blinking in surprise at his book on the ground.

Outrage propelled Exe to her feet. She wanted this kid to suffer for picking on Moth. *But how to hurt him without killing him?* Easy sprinted over to the center-stage duo before she could come up with anything good.

"Alex? Easy Parsell," Easy extended his hand, but Mongo ignored it. "I hit you up online yesterday, but maybe you didn't get the message." Mongo just stared at Easy as if deciding on the best way to butcher his carcass.

Still smiling, Easy dusted off the damaged book as he studied the cover, "I can see why this piqued your interest." Instead of returning the book to Moth, he offered it to Mongo. "What did you think about the author modeling the high school hierarchy after a Dark Ages feudal system?"

"Huh?" Mongo fumbled through the pages, glaring at Easy. "I don't– Higher what? Who'dya think you're talking to? I'm gonna crush you!"

Easy thumped Mongo on the back, "That's exactly what Morgan would say! Now do Ethos. Come on, it'll be beautiful."

Mongo frowned, "Wha– I'm not doin' character impressions. I'm threa–"

"Oh you should, you're fabulous at it. Are you into drama? You should meet my brother Thone. You're built for football too. My brother Seph's the man for that," Easy flung his arm over Mongo's shoulder.

"Who?" Mongo's bewildered gaze fell on the rest of the Parsell boys lined up behind Moth. In fact, every single student was standing and staring Mongo down.

"Moth here's a book lover like you. Were you wanting to get a discussion going on this one? I'd get in on that," Easy let go of Mongo and put his hand on Moth's shoulder. "You up for that Seph? Thone?" All of Exe's brothers, even little Charley, nodded in unison. The rest of the student body nodded in unison too.

Mongo surveyed the crowd and hung his head, "I haven't read it."

"That's alright. I'm sure Moth'll let you borrow it," Easy glanced at Moth, who shrugged his agreement and pulled a fresh book from his backpack. "Let me know when you're ready to discuss it. In the meantime, you up for a game of croquet? You a power player, or a finesse man?"

Clutching the book like a lifeline, Mongo let Easy lead him toward the small strip of lawn where the Prep Set had a game going. Exe flopped back down on the bench. *Leave it to my social guru brother to redeem the only potential bully in town.*

Exe lingered alone in the shadows of the prickly pear cactus patch on the far end of the cemetery, watching her brothers and their friends laugh and chat around the Friday night bonfire the Parsell Pack hosted every winter weekend. Viva's bleak warning that she was evil and dangerous warred with the sight of Easy chumming around with Mongo in the crackling glow of the blazing fire.

After escorting the former tormenter on an apology tour through the school to make amends for all of the cruel and malicious things Mongo had done in the past, Easy and the reformed bully stayed buddy-buddy. Seeing the strange duo around school had at first given Exe a stoic hope. *If only my own redemption could be achieved with such ease—if redemption is even possible for me.*

But the textbook had implied that Exe was born evil. That fact nagged at her, the way Velin's voice once did. *Is there such a thing as an evil twin? And is that evil twin me? Is that why Velin dedicated himself to forcing me to suppress my powers? Because I'm not just dangerous, I'm evil?* True, she hadn't been able to bring herself to do anything truly evil to anyone or anything yet, but each day without a signal to come train seemed to solidify Viva's vicious suggestion as reality—that Exe was indeed irredeemably evil and her birth parents intended to abandon her again.

Reason argued otherwise as she stared at the flames dancing on the burning logs. *Why would Rande and Caulder teach me dangerous defensive spells if I'm really evil? And why would Asher and Malina have sent me away to Velin at all? If I'm truly evil incarnate, why not just let their government execute me?*

Exe shivered in the crisp, February wind as she huddled deeper into her sweater and jacket—as if the layers could protect her from the darkness of her thoughts. If only she still had Velin to blame for them. *He'd probably relish being in my head right now as I debate how awful I really am. Maybe I should just ask him.*

CRACK!

Exe almost whirled herself into the cactus patch as she searched for whoever had volted into the cemetery, mentally prepared to face a Disimulata there to arrest her for her crimes. It took her a second to realize that it was just the sound of a burning log splitting open in the bonfire. The sudden flare of heat and the blast of brightness were dead giveaways. But the sudden brightness stayed, illuminating her face. The formless fear in Exe's belly tightened as awareness settled over her. Her necklace was glowing again.

Exe teetered between anticipation and outrage. She'd worried for over a month about why she'd had no word from anyone, but now that word had finally come, she no longer wanted to hear it. *Viva's told me the truth, what else is there to say? That's it. I'm not going!* The bitter anxiety and deep shame she'd felt after reading the textbook crystalized into one defiant thought, *Asher should've told me the truth from the start.*

Her birth father was so concerned about the safety of his own world, his own skin, and the daughter he'd kept, that he hadn't given one thought about Exe. Or Rande and Caulder. *What if had I accidentally killed them during training?!* Nor did Asher care that the Parsells were at risk every second they kept Exe around. He hadn't even cared enough to warn Exe about just how dangerous she was, or to answer any of her important questions, or– *I'm not going.*

But it's probably not Asher waiting for you in the field, Exe argued with herself. Viva was the first member of her birth family that she'd seen in months. There was little chance Asher or Malina would suddenly show up now. *It's Rande or Caulder I'm ignoring if I don't go.* Exe toyed with a long spine on the prickly pear cactus, idly contemplating how the painful prickers protected its sweet fruit. *Would either of them even agree to come back after what happened last time? Caulder played it off, but they were both disturbed by what I did. Well, whoever it is, they can wait.*

The warmth of the bonfire drew Exe out from behind the cactus. She sat down on an empty log across from Easy and a few of his friends to watch the flames, pondering how to respond to this latest summons. She let the minutes stretch while she played out every possible scenario in her mind: What she would say or do should she find Rande or Caulder waiting. Or Asher or Malina. Or Viva. *Confront them with the textbook or say nothing? Beg for more training or resign myself to getting Velin's help? Yell at them for leaving me in the dark for so long or demand that they finally start telling me the truth?*

"You were told to come as soon as we called."

Exe jumped at the sound of Asher's low, tense voice right behind her. Clearly, he'd concealed himself from everyone but her, considering that not one person around the bonfire had remarked on the oddly-dressed man suddenly joining their crowd.

"Find us a hidden corner to volte from. Now," Asher demanded.

Exe rose slowly, barely able to keep herself from confronting Asher over his high-handed manner. *What right does he have to talk to me that way, considering that I haven't even seen the man for the past three months?*

Her eyes met Easy's over the flames, the probing concern in his expression a clear indicator of the rage that must be written all over her face. *I need to calm down if I'm going to have any shot at getting answers out of Asher.* Drawing a deep breath, Exe forced her outrage into her private mind vault and unobtrusively tilted her head toward an empty alcove in her home's outer wall.

"It's nice to finally see you again, Asher," Exe said with a (hopefully!) calm smile as they entered the alcove, inwardly enjoying his flinch when she called him 'Asher.'

Asher gave her a curt nod as he grasped her shoulder, and Exe once again felt herself spiraling through pitch black, feeling splintered into a billion pieces.

CHAPTER TWENTY-ONE

BELATED

Exe stepped into the dusky field wholly unprepared for what she found. In the center of the velvety emerald mirage stood a pearly table set for four with silver-filigreed place settings. The most sumptuous feast Exe had ever seen surrounded a towering cake decked out in delicate sugared lilacs and other exotic blossoms.

Above this picturesque tablescape fluttered a host of phosphorescent fairies casting a luminous glow over the mirage. Their soothing light illuminated the faces of the duo observing Exe. When recognition lit Exe's face, Malina and Viva both smiled—one hopeful, one hateful. At Malina's signal, the iridescent imps hovering overhead scurried about spelling a message in sparkler-like lights: 'Happy Birthday, Exe!'

"Is this for me?" Exe took a few steps forward, despite the sticky tangle of confusion that made her legs feel like pulled taffy. "Today's my birthday?" Exe asked, hesitating when Viva's spiteful smile deepened. *If only we'd waited a month to celebrate my birthday, then Viva would've never known that I don't know when I was born.*

"Come find out for yourself," Viva invited insidiously.

"It isn't much, but we wanted to do something for you," Malina apologized as Exe stepped into the mirage.

"What do you mean? It's beautiful," Exe assured, unable to resist taking a fingerful of frosting from the decadent confection.

"Wait!" Malina called out.

Too late. The moment Exe touched the table, the illusion of a tasty banquet vanished. In its place stood a pathetic array of half-eaten dishes surrounding a few cake slices. *They brought leftovers to celebrate my birthday.*

"Please don't be disappointed, Experience. I only enchanted the buffet to show you how we would honor your birth, if we could," Malina confessed. "But I can't exactly order a second cake for you when you're supposedly–"

"Malina," Asher's tone warned.

"This is all that's left from my birthday bash," Viva crowed. "Yesterday."

"Yesterday?"

"Everybody was there," Viva gloated. "Politicians, celebrities, the crème de la crème. All the top Anacapians come out to celebrate my birth every year."

"When is my real birthday?" Exe puzzled, searching for a way to make this all okay. "Were we born around midnight or something? So Viva was technically born yesterday, on the eighth, and me today on February ninth?"

"I had you both sixteen years ago, yesterday."

"And you were born first," Asher frowned as Viva giggled. "Viva's our baby."

"You lied to me! You lied about everything," Exe glared at Viva.

Asher narrowed his eyes at Viva, "What else has she told you?"

"What you should have!" Exe turned on Asher. "You keep saying that Anacapia is too dangerous for me, but you won't say why. Tell me why!" *Tell me that infernal textbook is a lie!*

"Now is not the time," Asher hedged.

"Just say it! Why won't you tell me the truth?" Exe yelled. When they all just stared at her in silence, Exe scowled, "Forget it. I already know." Exe wished the crumpled wanted poster into her hand threw it at Asher's feet.

"Where did you get that?" Asher demanded, glaring at Viva.

"Asher, she needs to know," Malina murmured.

"Our government– our ruler– Jettaini wants you dead," Asher said flatly.

"Why?"

"There are a multitude of complex–" Asher began.

"Why won't you tell me?" Exe cried. *Are you afraid to admit that I'm evil?*

"It's because you're–" Malina started.

"No, Malina. Not now," Asher interrupted, casting a sidelong glance at Viva. "We need to enjoy this while we can. Tonight's our one chance to be together as a family. You'll be done with training long before your next birthday."

"What training? I haven't seen Rande or Caulder in weeks!"

"We're working on that," Asher answered. "But we risked coming here tonight so that we could celebrate at least one birthday with you. So let's get on with it before time runs out."

"We were lucky to get away at all," Viva scowled. "Our family is constantly monitored because of you."

"Your father's right. We want to celebrate you tonight. And what's a party without presents?" Malina plastered on a smile as she leaned in to whisper in Exe's ear, "I'll give you the truth when we next have a moment alone."

That's practically a vow that Malina will never be alone with me.

Malina motioned like a game show host to a stack of brightly-wrapped gifts that completely obscured the boulder. Exe stared stonily as the fluttery fairies whisked the wrappings away. Most of the bulky ones contained clothes—a whole wardrobe of outfits that looked exactly like the retro twenties and thirties-style fashions Viva always wore.

"Every time I take Viva shopping I think of what I'd buy for you. I finally got my chance," Malina beamed.

"They're lovely," Exe mustered a sour smile as she admired garments that she'd never have an opportunity to wear.

"That's from me," Viva's voice sang sweetly poisonous as the fairies opened a small box, revealing a vanity set with an ivory brush, comb, and handheld mirror. "They're enchanted to style your hair to look just like mine. Maybe you'll look halfway decent the next time we see you. If there is a next time..."

Exe glowered at Viva, then watched the fairies open the last package. The heavy box contained a thick leather book embossed with dozens of unfamiliar symbols. Struggling under its weight, the fairies lifted the tome to display the blank pages inside.

"It's an Entirety Tome. A rare treasure, and quite hard to find," Asher enthused, offering Exe a rare smile. "Simply speak the title of any Anacapian book to the pages, and you'll find the text inside. I've included a list of textbooks that will speed up your training. I even had Velin spell the Entirety Tome to work with all Ari Zona books too."

Because they never intend for me to ever return to Anacapia.

"So that's what this is really about," Exe stated, staring at the book as if it were a snake poised to strike her. "This is all stuff that'll help you get rid of me faster. Or are you just trying to make me more like the daughter you cared enough to keep?"

"Precisely!" Viva preened.

"That's not what this is about," Malina objected. "These gifts were meant to give you a piece of your homeland to cherish."

"So you admit it! These aren't birthday presents, they're goodbye gifts! You don't care about me at all, do you? You only care about how dangerous I am for you!"

"Don't you dare talk to your mother like that," Asher reprimanded.

"She's not my mother. You're just the woman who gave birth to me."

Malina winced, "That's not fair. It's your safety that we care about."

"Really? Then why did you send other people to train me?" Exe demanded, flushing. She hadn't intended to let them know that she'd been hurt that they'd abandoned her to other people. *Again. And why haven't they mentioned that Rande hasn't been able to train me? Why won't they talk about what's wrong with my powers?*

"Viva just told you why," Asher admonished. "We're too closely monitored to come frequently enough to train you ourselves. You're lucky Malina was able to persuade Rande and Caulder to help. It wasn't easy."

"It's not that we don't want to train you. Of course we'd rather have that time with you ourselves if we could. We're your family," Malina pleaded.

"No, you're not," Exe stayed stony. "A real family would care about *me*. My real family does. They gave me a fabulous birthday party weeks ago because—thanks to you—I haven't known my real birthdate for the past sixteen years. And my real family gave me presents that they knew I'd like. Because they know me. You gave me clothes I can't wear and a training manual disguised as a gift."

"Training is exactly what you came looking for, isn't it? We're risking our lives to provide that for you. And this is your thanks?" Asher voice was quiet and cold.

'Risking our lives to train you,' because I'm dangerous. So the textbook is true.

"You're right. Thank you," Exe looked Asher square in the eye. "All I want from you is training so that I don't hurt the people I actually care about. Or kill anyone again," Exe fixed her eyes on Viva, whose sneer quickly faltered. "Accidentally, that is."

"You don't mean that," Malina said.

"Yes, I do."

"So this is the stubbornness Velin spoke of," Asher broke the silent standoff.

"I'm stubborn? Look who's talking," Exe scoffed.

"I think we should sit down and discuss this," Malina pulled out Exe's chair.

"Thanks, but if you're not here to teach me, I need to get back home to my family. I've got a lot of friends over, and they'll be missing me," Exe backed out of the mirage, feeling behind her for her door. *It's not there! Because Asher volted us here.* In defiance, Exe lifted her chin, raised a brow at Asher, and wished her tower door to appear without taking her gaze from his.

"What about our gifts?" Malina asked as Exe opened the door.

With a little more wish magic, Exe brought her nightstand of stacked vintage suitcases into the field. Once the fairies had packed up the gifts, Exe wished the cases closed and sent them home.

"You didn't say any spell words," Asher stared at her. "Rande was right. You're not even trying to perform magic properly."

Ignoring Asher, Exe turned to Malina, "Thank you for sending Rande and Caulder to train me. Let me know if and when they're willing to continue. Actually, send word through Velin. I don't believe there's any need for me to see any of you again," Exe stated as she yanked the door closed. Tensed and seething, Exe stared at the closed door, waiting. But not one of them cared to come after her. *Not even Malina.*

Exe kicked at her brothers' outdoor playthings that always collected in the lower level of her tower. *So much for my own room—Ella and Rove stashed me in an oversized storage closet.* Exe instantly regretted the thought. It wasn't the Parsells she was mad at. Her magical family had shown their true colors tonight. Exe had longed for the Verelustres to see her as their long-lost daughter happily returned to them. But they didn't. *I'm only a dangerous nuisance to them. A problem they can't wait to be rid of.*

Visions of Viva's venomous glee enraged Exe even further. Just as she was about to defiantly wish her brothers' collected clutter into Viva's Anacapian bedroom (*I can just wish that I won't hurt her like I did with the boulder, right?*), the door to the cemetery burst open. A troupe of teens trailed Easy in from the bonfire, traipsing through her tower bedroom on their way to the kitchen for more s'mores supplies.

All of that carefree camaraderie pushed Exe over the edge. Unmindful of Easy's startled expression, Exe raced up the tower stairs, desperate to reach the solitude of the belfry. Halfway up the third flight she slammed into a human brick wall. The impact almost sent Exe headlong over the railing, but a firm hand stabilized her.

"Steady soldier, we don't need another near fatality up here." The brick wall was Rove. It took Exe a second to process exactly what he'd said. The second it registered, Rove fixed her with a stern stare, "That's right. Your brothers finally told me how the belfry railing got broken. That's not happening again. Not on my watch."

Exe finally noticed the hammer and nails in his hands. She choked back a sob, then almost smiled. The planks Rove had nailed over the trap door might deter the boys, but she could just wish them away any time she wanted.

"If I see you up there, if I catch just one little dust mote out of place because you've been up there, you're out of this tower," Rove warned. "You'll be in the balcony with your brothers faster than you can blink."

She couldn't hold back the sob this time as Rove strode down the stairs, swinging his hammer and whistling cheerfully. Exe sagged against the wall and slid down to the floor. *I'm robbed of everything.* A whimper forced itself out with every bump of her butt on the steps as she scooted back down the stairs to her bedroom landing.

As she crawled into bed, Exe's vintage suitcase nightstand tumbled over. Out spilled the Entirety Tome which plopped open to a marked page. Her damp eyes fell on the bookmark—a cheerful photo of Asher, Malina, and Viva.

One happy family. Without me.

CHAPTER TWENTY-TWO

PRACTICE MAKES PERFECT

Exe swirled her knife mindlessly, making figure eights in the crimson frosting. A tableful of sugar cookies awaited her attention. It was Valentine's Day morning, but the town wasn't hosting a hearts and flowers festival. In Nowhere, the romantic holiday played second fiddle to the fact that Arizona became a state on February 14, 1912.

Easy had signed the Parsells up for a bake sale booth at Nowhere's Sweetheart Statehood Shindig, so naturally he'd invited a whole crew of kids over to finish preparing the goodies. The house overflowed with teens wrapping candies, frosting cookies and cupcakes, and concocting crazy, last-minute confections on the stovetop.

Ignoring the stacks of unfrosted hearts, Exe reached for a tower of flag-shaped cookies and began slathering red on the top halves. Throwing herself into cookie decorating didn't stop her from reliving her birth parents' pathetic excuse for a birthday celebration. *They miss fifteen birthdays and that's the best they can do?*

While she had every reason to feel hurt and angry, Exe couldn't help but be embarrassed over the childish way she'd reacted. *Viva's probably reveling in my misery and sharing every minute detail of my immature outburst with Riven. And Rande and Caulder.* Exe blushed at the thought of Viva mocking her in front of Caulder. *Is that why they still haven't come to train me? Am I truly stuck with Velin?*

"Having a crush on a boy who doesn't feel the same way about you isn't easy," a familiar, honeyed voice flowed. Exe jerked to attention, blushing as if someone had been reading her thoughts (although that was impossible now). She scanned her fellow frosters. *Boho Babe.* The sweet, bohemian girl had her arm around a sobbing miniature version of herself. *She has a name*, Exe scolded herself. *Technically, I've been 'friends' with this girl for months.*

"Th-th-at's easy for y-you to say, C-c-cadence. Th-thone l-likes y-y-ou," the pint-sized flower child sobbed all over the heart-shaped cookie she was holding.

"You don't know how Moth feels, Calli. Have you talked to him?" Boho Babe, aka Cadence, hugged her sister harder when Calli's heart cookie crumbled to pieces.

"I-I-I c-can't! H-he b-barely e-e-even n-notices m-me," Calli hiccupped, rubbing pink frosting onto her face as she wiped away her tears.

"Moth isn't really into girls or dating yet," Exe offered, drawing the sisters' attention. "Sorry to interrupt, um, Cadence."

"You're back!" Cadence smiled at Exe. "You're so rarely around, and even when you are, you're so very rarely 'with' us. Have you met my little sister, Calli?"

Calli dried her sad eyes, "Sh-short for Calliope. From G-Greek mythology. She's the M-muse of eloquence and e-e-epic poetry."

"Tell that to Moth and you're golden. A name that evokes both history and literature? He'll talk your ear off," Exe encouraged.

"R-really?" Calli brightened, jumping up from the table to track down Moth. Cadence stopped her, daubing the pink frosting from her sister's face like a doting mother. Exe watched with envious eyes as an unwanted vision of Viva flickered.

"Young love. So sweet and silly," Cadence sighed, watching Calli dash off.

"I wouldn't know," Exe mumbled.

"None of our Nowhere boys have caught your eye, have they?" Cadence nodded, knowingly. "But someone has. Who is it?"

Exe blushed, "What? Oh, no one. I don't think about stuff like that."

"If you say so. By all means, let's not talk about boys when there's so many other interesting topics to discuss. Otherworldly things," Cadence tantalized.

"What?"

"Ghosts. I think your house is haunted," Cadence whispered, her eyes shining.

"Haunted?"

Cadence nodded knowingly, "An ill-fated history, a cemetery for a backyard—this place is primed for supernatural activity. And I've seen one. A ghost. Here. Today."

"When? What did he look like?" Exe's suspicions tingled.

"About twenty minutes ago. A dashing young man dressed all in white peeped at us over the balcony banister when we were wrapping candy. Like he was eavesdropping or something. At first I thought he was just another historical reenactor, but he was wearing 1930s duds, not an Old West outfit. Is it kooky to see a ghost in broad daylight?"

"Caulder," Exe leapt up, scanning the room for him as she headed for the balcony.

"Have you seen him too?" Cadence chirped, trailing her. Exe stopped and stared her down. "Oh, I see. You're leaving us again." The bubbly Boho Babe lost a little of her bounce, then smiled at Exe. "Until next time!"

Exe waited for Cadence to bound back into the chaos then raced up into the balcony. Even if Caulder wasn't there anymore, its height gave her a vantage point. It didn't take long to spot him casually lounging in the kitchen while laughing teens thronged around him. *He was right behind me while Cadence and I were talking! He saw me race up here the second I heard he was here.* He was watching her now.

Fanning away the embarrassed flush she could feel turning her beet red, Exe jumped up onto the balustrade and slid down the fireman's pole Easy had talked their parents into installing. She bit her lip and held his gaze as she approached, feeling caught between laughter and anger. "What are you doing here?"

"Observing the Vale," Caulder smiled, turning his attention to the chaotic crush of baking teenagers.

"Vale?" Experience leaned beside him.

"It's what we call this world. Most inhabitants of Anacapia would refer to these people as Hoi Polloi. A fictional race of humans who lack magic. You didn't come when I called," though softly spoken, Caulder's rebuke bristled Exe.

"I've been busy," Exe snapped, hating the bitter bite in her tone. "How was I to know to watch for my necklace glow this morning? Especially after what happened with my birth family on my birthday. It's been almost two months. I doubted that I'd ever hear from you again."

"Sorry about that. Last minute smuggling run for a hard-to-find item. Risked our necks, but it was worth it. Did you like it?" Caulder asked with an expectant side-glance.

"What?" Exe hastily ran through the magical gifts she hadn't looked at since shoving them into her suitcase nightstand. "Oh, umm, the book? Sure. It's pretty cool."

"Ugh, mission failure. I'm the one who suggested the book when Malina asked what I thought you'd like. Let me slink away in shame," Caulder hung his head.

"No, I love it," Exe laughed, grabbing his arm when he pretended to go. "It's just, I already have a tablet where I download any Arizona book. Access to Anacapia books would be awesome, but I don't know any titles to call into it."

"A tablet? Like a stone thing? I thought you didn't have magic in this land," Caulder frowned.

"We don't. We have electronics that can do some pretty magical things though," Exe laughed, digging into a kitchen drawer to show Caulder Ella's tablet.

"Fascinating," Caulder said, whipping through the e-book library and other apps as easily as Easy once Exe showed him how. "Don't sweat it, sweetheart. I'll get you an Anacapian book list. I'm surprised Malina didn't think to include one."

"Yeah. So shall we get to training?" Exe said, too embarrassed to admit that she'd never actually looked. *Didn't Asher say he included a list of Anacapian textbooks?*

"Go for it," he smiled secretly.

"Here?" Exe gaped at him. "Our technology can accomplish a lot, but these kids would freak if we started doing actual magic out in the open."

"I got to thinking, in all that excess time I had in the field this morning," Caulder chided, smiling when Exe sighed. "Pent up powers are difficult to control. Yours need regular use. So you gotta get used to performing spells here, even if you need to go stealth to do it. And as your trainer, I believe it's my duty to supervise."

"Are you saying you want to hang out in Nowhere doing random acts of magic?"

"Why not?" Caulder enticed, backing his way towards the front door. "Besides, I'm itching to see how the unpowered half lives. Don'tcha got the moxie to show me your town?"

"I'm not a fan of strangers taking my sister anywhere, are you, Seph?" Easy strolled over with a tray of frosted Arizona flag cookies.

"Nope. Seems to me this outdated dude should've asked first," Seph replied, managing to look menacing as he licked pink frosting from a knife.

"Doesn't seem safe to go wandering about doing who knows what with a guy like this," Thone added, menacingly pulling off his frilly apron.

"Velin," Exe muttered to Caulder under her breath. "He's not a stranger, he's a friend," Exe stated, staring down each of her older brothers in turn. "And frankly, where we go and what we do is none of your business," she added, knowing

Velin would hear her through her brothers. *Is Velin doing this because he wants to protect me? Or protect Nowhere from me?*

"I'm not fool enough to put Exe in any danger," Caulder added, catching on that Velin was eavesdropping on them through her brothers. "And should anyone dangerous happen along, you could quickly let us know, right?"

"Relax man, we're just messing with you," Thone smiled, introducing himself and his brothers to Caulder.

"You do know the gunfight is staged, right? We don't actually have to dodge bullets in Nowhere," Seph laughed, leading Thone back to baking with their friends. Only Easy remained, studying Caulder warily.

"I'm still no fan of strangers. I know every single person in this town, and I don't know you. So how do you know Exe?" Easy asked, intent on interrogating him.

"He's an old friend, in town for a visit," Exe answered before Caulder could respond, realizing that this was Easy talking now, not Velin.

"An old friend? Of yours?" Easy asked, embarrassing Exe with his incredulity. "You expect me to believe that?"

"I don't tell you everything, Easy."

"Oh, I am very aware. You need me, you call me, okay Exe?" Easy replied, still eyeballing Caulder.

"Okay, Easy," Exe sighed, pushing him until he relented and rejoined his friends.

"So, those are your brothers. Nice guys," Caulder twinkled his eyes at her.

"Three of them. They really are nice, just overprotective," Exe replied.

"And so, it seems, is Velin," Caulder regarded her thoughtfully. "Not as neglectful as you implied."

"He's not neglectful when it comes to keeping me from using my powers, just everything else," Exe glared up at Velin's house through the kitchen window.

"Well, hopefully he knows that there are no Disimulata lurking about waiting to capture you, or he'd have warned you already. Ready to go exploring?" Caulder asked.

Exe stared at him a moment, tempted by the freedom Caulder offered. *Imagine being able to use my powers here on purpose...* But visions of Bonnie's and Hastings' dead bodies killed that dream.

"I can't. You know I can't," Exe dashed into her tower bedroom, desperate to hide her tears from Caulder. He muscled inside before she could slam the door on him.

"Mind telling me what that was all about? What is it that I supposedly know that would keep you from using your powers here?" Caulder asked, murmuring a trigger word under his breath to lock both tower doors when a few teens attempted to straggle through.

"You know what happened the last time I saw you. I'm untrainable. And my magic is uncontrollable. And..." Exe sank down on the stairs. "I'm dangerous, Caulder. It's why Asher and Malina won't train me themselves. I almost killed Viva the first time they tried. Didn't they tell you?" *That must be why Rande got so mad. They didn't tell him how dangerous I am.*

"You're not untrainable. Rande overacted last time, and I guess I did too. Rande discussed it with Asher, and they realized standard training tactics won't work for you." Caulder took a deep breath as he sat beside her, "The reason your parents can't train you themselves is because they're being watched, and they can't risk the government finding you. Rande and I can come because we aren't tracked. Our smuggling business is an open secret. Too many people need the banned goods we supply. And your parents did warn us about the extent of your wish magic, but why do you think that makes you dangerous?"

"I've killed people with my powers. And not on purpose, either," Exe said stonily, waiting for the inevitable horror, but Caulder's expression didn't change.

"How?"

"When I was little, I wished my friend Bonnie dead. A week later she was."

"How?"

"She got hit by a bus," Exe hung her head to avoid his gaze.

"So you wished this bus to run her over?" he asked softly.

"No," Exe whispered. "But I wished her dead, and then she died within a week."

"Then you didn't kill her."

"What?!" Exe stared at him in stark astonishment.

"Magic doesn't work that way. Even powerful wish magic. It doesn't linger around for a week waiting for an opportunity to strike. If she'd dropped dead the moment you wished it, then maybe you'd be responsible, but you're not. It was just a coincidence that she died so soon after," Caulder put a comforting arm around her shoulders.

For a few moments Exe sat in stunned silence, then she leapt up, wished the door open, and stormed up the grave-dotted hill towards Velin's house. Halfway there she stopped, *I wished Bonnie dead, but she didn't die. That makes it the only wish I've ever made that hasn't come true. Right? Did Velin protect her from me? And what about Hastings? Did I actually have a hand in his demise?*

"What's wrong? I thought you'd be happy to know that you didn't kill your friend," Caulder asked when he caught up to her.

"I am. It's just– Velin let me believe I did kill her. For years he used the memory of her death to keep me from using my powers. How could he torture me like that?" Exe cried, fighting to keep her voice at a whisper so that no one around would hear.

"I don't know. It was wrong of him, but I'm sure he had a reason. Maybe it was to protect you, or maybe he was afraid that you would hurt someone if you kept using your out of control wish magic," Caulder took her hand. "I can't explain or excuse what Velin has done in the past. What I can do is teach you to use your powers properly now, which will give you the freedom to use your powers here in the future. So, do you wanna keep running up that hill to confront Velin? Or are you ready to learn how to take control of your powers—and your life?"

Exe didn't hesitate, "Let's go."

Bedecked in heart-shaped Arizona state flags, patriotic bunting, and cowboy cupids, Nowhere's Main Street already buzzed with costumed residents, although the Sweetheart Statehood Shindig wouldn't begin for another hour. The excitement in the air quickened Exe's step, but Caulder's faltered.

He pushed her back against the blacksmith's wall when a horse-drawn stagecoach cut across their path. Breath quickening he asked, "Wait, what time are we in? Velin wouldn't– He didn't–"

"It's just after nine a.m.," Exe checked the time on her phone, then caught the panic in Caulder's voice. Scanning the scene, she quickly realized that it was all the period costumes and the old-fashioned town itself that had him spooked. "It's okay, we're still in present day. This isn't some sort of time travel spell that Velin's performed on the town. Look, there's a kid with a camera, and a couple of tourists on cellphones."

"So all these ladies in long dresses and gentlemen in cowboy hats are just playing make believe? To what end?" Caulder kept her pressed against the wall protectively, as if he didn't quite believe her.

Exe couldn't help but laugh, "Everyone's just pretending to live in the past to preserve history. You know, like a live-action museum."

"All of these people are that dedicated to preserving the past? So it can't be erased? Or rewritten? Amazing!" Caulder relaxed and made to join the crowds, but Exe stopped him.

"If anyone here looks like a time traveler, it's you," Exe teased, giving his 1930s-style outfit the once-over. Caulder glanced at his clothes, whispered a word, and instantly his outfit transformed into a perfect cowboy costume. Exe burst out laughing, "Unless you want to spend the day learning Nowhere's history, I suggest dressing like a tourist instead of a performer." Another whisper, and Caulder transformed his outfit into a replica of the T-shirt and jeans her brothers always wore.

Over the next few hours, Exe was extremely grateful that she'd shown him Ella's tablet—because clearly Caulder thought that life without magic would be as rustic as all the Old West playacting depicted. When he lamented over the time and energy spent by a woman scrubbing clothes clean with a washboard and tub, Exe had to explain how washing machines worked. They had similar conversations at the water pump, the campfire cookout, the dressmaker's shop, the straight-razor barber, and the old time photo studio with its faux flash powder camera.

But mostly they enjoyed the nostalgia like sightseers. At first, Exe was a bit embarrassed by some of the tourist trap hokiness, but Caulder fully embraced the fun of the folk song sing-a-long (and exuberantly applauded Cadence when she won the $500 prize for knowing the most lyrics). He even teared up a bit at the statehood pageant and had Exe pull up the words on her phone so he could join in saying the Pledge of Allegiance and singing the National Anthem.

Spying Exe's indulgent smile, Caulder explained, "I can't help but be moved at the sight of so many people united by their love for their country."

For Exe, the best part was watching Caulder use his powers simply to amuse her. She couldn't help but laugh when he magically swapped the hats on the mannequins in the courthouse museum. The simple act drew chuckles from the crowds who quickly noticed the bonneted cowboy and the ten-gallon hat on the cow—not to mention the confusion of the security guards as they hunted for the trickster.

Caulder also performed a few altruistic acts that impressed her. Like retrieving and cleaning the fallen sugared fry bread of a sobbing toddler too young to talk. Now and then, Caulder hinted that Exe should try using her powers for fun too, but Exe refused. *Why is he tempting me? He knows I can only do wish magic that'll just hurt someone.*

As a thank you treat after their chuck wagon supper, Exe led the way to the ice cream parlor. It's electricity-powered refrigeration was one of the town's rare exceptions to strict authenticity. Officially, it was allowed because ice cream did technically exist at the time, even if there wasn't any in 1890s Nowhere. (In reality, they allowed electricity-powered food vendors for the money they brought in.)

"What do you mean there's no more Blue Moon?" Exe exclaimed, frowning at the bow-tied ice cream man as he explained that they were out of her favorite flavor.

"See for yourself. I can't scrape together a scoop outta that," the harried clerk pointed to an ice cream container with just a few pale blue stains inside.

Before Exe could pick a new flavor, Caulder whispered in her ear, "Distract him." Drawing everyone's attention to the sundown gunfight starting outside, Exe glanced back to catch the smears of blue ice cream sliding together and expanding to fill the container. (*Just like I did with my milk as a kid!*)

"Say, they must'a found some in back," the ice cream man scooped up a cone of Blue Moon for Exe then looked at Caulder expectantly.

Caulder turned to Exe, "What flavor would you pick if they hadn't 'found' more Blue Moon?" Exe scanned the refrigerated case and directed the clerk to give Caulder two scoops of Butter Brickle.

Arm in arm they strolled out of the shop in quiet camaraderie, away from the crowds crowing over the comically dramatic gunfight raging in the street. Trading licks sent a strange warmth shivering through Exe as she placed her lips on the cool, creamy scoop where Caulder's had been moments before.

"I thought our powers couldn't produce food out of thin air," Exe said a little too loudly in her embarrassment. But she didn't regret broaching the topic. The fact that you couldn't conjure something out of nothing had been one of Rande's first lessons. Seeing Caulder create more ice cream had actually been a relief, since she'd assumed that conjuring more milk as a kid was another sign that there was something wrong with her.

"From nothing is the key," Caulder explained. "I didn't conjure your scoop out of nothing; I grew it from the leftovers. A handy talent when food supplies are low, though not everyone has a spell for it or the talent to do it. Our family learned out of necessity."

"So it's not 'abnormal' to be able to do it?" Exe couldn't mask her relief.

"Nope, but that is," Caulder said, eying the strange, shadowy shapes of the old-fashioned playground equipment behind the little red schoolhouse. Exe trailed after him as he went to investigate, wildly entertained as he prodded the teeter-totter like it might fight back. He looked even more confused after she explained how it worked.

"It's just a playground to wear kids out during school recesses," Exe laughed and sat on the bench surrounding the spindly cottonwood tree in the center of the schoolyard.

Caulder threw her a mock glare, "I don't believe it. Let me see—light it up."

Exe crunched the last of her cone, "There are no lights back here to turn on."

"Call over some of those stringed ones I saw out front with a summoning trigger," Caulder suggested.

"You know I can't. I'll just end up wishing, and you'll wind up strangled by them," Exe idly traced UROK onto the bench. "Look, if you're worried that Rande or– someone will be mad that you didn't teach me anything after spending all day with me, tell him what I learned from your ice cream trick."

Sighing, Caulder called for the lights himself, keeping them illuminated without electricity. With envy-tinged contentment, Exe watched the twinkling strings entwine themselves in the cottonwood branches. Biting her lip to hold back tears, Exe thought, *I'll never be able to perform the simplest magical task without putting people at risk.*

"The fault was ours, you know," Caulder's soft whisper startled Exe as he moved to sit close beside her. "We should've asked you how your wish magic worked before we ever tried training you. Then we would've realized that visualizing the outcome wasn't the way to go. You see, for the rest of us, connecting with our vades to perform spells is instinctive—because without that connection, we have little power to perform. You don't have that issue. So with you, we need to focus on the connection, not the outcome."

"How do we do that?" Exe turned away to hide her damp eyes.

"Simple. We need to break you of the habit of believing that having powers is a punishment," Caulder nudged her jovially. "I'm gonna teach how you to enjoy magic. Come on, it's fun! You know how to have fun, don't you?"

Caulder jumped up and circled around the Witch's Hat ride. The spookily named apparatus was simply a full-circle swing attached by chains to a single, tall center pole, creating an upside-down cone shape that gave it its name. Its design allowed the ride to both rock like a swing and spin like a merry-go-round. Puzzled yet determined, Caulder took a flying leap onto one of the long benches—and promptly fell flat on his back.

"Plaything? That contraption's a torture device," Caulder feigned fatal injury, then winked at Exe.

"You really need two people for this ride." With a reluctant smile, Exe helped Caulder to his feet and showed him how to clamber onto the Witch's Hat together from opposite sides. "It's all about balance. We just need to work in tandem."

Exe demonstrated how to get it spinning by propelling it like a skateboard. Caulder caught on quick, so Exe upped the difficulty by daring him to stroll around circular seat as it spun, mirroring her movements to keep the ride steady. Exe toyed with him, moving suddenly faster, then slower, forcing him to keep a close eye on her.

"And what happens if I make a mistake?" Caulder teased as he deliberately lurched the wrong direction. Instantly, the Witch's Hat wobbled off kilter, forcing them both to find their 'sea legs' fast as the whirling circular seat rose and sank beneath their feet. But the ride didn't slow as it should have once it began to rock as well as rotate. Instead it swayed and spun unnaturally faster and faster.

Exe laughed, loving the tingling thrill running through her as the tame playground ride suddenly felt like it belonged in an amusement park. After a few minutes though, a sort of seasickness set it. Pushing down a wave of nausea, Exe called to Caulder, "Fun's fun, but let's get off now."

"You're the one who knows how this crazy thing works. It's up to you to stop it if you want to," Caulder returned, hanging casually onto one of the chains. Exe glowered at him, *Clearly he's keeping himself steady with magic, while I'm barely clinging on!* Exe could feel the strength in her fingers starting to give out, "I'm serious, Caulder. Slow this thing down, or I'll–"

"Or you'll what?" he challenged. "Whatever it is, do it now. My stomach can't take much more of this. Come on, do it! You can do it!"

Exe shook her head and mouthed the word 'no' just as her fingers gave way. The wildly-whirling Witch's Hat launched her at the cottonwood tree at warp speed. Exe bounced as she smacked into the suddenly rubbery trunk, then felt herself wafted gently onto the seat surrounding it. *But I didn't even wish. Caulder must've saved me.*

In the next instant Caulder was beside her, brushing the hair out of her face, "Are you okay? I'm sorry, I thought desperation would work. That it would force you to forge a connection. And once you knew what that felt like, you'd be able to do it on purpose."

Exe sat up slowly, "I think it did, once. When I forced Velin's voice out of my head a few months back. I remember it, but I don't know how to recreate it."

"Really? What did it feel like?"

"Electric." Closing her eyes, Exe tried to put herself back in that moment when Velin's tsunami of thoughts almost drove her mad. "Pulses pouring inward, like they were racing toward my soul."

"Hmm," Caulder murmured, turning to consider the playground. "Got it."

In a blink, Caulder was suddenly standing atop the towering metal slide. With a slow smile he glided down the slide, still standing, like a surfer riding a wave. Caulder ran back up the slide, sat down, then held out his hand. Exe climbed the ladder and, at the invitation in his eyes, maneuvered until she was seated between his legs.

"Close your eyes," Caulder whispered, nudging her until she leaned back against him. "I want you to think about that hat contraption we were riding and the trigger word, 'coruscate'—but don't say it yet. Focus on recalling the feeling you had that one time you used your powers properly. When you feel a similar connection, say the word."

"What's going to happen?"

"You'll see..."

Eyes closed, Exe concentrated on the Witch's Hat, 'coruscate,' and remembering the connection. She felt Caulder ease them forward until they started to slide together. As they picked up speed, Exe felt her necklace thrum as if electrified and a swoony sensation pulsing inward in search of her soul. She whispered, "Coruscate."

Caulder chuckled as they slid to a stop. Exe's eyes popped open and saw every inch of the Witch's Hat illuminated, the metal glowing as if it were made of white neon lights. Fists raised to the sky, Exe jumped up and whirled around triumphantly. Caulder caught her hand and pulled her toward the merry-go-round. Using the trigger word, Exe lit the ride up and hopped on. Caulder set them to spinning and joined her, laughing joyfully as Exe lit up everything she laid her eyes on: the slide, the swings, the monkey bars, the jungle gym, even the water pump.

"I did it!" Exe jumped from the still-spinning merry-go-round to admire her work. "But what if someone sees? There are people everywhere. And tomorrow–"

"Don't worry. I shielded us from discovery, and we'll 'turn out the lights' when we leave," Caulder skidded the merry-go-round to a halt.

Smiling in reply, Exe raced him to the glowing swing set. Laughing and chatting as they swang, Caulder reminded Exe of other trigger words to try. Exe's necklace thrummed against the base of her throat as as she repeatedly created that swoony sensation connecting her to her vade. Around the playground, the dead grass grew green again, the heat-bubbled paint on the teeter-totter smoothed out, the broken swing's chain forged back together...

Emboldened by her success, Exe cast about for a task to really impress Caulder and took aim at the spindly cottonwood. Pumping her swing as high as she could, Exe leapt off at the highest point, wishing for the tree to expand until it was tall and wide enough to shade the whole playground and for the twinkling lights on it to transform into large paper lanterns scattered throughout the branches. Unparalleled power soared within her as she flew through the air, watching the tree transform before her eyes—despite the fact that she had no trigger words for that type of magic. Exe realized what she'd done the second she landed. *Wish magic! Always wish magic!*

Choking on a sob, Exe ran, barely noticing as the playground dimmed to darkness behind her. She heard Caulder calling after her, saw Easy's startled expression as she dashed by the dwindling crowd on Main Street, but she didn't stop until she'd reached the silent, shadowed cemetery behind her home.

"Tell me where you're headed next time so I can volte. There's not much call for running where I'm from," Caulder gasped when he caught up to her, breathing harder than the sobs that still wracked Exe. "Mind telling me what spooked you this time?"

"The tree. I used wish magic. I can't escape it," Exe collapsed against her tower.

Caulder sank down on a tombstone across from her, "So? Exe, you've been casting properly for all of an hour, at most. You've relied on wish magic your whole life. Of course that's going to come more naturally. It's habit. You can make proper casting a habit too, with a little work. Don't discount the progress you made today."

"Don't you understand? I want it stopped! Don't you realize how common wishful thinking is? And how dangerous it is when I do it? I'd rather have no powers at all than spend my life afraid of wishing! Why can't they just bind up my powers so that I can't use them?" Exe banged her head back against her tower door when spotted that despised disquieted look on Caulder's face. "What? What is it? Stop looking at me like that! Why won't anyone tell me what's so wrong with me?"

"Exe, I can't–"

"What am I saying? Viva already told me, and no wonder she despises me for it. I'm surprised you even agreed to train me at all, knowing what you know about me. I should be grateful. It was quite brave of you, taking me on. Thanks for at least trying to teach me. I promise to try very hard not to hurt or destroy you," Exe bit her tongue to keep from saying more. *I've already said too much.*

"What are you talking about?"

Exe raised her chin and wished for the Anacapian history textbook that Viva had given her to appear. It fell between them, opening to the pages Viva had marked.

Caulder knelt down and scanned the pages, his frown deepening, "And you believed this? Coming from Viva?"

"Are you saying that she lied? That she– I'll get her for this!" Rage building, Exe jumped up, cast the 'postern' spell (brushing away relief when her necklace thrummed), and tore into the field.

The time has come to have it out with my dear, diabolical sister.

CHAPTER TWENTY-THREE

CRADLE TO GRAVE

Exe stood still at the edge of the mirage, halted by the unwelcome memory of that infamous 'Wanted Dead' poster. *If the textbook's a lie, then why am I wanted dead?*

Textbook in hand, Caulder appeared instantly beside her, but he didn't say a word.

"I can't go chasing into Anacapia to find her, can I?" Exe asked. Caulder shook his head. "Why not? Why is it safe for Viva and not me? Am I really–" *evil?* Exe didn't want to hear the answer to that question. *Not from Caulder.* Instead she asked, "Why does Viva hate me so much?"

"Viva doesn't hate you. She hates who she is... because of you," Caulder explained, carefully setting the textbook on the boulder before facing Exe. "Viva's an outcast in our world, and that's made her angry and bitter. But when Viva's truly being herself, she's all charismatic confidence. A clever communicator. An independent thinker. Daring, captivating, the epitome of pure joy. She's got the kind of personality that would, under normal circumstances, make her the adored center of attention. And that's what she would be if not for—"

"Me," Exe finished for him.

She tried to put herself in Viva's position: no siblings at home, the twin of a girl wanted dead by the government, parents preoccupied with their fight against that injustice. *Is she just as friendless as I am, because of me? But that would mean...*

Exe glanced at the textbook, "It's not just the government that wants me dead, is it? Viva doesn't have friends because everyone in your world believes that book, and hates me for it. And everyone hates her too, because she looks like me, don't they?"

"Not everyone," Caulder comforted.

"Thank you," Exe smiled at him then looked away. "But that doesn't help much given that you'll be out of my life once my parents think I've been trained enough. I thought that, if I could get my powers under control and prove that I wasn't dangerous anymore, I'd be allowed to return. That's never gonna happen, is it?"

"Not anytime soon."

Exe turned her back on Caulder, desperate to hide the tears pouring down her face, "I'm sorry. It's just difficult to accept that I'm destined to be alone for the rest of my life. I'm only sixteen!"

"Don't say that," he put a comforting hand on her shoulder. It took all of her willpower not to shrug it off.

"It's true. I'm kicked out of Anacapia, the only place to find people like me. And I can't get close to anyone in this world, or they'll find out about my powers!"

"So what if they do?" Caulder looked at her curiously. "I get that you wouldn't want to advertise your powers

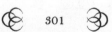

in a world without magic. People tend to get crazed and obsessive about those who have talent they cannot hope to gain for themselves—just ask Velin about that. But telling your family? Maybe one or two close friends? Why not?"

"Velin always stopped me from using or even talking about my powers. You think I could?" Exe turned to him with a budding hope, but the light in her eyes died the moment hers met his. "But I still don't get to see you," Exe blushed, then rushed on, "And I'll never get to experience my homeland. Nowhere is great, but just imagine if you knew nothing about Anacapia. Every time I look at this mirage while I'm training, I ache thinking about how little I know about where I'm from. Plus, I'll live my whole life on the run, looking over my shoulder. Knowing there's a whole world of people out there who'd kill me if they could. I'll wind up becoming a hermit, like Velin. Hiding from hate. Just waiting to die."

Caulder stared into Exe's eyes for a long moment, then took her hand and drew her through the mirage's waterfall. Exe teared up at the ache that hit her when they emerged in the Corpse Copse, "What are we doing here? I thought—"

"There's something you need to know. And I think you're only going to truly believe it, if you see it," Caulder said, leading her to a curly white tree with a trunk that looked as if it had been blown up like a balloon to the size of a phone booth. Opening a hidden door in the tree trunk, Caulder beckoned her inside.

Glancing at that tiny, enclosed space, Exe shook her head, "I can't get in that."

Seeing the stark, mindless terror on her face, Caulder stepped into the doorway and whispered, "Close your eyes."

Exe obeyed and felt his arms close around her. She kept her eyes clamped tight as she felt Caulder moving them into the cramped compartment. Her breath quickened at the thump of the door closing. Then she felt herself melting, tingling, the panic easing away. Another second and she felt like herself again as Caulder whispered in her ear, "You can open them now."

"Did you just volte me?" At Caulder's nod, she said, "It felt so different from when Asher volted me home."

Caulder smiled, "I've got a better spell. It's a talent of mine. Comes in handy when I'm volting delicate cargo."

Exe glanced shyly away, her eyes falling on a broken gravestone and a tiny, white coffin half-unearthed before it. Instantly, all the air felt sucked out of Exe's lungs as a deeply-buried memory seized her. *Screaming terror. Pinned in, unable to move. Breathless, choking sobs. Oppressive darkness. Clawing at satin.* Trembling, Exe knelt beside the half-buried, baby-sized casket and lifted the lid, exposing the torn, dirt-stained amethyst satin. *It's so tiny. I can't believe I was once buried alive in this coffin.*

"I guess this explains my claustrophobia," Exe joked to regain control. "It's bad enough just knowing that I was once buried alive; why did you feel I needed to see this?"

"That's not what I brought you to see."

Exe finally looked around to take in the whole scene. They were atop a lone, moonlit mountain in the middle of nowhere, with a dark, dangerous thicket surrounding them. But the clearing around her tiny, broken grave had become a sort of shrine. Someone had constructed a makeshift pavilion bedecked with thousands of ever-lasting roses in every shade of purple imaginable. The whole place overflowed with bouquets of flowers, wreaths, and fascinating trinkets adorned with amethyst ribbons. Tears welled as Exe took in the hundreds of images of herself, mostly that hated poster—with the word "Dead" obscured or torn off, so that it simply read, "Wanted."

"I have supporters? How many?" Exe asked, looking at the makeshift shrine.

"Thousands," Caulder said, then shook his head in answer to her next question. "Jettani's number in the millions. She clears this place on the eve of your execution every year and completely conceals it with that thicket. This is what your supporters have done for you in less than a week. It used to be guarded to keep this from happening, but now— I think she uses it to gauge the growing support for you and your family. You're not forgotten Exe, nor completely despised."

"I'm not?" Exe asked as Caulder picked an amethyst rose and tucked it behind her ear. "So Viva did fake that textbook? Everything in it is a lie?"

"Not exactly," Caulder hedged. "The textbook is real. But it's not the truth. It's just what our government wants people to believe. Viva never should've given that propaganda to you."

"Then what did happen? Why was I buried alive if the government wasn't trying to execute me because I'm... evil?" Exe sank down beside her open grave.

"The facts about what happened are true. Their story about why is a lie," Caulder knelt beside her. "Demaine and your parents plotted to fake your death because they knew Jettani was lying. She fabricated the doomed future she supposedly saw when she carried you into the Portal Portend as a baby."

"What's the Portal Portend? Some sort of crystal ball?" Exe asked. She'd heard of psychics and horoscopes, but she'd never thought prophecies could be real.

"Certainly not," Caulder denied. "Future-telling is not only an Inconceivable, it's absolutely impossible. There are too many variables that could change in a heartbeat. That's why Velin couldn't precisely reset time to its original state. He reset major events, but little things were different because he'd meddled with the past. That's why the future cannot exist in a way that can be foretold. Those who appear to predict the future merely possess the gift to interpret the hearts and minds of men."

"So what does the Portal Portend do?"

"As I understand it, the Portal Portend doesn't reveal a destiny set in stone. It simply shows you your true self. In our parents' day, they weren't carried through the Portal when they were born. Back then, it was a coming-of-age rite of passage meant to launch teens into adulthood with confidence in their ability to overcome adversity, independently and responsibly."

As Caulder explained it, when a teen was ready to be affirmed into their chosen path of magic, they would step into the center of the Portal—not to have their future dictated—but to learn of their potential. The Portal Portend opened each person up to clearly see the depths of their own soul, unclouded by emotion or delusion. The Portal exposed strengths and weaknesses, talents and fears, courage and cowardice. All of the potential within—both good and evil. When they stepped out of the Portal, they were filled with the knowledge of their own potential and the drive to pursue the path most suited to them.

Exe listened in rapt fascination. *It sounds like a sort of graduation, only more exciting. More personal.*

"My father says that, when the Portal Portend was used for its true purpose, it was always a positive affair meant to encourage the young to strive for their personal best. It was such a transformative experience that people would carry presages in with them to record this knowledge for future viewing," Caulder said wistfully. "All that changed when Jettani came into power. She's reduced the Portal Portend to a fortune teller."

"Even if the Portal could predict the future, why wouldn't Jettani use that knowledge to keep kids on the right paths? Why use it to condemn them to a life of Jettani's choosing?" Exe frowned. *Or death...*

"Power," Caulder said flatly. "There is no better way for a powerful woman to find potential rivals than to identify them at birth, before they realize their own power. Keeping kids from reaching their true potential makes Anacapia easier to control. Only Jettani's inner circle is allowed to go through the Portal as teens now, though even they do it on the sly. Presages are one of our top sellers to our wealthiest clientele."

They fell silent, contemplating the damage and deprivation caused by an unchecked government and too much power in the hands of a corrupt ruler. *Can nothing be done when a country's highest office turns its power against its people?* Exe had to stop herself from wishing that things could be different.

"Thank you for bringing me here. You have no idea how much I've been longing to see more of Anacapia. But this is it, isn't it?" Exe met Caulder's gaze across the grave, "This is the last I'll ever see of my homeland."

Caulder nodded, "We're working to change that. But it's slow, if not impossible."

"Inconceivable," Exe stood and moved into a rose-covered arch, straining to see as much as she could beyond the thorny thicket. The full moon illuminated the countryside, glistening upon the rippling waterfall mountain in the distance. The city atop it glowed like a bonfire, with a flickering, aqua-violet flame at its very center. *There dwells the woman who wants me dead. And there's nothing I can do about it.*

"Take me home," Exe called to Caulder, unable to bear the sight of Anacapia—the home she'd never know—for a moment longer. "How do we leave? We have to go on foot don't we?" Exe asked, remembering the long, dangerous walk she'd taken with Riven on her first visit.

Caulder shook his head and magically rolled a stone away from the mountainside, revealing a shallow cave. "We used this as one of our stash houses before your grave was discovered empty. Now it serves as a safe volting chamber for your supporters," Caulder explained, leading her inside.

Exe steeled herself, focusing on the magical feeling of volting with Caulder. When she opened her eyes, they were back in the Corpse Copse, and Caulder was pulling her through the cascade and back into the mirage.

"I guess this is it," Exe said.

"For today. We're not done yet. You've just figured out how to properly cast. I'll be back in two days for more training. Just me," Caulder said, letting go of her hand once she'd stepped out of the gathering pool. "I'd better go."

"Me too," Exe answered, but she stared after him long after he'd disappeared through the falling water. She'd been too heartbroken moments ago to really look at the homeland she was leaving behind, but now she was overwhelmed with the impulse to run back through the cascade.

Maybe I can convince Caulder to take me just to the edge of the Corpse Copse to see Anacapia one last time. But deep down, Exe knew that wouldn't be enough to satisfy her. *I want memories! If only it weren't so dangerous to look like me there. Although... Viva gets away with it. If only our eyes were the same color...*

With resolve, Exe gazed at the mirage from her tower doorway. *I may never be able to return to Anacapia openly, but one way or another, I'll find a way to explore my true home—before it's time to say goodbye forever.*

ALTER EGO

Exe stared at her aquamarine eyes in her dressing table mirror, comparing them to Viva's in the family picture Malina had tucked into the Entirety Tome. They were a perfect match. *I'm so glad I didn't scratch Viva's eyes out of the picture as I'd wanted!*

Contact lenses. The idea had come to Exe as she gazed after Caulder the other night. Wishing her eyes aquamarine was a risk she wasn't willing to take. (*What if they stay that way?*) And Riven had warned her that a temporary, active spell to change their color would be too easily detected. What she needed was permanent spell that would change her eye color only temporarily. While Exe didn't need glasses or contacts to correct her vision, Ella, Rove, and Moth did, and that's what gave her the idea. The rest was simple. She just ordered non-prescription lenses online, wished them the right color and voila—she had Viva-hued eyes.

Mimicking the rest of Viva's appearance might've been more of a challenge had it not been for the Verelustres' birthday gifts. The clothes from Malina were already in the right style, and Viva's enchanted brush took care of the hair. The hardest part would be convincing Caulder that she could pass for Viva in Anacapia.

Fooling him first was the wisest plan of attack, so Exe needed to get to their next private practice session early. *Or he'll know I'm not Viva when I arrive through the door rather than the cascade.* Slipping on sunglasses (just in case she happened upon a curious sibling), Exe sashayed down her tower stairs with a snotty swagger to help her get into Viva's snide mindset.

"Where's the clambake, kitten?"

Exe turned slowly at the sound of Easy's voice and spied him lounging in the doorway to the main house. Smiling, Easy said, "From the kooky costume, I take it that you're joining Monalea's efforts to start a Roaring Twenties Prohibition festival, despite the mayor's protests. But what's up with the strut? You look like one of those pompous, well-to-do ladies strolling down Fifth Avenue with a poodle, like in those old cartoons."

"Sorry, just trying to get into character," Exe muttered, resisting the urge to regard Easy over the rims of her sunglasses. "I'm gonna be out for a while. Tell Mom not to expect me for supper."

Easy nodded, "What else is new? You're back to being hardly here these days. Not ready to spill what you're up to? Okay. FYI, those shades aren't era-appropriate."

"I know," Exe smiled anxiously, waiting on Easy to leave—which he finally did after a shrug and a long sigh. As soon as he was gone, Exe properly performed 'postern,' strode into the field, and whipped off her sunglasses, scolding herself for overdoing her portrayal of Viva. *If Easy noticed that I was acting over-the-top, there's no way that I would've fooled Caulder.*

With a sudden panic, Exe realized that she had no clue how Viva normally behaved. *She can't be that awful with everyone.* She couldn't rely on appearance alone to trick Caulder, but she had no idea how to talk or act like Viva. Steeling her nerve, Exe tried to recall Viva's stance compared to her own, but every pose she tried seemed fake. As the minutes ticked closer to Caulder's arrival, Exe tried to remember how Caulder had described Viva to her. *Charismatic. Confident. Clever... Just like Easy.*

Exe mimicked how Easy had lounged against her tower door just as Caulder sauntered out of the cascade. His stride faltered when Exe tilted her head and half-smiled—as Easy so often did to her.

In a flash, Caulder was in her face, gripping her shoulders tightly, "What are you doing here? Do Asher and Malina know you've come? I swear, if you're trying to make trouble for Exe again, I'll—"

"You'll what?" Exe replied, with that convincing note of cloying menace in her voice that Viva did so well. Caulder let go of Exe and glared her down, "I'll have Asher and Malina bind your powers. It won't be so easy for you to torture your sister without access to your magic, will it?"

Exe turned away from Caulder and walked as casually as she could into the mirage, trying not to show her shock at this revelation. *Powers can be bound? Then why weren't mine? I asked them to, didn't I? Wouldn't that have been easier than training me?* As much as she wanted the answer, Exe would never ask that question. *I may have wanted my powers bound then, but not now.*

"Where is your sister, anyway? Her door is here, so she must be– Exe? Exe are you here?" Caulder paced the field as he called out, searching.

Exe sat down on the boulder, "I'm right here."

Caulder whirled toward the mirage, his eyes glancing over Exe then searching the foliage, "Where is she?"

"Caulder," Exe said to catch his attention. "I am right here."

Instantly, he was in her face again, staring hard into her aquamarine eyes, whispering a word she didn't quite catch. Once, then again. Horror tautened his face, "Exe? Tell me you didn't permanently dye your eyes to match Viva's."

"Nope. It's not a temporary spell, either. Rive–" Exe caught herself just in time. *Caulder doesn't know Riven's a double agent! Does he?* "Revealing my real eye color can only be done like this." Exe pulled aside one of her contact lenses so that he could see her eye's natural amethyst hue.

Smiling at the complete puzzlement on his face, Exe explained, "It's called a contact lens. The umm, what do you call them? The Hoi Polloi use contacts to correct their vision so that they don't have to wear eyeglasses. I take it you don't need anything like this in Anacapia? Which means no one will think to check for them."

Caulder's expression faded from fascination to dread, "No. You may have fooled me for a minute, but if you think I'm going to go marching you into Vianelle dressed as Viva? Not a chance."

"I'm not asking you to introduce me to anyone as Viva, but there's got to be a lot of places like my grave where people hardly ever go, right? Caulder, I know that I'm never going to be able to call Anacapia my home, but don't I at least deserve to learn a little about the country I'm from before I'm cut off from it forever?" Exe pleaded.

Caulder paused thoughtfully, "You'd be satisfied just seeing the countryside? Just locations and creatures? Creatures that can't talk," he qualified. At Exe's nod, he continued, "And you'd do exactly as I said while we're in Anacapia? Without question?"

"Did we need to interact much with others to enjoy Nowhere together?"

Caulder considered her for a moment, then said, "Alright, I'll show you a little of rural Anacapia, under one condition—you need to get Viva to agree to this."

"What?!"

"We never know when we're being watched. I'll not risk anyone realizing that there are two Vivas roaming around Anacapia. Do you realize how far the Disimulata can see with their telescoping sunglasses?" Caulder demanded. Exe bit her lip, *He's right. But I can't tell him that Riven's the one who showed me those sunglasses.* Caulder sat back with a small smile, "If you're masquerading as her there, then she'll need to be waiting for us here. It's the only way."

She'll never agree to that! Exe's mind screamed. Outwardly she remained calm, "Fine. Bring her to me, and I'll arrange it with her."

Caulder's surprise was gone in a blink. He stood and said, "Great. I'll go get her."

"Now?" Exe faltered.

Caulder sat back down, "Now. I'm not giving you time to come up with some clever way around my condition."

"Don't you trust me?"

"No," Caulder's warm smile took the sting from his reply. "You've got about five minutes to come up with your strategy to convince her. Good luck."

The second he vanished through the cascade, Exe considered every conceivable reason that might convince Viva to help her. But all she could envision was Viva's mocking, vindictive smile as she took cruel pleasure in saying no. All too soon, Caulder returned, followed by Viva—wearing a grin even more malevolent than Exe imagined. That grin faded at Viva's first sight of Exe.

"What is this?" Viva's eyes narrowed as she glanced accusingly at both Exe and Caulder. "You plotting to replace me or something?"

"Something like that," Caulder kicked back on the boulder with a wry smile.

Exe frowned at Caulder, confused by Viva's reaction until she remembered, *The contacts.* Viva launched herself at Exe, who instinctively stopped her with a blocking spell that knocked Viva flat on her back.

"Nice reflexes," Caulder raised a complimentary brow to Exe. Then he explained to Viva what contacts were. When Viva tried to start an argument over why Exe was wearing them, Caulder said, "Relax, Viv. We're just here for a copacetic confab. Your big sis has a favor she wants to ask you."

Viva rose, waved a casual hand to straighten her appearance, and regained her malevolent grin, "I wonder, would it be more fun to just say no now? Or let you plead your case, and then say no. What do you think, Exe?"

Exe clenched her fists to keep from slugging her sister. Taking a deep breath, Exe's aquamarine eyes met Viva's, "Look, we both know I'm never coming home. Anacapia is too dangerous for me, with or without Jettani in power. It'll never be safe for me. But it is safe for you."

Viva sneered, "I'm glad you've finally accepted the truth. But if you think I'm going to willingly swap lives with you—"

"Not permanently," Exe interrupted before Viva could walk away. "Not even swapping lives. Not really. It's just, sooner or later my training will end, and I'll be cut off from Anacapia forever. I accept that. But before that happens, I want to see a little of the homeland I'll never know. Not just in textbooks (Exe bristled at Viva's smirk), but in person. I want memories I can treasure once Anacapia's lost to me forever. Caulder has agreed to take me, only to places where we won't meet any people. But only if you agree to wait here while we're there—so that there's no chance anyone will spy two Vivas in Anacapia at the same time. So, what do you think?"

Viva stared at Exe stonily for several endless seconds. Exe's mind raced over all the bargains she might've made and the reasons she should've stated to persuade Viva, but it was too late now. *My fate is in Viva's hands. And I already have her answer.*

"I'll do it."

"What?!" Caulder bolted off the boulder to grab Viva's shoulders. "Are you nutso?! You're agreeing to let Exe go traipsing around Anacapia masquerading as you?"

Viva shook him off, "Absolutely. On three conditions." Hope imploding, Exe crossed her arms and waited. Viva said, "Condition one, you perform absolutely no magic while you're in Anacapia. If you do, they'll find you. Condition two, Caulder doesn't let you interact with anyone while you're disguised as me. I'll not have you making a fool of me by acting like a naïf in front of people."

"Agreed. And condition three?" Exe asked, ignoring Caulder's shaking head.

Viva's vicious smile was back, "I get to go exploring in your world as you, while you're exploring my world as me."

"Only if condition two applies to you too," Exe said, knowing that Viva would take this opportunity to make trouble for her if she could. "You don't interact with anyone while you're in Nowhere disguised as me."

"No deal," Viva smirked. "You're the one asking the favor, not me. I'm happy to just stay home. But if I'm going to be stuck here while you're off enjoying Anacapia, then I want my chance to make my own memories to treasure. Take it or leave it."

Exe hesitated barely a second before shaking Viva's hand to seal the deal. *Any damage she does, Easy can quickly fix, right?* She yanked her hand away when Viva tried to turn it into a strength contest and turned to Caulder, "Well? No time like the present."

"Surely you can't be serious?" Dumbstruck, Caulder turned from Exe to Viva, only to see identical, expectant expressions on their faces. "We need to plan this out! We can't just go waltzing in there!"

"What's to plan?" Viva shrugged. "You've got cruor-protected stash houses all over the countryside. Your little sister, Dodger, told me that the one by the Silver Sands is all but empty because you're overdue for a smuggling run. You can take Exe there right now. Relax, Dodger only revealed that information while trying to weasel details out of me about your mysterious absences with Rande. It really rankles her that you won't tell her where you disappear to whenever you're training Exe," Viva added to quell Caulder's outrage over his sister's slipup.

"If Asher and Malina ever find out, they'll murder me," Caulder caved.

Viva smiled in triumph and headed towards Exe's tower door, "Shall we meet back here in say, three hours?" Caulder nodded and led Exe toward the cascade.

"Wait!" Exe called out to Viva. Suddenly, everything was happening too fast. "What if you run into one of my brothers and act like you don't know who they are? Or what if someone tries talking to you about stuff that you should know? Maybe—"

"I'll wing it," Viva called back with cruel humor.

"You can't go into Nowhere looking like that!" Exe released Caulder's hand and dashed after Viva before she could open the door. Viva glanced down at her cool, Deco clothes and gave a nonchalant wave of her hand. Instantly, she was transformed into a bedraggled version of Exe, complete with violet eyes, rat's nest hair, ragged jeans, and a worn, holey concert tee (with Def Leppard spelled 'Deaf Leopard').

Flashing Viva a ha-ha-very-funny glare, Exe wished her sister into a better representation of herself, with properly brushed hair and a correctly-spelled shirt. Still, Exe was reluctant to let Viva go into Nowhere. *It'll take hours to give her all the information she needs!*

"We need to go now, before I wise up." Caulder paced impatiently in the mirage.

Unwilling to miss out on this opportunity, Exe ran back to the mirage, shouting instructions to Viva as she ran, "There's a family photo by my bed, upstairs in the tower you'll enter. Everyone's names are on back, but you may need to match them with the school photos that are pinned to the bulletin board above my bed. Easy's most likely to ask questions, but he doesn't know– No one knows I have powers, so don't go using them in the open! What am I forgetting? Oh, don't–" *read my diaries.* Exe stopped herself just in time. *Because that's the first thing Viva would do if I ask her not to.*

Exe didn't bother trying to think of more instructions because both Viva and the door had gone. With one last glance at where it had been, Exe turned an adventurous smile on Caulder and led the way into the cascade.

Exe didn't panic this time when Caulder pulled her into the volting tree. When she opened her eyes, she found herself on a wavy sea of snow—only the weather was too warm for that. *Silver sands.* Kneeling down, Exe let the silky, blindingly white sand slip through her fingers as she surveyed the endless horizon of silvery dunes.

A flash of red caught her attention, "Is that a fire?"

At the base of the silky sand dune they stood upon was an enormous, blazing pool. The sand around the inferno glowed red-orange in the flickering light reflecting off its rippling surface.

"The Lake of Fire," Caulder smiled and caught her hand, pulling her forward until they were slipping down the drift.

They came to a stop only inches away from the fiery lake. To Exe's surprise, the water wasn't actually on fire—or water at all. Instead, it was a lake of glassy pebbles, slightly larger and flatter than the micro-beads that made up the mirage's cascade. The stones in the center of the lake were pure bright yellow, which rippled into a circle of brilliant orange, which in turn darkened into a deep, fire-red. After an encouraging look from Caulder, Exe tentatively touched the pebbles. They were hot but not blazing to the touch and as silky as the mirage's 'water.'

After checking his pocket watch ("To ensure there are no Disimulata nearby."), Caulder conjured a blanket so that they could lay back against the sand dune. Once Exe was settled beside him, Caulder pointed up at the sky.

Exe gasped at the sight of three luminous tornados pirouetting across the dunes on the far side of the Lake of Fire. The trio of cyclones glided over the surface of the lake, their elegant tendrils intertwining lyrically. As they reached its yellow center, a large geyser shot up between them. Then another, and another. Suddenly, dozens of what looked like see-through seahorses glowing an iridescent blue sprang out, vaulting from geyser to geyser in a sort of dance.

"What is this?" Exe breathed, unable to take her eyes from the sight, only glancing at Caulder when he didn't respond.

"Mating ritual," Caulder confessed, suddenly shy under Exe's questioning gaze.

Blushing, Exe looked away and tried to think of a less-embarrassing subject. *I could ask where his stash house is, but then he might think I want to leave. What did Viva say about it? His little sister, Dodger.*

"I didn't know you had a sister," Exe blurted, cutting Caulder off as he muttered something about the sand. "Her name's Dodger? Why didn't you tell me about her?"

"Probably because Dodger doesn't like to be talked about," Caulder relaxed. "Her real name's Decany, but never call her that, or she'll sock you. Not that you'll ever—" Exe cast him a sidelong glance as he rushed on, "Dodger's eleven years old and she is the prettiest, daintiest little girl who'll ever curse your kneecaps off if you cross her."

"My brothers would love her," Exe laughed.

"She's been helping us with our smuggling business for over a year now. Trust me, we tried to keep her out, but— Well, she's smarter and craftier than us, especially when dealing with shifty characters. Dodger can elude any pursuer, unearth the best-paying buyer for even the most obscure objects, and she can spot swindlers and welchers every time. We haven't once lost money or goods since she's joined us. She handles the selling mostly, and Rande insists that one of us be with her whenever she's working. But she's pushing to go out solo. Says we chase off skittish buyers. Claims they're the big spenders, but that's just a ploy to persuade Rande."

"Wow, I never realized how big your smuggling business is. I guess I've never really asked about you. I'm too obsessed with my own issues," Exe scolded herself.

"It's true. And I don't know why," Caulder sighed dramatically. "It's not like you were buried alive after a faux execution. Or like you're wanted dead by a corrupt government. Or that you've been living on the run for your entire life. Or anything extraordinary like that. Compared to you, I'm fascinating."

Exe nudged him playfully and turned her attention back to the nature show, sighing as the reflected setting sun turned shimmery silver sand dunes to gold. As twilight rose and the dunes glowed blue under the moon, the cyclones dissipated. In the stillness, Exe whispered, "Are there many other places as beautiful as this?"

"There's little beauty left in Anacapia," Caulder murmured, staring blindly across the faintly glowing lake. "Don't get me wrong, much of Anacapia is picturesque. But it's tainted by oppression. Do you know why our smuggling business thrives? It's because so many magical items are banned here, and the only ones who can afford most of the goods we smuggle in are wealthy elitists. That'd be fine, if it weren't by design. It's rich politicians who purposely brought on this oppression to satisfy their lust for power. Our people are deprived on purpose, to make them easier to control. And each time I come back from countries unmarred by totalitarian injustice, I become more resentful of Jettani's tyranny.

"There are lands out there where people are free to come and go. Where they can learn all they want to learn. Earn as much as their strength and intellect can earn them. Where people are free to do, see, say, be. And each time I see the freedom in those places, I'm tempted to stay," Caulder's voice turned wistful. "To leave Anacapia for a land where freedom already exists. To abandon Anacapia's ungrateful inhabitants to the fate they seem so determined to deserve. But then, though I envy their freedom, those lands are not mine. For better or worse, Anacapia is my home. And if I must sacrifice body or soul, life or limb to keep her safe, then that's what I'll do."

Exe sat silent, gazing up at the billions of twinkling stars in the midnight sky, realizing for the first time that Asher and Malina's fight against Jettani wasn't just about her. Though he didn't realize it, Caulder had just reignited a flicker of hope. *No people can stand to be oppressed forever. Despotic dictators always end up overthrown. History has proven that out time and again. Maybe I can come home... someday.*

"We should go," Caulder pulled Exe to her feet and vanished the blanket.

"Now? We can't have been here for more than an hour. We've got two left," Exe said, trudging up the sand dune after him.

"We've got a ways to walk," Caulder held her hand to help her slide down the opposite side without falling.

Exe swiftly realized why they'd left so soon. It took the better part of two hours to cross the dune-waved desert. And while sliding down was always fun, it grew harder and harder to climb up the slippery sand. Eventually, Caulder led her to an outcropping of rocks at the edge of the desert, and effortlessly lifted a large rock as if it were made of Styrofoam. The seal on the faux stone popped like a cork as Caulder pulled it from its hole and beckoned Exe to crawl into the revealed tunnel.

Within a few feet, Exe was able to stand upright, but she halted at the soft sound of grunting up ahead. Caulder pulled the stone stopper into place and pushed past Exe, urging her into the shadows with a glance.

"Looking for something, Dodger?" He called out, conjuring a ball of light to proceed him into the chamber. It joined with another ball of light spotlighting a slight figure perched atop a stack of crates.

"Finally you showed, Caulder," a sweet voice cried. The merged ball of light illuminated the head of the tiny girl like a halo. "I called you over an hour ago! Why'd you bother with the door? Do you know where we left that half-case of presages? The Dankworths want another, although I don't know why. It won't change what was revealed about that pathetic son of theirs. Unless they're getting one for someone else. Schade's due to go through, I know. Riven already tried to buy one from me, but I refused to sell that scuzzball anything. Ah-ha! Here they are. Guess I just needed your luck, not your help. Who's that?"

Exe's breath had caught when Dodger said Riven's name, but she'd hoped it had gone unheard. *Clearly Dodger heard it*, Exe thought as she shrank further back into the shadows. The adorable, doll-like child kept her eyes riveted on Exe's shadowed silhouette as she bounced down the crates, her fairy-light dress floating around her.

"Viva? What are you two doing together?" Dodger flitted to a halt in front of Exe.

"Can't keep anything from you, can I, Dodger?" Caulder ruffled Dodger's curls and pulled Exe from the shadows. "We were just taking in the tornadoes, but we've gotta get going now. Sorry I didn't get your message, scamp."

"Oh," Dodger drawled knowingly, ribbing Caulder with the velvet-bagged presage that she held. "Is she why you've been so hard to find lately? Don't tell Rande."

"What is that?" Exe asked, eying the small velvet bag—a split second before recalling Caulder's graveside explanation of presages and the Portal Portend.

"What do you mean?" Dodger stared at Exe like she was crazy. "You know it's a presage. You've got one of your own at home. You made me swear not to tell— oops."

Caulder shot Exe a look of outrage. Then, realizing she wasn't actually Viva, flashed her an apology with his eyes.

Unfortunately, Dodger caught this quick shift in his expression. "Viva didn't tell you about sneaking into the Portal, did she? Or did she? Wait, what's going on?"

"Sweetheart stuff, Dodg. You wouldn't understand," Caulder said, putting his arm around Exe's waist. "Listen, I need to take Ex—ellent care not to vex Viva. You know how prickly she can be." At Caulder's warning squeeze, Exe shot him her best, Viva-like glare. Caulder then turned a stern eye on Dodger, "I don't care how well you know the Dankworths, you don't deliver that alone. Wait here while I volte Viva home."

"Why do you need to volte her ho– ohhhh," Dodger drawled knowingly again, making kissing sounds on her hand.

Caulder rolled his eyes, then Exe was melting, tingling, and suddenly they were back standing on the midnight banks of the river in the Corpse Copse.

"What took you so long?" Viva was already leaning against Exe's tower door when they came through the cascade, tapping her foot impatiently.

"We hit a Dodger-sized snag," Caulder smiled wryly. "So, we're dating now."

"What?!"

"What else could I say when she spotted us together?" Caulder asked.

Viva kicked the door and fumed, "Great, that's just what I need."

"Thanks for the complement," Caulder glowered at her. "It's for the best anyway. Dodger will spread it around, so it won't be suspicious if anyone does spot us together. Unless you're ready to call it quits."

"No!" Exe and Viva exclaimed in unison.

After a mutual glare, Viva demanded that they tell her everything that had happened twice over. Once Viva was satisfied that she could retell any detail of the trip if asked, she bounded toward the mirage.

"Wait, what about me? I need to know what you did in Nowhere," Exe called.

"You'll find out," Viva flashed her vicious smile and disappeared through the cascade. Before Exe could express her outrage, Viva's head popped back out through the falling water, "By the way? Velin knows."

As Caulder and Exe exchanged a shocked glance, Viva continued, "He knew I wasn't you almost immediately. He said if you want him to keep quiet, you'd better write every detail of your Anacapian adventures into your diary. He wants pictures too. Apparently you're some kind of artist? I can't imagine you having anything resembling talent. Abyssinia!" And with her Cheshire grin, Viva disappeared again.

Exe walked around on pins and needles the next day, terrified of what Viva might've done, but she needn't have worried. Velin must've told Asher (and Asher told Viva) that Exe preferred to be a loner—because all Viva did while in Nowhere was make a bunch of friends. As the weeks passed, whenever Viva played the role of Exe, she made sure to be the life of the party. Exe was surprised to find that she didn't mind at all.

True, it was a little annoying to have strangers coming up to her all day to discuss past fun, future plans, or just to chat about people and events that she had no knowledge of. It was even more irritating to have all of her brothers congratulating her for finally coming out of her shell and making 'real' friends. But in reality, Viva had actually done Exe a huge favor. *Not that I'll ever tell her.*

Now that Exe had her powers under control (a fact that became more evident with every training session with

Caulder), she wasn't feeling so dangerous or afraid of accidentally hurting anyone anymore. While she still took care to avoid wishing, her main reason for staying friendless was gone. And now she had a bunch of genuine friends— without having done the hard work of meeting them in the first place. *Viva just saved me from the embarrassment of asking Easy to help me make friends.*

Having friends and being comfortable in public was the icing on the cake to the most perfect spring Exe had ever experienced. Once or twice a week, while Viva was enjoying herself in Nowhere, Caulder took her on incredible adventures in Anacapia to see fantastical sights that Exe could scarcely believe were real, even while seeing them with her own eyes. Even being forced to write about these risky trips in her diary for Velin to scrutinize didn't dampen her spirits. (*Maybe he's not just prying or spying. Maybe he's just homesick and wants to experience Anacapia again through my entries.*)

Exe gazed up in wonder at the sparking cobalt cliffs that resembled a mammoth glacier. Known as The Deadening, here Caulder's father and others mined the infamous bluestone—a building material used to construct prisons and other structures because it sapped magical energy and prevented using powers completely (unless you wore specialized gear to block its effects). Under Velin's careful stewardship, Caulder told her, the mine had thrived as the bluestone replenished itself, albeit slowly. But now the stone was being depleted due to Jettani's thirst for the control it provided.

Exe marveled at the sight of dragons flying overhead as they perched upon a pitching mountaintop in the Craggy Sea. Caulder explained that they were actually floating on a sandy seabed that tossed the rocking mountains to-and-fro, and occasionally into one another. Both the unpredictable swaying of the range and the fierce dragons served as protection for Anacapia's southern border.

Caulder arranged a twilight escapade to show Exe the beauty of the Neon Beach. (Viva gladly agreed so that she could attend one of Easy's epic parties.) In the evenings, the ebony sand glowed deep purple and illuminated the cove like a blacklight. Within the waters, a multitude of psychedelic sea creatures gleamed neon, making them an easy catch for the fishermen (too far out to sea to notice Exe and Caulder).

Once he even took her close enough to view the waterfall mountain with the capital city of Vianelle at its peak. From a safe distance, Exe delighted at the sight of the ferries defying gravity and rushing water as they cruised up and down the roaring cascades to a dock jutting out of the mountaintop. When they reached the dock, the sideways-sailing ships were scooped up with what looked like a giant bubble wand so that they floated horizontally, allowing passengers to bustle on and off.

The telescope Caulder provided let Exe see some of Vianelle above the city's high walls. She was primarily fascinated with the palace where Jettani reigned. The soaring spires of Incendia had undulating walls made of violet fire falling into aquamarine water that cascaded upward like a fountain. A glistening mist formed in the center where the two contrary substances met. With a whispered command, Exe tried to refocus the telescope on the Portal Portend, but she could only see the tips of some ivory arches above the city walls.

As she strained to see it, something Dodger had said bothered Exe, "Dodger said Viva has a presage of her own.

She's been in the Portal Portend by herself. She knows what Jettani saw about her."

"Seeing her presage won't help you," Caulder took the telescope from Exe and nudged her back down the forested hill. "You and Viva are two very different people."

"I know that," Exe glared at him as he led the way into an abandoned cottage at the foot of the hill. "But if she can get into the Portal with a presage, maybe I—"

"No," Caulder said with finality as he opened a trapdoor in the floor. "It was enough of a risk showing you the city from a distance. Going inside would be suicide, no matter how good your Viva disguise is. They'd know you weren't her after talking to you for two seconds, and you couldn't avoid talking to people within Vianelle."

Resigned, Exe glowered at Caulder and let him volte her back to the Corpse Copse. As much as she wanted to argue the point, it wasn't worth jeopardizing future Anacapia adventures by reminding Caulder of the risks. And a disturbing thought had just occurred to her, *Apparently, everyone in Anacapia would know instantly that I'm not Viva. So why is it that no one in Nowhere suspects that Viva's not me?*

CHAPTER TWENTY-FIVE

CAUGHT DEAD

"Alright, kid. Show me what you got," Caulder challenged, bracing himself beside the mirage so that it could cushion his fall should Exe actually succeed in casting against him this time.

While Exe would've preferred to spend every moment with Caulder exploring Anacapia, Rande occasionally insisted on seeing her train to assess her progress. Luckily, despite the fact that they did more adventuring than training these days, Exe had proven to be a quick study now that she could connect to her vade—except today.

Today, Caulder was attempting to teach Exe how to use an opponent's protective forcefield against them. The spell was designed to strike the invisible shield with enough strength to break it, or push against it with enough pressure to force your opponent backward. Unfortunately, the trigger word was "winkler." Instead of properly casting, Exe kept dissolving into fits of laughter because every time she said the trigger, visions kept popping into her head of slow-mo

Fonz battling Mork from Ork on a particularly silly episode of "Happy Days."

Caulder's bemused expression as she'd tried to explain her amusement only made her laugh harder. The one time she finally did manage to get the trigger out, Exe hit his shield so hard that he went sailing through the cascade into the Corpse Copse. That sobered her up fast, as the comical sitcom scene was instantly replaced with flashbacks of Riven's shoulder impaled on the fallen log. And just in time too. When Caulder limped back into the mirage, he'd had Rande with him.

"Sorry, Exe. I was talking to your sister," Caulder apologized, motioning Viva forward instead. "Show me what you got, Viva."

Exe moved aside, glowering at Viva's preening as she stepped forward to show off. Unfortunately, Viva had convinced Asher and Malina to let her join Exe's training sessions. Viva said that she'd only asked to join the sessions to cover for her own absences from home while Exe and Caulder explored Anacapia, but Exe knew that was just an excuse. Viva really came along to mock Exe's inexperience. She never got the chance, though.

Exe used Viva's scornful presence as motivation to up her casting game. And once Viva realized how good Exe was getting, she insisted on joining in, determined to show her sister up. Exe was grateful to discover that she was more than a match for Viva on those occasions when Caulder had them duel one another.

Only Caulder and Viva knew that, though. Whenever Rande showed up, Exe had to downplay her progress so that he wouldn't call a permanent end to their sessions.

So, as galling as it was, Exe was forced to give Viva the upper hand under Rande's watchful eye. While Exe dreaded Rande's brooding presence, Viva found it absolutely delightful—because she could show off her 'superior' skills. And even though Exe knew that Viva wanted their twin swap adventures to continue as much as she did, it always felt like Viva was trying to provoke Exe into exposing her true power. Like now.

"Pay attention!" Rande snapped Exe out of her thoughts to watch Viva slowly but surely forcing Caulder backward into the mirage. "That's the kind of measured control you need to master. If you can mirror even a smidgen of Viva's finesse, maybe you'll quit casting every trigger like you're swinging a sledgehammer."

Exe bristled as Viva strutted by with genuine confidence in her own abilities—and Exe's expected failure. *And she's right for once.* While Exe outclassed Viva in power and stamina, Viva had her beat when it came to precision, restraint, and control.

Caulder smiled encouragingly as Exe stepped forward to take her turn, but he took extra care bracing himself against the edge of the mirage. Exe swallowed hard and tried to recall all Caulder had told her about reining in the force of her casts. *Take control of the trigger, like easing air out of a balloon instead of popping it. Release, don't fire.*

Tamping down the urge to use wish magic to make it appear as if she'd mastered control (*That would wipe the sardonic smirk off Viva's face*), Exe whispered, "Winkler."

WHAM! Caulder went flying toward the cascade again.

"Arrestant," Rande commanded. Caulder immediately ceased moving.

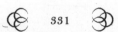

"Thanks for the save, Rande," Caulder called as he hung suspended in midair. He pulled himself out of the hold with an elegant backflip and landed on the emerald grass with catlike grace.

"You're still letting your magic master you," Rande reprimanded Exe. "I expected better after all the time Caulder's spent on your training. You'd do well to learn 'arrestant' so that you can save the victims of your overcasting yourself in the future."

"I'm so sorry. I don't know why I can't seem to control the force of my spells," Exe flushed at that half-truth. *You'd probably do better if you actually spent more time training and practicing*, Exe scolded herself, inwardly rolling her eyes as her conscience played Velin again.

"If I don't see improvement soon, we'll need to rethink our training methods. Again," Rande scowled as turned to go. "If I have to involve myself more—"

"She'll get the hang of it," Caulder promised. "We'll practice more tomorrow."

"That was magnificent!" Viva applauded the second Rande vanished into the cascade. "My sister, the sledgehammer."

"Yeah, magnificent that Rande's gonna involve himself more," Exe glowered, slumping down on the edge of the mirage.

"I'll talk him out of it," Caulder said, sitting beside Exe to give her a one-armed hug. "Actually, I'm glad you're in such a good mood, Viva. Maybe you'll say yes to letting Exe meet some Anacapians tomorrow?"

"What?!" Viva screeched. "Don't be demented. Just who do you think she could meet that wouldn't instantly know that she's not me?" Exe winced at the reminder that she couldn't pass as Viva, but her twin had no problem fooling the Parsells. Thankfully, Viva didn't notice.

"I want to introduce her to the Flaneur."

"Oh. Fine. But you'll owe me," Viva replied as she too vanished into the cascade.

"Who're the fla-newer?" Exe asked.

"You'll find out tomorrow," Caulder smiled mysteriously.

"Welcome to the Placid Pools," Caulder murmured, after volting them just inside the gated entrance to a glorious garden filled with grottos, fountains, ferns, and flowers—all surrounding a magnificent series of interconnected pools.

Every inch of the Placid Pools inspired serenity. Clear, sweet water rippled invitingly where the pools were fed by a natural spring. The silvery-opal mosaic pool tiles glistened enticingly against the moss-covered marble walls that completely enclosed the garden. Yet it wasn't the beauty of the pools that took Exe's breath away—it was the dozens of exquisite, vacant inhabitants floating and playing in the pools or lazing around the edges on chaise lounges.

"I didn't expect so many people," Exe edged behind a potted palm. "What if someone realizes I'm not Viva?"

"They won't. Even if anyone here was once a close, personal friend of Viva's, they wouldn't realize you weren't her. They wouldn't even remember her if she were here. Because these people aren't really people anymore," Caulder explained. "They're the Flaneur. People who've entered the pools to gain immortality, only to become prisoners, eternally compelled to remain. Here they are undying and un-aging, but they must stay forever within the confines of the Placid Pools. Forever satisfied, forever youthful, forever vapid. And completely incapable of leaving. If anyone did leave, they would die the moment they stepped outside the garden walls."

"Why did you volte us in here if we won't be able to leave?" Exe stared warily at the beautiful, listless creatures, yet felt strangely enthralled by them, and by the pools.

Caulder laughed, "Don't worry. We'll be able to leave when the time comes."

Exe only half-heard him. She was already slipping away into tranquility as she explored the gracefully arching alabaster pavilion that surrounded the pools. Under a vined pergola, several Flaneur languished on piles of plush pillows, entranced by the achingly ethereal songs of the Sirens that wandered amongst them. Others surrounded a majestic cornucopia overflowing with luscious fruit, which magically refilled itself as they ate. Small natural pools swirled in the corners of the garden, where more Flaneur were dipping in silver goblets to drink their fill.

Across the pools, a practically perfect young man lay draped across a jewel-encrusted chaise lounge atop a dais. Dozens of the listless creatures gathered at his feet, hanging on his every word as he slowly popped grapes into his mouth between phrases.

"Fainéant. The Teller of the Unending Tale," Caulder explained when Exe stepped toward the young man, caught in his thrall. "He tells the most mesmerizing saga ever heard. You'll never be bored by him, but his story never reaches an ending. It's fabulously fascinating. And absolutely frustrating. Care for a swim?"

Caulder was already diving into the pools by the time Exe realized that he'd magically changed into a swimsuit. Exe caught herself before using 'novaturient' to alter her own clothes, *I cannot use magic in Anacapia or I might get caught!* Clearing her throat to catch Caulder's attention, she gave him a look of impatient expectation.

"What are you waiting for?" Caulder smiled innocently.

Goaded, Exe dove in after him, feeling her clothes transforming about her just before she cut into the crisp, clear water. Time past swiftly as they ate and drank, listened to Fainéant for a while, and played amongst the Flaneur, occasionally drawing them into inane conversations.

Exe felt every fear, every worry, every desire, every thought drifting further away, until she found herself whispering, "I could stay here forever."

The split second she said those words, a searing, blinding, pain ripped through her, as if her insides were being boiled in hot oil. Her head plunged under the water as the blazing agony doubled her over. Water flooded into her lungs scorching her throat.

I have to get out of the water. Ignoring the shooting pain, Exe drove herself to the pool ledge, her hands clawing uselessly at the slick tiles. Suddenly, strong hands grasped her underneath her arms and hauled her from the pool. Hard thumps forced watery coughs from her lungs with every jerk. When she could finally focus her eyes, she realized that Caulder had pulled her beyond the garden gates.

"What happened?" Exe coughed as if she'd been breathing in smoke. Her insides ached. Though the scorching torment had finally receded, Exe thought she could smell the scent of burning flesh.

Caulder leaned over her, "Are you okay? I am so sorry! I should've warned you to pay attention to how you were feeling."

"What did you do to me?" Exe coughed again and rolled onto her side. She knew there was nothing left to cough up, but inside her throat, the fiery sting still lingered.

"I cast a 'time's up' spell on us both as a precaution," Caulder smiled sheepishly. "The only way to get stuck at the Placid Pools is to decide deep in your soul that you want to stay forever. The 'time's up' spell is a painful last resort to prevent that from happening. I can't believe I forgot to warn you that we had to leave the moment you started to feel like staying forever."

"That's okay. You didn't do any permanent damage. Did you?" Exe asked with half-amused suspicion as she let Caulder help her up.

Caulder laughed and half-hugged her, "No. Not yet anyway." Laughter fading, Caulder transformed them back into their clothes and leaned in. The quivery shivers running through Exe iced into terror as she heard a series of chillingly-familiar electric cracks. *That's the same sound Hastings made when he found Riven and I on the road.*

"The Jette Set," Caulder breathed, immediately pulling Exe to the ground and rolling them into a shrub covered in sickeningly sweet-smelling flowers. Through the leaves, Exe spied a half-dozen boys dressed in ebony Gatsby caps and black Cossack jackets lounging by the pool's gate. Standing tall amongst them was, *Riven!*

"Why'd we volte here, Schade? I thought we were settling the score at Progloria," Riven said in a drawl so jaded and superior, Exe barely recognized the voice as his.

A stockier, nastier version of Riven answered with an sinister smirk, "We are, big brother. Just here to get rumble ready, right boys?" Most of the boys flexed their arms and rubbed their hands together in gleeful anticipation. Only one kid looked nervous.

Riven checked his pocket watch impatiently, "Let's drift, Schade. I gotta report on duty soon."

Schade just laughed and scanned the Flaneur for a target, "Don't be a killjoy, Riven. What's that Verelustre dish gonna do-to-ya if you're late, bat her lashes? How that dame ranked general, I'll never know. Let's roll in. First to make one scream wins the head start."

When Schade and his friends strolled through the gate, Riven sighed, snapped his pocket watch closed, and followed. Exe glanced at Caulder, silently asking if they should make their getaway.

Caulder shook his head and whispered, "Don't move a muscle. That's the Torsade brothers, Riven and Schade, and their brutal buddies. Those two would kill you just for the sheer pleasure of it, let alone the reward and glory."

Caulder doesn't know Riven is a double agent, Exe reminded herself, biting her lip to keep from defending him. *What would Caulder say if he knew that I carry Riven's 'in case of emergency' coin with me on every Anacapian adventure, just in case.*

"Those twisted thugs, blitzing the Flaneur because they know they can't get away," Caulder said in disgust as the sounds of chaos wafted over the garden walls. "They're so far gone in oblivious tranquility, do you know the depths of torture it'll take to make one scream?"

"Like shooting fish in a barrel," Exe shuddered and kept her eyes fixed on the gate, silently pleading for someone

to scream. (*The temptation to wish for it to happen is almost unbearable...*) Suddenly, a haunting cry rang out as a beautiful girl ran through the garden gate. The moment she crossed its threshold, the girl aged in an instant, then crumbled to ashes. An eerie silence fell.

Whoops of triumph broke the stillness as the Jette Set thugs raced to the gates. "And the tyro wins the head start at Progloria," Schade pounded the nervous kid on the back in congratulations. "Let's blow, boys. Time to find out who's the big wheel and who's all wet. Unless any-of-ya wanna punk out?"

In answer, Schade and his friends volted away. Only the nervous kid remained. He fell to his knees in the girl's ashes, "I didn't mean to make her run. I just needed her to scream. I couldn't bear it if I finished last, and Schade– Is this murder? Am I gonna end up like those Gyve kids?"

"Scram, before I rat you out," Riven stalked up behind him. Still kneeling, the nervous kid vanished. Riven's eyes were riveted on the ash pile, his face twisted with inscrutable darkness.

"Look at him, sneering at that poor girl's remains as if she were worth less than nothing," Caulder's bitter whisper startled Exe.

He looks like he despises what was done to her, Exe thought, but she didn't dare contradict Caulder. Riven stretched his hand out toward the girl's remains, then hesitated. After a moment, Riven pounded his palm with his fist and vanished.

"I'd better take you home," Caulder said, helping Exe up out of the flowery shrub. "I'd intended to show you Progloria today too, but we can't risk that now."

Exe brushed herself off and frowned at him, "Already? We've still got several hours before Viva's set to meet us. What'll we do in the field all that time?"

"I don't know, maybe train? You know, that thing your parents think I'm doing when I come see you?" Caulder winked at her, then headed toward the gate. He knelt down by the girl's ashes, head bowed.

Exe bowed her head too. *The poor soul was so afraid of death, she chose to exist in mindless immortality, only to die so cruelly.*

With a whispered word, Caulder elevated the ash pile, floated it through the gate, and settled the girl's ashes into the earth around a plant blossoming with bleeding heart flowers. After a moment of silence, Exe gazed around in horror at the carnage. Everywhere she looked she saw urns overturned, seats smashed to smithereens, and exploded pillow feathers coating the destruction like snow. The bloody, disheveled Flaneur huddled against the walls in shellshocked silence. Only Fainéant droned on, though he hung askew off of his jeweled chaise which had been knocked off its dais. In deference to the traumatized Flaneur, Caulder whispered his triggers as he slowly worked to put the Placid Pools back together.

I really do need to spend more time training, Exe thought as she struggled to think of any trigger words she could use to help. Recalling how Viva had healed herself while Asher was freeing her from the boulder, Exe almost used 'Sospital' to heal a wounded Flaneur. She stopped herself just in time and turned to Caulder, "Is it safe for me help?"

"I don't think they track casting way out here. And I doubt they can discern who's casting what spells yet, either. That's probably why the Jette Set chose to play their sadistic game here. But still–" Caulder said. "Better not risk it. Besides, Viva would kill you if she ever found out."

With a sigh Exe stood back and let Caulder repair the damage alone. Once everything was put right, Caulder stood in the center of the grotto and said low and slow, "Somnifacient." One by one the Flaneur nodded off into a deep, healing sleep, including Fainéant, who began to snore midsentence.

Taking Exe's hand, Caulder led her into a secret alcove concealed between two fairy fountains. Pitched into darkness once the door closed, Exe let Caulder pull her into his arms, but instead of volting immediately, he rested his chin on the top of her head, "I need a minute. That took more power than I anticipated."

Leaning against him to hide her shyness, Exe asked, "What is Progloria anyway?"

Caulder gave her a squeeze, "An abandoned game field with a significant history that I thought might interest you. I'll take you there and tell you the story someday soon. We've got time—unless you're planning to suddenly improve. Your progress has been shockingly slow."

Exe playfully pinched him, "You know I've been faking in front of Rande so that he doesn't end our training."

"Oh really?" Caulder replied as Exe felt herself melting, tingling. "I say you're all moxie. Care to shut me up?"

When she opened her eyes, Caulder was already dashing through the Corpse Copse' cascade. Exe chased after him, lurching when he whacked her with a spell the second she stepped into the mirage. She hit him back with a barrage of triggers that sent him reeling as far back as the field's etched fence.

They sparred playfully, although Exe found she had to call 'time out' to rest more often than Caulder did. After an hour they took a longer breather on the mirage's boulder, and to Exe's surprise, Caulder recovered before she did.

"You've got a lot to learn, Moxie," Caulder said, bestowing the nickname on Exe with a cheeky wink. "You hit too hard and too fast for too long. That's why you get winded so quickly. It takes finesse to balance your casting, mixing in simpler spells that pull less power to distract and deflect. Unless you take your target down with that first intense volley, you'll always be beaten in the long game. Ready to try again?"

Exe nodded as she hit Caulder with an intense trigger, then dashed into the mirage's foliage to take potshots at him with less intense spells as instructed. By following Caulder's strategy, Exe conserved enough power to wear him down and get the upper hand. Caulder took to conjuring objects to serve as obstacles and cover. Exe did the same as they moved from outright battling to covert attacks.

"I knew it," Rande's chilling voice cut through their cheerful conflict.

I can't let him see me dressed as Viva! Exe dashed behind her tower door. Resorting to wish magic, Exe instantly changed into her Arizona clothes and removed her colored contacts.

"Rande? I thought you weren't training with us today," Caulder called.

Rande growled, "Since I knew you were both lying to me, I had no qualms about lying to you. No one as powerful as Exe could stay as consistently mediocre as she has—unless she was faking it. And now I've seen proof that I'm right."

"Of course I'm better when you're not around. Caulder puts me at ease. You make me nervous," Exe said, stepping out from behind the door. "If you've been eavesdropping long enough, you'll have heard Caulder telling me that I still have a lot to learn. I've got no finesse, nor any control over my casting intensity. Right?"

As Caulder nodded his agreement, Exe spotted the tower door's knob turning. She leaned back against it as casually as she could to keep Viva from coming into the field. *Rande can't learn that Viva's been spending time in Nowhere!* Leaving the door open a crack so that her twin could hear Rande, Exe hoped Viva would be wise enough to not force her way into the field.

"Nerves or not, this little battle proves that you're more than trained enough to keep your powers in check," Rande snapped. "And teaching you that is all we agreed to do. Velin can teach you the finer points of control. I know Asher's been working on him to take over your training. Of course, Asher and Malina will want to see for themselves that you've got your powers under control. That'll take some doing to arrange, but after that, we're done." Rande turned on his heel and marched through the cascade.

"What have you done?!" Viva burst through the door, catapulting Exe forward.

Caulder caught her before she hit the ground, "Rande caught us sparring while we were waiting for you. Exe wasn't downplaying her progress."

"It can't be over!" Viva and Exe exclaimed at the exact same time.

"Can we convince Rande to give us more time?" Exe asked.

Caulder shook his head, "Rande has always considered training you a distraction from the real fight. He wants it done as soon as possible. It's for the best. We were almost caught by the Jette Set today."

"What?!" Viva gaped at him. After Caulder explained what happened, Viva said, "You're lucky you weren't discovered. Perhaps it is best this is ending now."

"But today can't be the last time I see Anacapia," Exe exclaimed, shuddering at the memory of the Flaneur girl's death. "Rande said it'll take time to get Asher and Malina here to see my progress, right? Can't we risk just one more trip?"

Caulder and Viva exchanged a look.

"This Saturday night. I'm invited to a party," Viva glanced at Exe disdainfully.

Exe rolled her eyes, "There's always a party. And I'm always invited."

"I'm sure your brothers would rather have me there as you, instead of you. Right sis?" Viva mocked. "Or are you fine not seeing Anacapia again?"

"I'm sure they'd prefer you," Exe ground out.

"You should know that I've been invited to this one by a boy I'm– you're dating."

"A boy I'm what?!" Exe exploded. "Who?!"

"Figure it out for yourself," Viva flashed that Cheshire grin of hers. "I'll give you a hint—he's one of your online friends."

"Online? But I don't have any social media accounts."

"You do now."

"You got into my phone?!" Exe fumed but bit back a nasty retort. *I will not let her goad me into missing my last chance to see Anacapia.* They both turned to Caulder.

Caulder held Exe's pleading look for a long moment then said to Viva, "If it's at night, I'm taking her to The

Wendings." When Viva looked like she might object, Caulder added, "I'm sure it's practically deserted since the Gyve kids–"

"Fine," Viva glared at Caulder for a moment, then turned to Exe. "But you'd better remember conditions one and two if I let Caulder take you to The Wendings. No magic. No talking to anyone. You got that?"

After Exe nodded, Caulder and Viva disappeared through the cascade. But Exe lingered in the mirage, contemplating in bittersweet anticipation what The Wendings might be. It was a welcome distraction from the distressing realization that, *I'll soon be saying goodbye to Caulder—and Anacapia—for the very last time...*

CHAPTER TWENTY-SIX

Burden of Proof

Sprawled across her bed, Exe picked flecks of whitewash off the wall, watching the shadows of her balcony railings lengthen as the sun dipped low outside her window. For once her tower wasn't ringing with high-pitched giggles, but tonight the silence wrung Exe out like a dishrag. Only the occasional yawp from her younger brothers cavorting with friends in the cemetery cut through the quiet. The suspicious absence of her three eldest brothers meant that they were up to the kind of distracting shenanigans Exe needed right now.

Exe's anxious anticipation for Saturday night had become increasingly unbearable. All she could think about was Anacapia and her fear that Asher and Malina would end things before she had a chance to say goodbye to her homeland—and Caulder.

Unfortunately, Viva's new friends made waiting worse as they talked to Exe incessantly about the upcoming party. (*On the other hand, maybe I should thank Viva. Worrying about which Nowhere boy might be her date for Saturday night has been a welcome distraction.*) Exe spent the rest of her time buried in Nowhere's goings on, as the whole town was alive with expectant happiness over the coming Spring Festival and the last weeks of school. But the current stillness left Exe with too much time to run through every possible worst-case scenario that might prevent her last adventure.

As the railing shadows lengthened to prison bars, Exe dug her fists into her eye sockets. She jerked her hands away quickly when she felt a sudden coolness compressed beneath one palm as if her chilly pendant had somehow crept into her hand. One eye flew open at the surprise, but the other stayed shut—its lid held down by cool metal.

Exe plucked it off and stared at the twinkling sliver coin. *Like the silver dollars they place over the eyes of the dead.* Exe suppressed that morbid thought, recognizing the silver dollar as the one Riven had given her. *I must've subconsciously wished for it while thinking about my upcoming farewell trip into Anacapia.* Exe had been toying with the coin a lot this week out of desperation at the thought that she'd soon be stuck under Velin's thumb once again. During those hours spent contemplating the coin, Exe had studied the words and images imprinted on both sides.

Its etchings were amazingly detailed and lifelike, as clear as a tiny photograph captured in relief on shimmering silver metal. The back side of the coin depicted a stone colonnade sheltering three statues facing inward. If they were looking at something in their midst, Exe couldn't tell. This image was surrounded by three mysterious words: Rochda, Lasis, and Veresos.

As captivating as that monument was, Exe spent more time pondering the front side of the coin. Some of the terms on this side of the coin, like Seren and Rara Avis, were just as unfamiliar as the ones on the back, but the text under the exquisite woman etched onto the coin read: Jettani Invidia.

She was the most beautiful woman Exe had ever seen. Gracefully waved hair framed delicate features on a perfect, fragile face, tilted in such a way to seem both regal and approachable. The expression on that flawless face exuded a kindness and strength that said all was right with the world. *And yet this woman is the reason I can't go home.* Exe spent several sleepless nights staring at that angelic countenance, puzzling over why Jettani had targeted her.

Why? The thought ricocheted around her mind like the endless questioning of a toddler, until she felt as if she'd explode if she didn't get an answer. *What damage did I do as a baby that warranted a death sentence!? Would Riven tell me the truth?*

Exe contemplated the coin for several long moments as it glistened enticingly in a beam of fading sunlight. *How would Riven react if I dropped this right now and claimed that I summoned him by 'accident?'* But calling Riven wouldn't be right. She couldn't ask him to risk his life just to console her, not when it was all almost over. *Answers can't help me now.*

Exe crawled out of bed to put the coin away. She unhurriedly navigated the shadowy stairs, as if slowing her pace might help her come up with an excuse to use it. It didn't. With a sigh, Exe opened her mostly empty jewelry box. The coin Riven had given her was still there. Exe glanced back and forth between the two coins. *If this coin isn't mine, that could only mean it's–*

Exe raced down the last flight of stairs, performed the 'postern' trigger on her tower door, and flung it wide. There

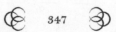

was Riven, pacing in the mirage. Exe sprinted into the field, intent on flinging herself at him like a drowning victim clutching at a life preserver. The glare he threw over his shoulder stopped her short.

"What took you so long?" Riven growled, still pacing.

"It took me a minute to figure out I had two coins," Exe bit out, hurt by his sullenness. "You never mentioned that you might summon me. Why did you?"

Riven stopped and faced her, "I need you to take me to your home. Now."

"Why?" Surprise edged Exe backward. Her eyes lingered on the Disimulata pin fixed to Riven's lapel, then flew to his face. Wild thoughts flickered within her as the image of the dead Flaneur girl surfaced.

"To dig up the graves of Hastings and Bates," Riven replied as if it were obvious.

"You want to dig up the dead Disimulata?" Exe asked in confusion.

"It's the only way, or so I'm told," Riven moved toward her, his pace deliberate. "Not that I agree. But I have to follow orders." Exe matched his pace, backing away from him until her spine hit the thin edge of the open door. Riven took the coin from her and strode on by, not meeting her eyes. "You coming?" Riven called, stepping into her tower.

"Not until you tell me why you want to visit their grave," Exe hedged.

"I need evidence to plant. Their pocket watches should do. Maybe their lapel pins too. It's the only way it'll be safe for Asher and Malina to visit you. Or so they say," Riven scowled, taking in the details of her tower bedroom. "Security's been tightened since those Gyve kids were caught. Now I'm the only one of the Sub Rosa who's not constantly watched."

Exe blinked at him for a moment, "I'm gonna need more than that. Who are these Jive kids?"

"You got any factions in your world that others detest and distrust just for being who they are? Well, we've got the Gyve, and they are universally despised," Riven sighed and leaned against the doorframe. "See, part of the problem is that no matter where the Gyve are born, they don't identify with that nation. They're loyal only to one another, not their country or their community. The Gyve are tight-knit, closed-mouthed, and nomadic. They aren't fond of obeying any laws but their own, either.

"At least, that's their reputation. So most countries run them out whenever too many gather in one place. We've got a lot of Gyve because Anacapia was forced to take 'em in from other countries as part of the surrender treaty Jettani signed to end the Horology Wars. Personally, I think it was all part of her plan."

"What plan? And what does this have to do with me?" Exe studied Riven, trying to piece together what this had to do with the dead Disimulata buried in their cemetery.

"Aside from vilifying you, Jettani and the Jetton Coalition—her political party—hold regular rallies and parades that malign the Gyve. She even shunted most of them to a derelict port called The Wendings where most Anacapians feared to go," Riven said.

The Wendings?! If this is true, then why does Caulder want to take me there? Exe caught herself before she asked Riven that very question.

"Jettani ratchets up fear and hatred of the Gyve to unite Anacapia against a common enemy. That way no one looks too hard at what she's doing to keep all Anacapians under her thumb," Riven continued.

"So she lies about them like she lied about me? The Gyve aren't as bad as she says?" Exe asked, outraged.

"Who knows?" Riven shrugged. "It'd be suspicious if I befriended any to find out. But they've done a fair job of fixing up The Wendings. Many Anacapians visit there now. Well, they did."

"So what did these Gyve kids do that got security tightened?" Exe asked.

"They put a costume on a statue," Riven answered flatly.

"What? You've got to be kidding!" Exe laughed.

"It isn't funny," Riven rebuked her. "They put a Tyrian costume on a Jettani statue, and they're going to die for it."

"Die? For a prank?" Exe's mind flew over all the stunts her brothers had pulled.

"Jettani's been putting the screws to the Gyve for years. Restrictions on where they live, how they travel, what they say, who they associate with, the types of jobs they can hold—even limits on the number of kids they can have. So some Gyve teens have rebelled by stealing Jettani statues and placing them in embarrassing situations, or dressing them up. The fools even put a Velin costume on one once, which is the real reason she's out to get them, in my opinion," Riven scowled.

"And Anacapians are okay with kids being sentenced to death for a joke?" Exe asked, wondering if the publicly given reason for her execution order was just as flimsy.

"The people of Tyria were mysteriously wiped out about thirty-five years ago," Riven replied. "So Jettani's legal team successfully argued that their wardrobe choice constituted a death threat—an act of treason punishable by execution in

Anacapia."

"That's ludicrous! Did Asher and Malina and the Sub Rosa protest? Is that why Jettani's coming after them?" Exe asked.

"Are you nuts? They'd be up for execution along with the Gyve kids if they did that. Most of the Sub Rosa work for Jettani in some capacity, so she using this 'Gyve uprising' and the missing Disimulata as an excuse to surveil any suspected subversives under the guise of national security. Your parents can't make a move without Jettani knowing because they're being 'protected' by the Disimulata. But if those kids are convicted of killing the missing agents..."

"Wait, you're going to frame those Gyve kids for the murder of the missing Disimulata just so my parents can make one visit here!?" Exe exclaimed. *They want to get rid of me that badly?*

"Not my idea," Riven defended. "I refused to do it until they were sentenced to death for the statue lark. It can't get any worse. For them. And if the disappearances are explained, Asher can leverage that to get the minders off the Sub Rosa's back."

"But any doubt Anacapians have about Jettani for killing innocent kids will be wiped away if they're found guilty of murdering her Disimulata. And what about the rest of the Gyve? Won't they be persecuted more after this frame job?" Exe argued, astounded that her birth parents would condone this.

"Those were my arguments to Asher and Malina," Riven nodded his agreement. "But your mom convinced me—although this may not be right, it's what's best for the cause. And that's true. Once it's done, they'll be free to fight Jettani more aggressively. And free to see you, too. Now will you take me to the bodies?"

"We can't get to the bodies yet. My little brothers are playing in the cemetery," Exe said, still reeling over what Asher and Malina were willing to do for their cause.

"Sounds like something my little brother would do. Schade has no respect for the dead. Or the living," Riven scowled.

"That's not fair," Exe defended her little brothers. "My brothers have a great respect for the dead. As far as they know, no one's been buried there for over seventy-five years, and I guarantee you that Moth's unearthed the history of every soldier interred in our backyard. Stories that everyone else has forgotten."

"Sorry, I guess I'm on edge at the thought of seeing Hastings' body again," Riven apologized, then relaxed and smiled for the first time. "So, how long do we wait?"

"It shouldn't take long. It's almost curfew," Exe replied. Riven's almost happy acceptance about the delay surprised Exe as he began poking around every level of her of tower, delighting in the strange, non-magical 'contraptions.'

"This your family?" Riven asked, indicating the photo on her vanity of herself and the Parsells in full costume that they'd taken at one of Nowhere's many festivals.

"Yes. We don't normally dress like that," Exe blushed at how ridiculous she looked in the picture with her bonnet and spectacles.

Riven just smiled as Exe urged him outside into the cemetery. (*Who knows what other embarrassing things he'll find!*) Waiting in the tower's shadow, they watched the moon rise over Velin's house, their eyes straying to the firefly flashlights marking her little brothers and their friends as they raced around the cemetery.

"Your brothers look like they're having fun," Riven breathed deep and closed his eyes, looking younger as his scowl-lined face relaxed. "I can't even recall a time when I was free to play. With a life like this, why did you ever come looking for Anacapia?"

"If you'd grown up with a cruel madman like Velin in your head, you'd go looking for answers too," Exe gazed up at Velin's house, dreading the too-soon day when he'd be her only contact with the magical world.

"I can't picture Velin as a cruel madman. People say that kids flocked to learn from him back in the day. But you wouldn't know that. I keep forgetting how little you know about us. We grew up hearing all about you, notorious naïf, " Riven lifted one lid to peer at her.

Exe shuddered as she thought about the awful story she'd read about herself in the textbook. Desperate to turn the topic, Exe said, "Asher must really trust you now. Sending you here, telling you about Velin."

Riven slid down the wall until he was sitting at Exe's feet, "He trusts the spell you suggested—the mind vaults work. I'm the guinea pig that proved it. Besides, it'd be just as suspicious erasing you completely from my mind, given how notorious you are."

Exe crouched beside him, contemplating how gray her life had become. As complex as her childhood was, the concepts of right and wrong, and good and bad, had still been black and white. Now everything she held true felt murky. "What makes someone evil?" Exe unintentionally uttered the dark thought aloud.

"I don't know," Riven said, eyes still closed. "Greed, anger, hatred, power, birth."

"Do you really believe that some people are born evil?" Exe shivered. *I thought I'd put this dark idea to bed. Why can't I quash it?*

Riven was slow to answer her, "Maybe. Look at my family. My mother is Jettani's closest confidant, my little brother lives to torment others, and my father pretends honorability, but he once betrayed his kin to save his own skin. And me?" Riven thumped his head back against the wall, "I'm preparing to frame a couple of innocent kids for a murder I committed. Does that make me evil? You tell me."

Exe could only stare at him as the blinding light of 'no' blotted out the dark, shadowy 'yes' that lurked within her.

"The lights are gone. Let's get this grave robbing over with," Riven interrupted her confused thoughts. Up the hill they trudged to the original grave where both bodies were now buried. Riven whispered a trigger and the hardened burial mound began to crack and crumble. Both Bates' body and Riven's briefcase arose from the dusty earth. Though no stench accompanied the corpses, Exe's nose wrinkled at the few bits of leathery flesh still clinging to Bates' dirty bones.

With tentative hands, Riven set the briefcase aside and rifled through Bates' black trench coat until he found his ebony pocket watch. The rasping rip of fabric split the quiet night as Riven tore the insignia off his fraying lapel. Pocketing the evidence from Bates' body, Riven set his briefcase atop the corpse, but he couldn't seem to make his thumbs flick open the latches.

"I'll do it," Exe offered, stepping up as Riven moved aside. Exe opened the case and closed her eyes, but not fast enough. The image of Hastings' squashed, waxy face with its grotesque, twisted lips and the gaping black holes that had once held his eyeballs burned bright against her closed lids. Beside her, she heard Riven retch. Three quick trigger spells and Exe opened her eyes to find Hastings' lapel pin and ivory pocket watch resting atop the closed briefcase.

A bright beam sliced through the darkness. Headlights from a car turning onto the dirt road beside their house briefly spotlighted Exe and Riven before moving on. Riven swiped up Hastings' belongings as Exe hastily reburied the bodies.

The car stopped in front of the house across the dirt road where an adorable elderly couple lived. Exe motioned for Riven to hide behind a tombstone as she spotted three stealthy silhouettes emerge from the car. The three shadowy figures tiptoed across the road—heading straight for them.

Riven and Exe huddled deeper into the shadows as a new swathe of light cut across the cemetery. Rove had flung her tower door wide and was now striding across the graveyard in his pajamas. A fainter ray spilled out from the house next door as her elderly neighbors toddled out in their bathrobes and slippers.

"I think my brothers just got busted for joyriding," Exe whispered.

"What's going to happen to them?" Riven's voice tensed with heightened alarm. Exe couldn't risk explaining. The elderly lady and Rove had caught up to her brothers right in front of the gravestones where she and Riven were hiding. The elderly man lingered by the vintage 1930s car that her brothers had stolen and returned.

"This isn't what it looks like, Dad," Seph began.

"What were you thinking?" Rove's voice boomed. "You're

almost eighteen, Seph. A few more months and you'd be convicted for carjacking as an adult."

"I'm impressed you got that old jalopy running," the elderly lady said, more amused than upset. "Ralph's hung on to that heap since we were courting."

"You've spent years training us to repair old vehicles, sir," Easy risked reminding Rove. "You had to know we'd be tempted by the Woolley's 1939 Lincoln Zephyr Coupe. With original interiors."

"Really?" A spark of interest broke Rove's stern expression, but only for a moment. "Do you truly think stealing a rare, classic car excuses your behavior?"

"We didn't jack it, sir. Just took the beauty out for a test drive," Thone rolled out.

"Never thought I'd see Betsy purring again," the elderly man had tears in his eyes when he joined them. "You boys must've spent hundreds on parts to get her running. Spiffed up her looks, too. How can I thank you?"

"Did they ask your permission to touch your car? To drive it?" Rove's hard tone said his sons weren't out of hot water just yet.

"We wanted to surprise them," Seph and Thone said together—as rehearsed.

"We didn't ask because we didn't want to disappoint the Woolleys if we couldn't fix her. We know how much you both adore Betsy," Easy's face beamed innocence.

"One good turn deserves another," Rove's own expression said he recognized that his sons were trying to pull a fast one. "Six months of yardwork ought to repay the favor, don't you agree, boys?"

"Ralphy and I are too old for yardwork. But I can still bake pies," Mrs. Woolley replied. "What flavors do you boys like?"

"You misunderstand. My brothers and I will be maintaining your yard to repay you for the privilege of fixing up your car," Easy explained.

"How wonderful!" Mrs. Woolley clapped her hands. "Landscaping's such a challenge for us these days. I think I will bake you those pies."

"That's some favor. I thank you. If you'll take over yardwork permanently, Betsy's yours to borrow anytime," Mr. Woolley seemed close to tears again.

"As long as you ask first," Rove added.

"Care to go for a midnight spin like we used to?" Mr. Woolley asked his Mrs.

"Oh Ralphy, I thought you'd never ask," she replied. Holding hands, the Woolleys strolled home and hopped into Betsy. Under Rove's watchful eye, Exe's eldest brothers marched inside.

"Twenty years locked up. That's what'd happen to them in Anacapia. Here they get yardwork and pies? You're lucky to live here," Riven jumped up as soon as Rove closed her tower door. "Shortly after I plant this evidence, Asher and Malina will be free to come see you, and then– I should go."

"That's it? Isn't this the last time I'm going to see you?" Exe hugged herself as Riven turned away, unbelievably hurt by his casual farewell.

"Do you care?" Riven glanced back over his shoulder. At Exe's tremulous nod, he said, "I got you a birthday present. I was going to give it to you when you used the coin to call for me. But you never did."

"I'm sorry. You said I should only use it if I was in trouble," Exe said.

"Or if you needed me. I guess you didn't need me," Riven shrugged then pulled a beautifully-wrapped box from his jacket and handed it to her.

Exe barely glanced at it, "It's not that I didn't want to see you; you said it would be dangerous. If it was safe, why didn't you come see me?"

"Couldn't risk showing up when another Sub Rosa member was hanging about, now could I?" Riven replied, then glanced down at the package in her hands. "Aren't you going to open it?"

Exe hesitated, torn between wanting to argue that he should've come to see her on his own, and feeling grateful that he hadn't come unannounced and discovered her secret trips into Anacapia with Caulder. Abandoning her inner battle, Exe tore into the giftwrap and revealed an enchanted snow globe with an exquisitely-detailed miniature version of Vianelle inside.

Riven took the globe from her, shook it, and the little city flickered to life with lights, traffic, and little strolling people. A flick of a switch, and the filigreed decoration atop the globe transformed into a magnifying glass. Gazing into the magnifier, it slowly dawned on Exe that she was observing the city's actual nightlife in full swing.

"It's a bird's-eye view of Vianelle in action," Riven confirmed her suspicions. "It's not detailed enough to make out who's who among the people, but you can explore every inch of the city. I thought you might like to see it, since you can't– Do you like it?"

"This is the best present I've ever received," Exe swallowed hard as she met his eyes over the snow globe.

"It's nothing. A tourist trinket. Street vendors sell them by the thousands," Riven ducked his head, then met her gaze again. "But I'm glad you like it."

"I love it," Exe hugged the snow globe to her. "It's a bit of home that I can keep with me forever."

"Forever. I guess this is goodbye," Riven murmured, taking a step back from Exe. "Those brothers of yours look tough. They'd never let anything happen to you, would they?" At Exe's nod, Riven added, "Velin did right, giving you to them. It's been swell, doll. Don't you forget about me." And in the next instant, he vanished.

CHAPTER TWENTY-SEVEN

RARE FORM

Regret echoed in every footstep as Exe paced her tower hour after hour early Saturday morning. Regret that she hadn't reached out to see Riven again these last few months. Regret that she hadn't invited him to stay longer on his last visit. And selfishly, regret that she hadn't asked him to stall planting the evidence until after her final Anacapian adventure. *But what reason could I have given without betraying Caulder?* Nothing short of the truth would've worked, and that would've only angered Riven.

Although she hoped that Asher and Malina wouldn't be free to test her today, deep down Exe's intuition said different. Exe had written so much in her journal these past few days about her regrets and her worries over what was happening in Anacapia, that Velin had deigned to send her yesterday's copy of Anacapia's newspaper. The headline article stated that the government's minder program had been suspended now that the Gyve teens had been executed for the murders of the missing Disimulata.

Of course they'll come today. My birth parents were willing to frame innocent teens because they want me cut off from Anacapia as soon as possible. But why is that so important? Because I'm in danger? Or because I am a danger? Exe pushed the dark thought aside and focused on the problem at hand.

If I'm right, if Asher and Malina do test me today, then they'll seal off the mirage when they're done, and I'll never see Caulder or Anacapia ever again. Her only hope was to find a way to stall them herself. *It's only one more night.*

Just then her necklace began to glow. With a deep breath, Exe grabbed her vade, performed 'postern' on her tower door, and stepped into the field to face down her birth parents who were determined to end everything.

Asher and Malina stood alone in the mirage. Resentment bubbled, seeing them standing there so casually after so long. Asher was guarded and mildly impatient, looking polished and remote in his double-breasted, herringbone suit. Malina was bright and carefully optimistic, looking as pressed and authoritative as Rove in her crisp, steely blue military jumpsuit.

Exe raised her chin defiantly and asked, "Are the flowers in bloom?"

"Only the roses," Asher's eyes narrowed. "Why do you ask that of us?"

Exe turned a small, flat smile on him, "Rande taught me well to always ask that of any strangers I meet in this field. Didn't he tell you all about that lesson in his reports on me? And after all, we are strangers."

"As obstinate as ever. I see gaining control over your powers hasn't improved your attitude," Asher's jaw tightened. Malina put a hand on his arm and tried to interrupt, but he simply covered her hand with his and pushed on, summoning

Exe's vade to him. "Since you have no interest in pleasantries, shall we simply get to it? Velin has transcribed new spells into your vade—without your knowledge. Again. You'd do well to leave the book in his keeping if you've no interest in securing it yourself."

"You have no say in what happens to my vade—or me— after today. Can we get on with this?" Exe returned.

Asher raised a brow and paged through her vade without touching the pages, "As I said, we've added new spells. I'll give you the trigger word, you'll properly connect to your vade, and you'll perform the spell."

"You aren't going to tell me what the spell is supposed to do?" Exe frowned.

"This way we'll know whether or not you're connecting properly," Asher leveled a steady gaze at her. "Rande has reported that you don't need to know what a trigger does in order to perform it. In some ways, knowing impedes your ability to connect to your vade, and you slip into wish magic."

Exe shrugged, "Fine. Let's go."

For the next hour, Asher called out unfamiliar trigger words and Exe performed each spell flawlessly, and powerfully. 'Petrogenesis' expanded a speck of dirt into a large rock, 'lugent' caused the stone to weep water, then 'buccellation' shattered it into a million pebbles. (*Just like Asher tried on the boulder when it fused with Viva's legs.*) 'Scathefire' conjured a small, wildly scorching blaze that Asher had her immediately freeze with 'gelicide.' 'Carapace' created a shield that blocked attack spells sent her way by Malina, then 'murklins' shrouded the field in a brief, deep darkness, giving Exe precious seconds to run with 'celeripedean' giving her a boost of speed.

When Exe took a quick break in the mirage to catch her breath and splash a bit of the refreshing microbead water on her face, Asher snapped her vade closed. Looking at Malina, he said, "There's several dozen more, but I think we've seen enough. She's clearly mastered control over her powers and is no longer a danger to those around her. Velin can take over her training from now on. When he's ready."

Malina folded her hands behind her back and regarded Exe with a look that was regretful, yet strangely speculative, "I'd have to agree. Her innate command is undeniable. With a little restraint and finesse..."

Exe sank down on the boulder, her mind racing, *They're going to close the entrance to Anacapia. I have to convince them to keep it open for just one more day!* With a nod to one another, Asher and Malina joined hands and stepped in front of her.

Asher handed Exe her vade then cleared his throat, "I'm sure you didn't expect– When you came looking for us– If things were different... I wish–" Asher cut himself off as he locked eyes with Exe. Clearing his throat again, he continued, "I regret that we have to part. But I'll rest easy knowing that you're safe and happy with a good family. You've the power now to do wonderful things for them. Let Velin guide you as to what's appropriate. In all things. He's a great man, underneath the bitterness. You'd do well to take advantage of the opportunity his tutelage provides. It's an honor that many have craved, but few have received."

"I've so longed to see you. And now that I have, it makes it a million times harder to accept that I'll not get the chance to know you," Malina reached out a hand to brush aside Exe's hair. "Please believe me, we are in this fight for

you. If Anacapia is ever safe, we'll come to you. I promise."
After a few solemn moments they turned to go.

"That's it? That's the goodbye I get?"

Asher stilled, "Sending you away the first time killed
something inside of me. Staying dead to emotion is the only
way I can think to survive saying goodbye again."

Slowly Asher held out an arm. Exe ran into their
embrace. Being hugged by them for those scant precious
moments felt both strangely uncomfortable and like coming
home at the same time. All eyes were damp when they
finally broke apart. There were no words left to say. Asher
and Malina eased back toward the cascade.

"Wait! You don't even– I don't even–" Exe glanced
around wildly. Her eyes fell on the boulder and an image of
Viva trapped in the stone flashed into mind. "I don't even
get a chance to say goodbye to my sister?"

Exe tried not to falter under Asher's penetrating gaze as
he said, "It's obvious that there's no love lost between you
two. Why the sudden desire to see her again?"

"You think I want it that way?" Exe balled her fists
to keep from lashing out to blame Viva's nastiness. "Am
I supposed to live happily ever after here, knowing that
I have a twin sister out there who hates me? Don't we
deserve the chance to mend fences, even a little?" Exe gritted
her teeth at the thought of ever trying to patch things up
with vicious Viva, *But I have to sell this.*

Malina seemed to consider the notion, but Asher said, "A
magnanimous idea, however we cannot keep access to you
open any longer than absolutely necessary. Our public axing
of the minder program has Jettani redoubling her efforts to
spy on us all. Should another Disimulata find their way to

you– We cannot risk it. We'll tell Viva that you wanted to reconcile. I'm sure she'll be grateful to know that... someday." And again Asher and Malina turned into the cascade.

"There's something wrong with me! And you know it!" Exe burst out, surprised by the sudden surfacing of this dark doubt that she thought she'd buried. Asher and Malina both glanced at her, then shared that familiar disquieted look Exe had come to despise. "I know that look. I know there's something– abnormal about my powers. You can't just leave me here in the dark, still terrified that I'll accidentally hurt someone."

"Asher, she has the right to know," Malina said.

Asher shook his head, "It isn't safe–"

"Safe for who?" Exe cut him off.

Asher ignored her and focused on Malina, "It's too dangerous. What if the knowledge should fall into the wrong hands? You know who I mean..."

"And what if that wrong someone approaches Exe with the knowledge?" Malina replied. "Is it better that she be unaware and unprepared? She needs to know."

"There isn't time. I'm due back," Asher pulled out his pocket watch. "They've tightened our schedules so they can keep near constant watch on us without minders."

"You could come tell me tomorrow, couldn't you?" Exe said, hope of seeing Caulder tonight flickering.

"I can stay," Malina said, closing Asher's pocket watch. "Riven is making sure my absence isn't remarked on." Asher nodded to Malina, gave Exe one last disquieted glance, and vanished into the cascade.

Exe stared nervously at Malina, suddenly aware that this was the first time she'd ever been alone with her birth mother. Her raw emotions fluctuated wildly between the desire to demand answers to all her unanswered questions, fear at the thought of learning what was wrong with her, and desperation to find a way to convince Malina to keep the entrance to Anacapia open just one more night.

When Malina hesitated to speak, Exe glanced away and fixated on the boulder, wondering if Malina knew what had happened. *Of course she knows. Asher would've told her everything. And Viva. My treacherous twin probably convinced Malina that I did it on purpose.*

"It wasn't your fault," Malina followed Exe's gaze, her melodious voice comforting as she sat down on the boulder and patted the space beside her. "It's been a long time since we've dealt with anyone new to magic. Asher forgot how much we had to teach Viva about her powers when she was young."

Exe gave the boulder a sidelong glance, and sat instead on the banks of the whirling aquamarine gathering pool.

"You were only one when we– sent you away," Malina murmured. "Already you'd learned to walk, but you insisted on my carrying you everywhere. Viva was my explorer, always off into trouble, while you, my cuddler, couldn't bear to be separated–"

"Why did you send me away?" *All alone*, Exe added silently.

"It was the only way to keep you safe," Malina's expression pleaded. "We would've been too easily found had we all run together. Then too, we didn't want to abandon our people to Jettani—even if most could not recognize her actions and agenda as evil. Fighting for what is right and good requires hard choices and sacrifice."

"So you sacrificed me," Exe couldn't keep the bitterness from her voice as she stared into the cascade.

"We sacrificed our personal freedom and happiness to keep you alive and to defend our country," Malina had a touch of military sharpness in her tone. "Is that sacrifice so hard to understand?"

"No," Exe trailed her hand through the calming microbead water, thinking of Rove and his dedication to God and country. "Is that why you were willing to sacrifice those Gyve kids instead of saving them? Or did you really do it just to be free to see me one last time?" Her birth parents' willingness to let kids get executed for murders they didn't commit disturbed her more than she cared to admit.

"There was no saving those children. Jettani was bent on executing them for daring to mock a statue of her," Malina bowed her head. "We hated to pin the deaths of those two Disimulatas on them, but in a way, justifying their executions with more serious crimes thwarted Jettani's plan to normalize the punishment and execution of innocents for trivial reasons.

"I'm sorry if Riven left you with the impression that we'd frame innocent teens for murder simply to make our lives easier. Perhaps I need to fill him in on the details. It's part of a much larger battle to bring Jettani down—and we framed them with their blessing. Asher and I made sure to meet with their families beforehand, who were then able to get the teens' approval of our plan. They were proud to die as martyrs who'd struck a blow against Jettani's dictatorship by killing two of her oppressive, brutal secret police rather than as punks who'd pulled a prank. They died knowing that their executions would not be the warning to 'obey or face the consequences' that Jettani wanted it to be. Instead, their deaths are a call to action for all those opposed to tyranny."

Exe stared blindly at the sparkling, soothing cascade, unable to fathom the bravery of teens willing to die a martyr's death.

Malina broke the silence that fell between them, "Your father mentioned that your wish magic is particularly powerful—can you show me? Perhaps fashion those stones into a little man?"

"I thought I wasn't supposed to use wish magic anymore."

"I think it's important that you do, this once," Malina replied.

Ignoring the rocks scattered across the dusty field, Exe glanced around the mirage with the artist's eye she'd learned from Thone. A purplish cattail for the body, silvery driftwood for arms and legs, a plump, pink berry for the head, diaphanous leaves for a coat, and a perky yellow flower cap. With a series of wishes, Exe watched her little man come to life all by himself, bound together by woven reeds. Once the little man was finished, Exe made him check his reflection in the swirling water. Cheekily, the little figure approved of his appearance. After performing a flashy tap dance, he bowed and doffed his flower cap. Winded but satisfied, Exe looked over for approval.

Malina's impressed smile couldn't hide that familiar unsettled expression. Exe wished her happy little man to fall to pieces, scattered across the emerald grass, "Are you ever going to tell me what's so wrong with me?"

"What you've just done shouldn't be possible," Malina's voice wavered. "You've written no spells to perform such complex magic. Let me show you the man I'd create with my own wish magic."

The pieces of Exe's little man jerked and wobbled. With great effort the driftwood formed a little circle. The cattail lumbered into place as the lopsided mouth. The leaves formed a lumpy nose, while the pink berry and yellow flower floated in as two wonky eyes. The twisted, broken reeds topped the lopsided face as a mass of untidy hair. Exe watched and waited, but nothing else happened. The sad little smiley face just sat there.

"That's the best I can manage without relying on spells. That's why your powers are so– surprising," Malina gasped, exhausted.

"My wish magic just grew strong because that's all I've been using for so long," Exe frowned. "I bet if you'd used nothing else for your entire life, you could make a man like mine too."

"Perhaps I could believe that—were that the only evidence," Malina said.

"Isn't there a way to stop me from using wish magic altogether if there's something so wrong with it? Caulder mentioned something that could block it."

"You're speaking of a Bind," Malina's unsettled expression deepened. "If you know the spell and have the authority, you can bind the powers of another, rendering the bound one powerless until the binder releases the spell or dies—although most of us have protected ourselves from a basic, one-person bind.

"Two or more can work together to create a complex Intertwined Bind. The bound one cannot be freed from an Intertwined Bind unless all binders release the spell or die.

Unless a Bind Breaker frees them. But there've been no Bind Breakers around Anacapia for almost two hundred years."

"Why didn't you and Asher bind my powers before sending me away?" Incensed, Exe thought of all the harm that could've been prevented.

"We did."

"What?! No you didn't," Exe turned to face Malina. "I've had access to my powers for as long as I can remember. And you and Asher aren't dead, so—"

"You're an Unbindable, Exe. Rara Avis," Malina said in a low voice, as if afraid of being overheard even though they were alone.

"Unbindable? So my powers can't be bound like most people's can? Why is that such a big deal?"

Malina drew a deep breath, "It's not just that you cannot be bound from using your powers—your powers themselves are not bound by the physical limitations that most of us have. True, you are not a god—your powers still have limitations, as you've experienced. Your power is simply much greater than most people's. That must be what terrified Jettani when she carried you into the Portal Portend soon after you were born. Back then, we thought you were targeted to attack us, because she was afraid that our growing popularity threatened her power. But it's you she's truly afraid of.

"In you, she saw a threat worth killing. So Jettani worked hard to convince the people that you were evil. She declared that within you was the power to destroy our whole world. It took almost a year, but Jettani was able to convince everyone that the only way to protect Anacapia was to kill you."

"Jettani was afraid of me when I was a baby just because I'm unbindable?" Exe struggled to understand.

"No. You were too young to recognizable as an Unbindable. She was only able to see an immense power within you. That was enough to scare her into ordering your death," Malina sat down beside Exe. "You see, being an Unbindable is both myth and legend in our world. Some said it was an impossibility. Others believed it was an old magical trait that died out long ago. Either way, being an Unbindable no longer existed in our world—until Jettani claimed to be one in order to take control. Had Jettani realized that you actually were what she claims to be, it would've terrified her into killing you while still within the Portal Portend."

"Rara avis," Exe whispered, pulling out the coin Riven had given her to see those words inscribed around Jettani's image.

Malina looked at the coin too, "When Velin escaped after the Horology Wars, he left Anacapia without a ruler. Jettani and her supporters claimed that she was a Rara Avis to push her into the power position. And it worked. Though Asher and I now doubt that she is an Unbindable."

"But people just believed her? Didn't she have to prove she was Unbindable to take control of a whole country?" Exe asked.

Malina tented her fingers, considering her words carefully, "Jettani is incredibly persuasive. To most Anacapians she is beautiful, fragile, mysteriously innocent. The most pure-hearted lady ever to be born into our world. She has eyes that show only gentle selflessness. Her aura inspires dreams of a goddess sent to look after your every need. She's worked hard to cultivate her mystique. Most have come to trust her in everything and are supremely grateful she deigns to guide our government. For that is all they see. They are blind to the fact that she is a maniacal tyrant serving her own interests. A nightmare disguised as a dream come true."

"So that's how she was able to persuade a whole country to agree to execute me as a baby," Exe shivered with the knowledge that such a powerful, persuasive woman was determined to see her dead. "But she doesn't know I'm Unbindable? Who does?"

"Only our family and Velin. And Demaine. He's the man who saved you from execution. But he... vanished long ago. No one else knows. And no one else should."

"Does being unbindable make me dangerous?" Exe asked tentatively, relieved to finally be asking the question that had plagued her for so long to someone who knew the truth— yet dreading the answer.

"It's not that you're dangerous," Malina hesitated. "It's that you're powerful. Some people, like Jettani, are afraid of power in others because they fear it will diminish their own. Others will want to weaponize your power for their own selfish gain, and they'll lie, steal, cheat, and even kill to get their hands on it. I'm honestly surprised it never occurred to Jettani to use you rather than kill you. But she'll not tolerate anyone who might outshine her. Even the brightest, wisest, and most talented of her closest followers are shunted into low-level positions so they can never overshadow her.

"But no one, no matter how wise or powerful should have limitless authority over others," Malina continued. "Everyone deserves the free will to choose their own path and make their own decisions, for better or for worse. No government or its dictator should be granted the control she has over people's lives—what they read, what they eat, where they work, where they live...if they live."

"Life, liberty, and the pursuit of happiness," Exe whispered, thinking of the freedoms guaranteed to her that her birth family didn't have. *What kind of demented tyrant wants that kind of power and control over people? How can they not see that her sinister authority and influence has convinced them to kill kids for her own personal benefit?* Subconsciously she pulled her amethyst pendant into her palm, taking comfort in its tingling, *I'm not completely defenseless against her.* Desperate to abandon the dark subject, Exe asked, "Where's your tetherstone?"

"It's here," Malina showed Exe her deep teal ring. "And here, here, and here." Malina continued, showing Exe her deep teal earrings, necklace, and bracelet.

"Doesn't that weaken it? Cutting it up like that?" Exe asked, admiring the jewels.

"No. It takes only a small piece to create a connection," Malina answered. "Plus, it's safer for soldiers to divide their tetherstones. Were I to lose my ring finger in battle, I'd be powerless if that were the only place I wore it."

"Have you ever been to war?" Exe couldn't envision her glamorous magical mother as a soldier, until she saw the strategic gleam in her eye.

"Skirmishes only. I was still a child during the Horology Wars when we lost so much and so many," Malina sounded melancholy. Seeing Exe's confusion, she explained, "The Horology Wars, the battle over time. A fight that's only dormant, I'm afraid."

"Velin caused the Horology Wars, didn't he? It's how he lost his role as leader of Anacapia. Rande told me."

"I know," Malina answered. "I trust you better understand now why Velin found it so hard to raise you and train you. We asked too much of him."

"I understand," Exe nodded, but her expression hardened. "But it's difficult to forget how he treated me. I don't think I can bear to let him train me," she said, half hoping she might still persuade Malina not to end her training sessions with Caulder.

"Jettani won't forget you're still out there. Ever. The older you grow, the harder her secret police will look for you," Malina said firmly. "Even now, the Disimulata's search expands. Should they find this world again, and you're not ready—"

Exe bristled at the warning, "Clearly you think I'm ready to fend for myself if you're willing to end my training just when you've become free to actually teach me yourself. I know enough."

"Do you? Then you can tell me the difference between ephemeral and infinity spells?" Malina asked, paging through Exe's vade.

Caught off guard, Exe thought fast, "Ephemeral and infinity? Ephemeral are temporary spells and infinity are everlasting, right? Like the speed spell is ephemeral, but the mindlock spell is an infinity, right?"

"Good guess," Malina congratulated her wryly. "How did you know?"

"Riven explained a little bit when I first met him," Exe smiled. "He cast an infinity spell to change my hair color back to black. But he couldn't do the same thing to my eyes for some reason."

"Actually, he likely used a permaspell rather than an infinity," Malina clarified. "The essences of both dissipate, so they cannot be detected once cast, but a permaspell is less powerful. Were I to blacken my hair with a permaspell, it would soon grow out to blonde again. Infinity magic would keep my hair black until death, or until I reversed the spell. Changing eye color with either would be too dangerous to try. Altering living tissue is challenging even for the best medicors. Repairing a wound is one thing, but manipulating eye color? You'd likely wind up blind."

"Wait, so would that make changing eye color an Inconceivable?" Exe frowned.

"Clearly there is more for you to learn," Malina smiled knowingly as she handed Exe her vade. "Changing eye color isn't a top priority, so whether it's Inconceivable or not, I don't know. I doubt anyone's spent much time trying to write such a spell. Inconceivables are spells of such great magnitude that it would take several lifetimes to write one, if it could even be done. Immortality, resurrection, foretelling, time travel, anti-binds—spells like these have been labeled Inconceivables because of the improbability of them ever being invented."

"So there are some things that no one can do no matter how powerful their magic? Even me?" Exe asked.

"There's some debate as to whether Inconceivable magic cannot be done, or should not be done," Malina hedged. "That doesn't stop some people from trying."

"Someone did. Velin, when he invented time travel," Exe glanced thoughtfully back at her tower door, pondering the skeletal old man who'd soon take over her training.

Malina followed her gaze, "Whatever else Velin has become, he is both powerful and wise. You can learn a lot from him. Promise me you'll try?" After Exe's nod, Malina asked, "Is there anything else you want to know before I go?"

A million questions came to mind, but in that moment, when the end felt so painfully near, only one thing mattered to Exe. She asked, "Can't you please leave the entrance to Anacapia open for a few more hours? I honestly do want to see Viva one last time." *So she can masquerade in Nowhere as me while I say goodbye to Anacapia.*

"Is it really Viva you want to see again?" Malina's gaze penetrated Exe's fib.

Biting her lip, Exe admitted, "And Caulder."

Malina gave her an understanding smile, "I suspected you might grow fond of him. He's quite the charmer. Though you should know, him and Viva—"

"I know," Exe interrupted, blushing. "It's not like that. We've become friends. He's the one person from Anacapia that I've spent the most time with. I want the chance to say a proper goodbye."

Malina considered Exe for a long moment, then said, "The gateway between our worlds has been open for centuries, I suppose a few more hours won't hurt. I'll send Caulder to see you tonight."

Exe tempered her excitement, "And Viva too."

Malina raised a brow, "Really? Even knowing that—"

"I'm looking forward to it."

Malina bowed her head in agreement then glided into the cascade.

As she watched her go, it suddenly struck Exe that this was the last time she'd ever see her birth mother. "Wait!" Exe cried out, startling herself. Blushing under Malina's expectant gaze, Exe tried to think of what to say. Finally, she blurted, "What's my middle name?"

"Liberty," Malina smiled. Exe joined her in saying her full name for the very first time, savoring the sound of it, "Experience Liberty—"

"Parsell," Exe said.

"Verelustre," Malina said at the exact same time.

A distance grew between them in the following silence, threatening to engulf Exe in an unrelievable sadness. She tried to joke away the tension, "Liberty, huh? I'll never tell my brothers, or they'll try to nickname me Bertie. I, uh, like it though. So, um, what's Viva's middle name?"

"Independence," Malina replied, a smile softening her bittersweet tone.

"That's fitting," Exe smiled wryly, thinking of how Viva was free to move about Anacapia without worrying about being executed on the spot.

"Actually, I think I got it backwards. Viva's desperate to be liberated from the confines of her life in Anacapia, and you– Well, if not for your independent nature, you never would've found your way home. And as difficult and dangerous as this has been, I'm glad you did." With one last, soft smile, Malina slipped into the cascade. Exe bit her lip guiltily as she watched her birth mother leave for the last time.

ALL'S FAIR

I'm an Unbindable, Exe thought as she nervously paced around her solitary tower door in the starlit field, overwhelmed by the vast cavern of uncertainty that had opened within her. *I should be feeling invincible,* she tried to convince herself. Instead she felt more isolated than ever.

Not only was she as much of a freak in Anacapia as she was in Nowhere, but Exe couldn't get past Malina's ominous warning that there were people out there who'd want to weaponize her abnormal powers. *And there's no one I can talk to about it. I can't talk to my family about this. They're disturbed enough by what little they suspect about my powers. And I can't risk telling Riven when he's already in so much danger as a double agent.* Sanity said that she should cancel this last adventure and spend her last few hours with Caulder talking this all over with him while Viva said her goodbyes in Nowhere.

But Malina did say that no one else but our family and Velin should know that I'm an Unbindable. That includes Caulder, Exe argued with herself. Deep down, though, she knew that was just an excuse to explore Anacapia one last time, despite her misgivings.

It's irresponsible to go into Anacapia now that I know how unusual my powers are, even there. I should just cancel and ask Caulder to help me come to grips with being an Unbindable. I bet Malina suspected I'd talk this over with him. It's probably why she agreed to send him.

Exe had just about made up her mind to cancel when Viva breezed into the field followed closely by Caulder. Ignoring Exe, Viva conjured herself into an Arizona-appropriate outfit that was prettier than anything in Exe's own wardrobe. Then she checked her hair in her compact, applied a little lip gloss, and opened the tower door.

Before Exe could say a word, Viva cast her a baleful glance and sneered, "Don't you talk to anyone. You don't know anyone, you don't look at anyone, and you certainly don't speak to anyone. Got it?" With one last satisfied glance in the mirror, Viva snapped the compact shut and disappeared into Nowhere.

Exe turned shyly to Caulder. Somehow Viva's primping for her own rendezvous made this night feel more like a date than any of their other outings. *I refuse to spend my last few hours with Caulder talking about what a freak I am*, Exe suddenly decided.

"Ready to experience The Wendings, Exe?" Caulder asked, his smile a mixture of excitement and melancholy. Exe nodded and followed him into the mirage, but hesitated at the edge of the gathering pool.

"Are you sure it's safe?" Exe asked, wondering if she should warn him that she was an Unbindable. *If I tell him, he may not take me.*

"I wouldn't take you if it wasn't sure," Caulder replied. "What's got you worried? The people? There won't be many after Jettani warned them away from the Gyve. And the carnies won't do more than ask for your ticket. After what's happened, they'll need what little business we provide tonight."

Reassured, Exe teased, "Can you afford it?"

"I've got smuggler money to burn, Moxie," Caulder smiled, pulling her through the cascade and into the volting tree. "It pays to trade in unreasonably banned contraband that's only dangerous to the government's tyranny."

Exe closed her eyes to savor the melting, tingling sensation of volting with Caulder. On opening them, she found they were in a darkened storeroom overflowing with intriguing magical gadgets, gizmos, and goods.

At the question in her eyes, Caulder said, "Outcasts need outlawed stuff too. Especially when they're banned for no good reason other than to guarantee continued government oppression. Gyve leaders lease us this space in exchange for discounted goods—which we make up by cheerfully overcharging Jettani's followers."

Caulder ushered her out of the hidden storeroom into a large warehouse where they wended their way through random ride parts, worn out candy carts, crazy character costumes, and half-assembled games—each more wondrous than the next. To Exe it felt like being backstage at Great America, the amusement park the Parsells had visited while stationed in Wisconsin.

Caulder tensed and gasped as he was easing the warehouse's exterior door open. Assailed by the inexplicably-nostalgic, salty-sweet scents of unknown fair food,

Exe failed to notice his hesitation. The glimpses of the fantastical amusement park that she could see over his shoulder enthralled her. Thrilled screams blared and faded as a coasting coaster whizzed by. The sky sparked with fireworks as riders zoomed around strapped to life-sized bottle rockets.

Screams? Riders? People. Exe gaped at all of the people playing games, ordering food at concession stands, and waiting in line to board rides. Turning to Caulder, Exe expected to see fear and was ready to argue against his determined insistence that he take her home immediately. To her surprise, Caulder smiled.

"They came. From small towns, farms, and ranches. In defiance of Jettani's 'request' that they boycott Gyve businesses. She may control the cities, but Jettani holds no sway over the countryside," Caulder swallowed hard, a tear in his eye.

"All these people. Do we have to leave?" Exe edged into his shadow, afraid to venture out into the carnival grounds, yet desperate to stay and enjoy this one chance to explore a magical amusement park.

"No, Viva..." Caulder said over his shoulder. "There's an unwritten twilight hour rule at The Wendings—embracing couples are not to be disturbed no matter how well you know them. As long as we hold hands, or link arms, or otherwise keep in close contact, no one will engage us in conversation. Think we can manage that? Or would you rather I take you straight home?"

"I should say, 'home,'" Exe chewed on her bottom lip in indecision. "But now that I'm here– Now that I've seen– We've got amusement parks in my world, but nothing like this. My brothers would love this place. It must've been amazing coming here when you were little. Even in Anacapia, this carnival must've seemed like a dream come true."

"Yeah," Caulder breathed, leaning against the doorframe. "I was seven. Came with my mom and never wanted to leave, so she brought me again the next day, even though we couldn't afford it. Now that we can, she's gone. She never did get to bring Dodger here, though I know she wanted to. Seeing someone experience this place for the first time, there's nothing like it. So, do I get to enjoy that experience tonight?"

"Maybe just one ride, one game, and one treat— No two, three—"

"Come on. We'll take it slow, avoid any crowds, and go the second either of us gets nervous," Caulder said, taking hold of her hand.

Like a shaken soda bottle ready to explode, excitement bubbled in Exe as Caulder led her through the 'Employees Only' aisles toward the main thoroughfare. Just as they were about to step out into the carnival's midway, Exe stopped short. Her very own face stared back at her from a ragged and ripped 'Wanted: Dead' poster tacked to a tentpole.

"You're not Exe, remember?" Caulder whispered. "You're Viva. And you're used to seeing these posters of your notorious sister plastered everywhere. Besides, most of the people here wouldn't turn you in even if they knew who you really are. No one who'd come here after the government's boycott order is any fan of Jettani's."

Despite his comforting words, Exe stayed nervous as they strolled the busy midway—until she realized that the crowd was mostly couples, who were too focused on each other to pay any attention to her and Caulder. Relaxing, Exe looked about at the magical games, whimsical refreshments, and intriguing souvenirs with the obvious awe of a first-timer.

Suddenly remembering who she was supposed to be, Exe whispered to Caulder, "Wait, has Viva ever been here before? Do I need to pretend to be all jaded, or–"

"Nope," Caulder whispered back. "You can express all the tyro joy you'd like. Just be jaded with any people who glance your way. Viva despises almost everyone for shunning her because she looks like–"

Me. Exe nodded. *No wonder Viva was irritated when Caulder decided to bring me here. She's lived in Anacapia her whole life, but I get to enjoy The Wendings before she does!* Delighted, Exe asked, "What shall we do first?"

"Feeling brave? I'll take you on the Roving Rambler," Caulder said, indicating the giant roller coaster that was coasting around the park while the coaster cars simultaneously zipped around on its track. "No, not the coaster yet. I've got just the ride to start with. It was my favorite when I was little. It's a bit corny, but you'll love it."

They joined a short line of cozy couples with eyes only for each other. While Caulder casually scanned the crowds for signs of trouble, Exe craned her neck to get a look at the ride ahead. All she could make out was a large, mountain-shaped ride covered in climbing vines and crimson, heart-shaped flowers. As they got closer, she noticed the pink, petal-dappled canal flowing into a tunnel filled with a gauzy, sparkling mist. Giant swans with feathers of white, black, pink, gold, or silver floated serenely on the waters, each carrying a cozy couch for two on their backs.

Exe glanced dubiously at Caulder, "This was your favorite ride as a kid?"

"Yeah, why?" Caulder said, finally taking a good look at the ride when it was their turn to board a giant golden swan (*A real, live swan!*) with its red velvet loveseat. "Wait, what happened to the Fantastical Fables ride?" Caulder asked of the carnie standing under a heart-shaped sign that read: Sugared Sagas.

"That's our daytime ride for families. Not much call for kiddie rides at night, so we change over to a tunnel of love in the evening. Hurry up, you're holding up the works," the carnie replied as he bustled them onto the ride. "Bird's trained to raise its wings into a canopy should you be needin' privacy. Just say 'redamancy.'" With a sly wink to Caulder and a soft chirrup to the bird, their golden, living swan boat sailed them into the misty, low-lit tunnel.

Exe and Caulder sat stiff on the cushy, sloping seat that had clearly been designed to cuddle couples right up next to one another. Overhead, fluttering, phosphorescent fyre fairies cast a flickering, romantic glow. A curious aroma on the twinkling mist conjured up an image for Exe of her and Caulder snuggling by a campfire in a rain-dampened forest of lilacs and cedars at twilight. Exe edged away from Caulder, mortified by the daydream. From the way he cleared his throat and looked away, Exe guessed that he'd had one too.

None too soon the swan sailed them into a lighted cavern where an all-too-lifelike diorama depicted a grand romance similar to the tragic love affair of Romeo and Juliet. Although the scene wasn't at all raunchy or risqué, Exe flushed with embarrassment. Normally, she would've loved the tragic tale woven by the alluring, animatronic narrator (had she been enjoying it with Ella during one of their girls-only, romance movie marathons), but it was absolutely awful viewing it with a crush that might've become a boyfriend if only their own story weren't as ill-fated as the one they were viewing.

The ride glided them through a seemingly endless series of romantically-lit tunnels and animated stories of high romance and melodrama. Damsels in distress and knights in shining armor. Brave maidens and imprisoned princes. Star-crossed lovers and fated soulmates. Halfway through the ride, Exe looked in horror at Caulder when he commanded the swan to canopy them with its wings.

"We're supposed to be a couple," Caulder whispered. "We can't let any passing riders see how uncomfortable we are." By the time they saw the light at the end of this painfully-awkward tunnel of love, they were both hanging onto opposite arms of the loveseat so that they wouldn't accidentally touch.

"Nice moves, tyro," the carnie smirked at Caulder as he helped them off of their swan boat. "You may actually be the first couple to break up on this ride." Caulder threw him a narrowed glare and a sarcastic smile as he led Exe away.

"Well, this is awkward," Caulder said as they walked down the midway as far apart as they could while still technically holding hands. Suddenly, Caulder moved close and slipped his arm around her waist. Exe almost jerked away, until she heard him whispering, "I'm so sorry. That's usually a kids' story ride. I wanted to show you those youngster yarns that I so loved when I was little. But you can still read them in your entirety tome. The book's called, 'Fantastical Fables and Funny Fancies.'"

"I'll read them to my little brothers," Exe gave him a small smile, hoping that the whole evening hadn't been ruined by that horribly romantic ride. "Now what?"

"I don't think there's any way they can ruin this next one with any overblown love stuff," Caulder smiled back as he took her hand again.

The next ride turned out to be a simple lighthouse-shaped tower as tall as a twenty-story skyscraper. Three large red and blue tube slides encircled the white tower from top to bottom, swirling upward like a barbershop pole. Each tube pulsated as it widened and narrowed, as if squeezing an enormous marble down a too-narrow rubber hose. At its base, laughing couples came shooting out of the tubes while others dashed in between them whenever the swirling tubes revealed the entrance into the tower.

Exe and Caulder joined the queue of chuckling couples and were soon galloping into the tower. Once inside, they hopped on one of the cabled elevators that hurtled them to the top with breathtaking speed. While most couples headed right for the slides, the soaring solitude of the observation deck enticed Exe to urge Caulder outside.

For many long, peaceful minutes, Exe looked her fill at the vastness of her homeland. Vibrant bits of color glowed along the coastline of the Neon Beach. Moonlight glistened across silvery sand dunes and glazed the surface of the fiery lake. In the distance, a few bursts of dragon fire illuminated the swaying shadows of the Craggy Sea.

Her eyes lingered for only a moment on Vianelle, the icily-glittering city atop the waterfall mountain, then her gaze fell on the wide, snaking river that flowed from its darkly churning gathering pool. The farther the river ran from the mountain, the calmer and sleeker its surface became. As Exe followed its glassy path toward where she stood, the mammoth river widened and fanned, splitting into the dozens of canals and streams that formed the expansive river delta on which The Wendings was built. Exe contemplated how clever the Gyve had been to transform what might've once been considered useless wetlands into a thriving entertainment destination.

Recognizing the midway on the longest, largest island, she marveled at how the varied attractions were constructed to accommodate the small size and odd shapes of the many islands formed by the wandering waterways. Hundreds of little footbridges connected the park attractions to one another, reminding Exe of the beauty and charm of Venice. On the streams and canals, pretty little magically-propelled boats meandered along, providing tranquil transportation to any parkgoer who'd rather sail than walk. Even the coasting coaster had been specially designed to zoom around the entire park without disturbing the waters or the visitors.

"Magnificent, isn't it?" Caulder breathed into the quiet, his face shadowed on the empty, unlit deck. "Jettani sent the Gyve here to destroy them. Outcasts abandoned in a wasteland. Instead, The Wendings is a testimony to the wondrous things magic can accomplish when not restricted and controlled by an oppressive, tyrannical government. Although this is technically part of Anacapia, the Gyve and this land are a country unto themselves—and they're thriving, while much of the rest of Anacapia lies in government-orchestrated ruins. It makes me ache to think of how great Anacapia could become if we ever succeed in freeing her from Jettani's destructive reign."

"But it's so beautiful here!" Exe exclaimed. "I can't imagine it ever being a wasteland with all the little rivers, and islands, and greenery."

"Let me show you what it once was," Caulder replied, pulling a pebble out of his shoe and placing it in her palm. With the pebble held in their clasped hands, Caulder closed his eyes and asked her to do the same. The moment hers closed, Exe's mind was filled with a vision of a vast swampland where The Wendings now stood. Images of the Gyve fighting to keep the shifting rivers from flooding makeshift hovels and struggling to grow food in muddy, sodden patches too often washed away. The vision went dark as she felt Caulder sag beside her.

"How did you do that?" Exe asked, concerned as Caulder leaned breathless against the guardrail. Caulder looked carefully around to make sure they were alone before answering.

"Aftsight," he whispered with a wink. "A rare talent that lets me replay the past if I'm holding something that existed during that time. You may have powerful wish magic, 'Viva,' but you're not the only one who's gifted. The majority of us simply hide our talents so they're not exploited by those in power." Exe returned his smile and bit her lip, resisting the temptation to tell him that she was an Unbindable.

High above the harmonious melding of carnival ride melodies, Exe felt a growing urgency to see and do as much as she could in the scant time she had left. With one look, Exe communicated to Caulder that she was ready to kick the magical amusement park adventure into high gear. Together they headed inside to one of the tube slides.

Directed by a carnie to sit on opposite sides of the tube instead of together, Exe was even more surprised to find this was no ordinary slide. Instead of a slick, solid surface, the interior of the tube was instead lined on all sides with interlocking metallic disks that whirred in sleek sequence like swiftly spinning gears. Before Exe could think how that might impact the ride, the carnie shoved them both down the slide.

Swhooshing alongside Caulder, Exe realized that they weren't just sliding but swirling up the sides—until she could no longer tell which way was up. The spinning disks pirouetted them around and around each other, sometimes so close that they could almost rub noses, at other times, so far apart that they couldn't quite touch fingertips. The disorienting dance of the slide soon became a game as they competed to be the first to tap or tickle one another whenever the the slide brought them together. All too soon they were shooting out the bottom in a tangled, giggling heap. Hand-in-hand they ran toward the midway, laughingly debating which ride to take on next.

The Wendings' Flummox Funhouse was like stepping into a series of M.C. Escher drawings. Escaping required navigating staircases to nowhere (magically walking sideways and upside-down too), sailing canals that impossibly flowed into one another, and staggering through dizzyingly-curved rooms with undulating floors that were filled with distorting mirrors, mind-bending patterns, and décor that looked identical no matter which direction it was hanging.

Braving the coasting coaster, Exe delighted in the disorienting sensation of soaring forwards and backwards at the exact same time, often while being whirled about or tossed side-to-side by the twirling, rocking coaster cars.

They couldn't stop giggling on a ride that looked like a gigantic Gyro Wheel rail twirler that whizzed them tight together as they rolled along its giant track.

The Bobbling Wobblers resembled an old-fashioned gumball machine filled with water and dozens of colorful, translucent balls jetting around at the direction of the riders inside. Hopping into an amethyst sphere with Caulder, Exe delighted in floating around inside the rubbery bubble like an astronaut in space. Even more entertaining was zooming up to burst through the water's surface, or colliding into other riders' bubbles. Being able to engage with other Anacapians as they played bumper bubbles without actually interacting with them made it Exe's favorite ride, *Except for the slide...*

In between the rides, they played magical games and ate a half-dozen charmed treats, all on the house—courtesy of the carnies who appreciated access to Caulder's black market goods. As their time ran down, Caulder bought Exe a set of Spectaculars, a pair of comical-looking goggles which would let her relive The Wendings experience after she went home, including all of the rides.

"My brothers will love these," Exe whispered when she was sure they were alone. "If I'm ever brave enough to tell them about this place. And my magic. Or maybe I'll just say they're a new kind of virtual reality glasses."

"Who needs magic when you've got technology?" Caulder laughingly whispered back after Exe had explained virtual reality. "Come on, we're almost out of time and I've got one last treat for you." Drawing her over to a candy vendor, Caulder asked for an order of Changelings and requested that they be served in 'the cellar'—which turned out to be a private, fairy-lit patio completely concealed by gorgeous greenery.

"The Gyve know well the need for privacy in Anacapia, so 'the cellar' is completely soundproof and visually impenetrable. I've conducted a lot of illicit transactions here," Caulder said as he set a giant golden box on the table between them. "So as long as we're in here, you can be you, Exe."

"This has been amazing, Caulder," Exe collapsed back on her chair and turned teary eyes on him. "I don't want to leave."

"I know. Sometimes I think it would've been easier if you didn't know what you were missing. Still, I'm glad I got this time with you," Caulder replied, his own eyes misty. "And while you're you, there's something else I want to give you."

Exe sat up straight, eyes riveted on the translucent, spiraled pyramid that glowed exquisitely iridescent in the twinkling fairy lights fluttering up above. Lifting her eyes to Caulder's, Exe said, "A presage. Are you–"

"No," Caulder answered with finality. "There's no safe way to sneak you into the Portal Portend. Even if you're disguised as Viva," Caulder added before Exe could interrupt. "I just thought that you'd like to have one, as a reminder to stay focused on what's best about you, and to do good with the power you've been gifted. You don't need to keep drowning in guilt because you have darkness within you. Darkness that we're all capable of. And never forget—all of us here that know you, and care about you, we're fighting every day to free Anacapia, so you'll be free to return. I'm determined to make it possible for you to use that presage someday."

Exe gently cradled the delicate presage in her hands, overcome with the tenderness of Caulder's gesture. Without thinking, Exe slipped the presage into her pocket and grasped him in a fierce hug. Just as she turned to kiss his cheek, Caulder turned to kiss hers.

Their lips met. Soft and serene. For a moment they both stood still, eyes closed, suspended in an untroubled moment of perfect connection. Almost in unison they pulled gently apart, unruffled and unembarrassed, yet both sobered by unspoken impossibility.

"Hey, while we're still here..." Caulder whispered, clearing his throat. Sharing a smile of understanding, they sat and focused their attention on the golden box.

Exe expected Caulder to open the lid of the giant candy box, but instead he pressed the jeweled logo on its top, and the papery side parted like a stage curtain. Out pranced a tiny sugared candy shaped like a dragon. The incredibly-lifelike treat soared no higher than their eye level, breathing fire and growling a pint-sized roar. As Exe clapped excitedly, Caulder caught the creature, gently pressed its jellied head, and set it back down. Instantly, the dragon began pirouetting and prancing across the table as a delicate music tinkled from the candy box.

Laughing uncontrollably at the dragon ballet, Exe was delighted to learn that the treats were called Changelings because they were all charmed with the personalities of every candy character within the box. When Caulder popped the dragon into Exe's mouth, the tiny paper curtain opened and another candy emerged. They took turns pressing their heads and guessing which personality would materialize.

When Caulder reached out to eat the last little flower fairy candy that was swaggering about like a pirate, brandishing her bouquet sword, Exe stopped him, "I want to keep her so I can remember—this."

"I should've saved one for myself," Caulder replied, showing her how to turn the candy personalities off and on by tickling their feet.

Exe wrapped the now-still candy in a bit of paper from the box and tucked it into her pocket. As they were leaving, Exe paused, "Can I bring a box back to my brothers? It'll make it easier for them to believe me when I tell them about this. When I'm ready."

Concealing the new box of Changelings inside his smugglers' coat as they stepped back out onto the midway, Caulder said, "We've time left for one last ride. Which one shall it be?"

"The Bobblers, I think. No, the sli–" Exe cut off when Caulder suddenly pressed her back into the shadows by the candy vendor's shop.

"What is she doing here?!"

The unexpected harshness in Caulder's whisper startled Exe. For a split second, she thought that Jettani herself had come to The Wendings—then she saw the tiny, doll-like child in her floaty, fairy-light dress, surrounded by five tall, intimidating boys wearing ebony Gatsby caps and Cossack jackets. *Dodger! And the Jette Set!*

"Well, lookee what we have here," Schade's sinister drawl rang out, drawing the attention of nearby carnival goers who quickly skittered away. "Out on your lonesome are you? No big brothers to protect the merchandise? Let's just see what illegal goods you've got on you. Hand it over and just maybe we won't run you in, smuggler twit."

Schade and his posse moved in. Exe stared in horror when no one came forward to help fragile, defenseless Dodger. *Not even Caulder.* Instantly, Exe was bombarded with images:

her head shoved in the dusty mud, cheek crushed under the stilettoed heel; pelted with trash by spiteful boys at Bonnie's direction; the clawing hands and power-mad faces of every covetous, wanna-be necklace thief. Reverberating like a death knell, the Jette Set's callous laughter (and a vision of that waif-like Flaneur girl disintegrating to death) drove every shred of caution from Exe's head.

"No more!" Exe cried out, shoving Caulder aside as she stormed out of the shadows. As the Jette Set turned on her, Exe wished into existence an invisible fist that jabbed Schade deep and hard in the gut. He doubled over, curling so tight he almost fell into a somersault.

Vindictively inspired, Exe wished him into an unnaturally tighter ball and bowled him into his friends. Against their will, they wound around him like a giant human snowball that rolled careening and screaming down the crowded midway. Shouts of terror echoed around Exe as she bowled the human ball hard against a fence.

"Viva! No!" Caulder shouted.

Exe recoiled instantly at the sound of her sister's name. Slowly, she realized that the crowd wasn't simply scared of getting rolled over, they were staring in terror—at her. *No, not at me. They think I'm Viva...* In that moment, the ball of Jette Set bullies collapsed in a groaning heap at the foot of the towering slide.

"What have you done?!" Caulder yelled as he stared at the bruised and bloody Jette Set struggling to rise. In the split second that Schade fixed his eyes on Exe, Caulder grabbed her and Dodger, and volted them away in a brilliant flash of blinding white light.

CHAPTER TWENTY-NINE

ENEMY TERRITORY

Jolted by the explosive sensation ricocheting through her (so unlike the melting, tingling she usually felt when volting with Caulder), Exe barely registered the series of stash houses he volted them through before the three of them landed in a jumble on the black banks of the Corpse Copse's creek.

"What gives, Cauld? I didn't need your help! And what'd you go burning the south gate stash house for? Say, where are we?" Dodger demanded, glancing about.

"It was the emptiest one, less to lose. I think I volted us through enough cruor-blocked locales to hide our trail, but just in case..." Caulder replied, hustling them through the cascade and into the mirage. Caulder's sober eyes met Exe's over the top of Dodger's head, "Do you know what you've done?"

"I had to do something! They were gonna hurt Dodger just like that Flaneur girl," Exe defended, shivering despite the lingering warmth in the spring air. "You just stood there!" The field appeared strangely frozen in the chill gray of the city-lit night sky. Stars glittered ominously overhead.

"There's a reason we call her Dodger, Exe. She didn't need our help. She voltes better, farther, and faster than even me. And I couldn't have done anything if I'd wanted to. Not with you there. But you weren't supposed to be YOU there, remember?"

"Dodger-x?" Dodger puzzled.

"I know, I know. I wasn't thinking. I just—wished," Exe replied.

A dark figure burst out of the cascade and stalked toward Exe. "What were you thinking?!" Riven thundered, whipping off his Gatsby cap.

Before Exe could reply, Caulder leapt between them, blasting Riven back into the cascade with a whispered trigger. Turning to Dodger, Caulder commanded, "Take Exe and volte while I hold him off! I'll find you when I can. Go now!"

"Who?!" Dodger asked as Riven stormed back into the mirage and blasted Caulder with a spell that sent him sailing, his back cracking hard against the boulder.

"No!" Exe evaded Dodger's grasp and threw herself between them. Spells shot around her as they continued battling. "Caulder, stop! Riven is on our side! He's a double agent! Riven, it wasn't Caulder's fault! I made him take me!"

"WHAT DID YOU DO?!"

The cacophonous cry froze all four in the mirage like a twisted tableau: Dodger grasping for Exe; Caulder with his shirt torn, bruises forming; Riven bleeding from the corner of his mouth; Exe with arms outstretched trying to keep them apart. All four turned to see Viva storming toward them in a towering rage.

"Jeepers creepers! There's two of you?! So, you weren't executed?!" Dodger's arms fell limply as she turned from Viva to Exe. "Or you weren't? Criminy!"

"These two swells decided to go capering around The Wendings with Exe dressed as you and ran into a little trouble," Riven wiped the blood from his lip and gave Viva a once-over look. "Though, given your get-up, I guess you knew."

"What trouble?" Viva demanded, instantly transforming her Arizona outfit into an Anacapian one with a whisper and a wave.

"We were just about to leave when we happened upon the Jette Set," Caulder avoided looking at Viva's fear-paled face as he repaired his own clothes.

"They were about to attack Dodger," Exe tried to explain when Viva's stark, stricken gaze turned on her.

"Exe is back and you all knew? So this is where you've been disappearing to, Caulder! You found Experience Verelustre!" Dodger sang, clapping her hands.

"So what?! That ninny of a nymph can fend for herself just fine. What happened?" Viva demanded, cornering Exe against the boulder.

Riven stepped between them. "She shouldn't have been there, Viva. This is on you. Both of you. What were you thinking?" he added, glaring at Caulder.

"We were always careful," Exe defended.

"Careful?! You rolled my brother up in a bloody ball of bodies!" Riven shouted, then paused. "Always? How often have you gone galivanting around Anacapia? Did you forget it's a country filled with people who want to kill you?"

"A ball of bodies?!" Horrorstruck, Viva sagged as if she just might faint.

"At the very least you could've bound Exe's powers before leading her into the lion's den," Riven raged at Caulder who had moved to support Viva.

Exe bit her lip guiltily under the weight of the secret knowledge that any bind Caulder might've attempted wouldn't have worked on her. Riven's demand revived Viva enough to glare at her sister. Exe recoiled from her raw hatred. *She knows! She knows I'm an Unbindable!*

"You did this on purpose!" Viva's weak whisper seethed into a roar. "That's why you manipulated Mom to make sure this night happened– you want me out of the way! Haven't I suffered enough because of you? Because of you, I have never belonged in my own world. Because of you, I can barely show my face in Anacapia. And then you came along, whining 'woe is me' when our parents sacrificed everything to save you. Crying about being abandoned when you have the perfect life! Friends, family, freedom. And yet you set about to take what little I had!"

"Perfect?!" Exe yelled, masking her shame with indignance. "You got to grow up in Anacapia—with our parents—where you were free to use your powers any time you wished! You never had to be afraid or ashamed of who you are! I've lived my whole life with a madman in my head, who convinced me I was a killer simply to keep me under his control. I was farmed out to a family who had no idea how dangerous I was. I've been forced to isolate myself, suppress my powers, and live every second in fear that I might accidentally murder my family!"

"And now you've murdered me! Do you have any idea what they'll do to me once I'm captured and taken to Vianelle?! You should be the one to stand trial for the crime

YOU committed!" Viva shouted as she lunged at Exe and wrestled her to the ground.

Riven and Caulder grabbed ahold of them, struggling to separate the twins. Dodger danced out of the way of the thrashing ball of bodies. Unable to free herself from Viva's vicious grip, Exe shouted, "I wish I could—"

BOOM! In that instant, a brilliant, deafening explosion entombed the four of them in a column of black fire that swelled into a dome of white smoke. Within the span of a nanosecond, Exe felt herself disintegrate into billions of pieces as if forcibly blasted through a microscopic sieve. Just as she felt herself reforming, she slammed into something solid and unyielding that suddenly flexed and hurled her backwards. She skittered to a stop on a slick surface.

Searching for the others in the lingering fog, Exe staggered to her feet, puzzled as to why the shimmering mist felt weirdly wet. An endless roaring filled Exe's ears as she careened toward the three dark shapes rising beside her, slipping on the damp slickness below her feet. Realization came slowly—they were no longer in the field.

Abject terror was frozen on the others' faces as it dawned on Exe: they'd accidentally volted right onto the docks at the entrance to Vianelle. Before she could react, Riven shoved Caulder hard in the chest, knocking him over the edge of the dock to plunge into the waterfall mountain's raging gathering pool thousands of feet below them.

A scream of shocked fury locked in Exe's throat as she witnessed Viva diving in after him. Distant shouts sounded over the roar of the waterfall as Exe turned on Riven, ready to rage at him. Before she could utter a word, Riven lunged at her, sending them both tumbling over the edge. They hit the water hard only seconds later. Liquid surged into Exe's lungs as she surfaced, coughing and struggling as Riven tried to drag her along as he swam.

It took Exe a second to realize that they'd landed in the giant bubble wand contraption that slowly scooped up the sideways-sailing ferries. Caulder and Viva had already climbed into the arching metal supports below the dock. Exe's battling against Riven had cost them precious seconds. They barely missed getting crushed while crawling into the arches as the docking mechanism locked into place.

What do we do now? Exe opened her mouth to shout the question over the roaring water, but the look on Riven's face silenced her. He put a finger to his lips and looked up. Over two dozen pairs of goon boots thundered overhead. Though they were shouting, Exe could only make out the words, 'invasion,' 'attack,' and 'capture.'

Exe's grip on the water-slick steel stiffened with cold and tension as several silent hours passed below the swirling black trench coats of the Disimulata pacing above. Once the ferries quit running for the night, their numbers dwindled until there were only two left. When the two remaining began their pacing patrol, Exe and the others took advantage of their momentary absence, maneuvering their heads close enough together to talk above the roar of the raging falls without being overheard.

"What do we do?" Viva cried, panic edging her voice.

"Can we volte through a bunch of cruor-protected locations like we did to escape The Wendings?" Exe shivered, the iciness of the slippery steel penetrating her bones.

Riven shook his head, "Even if we volted in four different directions, the Disimulata are on alert. They'd be at every location the instant we arrived. Besides, these beams are embedded with bluestone for security. We can't use magic here."

Exe's eyes met Viva's. *Will she confess that I probably can use my Unbindable powers here?*

Glaring spiteful condemnation at Exe, Viva asked Caulder, "Dodger saw us vanish and she heard us talking about Vianelle. She'll send someone after us, won't she?"

"Yes, but they'll search the city first. It'll take hours, maybe days before they'd even think to look for us here," Caulder replied, then turned to Riven. "You're one of them. You need to crawl up and lure them back toward the city gate. Then we'll climb up and volte away from the end of the dock. That should give us enough time–"

Riven was adamant, "If I appear on this dock without having volted in or exited from the city gate, they'll know I was involved with the disturbance and nab us all."

"How did we even get here?" Caulder asked, slipping as he shifted his grip. "It shouldn't have been possible to volte here from within the Vale."

Glancing away guiltily, Exe was grateful when Riven turned their attention by saying, "Asher and Malina will hear about the disturbance at the gate and figure out what happened. We have no choice but to wait here until they find us."

"Or the Disimulata do," Caulder added, his eyes on Riven.

"Or we plunge to our deaths," Viva stated.

They fell silent as a pair of goon boots passed overhead, each lost in hopelessness and desperation.

Exe closed her eyes, *Please don't let Caulder or Riven die because of me. Or Viva. And what will the Parsells think if*

I never come home? Will Velin tell them what happened to me? Or won't he know because he can't see inside my mind anymore? If only Easy, or Thone, or Seph were here, then Velin could see inside their minds and send help. What if my brothers WERE here? They've gotten themselves in tight spots pulling their pranks, and they didn't have magical powers to get themselves out of them...

Exe looked all around, trying to picture her predicament the way her brothers would to find a way out. Far against the mountainside, Exe spotted a dark, cavernous beacon of hope. A giant culvert hidden out of sight beneath the dock, and below it, almost obscured by the falling water, a ladder built into the mountainside.

"What's under the city?" Exe asked as soon as the boots above moved away. "If we can get to that culvert, can we volte from there?"

"Are you nuts?!" Viva exclaimed.

"No," Riven answered. "They're constructed from bluestone too."

"But we could use the tunnels to access the city—we've done it," Caulder said. "And there are safe places to volte from inside the city. If we could get to them."

"We can get there," Exe assured.

"Pardon me, bughouse Betty, but have you recently sprouted wings? How do you propose that we get all the way over there without volting?" Viva sneered.

"We climb," Exe replied. With a silent 'Thank You' to Seph for all of their spelunking adventures, she demonstrated the proper rock-climbing maneuvers they'd need to use to safely navigate the slippery steel girders.

"Do you think we all have ankyro arms? How do you expect us to reach anywhere but where we are?" Viva scoffed.

"It won't be easy, but it's doable. Only we'll have to slide farther down where the arches are closer together. There's a ladder under the culvert—do you think it goes all the way down?" Exe asked. Caulder nodded.

Riven frowned, "If it doesn't, then we're stuck down there and closer to the waterfalls where we're more likely to be knocked off."

"It does," Caulder answered. "A couple of my clients do dock maintenance work. With all the bluestone, they can't use magic so they have to crawl around just like Exe described. Only we won't have their safety harnesses."

"We'll use our belts," Exe replied, profoundly grateful that belts were a must-have Anacapian fashion trend. Using Riven's Disimulata pin they poked holes at their belt ends to make them wide enough to go around themselves and the delicate support beams. "These are for safety only, to give you precious seconds to adjust your grip should you happen to slip," Exe said, demonstrating how to anchor the belts above the rivets. "Don't rest your full weight on it as you maneuver down, or it'll break when you really need it. Once we get low enough, we'll be able to climb from beam to beam without them."

"We'd better move now before the first ferry run," Riven said.

"No, I won't go. This is madness," Viva replied, on the point of hyperventilating.

"I get it. You don't trust me," Exe held up a quelling hand when both boys appeared ready to interrupt. "You don't have to trust me. Trust Seph. He's the one who taught me how to do this."

"Okay," Viva reluctantly agreed.

With painful slowness Exe led the way down the slick steel arches rivet by rivet. She took extra care with her footing so that the others would do the same. About halfway down, the arches grew close enough to clamber from beam to beam. Exe dropped her belt into the seething waters below and inched her way toward the falling water.

Getting from beam to ladder proved more difficult than Exe expected as the rushing water threatened to whisk her off the slippery metal. Thankful that she'd gone first, Exe figured out how to shift her position on the support until she was facing away from the waterfall. Then she leaned back to hook her elbow securely over the closest rung before swinging her whole body around to get on the ladder. Making sure that the others saw her using her elbows to secure her position on each rung, Exe began the long, dangerous climb upward.

Exe's burgeoning hope faded when she reached the hatch overhead. It wouldn't budge. *Locked. Like my belfry back home.* Panicked, Exe had to stop herself from wishing the thing open. *Take a breath and think. It's metal and there's water everywhere. It's probably just rusted shut.* Keeping one arm tightly wrapped around the final rung, Exe pulled at the latch with every ounce of strength she had and shoved her head against the hatch. It flew open with a rusty groan and clanged loudly against the floor above. Exe froze and stared upward through the open culvert at the only bit of dock she could see about seven feet up. Two sets of boots. One lounging, the other slowly pacing in front of the entrance. *No alarm. They didn't hear it.*

Wet and shivering, Exe quietly closed the hatch after everyone reached the safety of the tunnel. Moving deeper in where the guards above couldn't overhear, all eyes turned to Caulder. His hesitancy was clearly visible in the dim light cast by the faintly glowing bluestone walls.

"Where to now?" Riven demanded of Caulder. "You're the one who claimed to know where to volte from within the city. None of you would be safe in the places I know of."

"I don't need to tell you and expose one of our safe houses to the Black Jacket Brigade," Caulder raised his chin. "You're free to go up into the city by yourself without any trouble. I'll get the girls to safety."

"You think I'm going to leave Exe's safety in your hands?" Riven bristled. "After you traipsed all over Anacapia with her, giving no thought to the danger?!"

"Oh, just forget about me, right?" Viva cried out. "I'm already dead thanks to this loathsome skag."

"I'm sorry, okay! I didn't mean to–" Exe defended, then took a deep breath. "Whatever we're going to do, we have to go now. It'll be getting light in a few hours, and daylight means more people. We'll be in more danger in a crowded city, won't we?"

"Exe is right. And I'm not abandoning any of you," Riven returned. "If you three want to get out of here alive, you're going to need me. Got it?"

Caulder reluctantly nodded, "Bogey's. Do you know it? I know it's not a Jette Set joint. The cellar doors around back are fake. It's a small stash compartment, but it's cruor-lined. You can volte Exe into the Corpse Copse from there without being detected."

"Exe?" Riven asked.

"You're right," Caulder replied. "Exe needs your Jette Set membership protection if she's going to survive Vianelle."

"Wait, how does getting to Bogey's get us out? Volting in Vianelle is restricted to only within city limits. So it's impossible to volte out of the city, isn't it?" Viva asked. "That's why everyone has to volte to the city gates to enter. And that's why we rebounded off the shield guarding the walls onto the dock, right?"

Caulder glanced at Riven and sighed, "We've spelled the cellar so that volting from inside it routes through the old tunnels, which we've also coated with cruor clay. Unfortunately, they've blocked off all direct access to those old tunnels from here, or we could avoid going up into the city altogether."

"Thanks for that, by the way. I've used those protected tunnels to craft my own undetectable access points into and out of the city," Riven smirked as Caulder scowled.

"And we'll volte where exactly?" Exe asked, glancing at Viva. It had suddenly struck her that her thoughtless actions had made it so that Viva couldn't just go home.

"Home. I want my mother," Viva demanded.

"Neither of you can go home to Asher and Malina," Riven replied. "Not after—"

"We'll all go to the Corpse Copse, then back to Nowhere," Caulder said. Exe cringed at Riven's expression when Caulder said 'back to Nowhere.' When it appeared that Viva might protest the plan, Caulder added, "Velin will know how to help us."

With a plan in place, Caulder led the way deeper into the winding tunnels. After what felt like an hour of walking, he stopped below a swaying chain ladder that led up to a manhole overhead. He said to Riven, "This drops you in the alleyway behind the Moonlit Quill. Bogey's is six blocks away. Can you find it from there?"

Riven nodded and grasped the swinging chain ladder, "You three wait here. I need to verify that the coast is clear before we attempt this."

Exe and Viva sat down on opposite sides of Caulder and leaned back against the glowing blue walls to wait. Shivering as the cold stone turned her wet clothes to ice, Exe couldn't help but think, *I wish my clothes were dry.* Instantly terrified that the Disimulata would detect magic in the bluestone-protected tunnels and burst upon them, it took a second for Exe to realize that her clothes were still sopping wet. *Why didn't that wish work? Does bluestone really prevent me from using my powers even though I'm Unbindable?* Exe turned to ask Caulder how the stone worked, and found him looking slightly sick, his head resting back against the wall. She asked, "Are you okay, Caulder?"

Caulder gave a slight nod, "It's the stone. Don't you feel it?"

I don't feel a thing, except damp and cold, Exe thought. *If the stone doesn't affect me the way it does Caulder, then why didn't that wish work? After what I did to Riven's brother, it should've been a cinch.* But as impulsive as the ball of bodies was, she had wanted to hurt Schade in that moment. She'd felt power surging through her as she concentrated on exactly what she was doing. This had just been a casual longing that she wished were true, but had no real intent or plan to make it happen. *Can I really have gotten my wish magic under control?* Glancing over again, Exe realized that now was not the time to share her momentary happiness about that.

As the minutes dragged on towards an hour, Exe's gaze drifted to Viva who sat with her head buried in her knees. *How much trouble is she in because of what I did? What if they ask her to demonstrate that ball of bodies, and she can't do it?*

Could she claim it wasn't her? No, everyone was looking at me. They wouldn't really kill—

As Exe blocked the sickening thought from her mind, Viva sat up straight and nudged Caulder, "Face it, he's not coming back."

Caulder sighed and opened his eyes, "I've been thinking that too. We can't wait anymore. It'll be getting light soon."

"Can we make it to Bogey's?" Viva asked, rising and grasping the chain ladder.

"If we stick to the shadows, duck into every alleyway we pass...maybe," Caulder replied, following as Viva began to climb.

"Wait!" Exe cried out. "We can't just go up there. We have no idea why Riven hasn't come back yet. And he will come back."

Viva just sneered and climbed another rung, but Caulder asked, "How can you be so sure Riven will return?"

"Riven wouldn't just abandon me here. I know he'll come back for me," Exe replied uneasily, disturbed that Caulder looked more upset about her secret relationship with Riven than he did by the thought that he'd abandoned them.

Viva's sharp gasp drew Exe's eyes upward—to a circle of light above. Terror barraged Exe, *The Disimulata! But no, wouldn't they just volte down here and grab us? Or can't they volte into bluestone structures? I should know that. I never should've come here when I know so little—*

Darkness blocked the circle of light. A soft whoosh grew louder as a strange, flickering glitter grew closer and closer. The odd object dropped over Viva with a quiet thud, knocking her from the ladder. For a moment, Exe panicked that Viva had been trapped in some sort of magical net, until Viva threw it off and held up a sequined evening gown. As she puzzled over the gown, a falling fedora thunked her on the head, while Caulder got conked by a gentleman's walking stick.

More and more evening clothes fell on them before the light above vanished. Riven slid down the chain ladder right after. Looking grim, he said, "They've connected the attack at The Wendings with the incident at the gate. The Disimulata's all over the city on alert for Viva."

Viva held up the second evening gown and mocked, "My hunters are closing in, and you want us to throw an underground cocktail party?!"

Riven glowered and began handing out the clothes, "Disguises. The only people out on the streets now are the elite coming home from all-night lounges. Get dressed."

Exe and Viva moved down to a bend in the tunnel to change in private. The moment they were alone, Viva asked in a harsh whisper, "How **did** we get here?"

"I'm not sure," Exe whispered back, slipping into her gown. "Your desperation to make me take your place here must've tapped into my wish magic somehow. Something similar happened with Velin once. That's how I found the entrance to Anacapia."

Viva said nothing more as they finished dressing and gathered their discarded clothes. When they rejoined the boys, Riven explained what had happened above.

"The Disimulata spotted me the second I stepped out onto the street. I was able to divert the first patrol, but more appeared every time I cast a bit of magic to steal this stuff. This won't be easy," Riven warned.

"If it's that bad, maybe you should go for Ash—" Caulder started.

"I did that first," Riven interrupted. "They're being interrogated. I thought of going for another Sub Rosa member to help us, but who? I don't know any. And as far as I know, no one else knows that I'm a double agent. So even if you told me who to approach, what are the chances that they would believe me? They'd assume I was sent to trap them."

"Can't we just wait down here until things die down? You can let us know when it's safe, can't you?" Exe asked.

Riven shook his head, "After the Disimulata have finished combing the city, they'll search here next. This is our best shot. I'll take Exe out first, then come back for you two once I get her back to the field. Wait twenty minutes then come up, but stay in the alley. I'll escort you both to Bogey's like I caught you out after curfew. If anyone comes along before I come back for you, pretend you're canoodling. If you're lucky, they'll pass you by..."

Worried about leaving a trail, Riven and Caulder stuffed all of their abandoned clothing into their pockets. Caulder paused while tucking away his jacket, and pulled out the damp, rumpled golden Changeling candy box. He handed it to Exe, holding her gaze in a silent farewell filled with bittersweet wistfulness. Not taking his eyes off Exe, Caulder said to Riven, "It's a gift for her brothers."

Uncomfortably aware of Riven and Viva, Exe fumbled with where to stash the candy box in her pocketless evening gown. Reluctantly she turned to Riven. For a moment he just stared at it, as if he would refuse—or worse. Finally he shoved it in his jacket pocket and said, "We gotta go now. It's getting light."

As Riven started to climb, Exe tried to form an apology to Viva and a final farewell to Caulder, but the words refused to come. *I'm never going to see them again. How can I just say goodbye? This is the end of everything.* With one last, regretful glance at Caulder, Exe followed Riven up the swaying chain ladder.

The agony of scaling an endless ladder that careened crazily as they climbed was nothing compared to the terror of emerging from the manhole into a city teeming with secret police on the hunt for her. It didn't help that hundreds of her 'Wanted: Dead' posters were plastered from top to bottom across the alley's dingy brick wall. It felt as if she'd accidentally entered a maze of mirrors.

It took a second for Exe to realize that not all of the posters had violet eyes. Dozens of fresh ones had vibrant aquamarine ones, with 'Wanted: Alive' emblazoned across the top. *Well, at least they won't kill her—or me—on sight.*

"Now you know what Viva deals with, living in your notorious shadow," Riven said, reaching over to adjust Exe's oversized fascinator. Then he froze, "Why is just one of your eyes violet?"

Exe reached up with her fingertips and realized at once, "I must've lost a contact in the rushing water. What do we do?"

Riven tipped her fancy hat even lower, "You need to keep your face covered, and should anyone stop us, just close your eyes and lean against me like we've been out carousing all night, got it?"

After casually strolling alone to ensure the street was deserted, Riven came back, hauled Exe up against his side and steered her out into the city, subtly staggering only now and again in a convincing late-night revelers act. From under the brim of the fancy fascinator that completely obscured her face, Exe spied alluring bits of the deserted city. Tensed and alert at every passing shadow, Exe marveled at the sleek chrome and streamlined Art Deco-style designs of the shuttered stores.

She smothered a gasp as they hurried across one wide street. At the end of the boulevard, Incendia loomed brilliantly in the brightening sky. *The Palace of Water and Fire.* For a split second, Exe paused to gaze in wonder at violet flames pouring downward to meet smooth jets of pure aqua water shooting up from the palace's base. *Liquid fire falling into sparkling spires.* The ever-undulating substances made the entire palace flicker on the horizon. Where they met in the middle, the water trapped the fire in lava-like droplets that dissipated into a glowing mist that shimmered aqua-violet light.

Jettani's in there. The woman who wants me dead. And now my sister too. A thousand plans to confront the twisted ruler with the might of her Unbindable powers surged through her in that instant before Riven urged her along. *I won't make the same undisciplined mistake with my powers again. When I take her on, I'll be ready.*

A few blocks more and Exe stilled once again at the sight of a familiar structure in the center of a fenced-in city park—a colonnade she recognized from the back of the coin Riven had given her. *The Portal Portend.* Suddenly Exe realized that this was her only chance to learn what Jettani had seen when she'd carried her through the Portal all those years ago. *And Caulder gifted me with a presage to preserve those facts this very night.*

Exe pushed Riven into a nearby alleyway, and in the next second he had her flattened against the wall. Glancing nervously over his shoulder, Riven asked, "What is it? What did you see?"

"The Portal Portend! Riven, I have a presage," Exe breathed. "It's in my clothes in your pocket. I carry it in there, and all this ends! Everyone will know Jettani lied about me! That she's nothing but a fraud who has no right to send a bunch of junior-grade thugs out to terrorize people. So no one will care what I– what they think Viva–"

"Are you cracking up? Your parents have been fighting for fifteen years to open people's eyes, and you think to do it in an instant?" Riven growled. "You can't seriously believe that Anacapians will instantaneously abandon their deeply-held devotion to Jettani simply by showing them the truth of her treachery. They'll cling to their belief in her until forced to see her duplicity in a dozen different ways. And even then, many will stubbornly stay loyal to her."

"Isn't there a chance that seeing the proof of my innocence might change people's minds about Jettani? Especially since she just had those Gyve kids killed? And now she's after Viva?" Exe pleaded.

"Maybe there is a slim chance," Riven conceded. "But how does that help Viva? She'll still go down for what you did. You'd only guarantee that by proving Jettani wrong about you right now."

"What if I confess–" Exe started.

"And get yourself killed after all your parents did to protect you?"

"Do you think they'd rather have Viva die for what I did?" Exe returned.

"I'm gonna do everything in my power to keep you both alive, so let's move. Caulder and Viv are sitting ducks in that alley," Riven shook his head in disbelief, "I've actually brought both Verelustre twins into the heart of

Vianelle at the exact same time. We're lucky if any of us survive this."

Yanking her against his side again, Riven rushed her the last two blocks onto a dimly-lit street in a shadier part of town. Ducking under the dingy green neon "Bogey's" sign (with its flickering 'B'), Riven hurried down the alley and flung wide the cellar doors just as the golden light of dawn threatened to expose their position. Instead of a staircase, the doors revealed a shallow hole liberally coated with the crimson cruor clay. Exe curled awkwardly on the ground in her long, heavily-beaded gown, shifting to accommodate Riven as he crawled in beside her and eased the door shut above them.

As Riven wrapped his arms around her, Exe sensed an odd electricity that left her feeling as if she were betraying Caulder, even though Caulder knew that Riven would need to hold her to volte her. Riven waited precious seconds for Exe to meet his gaze. The moment their eyes met, that sparking, electric connection between them exploded into fireworks that emblazoned every inch of Exe. She'd never volted with her eyes opened before, and the experience seemed to sear a inexpressible bond between them.

A silky liquid cooled Exe's heated skin. Riven had volted them into the aquamarine stream flowing through the Corpse Copse, just inches from the fallen tree she'd accidentally impaled him with on the day they'd met. They stayed locked in their embrace within the soothing waters for only a moment. Then Riven dropped his arm, jumped up and hauled her to her feet.

Without a word, Riven hustled her through the cascade and out into the mirage. After a quick glance to verify that the tower door remained to take Exe home, Riven turned to go, then paused.

Without looking back, he said, "If you were so desperate to see some of Anacapia, why didn't you call me? I was a coin toss away the entire time. With my connections and status—and a proper disguise for you—I could've taken you anywhere and you would've been safe. Instead, you put everything at risk time and again. And now you've probably killed your sister." Tossing Exe's clothes at her feet, Riven hesitated as he pulled out the bedraggled golden candy box. As he threw the box down on the pile, he said sourly, "I hope it was worth it."

When Exe looked up from the pile, he was gone.

CHAPTER THIRTY

RADIO SILENCE

"**W**hat could've happened? Do any of you boys know?" "It's been three days. Maybe I should order her out of bed." "She's barely had anything to eat or drink." "Where in heaven's name did she get that gown?" "Mom, Dad, just give her time. She'll tell us what's the matter when she's ready."

Exe barely heard a word of her family's whispered concern as she lay curled in bed, still wearing the beaded gown, hugging her discarded clothes and the battered golden candy box to her chest. She was lost in one solitary thought (the last thing Riven had said to her): *I've killed my sister.*

In the hours she'd waited in the field after Riven dropped her there, Exe had constructed one fantasy after another of a future with Viva and Caulder in exile with her. With her hopes pinned on Riven rescuing them too, Exe envisioned begrudgingly sharing her tower with Viva, telling fanciful stories to fascinated friends on how they'd reunited after being separated at birth. Caulder would bunk with her brothers, or maybe even keep Velin company in that decrepit old house. Perhaps Asher and Malina would come too, and find a little house in Nowhere for themselves and Viva, where Exe could easily visit without abandoning her own family.

But those dreams grew more futile with every passing moment that Viva and Caulder failed to appear. Exe had even remained hopeful when she finally went home through her tower door, telling herself that Viva and Caulder had the power to volte themselves to Nowhere when they eventually escaped. But when the next day dawned without any sign or signal, Exe had withdrawn into the darkness of her deepest fears.

Whatever happens, I'm responsible. I can't even hang the blame on out-of-control wish magic this time—I did this. There were a dozen other ways I could've protected Dodger without repercussions to Viva. But in spite of everything Rove has ever taught me about discipline, and situational awareness, and remaining calm when in dire straits, I let myself be ruled by emotion and caved to impulsivity and rash action. I killed my sister. And Caulder... Her mind balked at the thought of Caulder. She couldn't bear to think about what might be happening to him. And so round and round the dark thoughts spun on an endless loop.

A sudden creak on the stairs below tore her from recriminations. Someone was climbing the stairs. She'd been so lost in thought, they were already on the flight just below her. *The Disimulata! Viva's told them where to find me!* Exe crawled out of bed and tucked herself along the wall. The creaking was coming closer. Whoever it was, they were making no effort to hide their approach.

"Exie?" Charley's small, frightened voice released Exe's tension. "Exe? Where are you? I'm scared!" The shadow of his head bobbed upward as he struggled up the steps, half-tangled in his security blanket.

"I'm right here, Charley," Exe called, crawling back into bed. "What are you doing up here in the middle of the night?" she asked, although she already knew the answer. For the last few weeks, she'd been delighting him with tales of her adventures into Anacapia disguised as make-believe bedtime stories. She slid to one side leaving room for him to join her and held up the covers invitingly. Charley didn't hesitate before plowing in.

"I missed you," Charley whispered.

"You wet your bed again, didn't you?" Exe whispered back.

Charley nodded, "How'd ya know?"

"You forgot to change your pajamas," she answered. Exe helped him peel off his wet bottoms and change into the dry ones she kept handy for just such an occasion.

"Tell me a story, Exie," he pleaded as the stairs creaked again.

"Is she going to?" Henny-boy called out softly, the shadow of his head peeking over the top of the staircase.

"Yes," Charley called back in a not-so-quiet whisper. Henny-Boy, and Moth too, plopped down on the foot of the bed. Exe waited a few minutes more for Seph, Thone, and Easy to take up their positions around her bed.

After Charley's second midnight visit to her, Henny-Boy had started tagging along to hear Exe's stories too, explaining that ten-year-olds weren't interested in fairy tales—he was just making sure Charley was okay. The time after that, Moth had joined. And then the rest of her brothers had started coming to hear her stories about what they considered to be an imaginary land. Although, from the strange looks Easy shot her during the stories, she thought he might suspect the truth. *Perhaps because of our trip to the field?*

While she'd at first resented Velin's demand to write down her Anacapian adventures in her diary (and draw him pictures too), Exe had to admit that she was glad to have those memories preserved in such detail now. And the paintings certainly helped appease Charley's incessant demand for details. While Exe did consider herself an amateur artist, she didn't have the skill to capture Anacapia the way she wanted. Luckily (and suspiciously), she'd found a spell in her vade to enchant her art supplies into creating photorealistic paintings of every location she'd visited. *Except The Wendings...*

Exe thumbed wanly through the stack of drawings on her bedside suitcase stack, debating over which adventure to retell, only her mind was filled with that last fateful night in Anacapia. Unable to focus on anything else, Exe told them everything that had happened that night. She lingered over details of The Wendings and answered all of their questions about the fantastical amusement park, although she was shy when describing her interactions with Caulder. When she reached the part where they'd shared the Changeling candy, Exe's voice caught and she trailed off.

"What's next, Exie?" Charley demanded, as Exe realized that all of her brothers were waiting impatiently for her to finish her story.

"She went home," Exe said abruptly.

"That's it? I thought they were going on one more ride," Moth, the story stickler, said. "It's kinda anticlimactic. Does she plan on going back?"

"I'm not sure," Exe hedged, Moth's question stirring an anxious uneasiness.

"What do you mean, you're not sure?" Henny-boy demanded. "It's your story. Don't you get to decide what happens?"

"I don't know! I don't know what I'm supposed to do now," Exe cried.

"Let's give our storyteller a break, shall we? It's hard work inventing all of these fantastical things," Easy said, looking at Exe like he knew they weren't imaginary. "We can wait to find out how the story ends, right? Let's get some shuteye."

As her brothers all settled in to sleep right where they were, Exe realized that they all had bedding ready to go— and it looked well-used. *Have they been bunking up here with me the entire time and I didn't even notice?* Though sound sleep had eluded her since her return, Exe now slipped easily into slumber, surrounded by her brothers' love.

The next morning, Exe awoke to another creak on the stairs just below and opened her eyes to the sight of Rove and Ella peeking at their children over the top step. They brightened at the sight of Exe's timid, yet well-rested smile and came up onto the landing. One sharp "Attention!" from Rove and her brothers were instantly awake and neatly lined up along Exe's bedside, all grinning broadly.

"I believe I called you all to attention," Rove leveled Exe with a stern look.

Exe scrambled out of bed and took her place in between Easy and Moth. When Rove called out "About face," Exe turned toward the down stairs, but her brothers all turned toward the up stairs. Turning around just in time, Exe kept time with her brothers when Rove called, "Forward harch!"

Up the narrow stairs toward the nailed-shut belfry they all climbed. When Seph reached the ladder he stood aside as did the rest of her brothers, but when Exe joined the line, Rove beckoned her forward, "You first, soldier."

Puzzled, Exe climbed the ladder and popped open the trap door. It fell with a thud as Exe gazed around in amazement. Her family had transformed the belfry into her own private paradise. Along the entire outer wall was a low, cushioned bench with storage bins underneath stocked with every type of clothing, accessory, cosmetic, jewelry, and more that a girl could desire. (Glancing at the odd assortment of items, Exe was sure her brothers had a hand in the shopping.)

Around the giant bell were bookcases stretching floor to ceiling stuffed with all of her favorite books and her vintage videotapes. Rove had maximized the space between the bench and the bookcases, finding room for a desk (complete with brand new computer) and a wall-mounted flatscreen with cushioned seating below. ("I figured out how to hook an old VCR to it," Henny-Boy boasted.)

Exe took it all in with a sweeping glance before her attention was captured by the brand new windows. All of her paintings of Anacapia had been turned into exquisite stained-glass windows. Glistening in the Arizona sunlight, Exe marveled at the mirage; the Silver Sands and the Lake of Fire; the Placid Pools; the silvery home where Asher; Malina, and Viva lived; even Vianelle atop the waterfall mountain.

Overcome, Exe threw herself into Rove's arms, her eyes fixed on the stained-glass image of Vianelle. Tears began to fall as Exe envisioned Viva and Caulder there (and what might be happening to them), until she was weeping uncontrollably.

"You haven't even seen the balcony repairs yet," Rove patted her awkwardly.

Ella embraced them both, whispering in Exe's ear, "It's okay, honey. We've missed you, but you're home now." Exe just sobbed harder. Her brothers joined the embrace, hugging any bit of Exe they could reach. They broke away when Exe finally grew silent, and Ella motioned her sons to head out.

"Entrance to this room is by invitation only, boys. And if any of you ring that bell while Exe is up here, I'll tan your hide," Rove called over Exe's shoulder. Only Easy lingered, halfway out of the trap door, as Rove and Ella loosened their embrace and waited for answers.

"We know you've been going through something," Ella started. "We've tried to be patient, but I think it's time that you tell us." Exe looked back and forth between them but couldn't speak.

"Look, Exe, I've known for a long time that you'd eventually have to deal with things that my other children wouldn't," Rove said. "I've done my best to train you to face whatever that may be. And I've prepared myself to help you when the time came. But I can't help you if you won't tell me what's going on."

"I'm okay. I promise," Exe wiped her tear-damp face with Rove's handkerchief. "I know I need to tell you everything, and I will, but–" She almost starting sobbing again as she glimpsed the stained-glass image of Asher and Malina's home. "It's too much right now. I need time."

Sharing a concerned look, Rove and Ella let Exe go and headed for the trap door. Making way for his parents, Easy hopped up to sit on the floor, legs still hanging down through the trap door. Rove let Ella go down first, then paused.

"You know, Exe, moving to a new place and attending a new school is always a struggle," Rove said slowly. (*Does he really think I'm just having trouble adjusting?!*) Smiling slightly at Exe's incredulous look, Rove continued, "Thanks to Easy's social skills, we've never had to worry about our boys. Only you. But Easy may have done them a disservice."

"Hey!" Easy objected pleasantly.

"Seph and Thone are nearing the age when they'll strike out into the world on their own. Will they be ready to do so after relying on Easy's help all of these years? I don't know. But I don't worry about you. You've never taken the 'Easy' path. Ever. And while I've often worried, I've always admired you for that. Whatever you're struggling with, I know you'll do what's right. Even if it isn't... easy."

As Rove stepped down another rung, Exe cried out, "I'm afraid!"

"You say that like you're ashamed. What have I taught you about fear? It's only detrimental if you let it rule you. A healthy fear is a wise thing. It fuels caution, guides instincts, and teaches restraint. And it's frequently the key to survival. Fear is also a powerful tool. It can paralyze you, terrorize you, lock you in, bar you from taking the risks that come with living. If you let fear rule you, anyone can control you. I've raised you to control your fear and do what's right, even if that requires risk. Can you do that?"

"I don't know," Exe bit her lip. "How do I know what's right?"

"I can't answer that until you're ready to tell me what's wrong," Rove said. When Exe just dropped her head, Rove sighed and continued down the ladder.

As soon as he was gone, Easy cleared his throat and said, "When you're ready to talk, Exe, I'm ready to understand. I know more than most, you know. I was at that field with you. And I know that Caulder kid is no 'old friend.'" When Exe teared up again and didn't answer, Easy headed out the trap door, too, saying, "You know where to find me."

I can't just sit here anymore. I have to do—something. But how can I know what's right until I know what's going on? Surrounded by the stained-glass windows depicting the home she'd never see again, Exe was almost overcome by an anguished urge to smash them. Desperate to escape the irrational desire to destroy her family's gift, Exe stepped out onto the balcony. Her eyes fell on Velin's house silhouetted against the sunrise. *I can't face Riven. And I can't go back into Anacapia to find out for myself.* There was only one person left that she could ask for help.

The desert-warmed spring breeze rattled the nine still hanging down like a six on Velin's weathered house. A drop of sweat dripped onto the framed paintings Exe held as she stood indecisively on his front porch, desperation and dread warring within her.

It had occurred to her a few hours before, as she'd stood on her belfry balcony puzzling over how to best approach Velin, that he'd never seen the pictures he'd insisted she make to accompany her diary entries. Wanting to make a proper peace offering, Exe had spent the morning in Ella's art studio framing the paintings. *He asked for them, but never asked to see them. Did he only want them so he could have those stained-glass windows created for me? Did he use my family to gift me the windows as a way to keep my memories of Anacapia close after I was cut off from it the way he is?*

Exe had no answers for the questions that had tumbled through her as she worked. And although she'd convinced herself that the gesture was magnanimous, doubts were creeping in now that she stood on the threshold of facing him again. Exe placed her hand on the doorknob, then decided to knock instead. *I can't offer a peace offering after barging in, can I?* She'd only rapped one knuckle on the faded door when it creaked wide open. The dusty hallway held only sheet-shrouded furniture that stayed still as she tiptoed toward the golden light beaming from the open door at the end of the darkened hall.

"Well?" Skeletal old Velin faced her across his desk, eyebrows raised, hands folded behind his back.

Exe set the framed paintings of Anacapia on the desktop and stepped back, "I thought you'd want to see these. Have them, now that I've got the stained-glass windows of– Were they your idea? Or– you did ask me for these, right?" Exe was suddenly suspicious that perhaps Viva had lied to her about Velin's request. *Did she just want me to write what I did in Anacapia down so she could read my diaries later?*

"I wanted the pictures, and the entries," Velin confirmed, not even glancing at the paintings. "Their existence merely assisted your family when your brothers came up with the window idea. What you're here for is over there." Velin jerked his head toward a strange newspaper displayed on an ornate podium then turned his back on Exe. His gaze brushed over the paintings as he turned, and Exe could've sworn a grimace of pain creased his face in that moment.

Exe approached the podium with apprehension as she saw 'The Anacapian Argus' emblazoned across the top of the newspaper and the headline: 'Viva V. Trial Tomorrow.' A sickening chill seeped through Exe as she read that Viva was not only accused of attacking the Jette Set kids at The Wendings, but she was also suspected of having been switched out before 'The Execution,' and was in fact Experience Verelustre! Not a word was mentioned about Caulder.

"Simply swipe the date to view earlier editions if you want news of that boy you went adventuring with," Velin said over his shoulder. Exe swiped and saw that the previous day's paper said Caulder had been released with a warning for interfering. She barely listened as Velin continued, "That's the only paper of its kind, you know. I got the idea to modify it from the Entirety Tome you were gifted and that tablet device your brothers often play with."

Scanning the story about Caulder's involvement, Exe was surprised to discover that no one had reported seeing 'Viva' and Caulder together at The Wendings before the incident. Instead, he was described as a passerby who had been about to defend his sister when 'Viva' attacked. Some of Jettani's concilium even hailed him as a hero for deescalating the incident by whisking Dodger and Viva away. ("After all, we might have Jette Set members on trial now had they instantly killed Viva in retaliation.")

"Rande intervened on his brother's behalf," Velin said, as if he could still read Exe's mind to know that she was puzzling over the praise heaped on Caulder. "That brazen young man threatened to cut the Vianelle elitists off from all their black market goods should anything happen to Caulder. So he was let off with a slap on the wrist."

"This paper doesn't say any of that. How could you know?" Exe asked.

"Your other young man, the one you were skulking around graverobbing with that night your brothers 'borrowed' the neighbors car," Velin replied. "He was here just this morning, and he filled me in on some of the details."

"He was here?" Exe turned and found Velin watching her carefully. *Riven came to Nowhere, but he didn't come see me.* Desperate to hide her hurt from Velin, Exe said, "Only one of its kind? What kind of newspaper only prints one copy?"

"There are millions printed. Every household in Anacapia is mandated to have a copy and read it daily. No need to buy a new one; those editions change daily to the current news," Velin explained. "This force-feeds every citizen the current propaganda, and erases any record of past propaganda so none can see how it's changed. While the news vanishes daily for the masses, Jettani's propaganda department keeps a copy of all previous papers to keep track of what they're telling the public. I spelled mine to access them so I may keep a permanent record of Jettani's shifting disinformation. All the lies she spews as 'fact' to deceive and control an entire population."

"Like the way you lied to me? Making me believe I'd murdered Bonnie with a wish simply so that I'd be easier to control?" Exe demanded, scolding herself for antagonizing him when she needed his help so badly.

Velin's considering gaze grew cold, "I'd hardly equate that to this propaganda. Its sole purpose is to subjugate an entire people to the iron will of the state, regardless of their wishes or welfare. I manipulated you to protect you. You were a stubborn, willful child who continued playing with your powers no matter how much I tried to stop you. And I had to stop you. Your life depended on it. When Bonnie died in that accident, I took advantage of the opportunity to drill home that you must not use your powers. Every time you used them was an opportunity for the Disimulata to find you. So it was either let you believe that you'd killed her, or tell a ten-year-old that she's being hunted by a relentless police force sent by a powerful, corrupt government who wants her dead. What would you have done?"

Exe tried to imagine herself at ten, finding the 'Wanted:Dead' poster and dealing with all the fear and suffering that came with it when she was that young. Finally she said, "I would've let me believe that I'd killed Bonnie to keep me from using powers that the Disimulata could easily track."

Velin inclined his head, "I am sorry that it had to be done. I could see no other way to keep you safe. While the Corpse Copse is the closest passage between our worlds, it's by no means the only one. Moving you frequently was another measure to keep you safe, but I could not risk anyone finding you when you were so far away. Here in Nowhere I can volte to you instantly, but in other countries—it'd take several voltes over several minutes. Quick, but not quick enough."

Comforted yet uncomfortable by the truce that had settled between them, Exe's tumultuous thoughts turned back to Viva, "They're going to kill my sister, aren't they?" When Velin sighed and nodded, Exe asked, "Why haven't they done it already?"

"Even a kangaroo court requires time to play out, despite the fact that the outcome is predetermined," Velin answered. "The court of public opinion is undoubtedly more important to a tyrant than a court of law. Judges and politicians can be blackmailed and bribed to do as ordered. But an unruly public, energized by justice and outraged by oppression, can easily overwhelm even the most brutal dictator, no matter how broad his reach or how big his army."

"So, can you teach me how to defeat an army by tomorrow?" Exe asked, blinking her tear-damp eyelashes.

"What?" Velin frowned in confusion.

"This says that they'll sentence Viva to death tomorrow, and they won't wait to execute her, will they? And it'll be my fault!"

"Your actions at The Wendings are the means, not the reason," Velin replied, his tone cautious, measured. "It was inevitable that Jettani would one day use Viva to take down Asher and Malina, the same way she used you. They're her only opposition. Jettani's only hesitated until now because she's afraid that once your parents are completely ousted, they'll return with you and use you as a weapon against her."

"That's it?! You expect me to just sit here and accept that my only sister is about to be executed for something I did?" Exe shouted, resisting the urge to destroy his study with the flick of a wish.

"What's done is done. You cannot change the past."

Amethyst clashed with sapphire as they stared each other down.

"I can't change the past, but you could," Exe dared with a tilt of her chin.

"No one but God should have the power to change or control the whole world."

"I'm not asking to change the whole world. I'm asking you to save my sister."

"And when would you have me go back to in order to do that? Shall I simply stop you from going to The Wendings? Stop you before your first ill-conceived Anacapian adventure? Or perhaps stop you from ever going into Anacapia in the first place? Have you even paused to consider what else would change if I meddled with the past? Yours is a selfish request."

Exe had to bite her tongue to keep from calling him selfish in return. *He only invented time travel to save his brother's life because he didn't want to rule Anacapia.* But Exe recognized the lie within that truth the moment she thought it. *I can't know that his reasons for saving his older brother were wholly selfish, but I do know that traveling back to end his life again was a purely selfless act.* The heartbreaking vision of adult Velin drowning his own older brother to return the world to the way it had been—despite the fact that it had resulted in the loss of Velin's own son—humbled her. *But still...*

"I shouldn't have implied that you should use time travel to help me. But you can't expect me to sit here and do nothing," Exe challenged.

"Make your peace with the past and move on. That's all that's left to you now," Velin muttered, sinking into his leather armchair before the cold, empty jade fireplace and burying himself in a book. Helplessness surged into outrage as Exe gaped at him.

"NO!" She cried out, gasping through incredulous tears, Rove's lesson on fear and action ringing in her ears. "For years I sat back and did nothing because YOU were afraid. That's why I struggled so much growing up. Your constant nagging kept me sidelined when it goes against my very nature. You can spend your life lamenting all that's gone wrong if you want, afraid of where risks or mistakes may lead you in the future. But I refuse to do so any longer! It's always right to fight for freedom and against evil—no matter what the risks. I'm responsible for Viva's arrest, and I have to find a way to fix it. Why won't you help me?!"

Velin just sat there reading, unmoved by her impassioned plea. Infuriated, Exe fled toward the door, her mind blank on where to turn next.

"I did attempt to raise you, you know," Velin said softly. Exe stilled in the doorway, listening as he continued, "You lived with me here for a year before I placed you with the Parsells. You were miserable. Always crying, interrupting my studies with your demands for attention, for necessities. I was the same way with my own son," Velin's voice cracked.

"You remember your life with him?" Exe asked tentatively.

"Faded memories of endless failings. I neglected my wife and my son because I was too absorbed in my studies," Velin whispered. "I pretended that my decision to revert the past to its original state was a wholly magnanimous gesture, but in part I returned to the status quo because of the disaster I'd made of my own perfect life. So I understand what it's like to regret a massive mistake. But even if you could correct the past, you'll always make more mistakes. Time travel cannot fix the past—it can only end the future."

"Refusing to act ends the future too," Exe's reply was both gentle and firm. "You cannot truly live if you let yourself be paralyzed by fear and doubt." When Velin's answering silence stretched toward a minute, Exe again turned to go.

"I always intended to train you," Velin's quiet words uttered almost as an apology for past failings halted her once again. "That doorknob wall. Each is enchanted with a lesson that operates similar to those virtuous reality glasses your brothers play games with. The room through that door is filled with them too."

Exe glanced over at the wall covered from floor to ceiling with its eclectic array of doorknobs and handles, then said, "So you do know how to act when it matters. You just always wait until it's too late."

"I delayed bringing you back here to train because I kept inventing new lessons," Velin continued softly, ignoring her barb. "And I was haunted by the memory of how I'd treated my son. You were so happy with the Parsells. The thought of bringing you back here, telling you about the dangers you were facing... Answering for my own mistakes. I waited too long."

"For what it's worth? Thanks," Exe replied, her back still to him. "For giving me to the Parsells. I was happy with them, despite how miserable you made me. It's thanks to them that I know how to stand up for the people I love, no matter what it costs me. I will figure out a way to make things right, even without your help."

Although Exe didn't look back, she could feel Velin's eyes on her as she left.

Presage. Vade. Wanted poster. Entirety Tome. Textbook. Spectaculars. Candy box. Vianelle globe. Coin. Exe gathered all the evidence that she might need, slung her backpack over her shoulder, and slipped out into their spacious nave living room.

The house was surprisingly packed for an afterschool afternoon, and it suddenly occurred to Exe that the house had been unusually quiet lately—until today. *My family closed ranks for me even though they didn't know what was wrong.* Her brothers were certainly making up for lost time, using the whole house as battlegrounds for a raging pillow fight.

At that very moment, Easy came spinning down the fireman's pole from the balcony, swinging his pillow at anyone in range. "We got 'em on the run! Let's go, Wolverines!" Easy shouted, wiping the sweat from his brow with his red bandana. The second he spotted Exe, Easy dropped his pillow and handed his bandana off to Thone. "Take over, I've got another mission to tackle. We're up by seventeen."

"Sweet! I was just down by that much. Wolverines, huddle! I'm the captain now," Thone said, ripping the blue bandana off his arm and tying on Easy's red one.

As Easy caught his breath and looked at her expectantly, Exe debated where to have this earthshaking conversation. *Might as well plunge him into the deep end.* Leading the way into her tower, Exe locked the interior door after them. Then she crossed to the door to the graveyard, whispered 'postern,' and opened the door into the field.

Easy released a long, slow breath, "So this is how you've been getting here. I figured this field is where you've been disappearing to, but I never imagined..."

"I take it you've known for a while that I have– magical powers?"

"You've been my sister for thirteen years. How could I not know? We just figured you'd talk about it when you were ready," Easy said, easing the door closed after following her into the field.

Exe watched him carefully as he prowled around the lone door and scanned the field, gazing right through the mirage.

At a loss for a spell that would reveal it to him, Exe simply wished. From his gasp, Exe gathered that he could now see it. She sat down on its crisp emerald grass, legs hanging over the side of the oasis and waited for him to take it all in.

Soon he sank down beside her and said simply, "So, you have a twin sister."

"You know that too?" Exe was aghast. "Does the whole family know?"

"Seph and Thone figured it out, after me. And I'm pretty sure Mom and Dad suspect, though she didn't engage with them much. The younger boys, though, they just think that Nowhere made you super cool," Easy joked, laughing at the outrage on Exe's face. "Relax, she's family too now. You gotta expect us to tease. Don't worry, we'll razz her too about how much better you are."

Easy's casual expectation of seeing Viva again broke Exe down, and when her sobs subsided she told him everything. Starting all the way back with the 'Wanted Dead' poster ("So that's where you got that thing."), how Velin had been manipulating them all of these years, ("You mean that ghoul living behind us is planting ideas in our heads?!"), and how how their road trip to the field helped her find her way to her birth country.

Exe didn't leave out a thing. She told him all the gory facts about helping Riven frame the Gyve kids ("So that's the guy I spotted you skulking around the cemetery with that night."), included every detail of training sessions with Caulder ("Told'ya that kid wasn't an 'old friend' I didn't remember."), and their risky adventures to Anacapia. She even told him everything Malina had told her about her unbindable powers.

Easy took his time paging through the deceptive textbook and her vade, and was delighted to find that he could call books into the Entirety Tome despite lacking powers. He asked quite a few questions about the real-life locations that had inspired the stained-glass windows, and probed to verify her stories. When they finally got to The Wendings, Exe delayed the inevitable by letting him virtually explore the amusement park with the Spectaculars and sample the Changeling candy. But finally Exe had to admit what she'd done to the Jette Set—and the consequences Viva now faced for her actions.

"And?" Easy asked when she'd finished.

"And—I don't know what to do!" Exe cried out.

"Yes, you do," Easy replied quietly. "Exe, what if it were me on trial for something that you'd done?"

Crumbling under the weight of the absolute conviction of the answer that crystalized in her mind, Exe grabbed Easy into a fierce hug. Easy met her halfway.

"I can't believe I'm advising you to turn yourself in to a government who wants to execute you, but you can't let your sister die for you," Easy said, wiping his tear-damp eyes when they finally broke apart. "But just because you need to be brave and do it, that doesn't mean you have to be stupid about it."

"What are you saying?" Exe asked, wiping her own eyes with her vintage tee.

"I'm saying, it's time to put my mastermind planning skills to better use," Easy replied, suddenly sounding a bit like Rove. "Now tell me every single detail about what we're facing. Who we're up against, who our allies are, and our assets. We need to look at every angle, consider every option. We'll devise a way to save your sister and get you both out of there alive. Wait a sec, we'd better enlist Seph and Thone's help."

Overwhelmed by Easy's immediate assistance and absolute confidence, Exe was speechless as she followed him back home. He ended the evening's events swiftly, gathered his elder brothers, sent his younger brothers off to play, and led the way back into the field just as soon as Exe magically opened the door. Exe braced herself to retell everything to her older brothers, but Easy made short work of that, giving them just the bare essentials before detailing the mission at hand.

"We should bring Dad in on this," Seph said, once he'd heard what Exe was up against. "And Mom should know too."

Thone shook his head, "We don't have time. They'd kill us if they knew what we're helping Exe do—even though they'd eventually admit it's the only option."

At first, Exe just listened to her elder brothers debate every possible plan of attack, pulling a bunch of ideas from past pranks and stunts that she remembered fondly, even if she hadn't participated. But soon enough she was offering ideas of her own. It was her idea to use Riven's gift of the snow globe to study Vianelle's layout and the location of the Portal Portend up close. The Entirety Tome came in handy too, letting them look up answers they needed about Jettani and the inner workings of Anacapian justice in the reference books on Caulder's list.

Dusk crept close as her brothers made her review the plan one last time. Satisfied that Exe had it down pat, Seph said, "And if anything goes wrong, just use those unstoppable powers of yours to knock everyone out, grab Viva, and your parents probably, and bolt yourself out of there."

"I'm not sure they're exactly unstoppable," Exe replied, her smile slightly unsteady, yet confident.

"Exe, you raised me from a fake grave, then exhumed like thirty corpses right afterward—I know that you can knock a bunch of unsuspecting people silly and make your escape with your other family. If you have to," Easy encouraged.

"You won't have to," Thone intoned candidly, lounging beside the cascade's gathering pool. "You've rolled with me long enough to know how to keep your cool under pressure. You'll play these people like a fiddle and be back here dancing with me tomorrow afternoon."

"We've planned for every contingency and armed you with an emergency exit strategy. Now it's up to you to execute– Sorry," Seph apologized.

"You sure comms won't work there? I'd prefer to be in your ear should you get in a tight spot," Easy said.

Exe shook her head, "I'm pretty sure tech won't work there. And for the last time, no. I can't take any of you with me. Look, I know you're all used to coming to my rescue, but not this time. Without powers, you'd just be a liability that'd distract me. I've got to have full focus to pull this off."

Ignoring their continued objections, Exe reached into her backpack and handed the Spectaculars and the Changeling candy over to Easy. "Share these with the younger boys when you explain everything. And tell Mom and Dad–" Exe's voice cracked. "If I don't come back–"

When she was unable to continue, Easy half-smiled, "We'll round up a squadron and come after you. That Veling guy can get us here, can't he?"

"He could, but I don't know that he would. I bet he'd be willing to wipe me from your minds if I don't– if it's mission failure."

"No way," Exe's brothers immediately replied as they engulfed her in a bear hug.

Bolstered by their strength, Exe whispered into Easy's shoulder, "I'm not scared, you know. I'm not afraid to die. I know what I believe. We're all born for a reason, aren't we? I just regret that I didn't accomplished more. But maybe this is enough. Saving my sister. If I can..."

"You can," her brothers said in unison.

As Exe led her brothers back into her tower, Easy quipped, "You know, we really should've insisted that Exe help with our prank planning all these years. You've got a real knack for subterfuge, little sister. We'll have to use your talents and powers for future pranks—WHEN you return."

Exe sat alone in the still quiet of her darkened belfry sanctuary, her eyes fixed on the presage Caulder had given her. The delicate glass pyramid glistened in the glow emanating from the spotlit stained-glass windows. Turning the coin Riven had given her over and over in her hands, Exe ran through the plan one last time, letting the strains of Don McClean's "Babylon" wash over her through her vintage Walkman headphones.

Once the last notes faded away, Exe ejected the tape, pocketed the presage and the coin, and took a last look around the gift her family had given her. She'd already said a tremulous goodbye to her puzzled parents, and given a dozen extra kisses to her little brothers, though they were annoyed at her disrupting their video game. Seph, Thone, and Easy had stoically refused anything resembling a goodbye.

Stepping softly out onto the belfry's balcony, Exe savored the warm desert evening breeze, the calming whir of the cicadas, even the piercing, solitary howl of a lone coyote. Exe took her time gazing at the big city glittering in the distance where the entrance to Anacapia lay. The far-off jangle of the saloon's piano brought a small smile as she looked out at Nowhere silhouetted against the moonlight.

Coming around at last towards the cemetery, Exe traced the shadowed path through the gravestones to Velin's dark and silent house. Idly she wondered what he thought of their plan, assuming he'd eavesdropped on it through one of her brothers. When questions had arisen that she couldn't answer while they were forming her course of action, Exe had thought about involving Velin, *But no. He chose not to help me. I'll leave him out of it.* Still, Exe was certain Velin must've popped an answer or two in her brothers' heads when they'd been unable to find it themselves.

I know you think it's wrong to meddle in the past, Exe thought as if Velin could still hear her. *What's done may be done, but the consequences can still be undone. Even without time travel. Fixing the future is always possible, if you're not afraid to act.*

Drawing a deep, fortifying breath, Exe pulled out Riven's coin, caressed it as if rubbing it for luck, then flicked it. Her eyes followed its descent until it vanished. A few minutes later Riven appeared close beside her.

Exe met his stony, guarded gaze and said simply, "I need you."

CHAPTER THIRTY-ONE

Coup de Grâce

Exe watched Riven's rigid back warily as she followed him across the moonlit field towards the mirage. Until he volted her into Vianelle, there was always a chance that he'd change his mind and refuse to help—and Riven's assistance was essential to her plan's success. It had taken her over an hour to convince him. Exe's brothers had coached her on how to counter his every objection. Yet in the end, Exe had to resort to the tactic she'd used against Riven the first time they'd met: she threatened to go without him.

Even though he'd been so angry that he'd kept his coin so that Exe could never call for him again—Riven didn't call her bluff. *He must not know that I can't get to Vianelle in time without him*, Exe thought. Time was of the essence and journeying to Vianelle without volting would take far too long. Yet as they neared the volting tree, Exe pulled back, suddenly feeling that volting with Riven was somehow a betrayal of Caulder. *But even if I could get Caulder to take me on this dangerous mission, it's Riven's protection I need tonight, not his.*

Riven mistook her hesitation, "Want me to go first to make sure all's clear?"

"No, I can't volte without you," Exe replied, lost in thought. Recovering quickly, she said, "I mean, I'm new at it. I'm not confident I could navigate through the old cruor-protected tunnels into Vianelle unscathed. But I will if I have to."

"You sure I can't talk you out of this?" Riven asked, wrapping one arm around her waist as they entered the darkness of the hollowed-out tree.

"I'm sure," Exe whispered, trembling as the electrifying fireworks of Riven's volting seemed to fuse them into one.

Moments later, the musty scent of dried clay invaded her senses. They were back in the faux cellar behind Bogey's. Lifting the cellar doors just enough to slip out, Riven ordered, "Wait here. Jettani's giving a speech tonight to whip up support for Viva's inevitable execution. Attendance is mandatory, so the city should be deserted, but I want to make sure."

Exe hesitated only a moment before following him. *If I wait in here, he might volte me back out of Vianelle on some trumped up excuse.* A riotous cacophony of crazed rantings, smashing glass, and terrified screams assaulted her as she edged her way toward Riven, who crouched catlike in the shadows of the alley's entryway.

Acrid smoke wafted over them causing Exe to cough. Riven's hand covered her mouth before hers could, "We need to leave. Now. Jettani's speech has already ended and whatever she said whipped people into a frenzy. They're destroying all Gyve businesses and attacking anyone even perceived as opposing Jettani. You're sure to get caught if you try to use the Portal tonight. We'll try again tomorrow."

"Tomorrow's too late. And it doesn't matter if I get caught—after I use the Portal. Facing Jettani at Viva's trial is part of the plan," Exe said softly, bracing herself.

"WHAT?!" Riven's whispered wrath was palpable. "I never would've—"

"That's why I didn't tell you. I'm going into that Portal tonight. And no matter what happens, you have to get my presage into Viva's trial tomorrow. Got it? I know you hate this, but I need you, Riven," Exe begged.

"Are you insane?! Have you forgotten that you are Wanted DEAD? They will kill you!" Riven's seething whisper rang within her as if he'd shouted it.

"No, they won't. They think Viva might be me now, right?"

Riven shook his head, "That's just a lie they're selling to make Viva's execution more palatable to the public. At this point, which Verelustre twin you are won't matter. They'll kill first, and ask questions later. And I cannot step in to save you, Exe. My role as a double agent is too valuable to the cause to expose myself. Even for you."

"I'm not asking you to save me. I just need you to keep them from killing me on sight," Exe stated, touching Riven's cheek when he tried to look away. "Jettani will want answers for what Viva did in The Wendings to those— for what I did to your brother. Should someone discover me in the Portal Portend, you need to convince them that Jettani wants to interrogate me before they have a chance to kill me."

"You want me to—apprehend you? Arrest you? Turn you over to be—"

"Yes. Believe me, there's a good reason behind all of this. You've just got to trust me," Exe said with quiet confidence.

"This madness will not save your sister, Exe. Even if you get the chance to say your piece in court, Jettani will still have you both killed," Riven replied, looking as if he wanted to wrestle her back into the faux cellar.

"Not if I can help it. This is all my fault, and I need to fix it," Exe said.

"It's not all your fault. Caulder and Viva bear just as much responsibility because they agreed to help you sneak in here," Riven replied ruefully. "Like I do, for this."

"No. They both took precautions and set conditions to ensure that my visits to Anacapia were safe. I ruined everything because I let myself be ruled by emotions while in enemy territory. From toddler age, I've been raised to have situational awareness and exert discipline in stressful situations. I knew better than to retaliate."

"And for that you deserve to die?" Riven asked.

"I cannot let Viva die for what I did. I need to confess and save her, no matter the consequences. But I'd much rather be armed with a presage that proves my innocence when I do it," Exe replied. "Riven, I've thought this through, planned for every contingency. It will work. But only if you'll help get both me and the presage into that trial tomorrow unscathed. Will you?"

"You're not leaving me much choice," Riven fumed. "Fine. But we wait until these rioters move off. It'll draw the Disimulata away from here."

"Fine," Exe replied, seating herself on a barrel tucked into a dark corner while Riven watched the street from the shadows.

After what felt like hours, Riven finally beckoned her forward. The raucous roar of the rioting mob was distant now. Only a fiery blaze remained, silhouetting the destroyed street as if sunrise had already come. Plumes of smoke and crackling embers of burned-out buildings were the only signs of motion as Riven led her onto the street, muttering over his shoulder, "You should've at least let me disguise you."

No. I need to be myself if I'm going to pull this off, Exe thought, but refrained from replying. The only gesture she'd made toward disguising herself was to pop in the aquamarine contacts that made her eyes the same color as Viva's.

Hanging back so that no one would suspect they were together should they be spotted, Exe followed him down the eerily-vacant, debris-strewn streets. Their careful footsteps ricocheted off the gutted shops like gunshots, despite stepping carefully to avoid the shattered glass that glistened ominously in the broken, flickering streetlights.

Up ahead, beyond a towering, formidable fence, the pearly, luminescent arches of the Portal Portend glowed like a beacon. Bypassing its ornate, padlocked gateway, Riven veered off the silvery walkway into the high hedges surrounding the fence. Stopping halfway down, Riven waited in the secrecy of the shrubbery for Exe to catch up.

Exe glanced around, puzzled as to why he'd stopped before reaching the secret entrance. About a foot overhead, Exe noticed subtle soldering marks on the solid metal bars of the fence. Smiling, Riven swiped his hand through the shimmering metal—they were merely an illusion to hide the hole where the bars had been cut away.

"It's surprisingly big for a secret passageway," Exe murmured, wafting her own hand through the space that was big enough for two people to easily pass through.

"Anacapia's elitists refuse to skulk, even when they're blatantly breaking the law. They shamelessly stroll right in with their heads held high, despite the fact that they reek of deceit. You're on your own now, doll," Riven replied, gently nudging her chin with his knuckle. With one last long, unfathomable look, he stepped aside.

Feeling suddenly alone, even though Riven still stood less than a foot from her, Exe drew a steadying breath and stepped through the fence. Once inside, the beauty of the Portal Portend drove away all of her fear and anxiety.

Three breathtaking, platinum statuettes stood in a wide circle, facing each other. Iridescent water ran down their silvery robes, feeding into three, perfectly-circular, intertwined streams. *Like a Venn Diagram.* Between these ring rivers were three curving, geometric ponds that, like a three-petaled flower, formed a rounded triangle platform at their very center.

Fear faltered her steps as she gazed upon the pure beauty of the statues. She'd read in the vile textbook Viva had given her that these weren't actually statues, but the entombed bodies of the three legendary women who'd founded Vianelle atop the waterfall mountain. Their preserved, ancient magic powered the Portal to see into the very soul of anyone who stood in their midst, and recorded their insights onto a presage—should one be present.

The purity of the Portal unearthed the familiar fear that refused to remain buried. *What if Jettani told the truth? What if the Portal reveals that I actually am evil or dangerous? Maybe I really would bring destruction to this land...* Exe immediately squelched the thoughts. *It's too late to turn back now. If that's what I learn, so be it. At least I'll clear*

Viva's name—even if I have to sacrifice myself. With a shaky, uncertain sigh, Exe pulled out the fragile, spiraled-pyramid presage Caulder had gifted her, bucked up her fading bravado, and approached the Portal.

The moment Exe strode onto the platform, the eyes of the statuettes sprang open, revealing sapphire, violet, and aquamarine eyes. Unaided, the presage pulled Exe's arms upward until she held it high overhead. Streams of illuminated water arced out of those jeweled eyes, etching their wisdom onto the glistening pyramid. The power of the water-beams burning into the presage held her upright, her fingers locked in place. The glowing water poured down over Exe's head and ran back into the ponds.

Instantly, a brilliant white light enveloped Exe as inspiring visions avalanched over her, almost knocking her to her knees. Her mind was inundated with images of herself succeeding, achieving. All her weaknesses were revealed, yet she felt emboldened to overcome each one. Her revealed strengths humbled her, instilling within her a great desire to accomplish as much as she could within her lifetime. The indescribable wondrousness coursing through her left her breathless, blessed, liberated.

When the shafts of illuminated liquid finally fell away, Exe stepped lightly off the platform feeling exhilarated and capable. Nothing could ever crush her. In that moment of euphoria, Exe understood exactly what had so terrified Jettani into ordering her execution: *I'm not a threat to Anacapia—I'm a threat to Jettani's tyranny.*

The instant Exe moved beyond the protection of the statues, the park went pitch black. Scores of Disimulata swarmed her, their ink-black trench coats and fedoras obscuring their figures and faces. *Riven!* Her mind screamed, but she stopped herself from calling out to him.

"Carapace!" Exe shouted the trigger just in time. A barrage of spells bounced off her forcefield, which quivered under the intensity of the attack. *They're already attempting to murder me! Riven, where are you?!* The struggle to protect herself tumbled the presage from her fingertips into the depths of the ponds.

"HOLD!"

Exe almost collapsed at the sweet sound of Riven's voice, but she held onto her protection spell until she felt the attacks against it subside. Deliberately blanking her face, Exe watched as Riven muscled his way through the black-trenched mob which melted back into the shadows in the face of his commanding authority. Only the three high-ranking Disimulata remained to surround Exe as Riven approached. As he drew near, Exe spotted a rank-and-file Disimulata agent edging out of the shadows to magically fish Exe's presage from the Portal's pond. Her eyes screamed a warning at Riven.

Riven barely glanced at Exe before turning on the thief. He held out his hand imperiously, "Hand it over."

The agent froze just as he was about to secret the spiraled pyramid into his pocket, "I got as much right as any of you to keep what I loot."

"You have no right to view what that presage has recorded. Do you presume to know as Seren Jettani does?" Riven reprimanded. Exe fought to hide her astonishment when the agent meekly handed over her presage.

"You've no right to order us about," the senior Disimulata barked. "Planning to claim the reward for the Bantling Destroyer's execution for yourself, Torsade?"

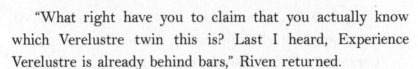

"What right have you to claim that you actually know which Verelustre twin this is? Last I heard, Experience Verelustre is already behind bars," Riven returned.

"Back off, Riv. You know that's just a story invented to—"

"Don't you dare presume what I know. You forget who my mother is," Riven's superior stare intimidated the senior Disimulata agent. "This girl is to be brought before Jettani so that the concilium may determine which twin is which."

When the senior Disimulata immediately nodded his assent, Exe thought, *Riven's only a junior member, and yet high-ranking Disimulata defer to him. No wonder he's so valuable to the Sub Rosa.*

"Shouldn't you fellas be wrangling that mob before they tear the whole city to pieces? I'll take care of turning this sister in," Riven commanded.

The senior Disimulata agent balked, "If this dame's as dangerous as rumored, I can't condone leaving you alone with her. The three of us best accompany you to the Stocks. The rest of you, get back to rounding up the rioters."

"Suit yourself," Riven shrugged and roughly grabbed Exe's arm. The three Disimulata each placed a hand on Riven's shoulder and in a twist of black, all five of them vanished.

WHAT ARE SISTERS FOR?

Although she knew they'd reached their destination, Exe kept her eyes closed tight as she took slow, shallow breaths to keep from heaving. Volting with the Disimulata was like having toxic ice water injected into every cell of her body. When she finally opened her eyes, the agents looked supremely disappointed that she hadn't vomited.

Brushing them off with a defiant glance, Exe focused on her surroundings. They were standing on a dreary path that dead-ended at a grim, windowless cement block that towered ten stories tall. When the senior Disimulata touched his lapel pin insignia and swiped his hand over the rough wall, a seamless door slid open, revealing a dank, dark prisoner processing office. The three senior Disimulata agents stood aside, allowing Riven to march Exe inside.

"Don't forget to give us some credit, Torsade," the senior Disimulata agent snapped, flanked by his frowning fellow agents.

"Consider yourself lucky if I forget that you almost killed this one before Jettani had a chance to interrogate her," Riven sneered. As the door slid closed, he shoved Exe toward the female agent manning the desk.

The woman went stark with fear the second she laid eyes on Exe's face. Reeling backwards, the agent swiped her hand across the large, empty Art Deco-style picture frame hanging behind her. Instantly, the image of a young female inmate sitting on the floor of a tiny, stark cell appeared. The girl had her head buried in her knees and looked sickly in the faint blue glow emanating from the walls.

"Eyes up! Now, Verelustre!" the agent commanded, pressing a button on the frame that spotlit the girl in a blinding beam of light. Viva slowly raised her head, glaring venom into the beam with her narrowed, aquamarine eyes, as if she could see the woman watching her. Another button press shut off the light beam and a hand wave vanished the image of Viva.

The agent's sigh of relief was short-lived. Leaning in to better see Exe's eyes, the woman gasped, "You've caught the other one!" At Riven's sharp nod, the woman asked suspiciously, "How come they both have aqua eyes?"

Riven glanced at Exe as if he'd only just noticed, then shrugged, "No idea. I trust you can handle her?"

"Of course, Mr. Torsade," the woman breathed, roughly grabbing Exe's arm and manhandling her into a phonebooth-sized chamber.

Just before the door snapped shut, Riven fixed Exe with an unfathomable stare that she might've mistaken for hatred if she didn't know better. Through the filigreed silver covering the plate glass door, Exe watched as Riven snapped his heels together, gave the desk agent a salute, and strode out the prison's door. Although this was all part of her plan, Exe felt as if the very air was being sucked out of her when Riven left.

Suddenly, she realized that air actually was being sucked out of the chamber she was locked into. Closing her eyes tight, Exe felt her aqua-tinted contact lenses fighting to slip through her eyelids. Unthinkingly, she quickly wished for them to stay put. They did. Only a few souvenir pebbles from her Neon Beach jaunt flew out of her pockets and vanished into the vents below her feet. The vacuum molded Exe's clothes to her to verify that she had nothing else on her.

Before Exe realized what was happening, she felt a white hot heat burning into her hairline—over top of the many scars that marred the back of her neck. Exe grabbed for her smoky amethyst pendant too late. It too was sucked downward into the vents. Though still fully clothed, the loss of her tetherstone left Exe feeling naked and exposed.

The vacuum pressure ceased and the chamber hissed. Still locked in the coffin-tight space, Exe watched the desk agent pull a small glass case from the booth that contained her belongings. She stuck the case into a wall of sleek chrome safety deposit boxes and labeled it Experience/Vivacity Verelustre. A sickening look of cruel anticipation on the woman's face told Exe that the worst was yet to come.

The agent slammed her hand down on a lever protruding from the chamber door. Instantly, Exe felt a sharp, sliding sensation across every inch of her skin—uncomfortable but not painful. The woman's malevolent smirk faded as she was obviously disappointed by Exe's lack of reaction to whatever the lever did. Her expression soured further when she saw that Exe's eyes were still aqua. Keeping her face carefully blank, Exe smiled to herself, grateful that at least this part of their strategy was going as planned.

Continuing to sneer at Exe through the glass door, the woman flipped a series of switches, turned a few cranks, pulled a number of knobs, then spun a final dial. Instantly, Exe was sucked through the ceiling of the chamber into a dark tube that shot her upward. After careening through the tunnel for several seconds, Exe was propelled upward through a metal floor that liquified seconds before her head rammed into it and solidified the second her feet cleared.

Dizzy and disoriented, it took Exe a second to get her bearings. She was in a small cell, identical to Viva's. A pale blue light emanated from the bluestone of three imposing brick walls. A floor-to-ceiling silver grate covered the fourth wall.

We didn't plan for this, Exe thought, subconsciously rubbing the spot at the base of her neck where her pendant usually hung. Not for a second had she considered that they might remove her necklace. *Will my wish magic still work without it? My powers are within me, right? Not in my tetherstone?*

A cackling beyond the grate sent chills down Exe's spine. Pressing her eye against the tightly woven grate, Exe spied the desk agent. *Clearly she has a faster, pleasanter way to get here. But it can't be volting, can it?* Noting the long, twining chrome coils she wore over her sleeves, Exe suspected that they protected the woman from the effects of the bluestone. *I won't give her the satisfaction of asking.* A second later, she was glad she hadn't.

"Well, well. Both of the notorious Verelustre twins here at my mercy," the woman chortled, strolling back and forth in front of Exe's cell and the one next door. "What sort of torment shall I entertain myself with tonight? With your trial tomorrow, I can't starve you, or scar you—at least, not your faces. Want to drown for a while? Or maybe a slow roast?" Water suddenly began to seep into Exe's chamber through the floor below. At the same time, the wall to her left throbbed with heat.

"Touch one hair on our heads and I'll rave like I've gone screwy, unable to answer any of Jettani's questions," Viva bellowed. "And my sister'll testify that it's due to your torture. You willing to answer to your revered Seren for what you do to us?"

"You wouldn't dare!" the agent raged.

"Try me," Viva laugh-screamed and repeatedly threw herself against her grate.

"She won't care if I maim the one of you who's supposed to be dead already," the infuriated woman fumed.

"Maybe, but which one of us is which?" Exe challenged. Bested, the angry agent stalked off.

"Viva—"

"SHHHT!" Viva hissed. "Lie down and go to sleep, you nitwitted naif!"

Outraged at Viva's attitude, Exe kicked at the bluestone separating their cells and sank down against the opposite wall. *Not even an ounce of gratitude despite the fact that I risked my life to save her.*

"SSSST."

Spotting Viva's eye starring at her through a small vent near the floor, Exe started to get up. "Don't make it so obvious!" Viva hissed.

Exe stretched and explored her cell before curling up on the floor in front of the vent. Narrowed aqua eyes clashed with worried faux-aqua eyes.

"You okay?" Exe asked.

"What are you doing here?!" Viva's words scorched despite her low volume. "Couldn't you at least grant me the chance of dying without your shadow hanging over me!? No, you have to martyr yourself so that whenever anyone talks about this, all they'll say is that the notorious Exe Verelustre was finally apprehended and executed. I'll be lucky if I'm a footnote."

"Don't be so dire. If all goes to plan, both of us will get out of this unscathed. I'm gonna show everyone that Jettani is not as benevolent as she pretends."

"Surely, you can't be serious!" Viva snorted. "Have you actually deluded yourself into believing that you can do in an afternoon what the whole of the Sub Rosa hasn't been able to accomplish over the last fifteen years?! You can shove your plan, naïf."

"It's not my plan," Exe hissed back. "Easy, Seph, and Thone came up with it. You trust them, don't you?" Taking Viva's silence for agreement, Exe gave her a quick rundown of the plan as quietly as she could. Viva remained silent long after she'd finished. "Well? Any thoughts? Suggestions?"

"Exe, this isn't some silly prank that you can just talk your way out of. The Jette Set may be junior officers, but they're considered on the level of law enforcement," dread dripped from Viva's words. "Even if you confess to doing what you did, they won't just let me walk free. Jettani will have us both executed."

"Look, I'm not about to let you die for what I did. No matter how nasty you are. I had to try to save you, didn't I?" Exe asked.

"I wouldn't have if I were you."

"You hate me that much? You would've let me die for something you did?" At Viva's stubborn silence, Exe continued, "I'm sorry for landing you in here, but you hated me long before this happened. And I didn't deserve that any more than you deserve this."

"You ruined my life," Viva's voice sounded small and teary. "You're always ruining my life."

"No, I'm not. Jettani ruined both of our lives. But I'm not sorry."

"What?!"

"No matter how vile her actions, no matter how upset I am that I didn't get to grow up here with all of you, I can't resent or regret the past. Sure, some stuff might be better if things had happened differently. Maybe you'd even be as popular here as you made me in Nowhere. But some things would be worse too. If our parents hadn't spent the past fifteen years opposing her, Anacapia would probably already be buckling under Jettani's tyranny. This way, at least we've got a fighting chance for freedom someday," Exe explained. "I wouldn't have the Parsells as family, either. And neither would you. They know about you, by the way. That we're twins. Would you really be better off without my brothers in your life?"

"We're never going to see our brothers again, are we?" Viva's dread-dampened eyes matched the bittersweet tears that sprang into Exe's when Viva said 'our brothers.'

"If we managed to touch fingers through this vent, could you use my 'unusual' powers to volte us out of here? If my powers even work amongst bluestone. Or without my tetherstone," doubt colored Exe's voice. "I accidentally made a little wish when we were in the tunnels under the city, but it didn't come true. At the time, I though I'd finally gotten my wish magic under control, but now? I don't know. Do you think my powers would work?"

"I doubt it. Without my tetherstone, my powers are next to nothing. Besides, my powers were bound in the prisoner intake chamber," Viva said.

"If you could volte away and leave me here, would you?"

After a long silence, Viva said, "No."

"I owe Easy five bucks," Exe gave her a small smile. "That was one of our contingency plans. Me setting you free and facing Jettani alone. I was sure you'd jump at the chance. Easy disagreed."

"He knows I don't want to be a fugitive," Viva replied with a trace of haughtiness that Exe now recognized as a defense mechanism. After another quiet moment, she added, "You didn't have to come, you know."

"I know."

"No, I mean, Dad is defending me tomorrow. He planned to say that I didn't perform some unheard of, unregistered spell. He'll claim that the spells Caulder and I both cast to protect Dodger collided. He even sent Riven to have Velin write spells into both of our vades that, when combined, would've resulted in a ball of bodies. I don't know what he'll do now, with both of us here," Viva said. Then she giggled, "I really wish I could've seen Schade rolling around like a bloody snowball."

Exe reveled in sharing a laugh with her twin for the first time—even if their amusement bordered on hysteria.

Sobering, Exe asked, "Asher had a plan? And I've ruined it. Do you really think he could've gotten you off with punishment instead of being executed for attacking those bullies?"

"After the Gyve kids? Yes." Returning to her usual unpleasant self, Viva added, "So you had better save us both tomorrow. Not that I care about you. But if you die and I live, I just know Mom and Dad will find some way to blame me."

With that, Viva put her back to the vent.

"Sis?" Exe whispered into the oppressive stillness. "How were the Gyve kids executed? I mean– Did they suffer? Was it– painful?"

"No," Viva murmured. "A lot of Jettani's supporters wanted them tortured to death, but the concilium decided that they'd best make it as peaceful as possible, since they were kids and it was a public execution. So they just stopped their hearts. Alive one moment, gone the next."

"Gone the next..." Exe repeated softly, slowly accepting that these were likely the last few hours of her life. "I'll do everything I can to keep them from killing you too."

"I know," Viva replied, her thanks unsaid, but still there on the air. A warm and sweet thread forever linking them.

Viva's breathing soon slowed with sleep, but Exe couldn't find rest. Two troubling images ricocheted through her mind: her wish for dry clothes not working in the tunnels below Vianelle, and Easy using her Entirety Tome despite not having any powers himself. The thought that crystalized terrified her, *Is it really objects that hold magic more than people?* She didn't know the answer. *Despite all that training, I know so little about how my magic works.* It was a chilling realization.

Are my powers primarily due to my tetherstone? Am I still an Unbindable without it? Was it actually my necklace that I couldn't control, not my wishes? Now here I am, without my necklace, surrounded by bluestone, and bound by that chamber, too. Will my powers still work? She was tempted to test them now, but it was too risky.

Suddenly, the plan that had seemed airtight in Nowhere, now felt childish and idealistic. *I may not have the power to save either of us.*

CHAPTER THIRTY-THREE

TRIAL BY FIRE

A swift, vicious kick to her gut jolted Exe from a restless sleep. She sat up, peering past the maliciously-grinning desk agent to see Viva waiting in the corridor, her wrists encased in platinum handcuffs embedded with bluestone. Exe glared at her, "You could've shouted me awake instead of letting her boot me."

Viva shrugged and grinned a bit maliciously herself, "Why should you get better than I got?" Before Exe could reply, the desk agent hauled her to her feet and magically slapped bluestone cuffs on her, without ever touching her. *Clearly, those coiled chrome arm bands do protect her from the power-sapping bluestone.*

As the desk agent marched them down the cell-lined, bluestone corridor, Exe tried to run through her brothers' plan once again, but last night's doubts clouded her mind. She could only form one stark thought, *What if I can't save us?*

The chrome door ahead melted away as they approached, reforming behind them after they'd entered the cold gray hall beyond it. Amid a squad of black-clad Disimulata, Asher stood waiting for them, his attention focused on a handful of court papers. Shock reeled him backwards when he looked up to find both of his daughters before him. From the glance that passed between the Disimulata, Asher's reaction was unexpected.

"Why was I not informed that you found my other daughter, Experience?" Asher demanded, before glancing more closely at their eyes. Confused, he looked back and forth between them, "Experience?"

Exe shook her head at him, and thankfully Viva did the same. Turning to the head Disimulata agent, Asher said, "I'm not prepared to defend both of my daughters today. I demand more time to sort this out."

The senior Disimulata agent (who Exe recognized from last night) refused. With quick efficiency, the agents surrounded Exe and Viva, grasped them by their shoulders, and vanished. When the swirling black trench coats parted, they were standing just outside an imposing palace.

Exe gasped at the sight of pure aqua water geysering upward into falling violet fire. *The Palace of Water and Fire. We're not being tried in the courthouse we read about in the Entirety Tome, we're facing Jettani in Incendia!*

The senior agent reached out, almost touching his palm to the fiery wall. Instantly, water shot up to part the flames, forming a watery archway into the palace. Down a long, wide corridor the agents marched them, its imposing, mother-of-pearl walls gleaming as coldly as the silvery sunburst archways that loomed like guillotines overhead. A sound like a great flock of angry chickens assailed Exe as they grew closer to a massive ebony door inlayed with glass and chrome.

Swinging magically open as they drew close, the doors revealed a Great Hall with towering columns of luminous aqua water and violet fire supporting the vaulted firewater ceiling. The feverishly clucking crowd hushed and parted as the Disimulata marched Exe and Viva toward a seven-foot, bluish-glass cube at the far end of the hall.

Feeling the heat of thousands of eyes on her, a pit of dread opened within Exe, *Our emergency escape plan accounted for only a few people in a small courtroom. Even at full power, I couldn't knock out this many people, could I?* Closing her eyes, Exe hoped that Easy's carefully calculated arguments might still save them.

Opening a small door in the back of the glass cube, the Disimulata enchanted off their bluestone cuffs and muscled their prisoners inside. Seating herself on the bluestone bench next to Viva, Exe realized that the glass itself was thinly sliced bluestone covered by a superfine chrome mesh to protect those outside the prisoners' box from its effects.

"I don't know why they bothered with the chrome," Viva whispered, barely moving her lips. "No one is allowed into Incendia's Great Hall without having their powers bound first—except Jettani, the Disimulata, and the concilium—who'll pass judgement on us."

"The whole concilium?" Exe replied. "Why didn't you tell me this last night?"

"I didn't know. Dad said it was a tossup if Jettani would want me tried quietly, or paraded out as a public spectacle. Look on the bright side. He said it was less likely that she'd have me executed if my trial was open to the public."

"What about me?!" Exe whispered furiously, as the crowd pressed in on the cube for a closer look at the notorious Verelustre twins. Viva just shrugged.

Viva blasé gesture burned Exe up—and made her grin. *I'd rather be angry at her antics than numb with dread.* Anything was better than the trickling terror that tore at her last night as she'd ticked down the last moments of her life. *And I used to think the monsters in horror movies were scary. But there's nothing more horrifying than facing down a corrupt government who's granted themselves the right to murder you.*

Exe gave herself a cold, sobering shake and, ignoring the vindictive crowd pressing their faces against the glass, turned her focus forward. She was surprised to see only a stark, marble wall—until she looked up. A low balcony just above them formed a half-circle around their cage. An intimidatingly long, ebony table and thirty chairs stood upon it. *Perfectly positioned so that they can look down on us as we plead our case, while we gaze upward at them, as if we're already admitting guilt and begging forgiveness.*

Exe hid her disgust as narrow ebony doors on both ends of the balcony swung wide. Fifteen gray-robed politicians strode out of each door, followed by fifteen black-clad Disimulata. The Disimulata agents stepped back in unison, taking their stoic positions in thirty alcoves imbedded into the marbled wall—one behind each politician. *Guards? Or their minders?* Surprisingly, the thirty politicians seated themselves before Jettani had appeared. *Why didn't they stay standing as a sign of respect?*

Exe's question was answered when the delicate platinum doors in the center of the balcony slid open to reveal Jettani. A reverent hush swept over the crowd as the ethereal woman glided serenely through the doors—she was barely taller than her seated concilium members. Exe's breath caught as she gazed at the achingly beautiful ruler who moved with the regality of a queen, yet exuded an aura of delicate gentleness.

The silky platinum waves of Jettani's hair glistened as if adorned with a million twinkling stars. Her resplendent, iridescent gown wafted about her as she floated forward, each step achingly solemn, proclaiming to all who looked upon her that she was indeed someone rare and precious to behold.

Exe had come prepared for Jettani's blinding, ageless beauty, but the ruler's expression astounded her. A tiny frown marred her perfect brow, her head tilted ever so slightly down as if bereft, wounded. And the midnight shine of her silver-laced onyx eyes reflected a deep sadness and regret as she gazed down upon her prisoners.

As Jettani approached the open space at the center of the curved table, an onyx throne inlaid with sleek silver starbursts arose behind her. Once she'd gracefully perched on its velvety seat, the throne ascended until she was high enough to look down on her assembled concilium. The center of the table rose too, accordioning upward to form a stepped podium in front of her. Once the table locked in place, two glass cases materialized upon it. *Our personal effects*, Exe thought, spying her necklace in one case.

As four more Disimulata agents arrived to flank Jettani's elevated throne, a lesson Rove had once taught her blossomed in Exe's mind: *A true leader has no need to elevate themselves above their followers. True leaders exude authority without making a pompous display of their might and power. Hubris exposes weakness.*

Yet the seemingly pure sincerity radiating from Jettani almost strangled Exe's last shred of hope that her plan might succeed. That's when she saw it. A lightning-quick gleam of triumphant hatred flashed into those steely-black eyes a moment before Jettani spoke, in a beguilingly melodious voice: "It seems your trouble in this travesty has doubled, Asher. Two daughters stand accused. My heart aches for you, Malina."

"I cannot mourn this day, Seren Jettani. For this is the homecoming of my long lost daughter. I was robbed of her by this concilium—who issued a death warrant against a baby, based solely on fearmongering, not evidence," the resolute strength in Malina's voice soothed some of Exe's fears. Glancing around, she spotted her mother, proud and brave in full military regalia, emerging from the crowd to stand by her daughters' silver-gilded cage. Her twin didn't seem to notice Malina, though.

Viva's eyes were fixed on Asher as he rose from his concilium seat several chairs down from Jettani. Flinging off his gray robe, Asher's footsteps echoed ominously in the vastness of the silent hall as he strode down the curved stairs to join Malina in front of their caged daughters.

Asher's minder sneered down at him as he magically folded Asher's discarded robe and levitated it onto the table in front of his empty seat. *As if it's awaiting someone to take Asher's place*, Exe shivered, disturbed that her careless actions at The Wendings might ultimately harm her parents also.

"Before we begin, I must protest the unprecedented illegality of failing to inform me that both of my daughters were standing trial today," Asher's voice rang with authority. "Not only have I had a criminally short time to prepare to defend one daughter against the incident at The Wendings, I have been granted no time to prepare a defense for my second daughter, whose presence I only learned of moments ago."

"You've had fifteen years to formulate your defense of Experience Verelustre, who by rights should already be dead," a reedy voice slithered on Exe's far left. The squat, bulbous concilium member's obsidian eyes were narrowed in accusation. His hands writhed over one another, as if salivating over the idea of personally strangling her.

"That may be true, Welmish, but which one? How is it that they both have aqua eyes? Haven't their powers been bound?" a nervous, bespectacled woman seated on Exe's right worried, sliding her glasses back up her sharp, pointed nose. Instantly, the crowd pressed in on their glass cage again, trying to catch a glimpse of their eyes.

Exe barely noticed the added scrutiny as she studied the woman who had just spoken. She swallowed a gasp as recognition hit, *That woman was at the Sub Rosa meeting I interrupted on my first trip into Anacapia!* Scanning the rest of the concilium, Exe spotted a few more familiar faces—including the sunny, rotund man seated on Jettani's immediate right.

"Yes, the infant that ought to have been executed by the deceiver Demaine was supposed to have amethyst eyes, was it not?" the bulbous Welmish replied as if both Exe and Viva were less than human.

"What difference does it make?" a nasally man intoned, his head slunk low in his robe, like a turtle trying to hide inside its shell. The nervous, bespectacled woman beside him turned to argue, but Jettani's gently raised hand quelled her concilium.

"Fusty's question requires answering," Jettani murmured with a nod toward the nervous, bespectacled woman. Then she glanced down at the sunny, rotund man beside her, "Tell me, Mahidable, how might eye color remain altered after one's powers have been bound? Only a permaspell might survive a bind, yet permanently modifying living tissue is an Inconceivable, is it not?"

The sunny, rotund Mahidable solemnly tented his fingers, "I can think of only one other way that artificial eye color might survive a bind, but that too is unthinkable."

"It's not– I can't– I mean, I can. Magic– My eyes..." Exe stumbled over her words, panicking as every eye in the hall riveted on her, *Why didn't our plan account for the fact that I can't talk to people!*

"Don't muck this up!" Viva hissed in a whisper. Exe tried to reply but no words would come. Viva grabbed her hand, squeezing it bloodless. Whether borne of anger or an attempt at reassurance, the gesture bolstered Exe's courage.

Taking a deep breath, Exe called out calmly over the impatient rumblings of the crowd, "It's not magic. I'm wearing contacts."

Silently wishing that her last wish magic act hadn't permanently fused the aqua lenses to her eyeballs, Exe reached up with her free hand. With a little effort, the sleep-dried contacts peeled away, revealing her amethyst eyes.

The surrounding crowd gasped and shrank back as if Exe had just opened a black hole that would suck them all into oblivion. Above her, nervous Fusty fearfully fainted as the concilium blustered their outrage. Only Jettani sat motionless, her expression impassive—although her dark, silver-shot eyes gleamed with masked malice.

"State your purpose in deceiving us with those unworldly eye shields," the nasally turtle-man wheezed. "Did you intend to replace your sister? Planning to plot our destruction, working against us from the inside? Who sent you to do this?"

"They're called contact lenses, not eye shields," Exe rolled her eyes, mimicking Easy's casual confidence. She looked pointedly at Fusty's glasses, "They're like eyeglasses you wear in your eyes to correct blurry vision where I'm from. I just use them to change my eye color."

"You haven't explained why," sunny Mahidable prompted over the fearfully awed rumblings of the crowd.

"To make my eyes look more like– my sister's, I guess. Although, I didn't even know I had a twin sister when I first got the lenses," Exe explained, grateful for the help in getting her rehearsed story out. "I never knew why I had to hide my eye color. I just had this endlessly nagging voice in my head commanding me to disguise my eyes, so I did. I suppose that's why those bullies picking on that little girl at that amusement park mistook me for this girl. So I'm the one you want. Not my sister. What's your name by the way?" Exe glanced shyly over at Viva.

Viva returned Exe's tentative smile with teary eyes, "Vivacity, Viva. And you're Experience! Although, I always called you Exie when I thought of you, which wasn't often. I didn't dare let myself believe that you'd actually survived your infant execution."

Exe turned back to gaze up innocently at Jettani, silently admiring Viva's skill in acting out the touching scene they'd quietly rehearsed in their cells last night. Making a moving emotional appeal had been Easy's idea, but this added icing on the cake was all Viva's doing—including using Charley's sweet nickname for Exe. Even now, Viva was noticeably swinging their hands as if she were thrilled to be reunited with her twin.

"So now we can tell who's who. The one's already sentenced. Let's pass judgement on the other and end this accordingly—with twin executions," the weaselly slug Welmish writhed his hands gleefully, as if the verdict on Viva was predetermined. The surrounding crowd murmured uncomfortably at this callous proclamation.

"Sentence my sister for something I did?" Exe's righteous indignation echoed as the hall fell silent. "I've confessed to the crime Viva is accused of. Let my sister go."

"As you wish," Jettani smiled.

At Jettani's nod, two of her throne guards marched off the balcony. They ripped open the cubed cage's door, yanked Viva out, and slammed it shut, leaving Exe alone in the bluestone box. Viva ran to their mother and buried her face in Malina's shoulder, as if she couldn't bear to witness Exe's fate. Exe rubbed away the pain from Viva's tight grip. *There goes my escape plan to volte out of here if things go bad. But I've accomplished my mission. I've saved Viva from the consequences of my actions.*

"It is admirable that you've come here to proclaim your sister's innocence," Jettani murmured, her face a perfect picture of regretful admiration. "But what are we to do with all of the evidence that says otherwise?"

"What evidence?" Exe demanded.

Jettani turned to the stunning, statuesque woman on her immediate left, who regarded Exe coldly with hard, deep sea blue eyes. (*Just like Riven's eyes. That must be his mother, Azura Torsade!*) With a wave of her hand, Azura Torsade commanded a near-invisible door in the white wall below the balcony to slide open. Riven and another Disimulata agent forcibly escorted Caulder and Dodger forward. Schade and the other Jette Set boys Exe had attacked at The Wendings followed them, pompously preening to be a part of the Verelustre twins' show trial.

Ignoring Riven entirely, Exe glanced only once at Caulder, afraid of revealing just how well they knew each other. *Please don't say anything,* Exe thought over and over, regretting that she couldn't plant the thought in Caulder's mind the way Velin had so often planted thoughts in hers.

"You were seen at The Wendings in the company of Caulder Ishkabibble, who would've known you weren't Viva," Azura stated with convicting authority. "And you attacked my own son in defense of Caulder's little sister—after mistaking their innocent questioning of this child's illicit activities for an assault. You could not have masqueraded as your sister if she had not coached you first. Since it's clear that she did, we can only conclude that your parents were apprised of your intentions. Perhaps this Caulder Ishkabibble even knew that you were really Experience Verelustre all along."

They're still looking for a way to convict my whole family, and Caulder too. They'll take down half the Sub Rosa for what I did if I can't stop this, Exe thought.

"Hold," Malina called out. "As instructed, my men questioned every single person in attendance at The Wendings that night, including your son Schade. I was not involved in the questioning, but I did read the report. Not one person recalls seeing Caulder together with Viva before the incident. Although, I guess it was technically Experience."

But dozens saw us together. The Gyve are so loyal to Caulder that they're willing to protect him from government persecution?

Exe caught Caulder's gaze for the briefest of moments in silent apology before she said, "Actually, I did talk with this boy for a short while that night. Although, I didn't know who he was. And I didn't realize until now that it was his little sister that I rescued from that pack of bullies."

Azura visibly bristled at Exe's description of Schade and his friends, but Jettani spoke before she could retort. Gently reproving, Jettani said, "So you admit that Caulder Ishkabibble lied about knowing you?"

"How can I know what that boy said when you interrogated him?" Exe shrugged casually, though she chose her words carefully. "A few minutes before those boys attacked, that Caulder kid caught me looking at a tattered old poster with my face on it. A poster that said I was 'Wanted: Dead'! He acted like he knew me, but also assumed that I wasn't the girl on that poster—so I pumped him for as much information as I could. That's how I found out about the Portal and the little pyramid thing I needed to use it. When I asked, he gave me a presage. Now I realize he must've given it to me as a reward for helping out his little sister."

Both Azura and Jettani beamed as if Exe had just walked into their well-laid trap. (*Although Jettani's hiding it better.*)

Azura practically sang with glee as she said, "You don't need a presage to use the Portal Portend. A presage merely records what the Portal reveals. The only reason you'd need a presage is if you intended to use it as evidence here today. And if you plotted to procure evidence for your twin sister, then you must've been working on behalf of your family. It's the only way to explain how you entered this well-protected city undetected—you had your family's help."

"Well protected?" Exe laughed coolly, grateful that Easy had practiced these lies with her so that she could tell them without stuttering. "It was a cinch to volte myself up into the beams of that dock outside the city. Then I used the tunnels below the streets to find my way to the Portal. Those Vianelle snow globes they sell at The Wendings made plotting my path easy. And I went undetected because the streets were deserted for most of the night, until those rioting mobs started destroying the city."

"So you say that the Verelustres were not involved in your penetration of our defenses," Jettani frowned delicately. "But why then would you risk entering the capitol of a country who wanted you dead, if not to obtain evidence to clear your sister's name? And to clear your own as well?"

"For the good of this country, of course," Exe said with a small, satisfied smile that clearly said Jettani had just walked into Exe's own trap. "Imagine my dismay when this Caulder kid told me that this government intended to execute me as a baby because I posed some sort of threat. A baby labeled as a danger to a whole nation? I couldn't believe it. But what if I was? I'd only been adventuring around Anacapia for a short time before I stumbled upon that magical amusement park. I had intended to continue exploring my newfound homeland, but not if I would endanger people. I entered the Portal to find out the truth about myself. So that if I did pose a danger, I could leave this place and never return."

"How very noble of you," Azura sneered. But a dawning horror crept over Jettani's delicate features. Exe grinned at her triumphantly.

"Thank you," Exe deliberately mistook Azura's sarcasm as sincerity. Then offhandedly she added, "I find it curious that both you and your leader just stated with such certainty that my presage will show evidence of my innocence."

Azura paled, "I speculated on your intent. I never claimed to know what you saw. Only Seren Jettani knows what the Portal Portend revealed about your nefarious future."

"Now I know, too," Exe challenged.

"I imagine that facing certain death would tempt you into deceiving us about the darkness the Portal surely revealed in you," Azura blustered.

"I have no need to lie," Exe said brazenly, ignoring the half-truths she'd been sharing by focusing on this absolute truth. "I am unafraid to show everyone present the uplifting wonder of my experience in the Portal Portend."

"Such a shame that we cannot expose what you saw to our audience," Jettani murmured softly, subtly emphasizing the word 'expose.'

Salvaging her composure to do Jettani's dirty work, Azura bit out, "No presage was recovered when you were captured—I doubt you even had one in the first place. The Disimulata present here today can attest that you did not have a presage when they apprehended you in the Portal Portend."

"Perhaps the one who found it intends to keep my presage for himself," Exe replied, refusing to look at Riven. *Please let him forgive me. And please don't let this get him in trouble.*

Azura chuckled mercilessly, "All of those Disimulata agents are here today to refute your lies. Come now, if any of you recovered the presage Experience Verelustre claims to have had with her in the Portal Portend, present it now." The crowd rustled in anticipation as Azura confidently cast her gaze around at the stoic Disimulata stationed throughout the hall.

Keeping her eyes locked on Jettani's, Exe silently pleaded, *Please Riven. I need you.* Finally, Exe lowered her gaze to

Riven's stony stare. Only when Exe opened her mouth to call him out did he step forward and pull the presage from his pocket.

The crowded hall roared in shocked curiosity and restless outrage as Riven held out the fragile, spiraled pyramid in the palm of his hand. Exe almost feared for Riven's life when she caught the murderous expression on Azura's face. Schade appeared as equally capable of violence when he turned from Riven up to the nasally concilium member, who now resembled a sunburned turtle burrowing deeper into his robes.

Could that weak-faced man really be Riven's father? Exe wondered.

When the hall had fallen silent once again, Riven cleared his throat, "I had no idea this presage was the property of the nefarious naïf when it was fished from the Portal's ponds. I merely claimed it so I could gift it to Schade. I'd been unable to obtain one through the usual channels." Riven gave Caulder a vicious shove.

Caulder balled his fists in reaction but stayed silent.

"We did not seek this evidence, but it is evidence all the same," Asher stepped forward, reaching for Exe's presage. "It's incumbent upon us to reveal what this presage has recorded to all those assembled—no matter how its secrets may impact my daughter's fate."

Worrying her thumbs against the palms of her hands, Exe braced herself to face one of the unknowns she and her brothers had been unable to plan for. No matter how wonderful the knowledge imparted by the Portal (and her brothers had adamantly insisted that it would be a positive experience), Exe was worried. *Will Jettani be able to distort what the presage recorded?* Exe forced herself to relax and smile, suddenly aware of the many eyes that were glancing back and forth between her and her presage.

Asher whispered a trigger word. Three streams of illuminated water instantly shot out of the tip of the presage and enveloped the entire hall in a brilliant white light. Exe's tension faded as comforting, inspirational visions began flooding out over the whole assembly. Yet the awed, uneasy sighs of the crowd signaled that they were unsettled by what they were experiencing.

CRACK!

A thunderous boom resounded off the walls and the room went dark. Exe could just barely see Riven in the eerie, aqua-violet gleam of the firewater columns. Her presage had shattered in his hand. Its shards dotted his face with thousands of glass slivers and tiny rivulets of blood.

Just like Ella and the water glass. That second of silence stretched endlessly as Exe stared at the wreckage of her presage pinpricking Riven's face. *If I wish it whole, they'll know. They'll have no doubt then that I possess the immense powers of an Unbindable. And they'll probably execute me for it. But if I don't, they'll kill me anyway. Maybe if people see the contents of my presage, some will realize how deeply they've been deceived by Jettani. At least then my death won't be in vain if my presage helps the Sub Rosa expose her twisted tyranny to the masses. But will my powers work?*

Exe almost smiled at the irony, *I've spent most of my life wishing that I didn't have magical powers, and now that I'm likely without them, I'm hoping that my wish magic still works.* Refusing to waste a moment more, Exe concentrated every thought on reassembling the shattered presage. Every inch of her body thrummed with power as she envisioned the shattered glass returning to its place.

Exe felt herself weakening with the amount of effort it took to fight off the effects of the bluestone without her tetherstone—but her wish magic worked.

Every glittering speck of glass soared back into place as the pristine presage reformed in Riven's palm. Exe wanted to collapse in exhaustion as the thrumming subsided, but she didn't dare. *I won't let them see how much this has weakened me.*

Exe slowly raised her gaze to see the triumphant gleam in Jettani's silver-black eyes—and the wary terror lurking in their the inky depths. Exe tilted her chin upward in a defiant challenge and awaited her judgement.

"What dangerous, demented powers lurk within you, that allows you to cast without your tetherstone? Only a malevolent magic could defy the complex bind performed on you by our prison and overcome the power-sapping bluestone," Jettani murmured as if devasted by her pronouncements. "As heartbroken as I am to draw this conclusion, I must declare that the concilium was right to–"

"Assume a mere teenager is capable of all that? And a bound one to boot? One might've expected such an esteemed concilium to look for the most believable explanation, rather than grasp at the most convenient one," Velin's voice boomed.

Exe's knees went weak with relief as Velin strode through the parting crowd toward her glass cage. *So Velin was eavesdropping on our planning session. I cannot believe that he decided to come here to help me.*

Shouts of outrage and demands to 'Seize him,' rang from the balcony, but Velin simply whispered a few trigger words under his breath. Instantly, all the doors in the hall audibly locked themselves, and a barely visible barrier arose in front of the balcony, effectively sealing the concilium and the Disimulata inside. More triggers sucked the agents on the main floor through the doorway below the balcony and locked them in. Only Riven remained, frozen where he stood with Exe's presage resting in his palm.

"For those too slow to catch on—I reformed that presage," Velin declared.

Jettani halted the concilium's efforts to free themselves from the balcony and called out to Velin, "So it was all you. You resented my rule, and you wanted revenge on the people of Anacapia for ousting you over your role in the Horology Wars. So you plotted with General Demaine to rescue Experience Verelustre from her execution. You raised her, and now you've returned her here to destroy Anacapia."

"Do I pluck off fairy wings for pleasure too? Or perhaps I execute innocent children for the crime of perpetrating an amusing prank—after framing them as murderers with questionable evidence, of course," Velin scoffed. "Your charges are foolish. You know better than most that I have no love for Demaine. I would never associate with that untrustworthy traitor, even to save an innocent child. Nor would I deign to raise anyone else's brat."

Velin hates Demaine? The man who's rumored to have saved me? Then how did I get to Velin if they didn't work together?

Jettani rose slowly. Managing to mask her outrage behind a façade of innocence wounded, she murmured, "You claim that you did not rescue Experience Verelustre from execution. Nor has she been in your care these many years. If it's true that you have no involvement in this girl's life, then why risk your own by coming here to save her?"

"You mistake the reason for my arrival. I've come to introduce Anacapia to my latest discovery," Velin drawled, tossing a copy of 'The Anacapian Argus' onto the floor. The newspaper's front page was filled with the headline: 'Verelustre Trial Today.' Casually, he added, "Interrupting this concilium's campaign to murder a young girl is merely good timing."

Velin's last statement threw the entire hall into an uproar. Screams, gasps, and accusations burst forth, not only from the concilium this time, but from within the crowd.

Is he trying to get us both killed? Exe thought wildly. But she quickly realized that most of the rage was coming from a handful of agitators scattered throughout the throng. The majority of the people appeared more curious or mildly concerned, instead of angry or afraid of Velin.

"I admit only to being homesick for my homeland these past decades. Keeping up with our country's news has helped keep me close to Anacapia. But I've grown troubled with what I've been reading," Velin picked up the paper and held it aloft for all to see as he scrolled through a series of disturbing past headlines. "Prominent citizens abducted or otherwise disappearing, not to mention the trouble with the children."

"What do you mean about trouble with the children?" a concerned mother called out, supported by the agitated mutterings of the crowd behind her.

"Setting aside the fact that Anacapians stood by while the government attempted to execute Experience when she was an innocent infant... Let's look at those 'accidental deaths' that allowed Jettani to end the graduation trials. That annual contest once allowed every student the opportunity to showcase their magical talents. But no longer. It's awfully convenient that those youngsters died just when Jettani was lobbying to end the graduation trials.

"Do you recall those youngsters who 'accidentally' volted themselves into a pack of lycanmere, irreparably fusing themselves with the creatures? That incident expedited Jettani's oppressive restrictions on volting," Velin swiped the date on his paper to expose every story as he spoke. "And let's not forget all of the children that went missing when Jettani's own hometown was wiped out—right before she was declared Seren. It's amazing how blatantly the evidence stands out, when you're allowed to examine the past for yourselves—history that Jettani's government has gone to great lengths to erase."

Jettani sank onto her throne as if overcome with anguish at Velin's accusations. Seeing her distress, Azura raged, "Are you attempting to accuse our revered Seren of crimes against her own people?"

From the disturbed rumblings of the crowd, Exe worried that perhaps Velin had pushed his accusations too far.

But Velin bestowed a benevolent smile upon Jettani, as if he were soothing a naughty toddler, "I would never think to accuse Anacapia's revered Seren. I have always believed that these acts occurred under Jettani's rule because she was under the influence of the destroyer Demaine in those early days. I became concerned when I discovered that incidents like these were still occurring—even though Demaine had fled after his treachery had been discovered. Why had no one in Jettani's concilium, or even any of Anacapia's good citizens, spoken up against these disturbing incidents?"

Velin held them all enthralled. The crowd that had cringed away when he'd first arrived now ebbed forward, nodding their agreement and whispering piously that they shared his concerns over these unsettling events. Though still thin and frail in appearance, Velin no longer appeared embittered or decrepit. Exe stood in awe as she observed this glimpse into the graceful orator and selfless leader Velin had once been as he continued:

"Then I realized that I was the only one with the tools to notice this continuing pattern of dark and dangerous deeds operating in the shadows to erode the rights and freedoms of Anacapia," Velin lowered is voice, drawing them in. "For one of Demaine's first acts was to command that our newspapers show only the news of the day. No one but his bureaucrats were allowed to view the archives recording our history. Anacapia's good citizens were permitted to view only the latest propaganda. A sinister plan devised by the great manipulator to keep Anacapians ignorant of their own history.

"That leads me to my latest invention. As of today, every copy of 'The Anacapian Argus' operates just as this one does. Simply swipe the date to scroll through every edition, every article ever printed. And for good measure, I've made it impossible to destroy these papers, or even remove them from people's homes. You are now free from this small piece of Demaine's subjugation."

Ecstatic cheers rose as they passed around Velin's scrollable newspapers that magically appeared throughout the crowd. This taste of freedom so exhilarated the masses that it took several minutes for them to notice that their beloved Jettani was waiting to address them.

When quiet finally fell, Jettani murmured, "We owe you for this service to our people, Velin." Though her tone was courteous, Exe was close enough to see the rigidity in her graciously tilted jaw and the hardness behind her gentle eyes.

"It is but a small repayment for the debt I owe to all Anacapia," Velin interrupted smoothly before Jettani could continue. "I know all too well how difficult it is to fairly rule a nation when you've a tricky quisling in your midst. My fear is that you still have some traitors among you. The foul deeds done when Demaine had authority here can be attributed to him. However, it appears that he still has influence. Why else would your concilium be so determined to put Experience Verelustre to death? And her twin too?"

"Of course!" Sunny Mahidable breathed in sudden revelation. "Asher and Malina were both staunch supporters of yours, Velin. When the young Verelustre couple began rising in position and popularity, Demaine decided to target their infant daughter in order to diminish their influence on Jettani. Little Experience was never a threat to Anacapia or Jettani—her parents were a threat to Demaine!"

A collective sigh of stunned enlightenment rolled through the hall. Suddenly the hostile eyes on Exe were now apologetic, even welcoming.

Nervous Fusty teetered to her feet and proclaimed, "The deceiver Demaine has done enough damage to our country. We cannot allow his deceitful influence to continue. I hereby call on the concilium to lift the death sentence that was so unjustly leveled against Experience when she was but a babe. All in favor, say aye."

After Velin's impassioned speech that subtly accused the concilium of doing Demaine's bidding, most members were quick to say 'aye.' Only the sinister slug Welmish and the irate Azura hesitated, until the weight of suspicion forced them to agree.

When Jettani hesitated to act, Velin cocked a brow at her, "Of course, if there's any doubt as to whether or not Experience poses a danger to Anacapia, we can always view the entirety of what was recorded on her presage now that I've restored it. I admit to being curious myself, although what we've seen so far seemed rather mundane."

In the face of Jettani's continued silence, Exe addressed Velin, "I find I'm more curious about who shattered my presage in the first place. All of us down here have our powers bound. And why would you reform it if you were the one who shattered it? No, the only ones with the power to shatter my presage are those up on the balcony. But why would they do it? Why do they not want anyone to see what's on my presage?"

Velin considered this, "That is curious. Perhaps we should show it. But I suppose whoever attempted to destroy it might claim that it's now flawed and its recording unreliable. Should that argument be made, we could always find another one. Or perhaps Jettani would prefer to go into the Portal with you herself. What say you, Jettani? Are you as willing as Experience to expose the depths of your soul to this eager audience at your late age?"

Velin's subtle taunt almost wheedled a sneer from Jettani. But when her audience began stirring discontentedly, a beatific expression of benevolent relief settled on her face. Appearing joyously pleased, she declared, "From this day forward, I hereby dissolve the death warrant issued against Experience Liberty Verelustre. Your family may take you home without any fear for your life."

At this pronouncement, Velin whispered a trigger word that ripped the door off of Exe's cage. The moment she stepped free and ran into Asher and Malina's embrace, Velin disintegrated the cage into a pile of blue sand. The chrome crumpled on top like a giant ball of tin foil. The cheering crowd surged forward in victory, immediately eager to welcome Exe into their midst while cursing Demaine.

Exe met Velin's gaze across the destroyed cage and mouthed a tiny 'Thank you' to him. Acknowledging her thanks with a microscopic nod, Velin volted. The moment he vanished, the shield imprisoning the balcony dissipated. The Disimulata immediately raced off the balcony and vanished too.

Giving chase, though I doubt they'll catch him, Exe smiled at Caulder as he joined their family celebration.

Out of the corner of her eye, Exe noticed Riven up on the balcony, arguing with his mother. From their furious gestures, Exe gathered that Azura Torsade wanted Exe's presage, but it had apparently vanished from Riven's palm when Velin volted. As the throng began flowing the now-lauded Verelustres toward the door, Exe saw Jettani draw Riven and Azura's attention. After listening to only a few moments of Jettani's rapid whispers, Riven's head whiplashed toward Exe, with a stark alarm in his eyes that she hoped no one else would notice.

"Detain Experience Verelustre," Azura commanded the Disimulata agents emerging from below the balcony. "She must answer for the crime that she has confessed to committing. She must bear the consequences for her attack at The Wendings and the harm done to the junior agents of the Jetton Coalition."

Exe patted Malina's shoulder reassuringly when her mother tried to stop the Disimulata from grabbing her daughter again, and shook her head at Asher when he stepped forward to intervene. Nothing else had gone to plan, but this she was ready for.

"Since when is it a crime to protect little kids?" Exe called out as the Disimulata muscled her forward. "That's all I did, no matter what story your son may have spun."

"We are willing to set aside any discussion as to whether or not the attack was justified," Jettani said magnanimously. "What's at issue is the magic you used. No child is authorized to weaponize spells against authority figures, nor even possess the type of attack spells you used. We must also address the fact that no such attack spell exists that could do as you did. At least, not one that's been legally registered with our government. As required by law."

"I see. Those do sound like very serious crimes," Exe said gravely. "However, how was I to know that they were crimes? There's no way that I could know the laws of this land because I was spirited away fifteen years ago to prevent you from executing me. I'm simply a girl who found her way home, stumbled on a fascinating amusement park, and stopped some unknown thugs from hurting a little girl. Where I grew up—away from my family because of the crime committed against me—we protect children from those who'd seek to harm them."

"You must be punished for the harm you caused," Azura sneered.

"What harm? They look fine to me. Well, at least they don't look hurt," Exe smiled a challenge at Schade and his Jette Set as they cracked their knuckles menacingly.

Jettani nodded her agreement, "Thankfully, our young agents suffered no permanent damage. But that does not explain why you had such a spell inscribed in your vade in the first place? Who would give you access to such a violent spell? And for what purpose? If not with Velin all of these years, who were you with? And what were they training you to do?"

Though Jettani pretended only curiosity, Exe sensed the subtle vindictiveness behind her questions. Thankfully, her brothers had prepared her for this.

"Stick to the truth as much as you can," Easy had advised. Seph had added, "It's easier to remember to omit things that you want to keep secret, than it is to remember completely invented lies." Thone had followed up with, "When in doubt, say as little as possible and let people assume those things that you don't say."

So that's exactly what Exe did.

"I have no idea where my 'vade' is or what spells are written in it. I've spent my life in– what did you call it? The Vale? The family who raised me has no powers, so I've had no one training me to do anything. All I know about magic is due to a voice in my head that I thought was my own— until a few months ago. It told me crazy words and what they'd do. I said them, and those things happened. Since I'm the only magical person I've known until now, I thought I was just making it all up.

"For all I know, that voice was this Demaine guy you've all been talking about. All I know is, once I realized that voice belonged to someone else, I stumbled on a spell planted deep in my subconscious that allowed me to block that voice permanently—but not before whoever it belonged to had inserted knowledge of Anacapia in my mind. I don't think it was nefarious, like you're suggesting. I was only 'told' that Anacapia was my homeland and how to get here. The voice didn't even tell me that my birth family was still alive, or that I had a twin sister."

"Where is this entrance that led you to Anacapia?" Jettani's soft question held a sinister edge. "If we are to find who took you, who holds your vade now—"

"I, too, want answers to these questions. However, my daughter has had a target on her back up until a few minutes ago," Asher cut her off. "I cannot condone publicly revealing the location of the Vale family who raised Experience, when those innocent people may become a target for any who are not willing to accept my daughter's innocence. Or worse, by any of Demaine's loyalists."

"Your reluctance is understandable," Jettani began. "But this is a matter of national security. We cannot allow your daughter to go free unless she gives us answers."

Malina stepped forward, saluted, and said, "As an officer in charge of national security, may I point out that whoever did rescue Experience from her execution acted in defense of our family. They also prevented our government from committing an egregious crime against us. I am not convinced that we need protection from whoever it may be, but if needed, I will see to it. And I will also secure my daughter's adoptive family from any harm that might be plotted against them. It's my sworn duty as an officer, and my responsibility as her mother."

When Azura looked as if she might protest, Asher halted her, "We are not refusing to answer the concilium's questions. Nor are we opposed to providing details of

Experience's past on a need-to-know basis. We object to the timing. Our daughters have been through enough trauma today. And we haven't even had a moment to ourselves to welcome Experience back into our lives. As my girls have been cleared of all charges against them, I insist on taking them home. We will make ourselves available to satisfy the concilium's curiosity about Experience at a later date."

No one on the balcony above said a word. After a few tense moments, Asher extended his hand and stared pointedly at the packages on Jettani's podium. At Jettani's nod, the packages floated down into Asher's hand. Two Disimulata agents stepped forward, locked eyes with Exe and Viva, grasped their wrists, then whispered a complex series of commands. Exe barely felt a strange pressure slide over her skin, but from Viva's relieved sigh, she guessed that the strange ritual had released them from the bind put on their powers in the prison.

Once this was done, Asher moved behind Viva, and Malina stood behind Exe. Feeling the cool tetherstone against her chest and the light weight of its chain slipping over her neck somehow made Exe feel safe again. As the heat of fusing metal warmed her neck, Exe silently wished that her necklace would never be taken from her again.

Feeling its power thrum through her, Exe raised her eyes to meet Jettani's. Though seemingly serene as she watched the scene unfold below her, Exe sensed a calculating appraisal in Jettani's expression. It left Exe feeling as if she'd been dissected.

As Asher and Malina led their daughters away through the swarming crowd, Exe ran through all that had just happened, suddenly afraid that she'd revealed something that she shouldn't have. *Does Jettani suspect that I'm an Unbindable?*

MAKE A WISH

The surging crowd engulfed Exe and the Verelustres as they fought their way out of the Great Hall. Disimulata agents melted out of the pristine, mother-of-pearl walls as they drew near Incendia's grand entrance, but Exe was sure they weren't there as a protective escort. When they stepped outside the palace into a thronging wall of people (who gasped and glared at Exe with fearful suspicion), the agents tailed them—but they didn't intervene when several people spat and struck at Exe and Viva.

The outcome of the trial rippled through the mob as the audience from inside Incendia mingled in with them. Over the cacophonous roar, Exe heard her own name and Velin's repeatedly shouted in various shades of outrage and astonishment. Dozens of paparazzi pushed forward, snapping endless photos. They kept shouting "Notorious Naïf" at Exe to draw her attention. Keeping their daughters between them, Asher and Malina rammed through the masses until they reached the street.

As their parents shunted them into one of the waiting taxis (that looked like it had driven right out of the film 'Casablanca'), Exe asked, "Why didn't we just volte out of there instead of wading through that bedlam?"

"Volting is strictly controlled within Vianelle and is only legal through state-owned vehicles," Asher explained, wrestling the car door closed against the paparazzi's efforts to question them.

Oblivious to the rioting crowd surrounding his car, their bored taxi driver didn't even look up from reading his paper. Engrossed in the headline article that was still emblazoned with 'Verelustre Trial Today' he droned, "Where to?"

"West gate," Malina instructed. Adding to her family, "It'll be less crowded."

"Names?"

"Verelustre," Malina told him. "Asher, Malina, Vivacity, and Experience."

The driver's eyes jerked up to view them through his mirror, and he almost dropped his paper when he realized that Exe was in his taxi. While the driver was busy gawking at them, Exe watched his paper's headline transform to 'Exonerated,' above a giant, cringing photo of herself taken outside the palace just moments ago, all black and white—except for her amethyst eyes.

Viva also spotted the newspaper's changed headline. Glaring at Exe, she said, "Like I predicted. You've made me a footnote in my own story."

"It's not my fault," Exe retorted hotly.

"We're in a hurry!" Malina barked at the driver.

Recovering himself, the driver added Exe's name to the meter and hit start. A second later, Exe experienced a strange, electric darkness followed by a blinding white light. Then another and another.

Shielding her eyes, Exe realized they'd been volted into another cab in a calmer part of the city. The flashes weren't part of the auto-volting, though. They came from this driver's camera, who'd read their names on his meter before they'd appeared in his cab.

"No one's ever gonna believe me without proof," the awed young driver breathed as he snapped another photo of Exe and her family.

Ignoring him, Asher rushed his daughters out of the taxi. Malina dashed after them, her head on a swivel, looking for any signs of danger on the mostly deserted street that led to the west gate. Passing a wall still plastered with Exe's 'Wanted: Dead' poster, Asher muttered, "They can change newspaper headlines instantaneously, but they're still advertising for Exe's execution."

As the Disimulata guarding the west gate dawdled through security checks on the Verelustres, a crowd began gathering. While some shouted insults at Exe, others were more curious about how she felt, and where she'd been all these years. A few even begged for permission to touch her, as if she were some kind of totem. Without waiting for Viva or Asher to get through the city's well-guarded exit, Malina ushered Exe into a volting chamber that had an accordion door, similar to a vintage phone booth.

Malina wrapped Exe up in a hug and volted them home, embering in Exe a sensation that was comparable only to those moments when she'd first held baby Charley. When she opened her eyes, she and Malina were standing on the Verelustres' terrace overflowing with its lush, impossible foliage and its sparkling series of ponds. Though they were home, Malina's hug continued. And when Viva and Asher arrived, her father enfolded them all into one long embrace.

When they finally broke apart, Malina led the way inside through the burnished silver doors set in the middle of the windowed wall. Exe ached inexplicably at entering through the front door this time, instead of sneaking in through the back door.

Taking her hand, Malina led Exe toward a floor-length, life-sized portrait of a flapper girl dressed in violet, standing alone against a black background. Triggering the painting to slide, Malina revealed an etched silver door and urged Exe to open it. "Your father and sister laughed at me for constantly updating this space, but I was determined that you'd need it one day."

Exe opened the door into the most magnificent bedroom she'd ever seen. A silver-plated vanity table with a velvet pouf stool stood by a bay window overlooking the softly glowing gathering pool below. Leather-bound books filled the shelves lining the niche where a tufted chaise lounge awaited hours of comfortable reading. In the very center of the room, a plush bed beckoned from beneath a tented canopy, overflowing with soft pillows and cozy silk comforters in Exe's favorite pale, dusty violet. It was the personal, private bedroom of her dreams. *But it's not home.*

"Welcome home," Malina whispered.

"I– thanks. But I can't live here," Exe blushed uncomfortably at the sight of Malina's crestfallen expression.

Asher just looked angry. "After all of this. After all we risked–"

"I'm sorry. I want to know you, and I'm sure I'll sleep over sometimes, but I have to go back to my family..." Exe trailed off when Malina winced. "They've always stood by me. I won't abandon them now. I need to go home. Immediately."

"Fine then. Leave," Viva glowered. "I don't care if you never come back."

"I'm not just taking off like some ungrateful brat," Exe protested Viva's snide implications. "My brothers know where I am and the danger I'm in here. I need to let them know that I'm okay. Right now."

"She's right. Our brothers need to know that we're okay," Viva brightened.

"Our brothers?" Malina asked weakly.

"You challenged Jettani to secure your return," Asher thundered. "And now you think you can just waltz in and out of Anacapia as you please?"

"Look Dad, Jettani and the Disimulata never have to know whether Exe is here or not. We can get me some of those contacts in violet, teach Exe to volte, or whatever we need to do to work it out. But right now, we've got to go let our brothers know we're safe," Viva said, holding her hand out to Exe.

Exe could've hugged her twin if not for the sly, Cheshire grin on her face. *I bet she's already thinking up ways to embarrass me, traipsing around Anacapia in those violet contacts.* Turning to her parents, Exe stated, "You two are just going to have to accept that you haven't simply regained your daughter. You've also added six sons and another set of parents to your family."

"Hoi Polloi sons and parents," Viva added.

"Right. Thanks for sticking up for me staying in Arizona with the Parsells," Exe said sincerely to Viva.

"I'm not doing it for you," Viva sassed back. "I don't want to live here with you twenty-four seven. Besides, I plan on spending a lot of time in Nowhere too. Like to attend school for instance."

"What?!" Exe exclaimed as Viva grabbed her hand and volted them into the Corpse Copse. Volting with her twin felt like stepping inside a bonfire, and from Viva's knowing smile, Exe was pretty sure she'd made it painful on purpose. But she didn't bother stopping for accusations. *Seph, Thone, and Easy have to be frantic by now!* Exe chased after Viva who'd already dashed through the cascade.

"Where are they?" Viva exclaimed on finding the mirage empty.

"Follow me. I know where they'll be waiting," Exe commanded, dashing through her tower door. Though they'd wanted to wait for her in the mirage, Exe had insisted that they go home, afraid that they might be stuck there if she never returned. *But I know they'd want to wait for me as close as they can get to Anacapia.*

Exe raced up her tower staircase, ignoring Viva's insistence that volting would be faster. *I'm not letting her volt me again, and there's no way I'm letting her get to my brothers first. She'd probably tell them that I'm dead.*

Seph and Thone were anxiously pacing the belfry, staring at the stained glass windows of Anacapia when Exe burst through the trapdoor. Easy sat nearby, too focused on describing what he was seeing in the Vianelle snow globe to notice Exe at first.

"Oh thank God!" Seph burst out, grabbing Exe into a bear hug. "Now we won't have to tell our parents that we sent Exe to her death!"

"We'll just have to explain why there's suddenly two of her," Thone quipped as Viva volted herself into the belfry.

"I'm pretty sure they already know," Easy winked at Exe before hugging Viva. "I'm so glad you're both okay."

"I gather you boys are in part responsible for Exe's reckless appearance in Vianelle," Asher's voice boomed as he volted into the belfry. Seph and Easy immediately shoved Viva and Exe behind them to shield them from the stranger who'd suddenly appeared in their home. Asher grinned on seeing the protective gesture, "Nicely done, boys. But against someone like me, you'd be wiser to stand behind my daughters. Luckily, we're all on the same side. I'm only here to inform you that Malina is hosting an impromptu 'Welcome Home' party for Exe in the field—and you're all invited. Let's call it a family reunion. Or should I say, family union."

Viva squealed with delight and asked, "Can I take them with me, Dad?"

Asher nodded, "Just down to invite the rest of 'our' family. We'll join you soon."

With a gleam in her eye, Viva turned to the Parsell boys and extended her hand, "Hands in, boys. You're about to experience the full magic of an Anacapian celebration." With thrilled grins, the boys piled their hands on top of Viva's. In a blink, all four of them had vanished.

Exe glowered at Asher, impatient to explain things to the rest of her family—especially Rove and Ella. Asher frowned back at her for a few silent moments, then said, "We need to have a serious discussion about the risks you took coming into Anacapia the way you did. There needs to be consequences for your actions."

"You want to punish me for accomplishing in one day what your inaction failed to accomplish for over fifteen years?" Exe scoffed in astonishment. "I know that the wheels of justice move slowly, but that's often because those who seek justice are too afraid to take the risks required to achieve it."

"Perhaps that's true," Asher smiled ruefully. "But the risks you took were unnecessary to achieve justice in this case. We already had a plan to save Viva from the consequences of your reckless behavior. For you to have ventured into the heart of Vianelle with a death warrant hanging over your head—"

"I had to do something to save Viva. I couldn't let her die because of me," Exe retorted. "And no one bothered to come tell me that you had your own plan to save her. Maybe we need to discuss your bad habit of keeping things from me."

"I was about to commend you on your bravery," Asher raised a brow at her. "Still, I must insist that you not take risks like that again. You're still in danger in Anacapia."

"No one can legally kill me now, so I think I'll survive," Exe snapped.

"Do you think that a law can prevent death? Removing the bounty from your head simply changes your demise from an execution to murder. Believe me, there are precious few who would demand justice were you to be murdered."

Exe stilled, "Jettani still wants to see me dead, doesn't she?" When Asher nodded, Exe added, "I'm afraid Jettani knows that I'm an Unbindable. I didn't think about keeping that secret when we made our plans to save Viva."

"She may be speculating, but she doesn't know. The presage shattered before it could fully reveal that fact. But you must not tell anyone, not even any Sub Rosa members that you're an Unbindable," Asher cautioned. "After what was done to Velin when he invented time travel, I can only imagine what people might do to exploit your considerable powers. Even our own people."

"Now I'm glad that the presage shattered. Did it break because Jettani tried to distort what it was revealing about me?" Exe asked.

"I destroyed the presage."

"What?! But why did you reveal its recording at all if you intended to destroy it?"

"I didn't realize how swiftly the presage would expose your Unbindable abilities. Those streams of liquid light that mimicked the Portal itself and the accompanying euphoria did exactly that—although Unbindables are so rare that I doubt anyone will realize what they saw," Asher explained. "So I destroyed it as soon as I was confident that people had seen enough to know that you're a positive asset to Anacapia, not a danger. Unfortunately, it was also enough to make Jettani suspicious."

"If Jettani suspects that I'm an Unbindable, why didn't she agree to go into the Portal with me to find out for sure?"

"She might have, if doing so would've allowed her to order your execution. But Jettani realized that public opinion had shifted in your favor—thanks to Velin's careful targeting of Demaine. And while she may have been tempted to use the Portal to discover the extent of your powers, entering it with you now would expose her own limitations to you. That's a risk she could not take."

"So, with Velin's help I removed the death warrant hanging over my head, but by confronting Jettani, I've put an even bigger target on my back, haven't I?" Exe stated.

"Yes. But I don't want you to live in fear. I simply want you aware of the fact that you'll never be completely safe in Anacapia. Or anywhere, while she's still in power. It's vital that you be on your guard," Asher cautioned.

"Don't worry. I've been raised to be on alert," Exe said.

"And a shrewd debater too," Asher said seriously, though Exe heard a hint of a smile in his voice. "I'm glad that you were skilled enough to talk yourself out of a death sentence, but I'm quite concerned with how easily you lie."

"I didn't actually tell that many outright lies," Exe blushed. "Most of what I said was truthful—it just wasn't the whole truth. I didn't know who Velin was when he gave me away to a Hoi Polloi family, or that he was the voice in my head. I didn't know what a vade was when I performed the spell to lock my mind. And I currently have no clue where my vade is, since Velin's always stealing it."

"You'd make quite the politician," Asher grinned.

Exe laughed, "Easy calls it selective sharing. He coached me to tell only the parts of the truth that would protect everyone."

"Selective sharing? I'll have to remember that. It'll definitely come in handy in my line of work," Asher replied.

"So, can I go clear things up with the rest of my family now? Goodness knows what lies Viva's telling them," Exe pleaded. Asher nodded and volted them down to the lower level of Exe's tower. "Wait here," Exe called over her shoulder to him as she ran into the living room where a debate was raging.

An overwhelmed Ella sat on the couch being peppered with questions by Charley, Moth, and Henny-Boy. Stone-faced Rove stood nearby, surrounded by Seph, Thone, and

Easy all attempting to explain at once. Viva stood between them all, shouting above the chaos, "You don't understand. I'm not your daughter!"

Astonishment reigned as Exe skidded to a halt right next to Viva. Their eldest brothers grinned while the rest of the Parsells gaped at the twins. In his surprise, Charley's glass of milk flew up into the air.

"Arrestant! Carapace!" Exe called out, instantly freezing the milk mid-spill and creating a forcefield to shield the couch. Then she said, "Winkler," to scoop the milk back into the cup and place it into Charley's hands. The Parsells— including Easy, Thone, and Seph—watched in stunned silence. Clearly, knowing that Exe had powers hadn't prepared them to actually see her magic in action. Ella and Rove shared that familiar, disquieted look that (to Exe's relief) swiftly melted into acceptance.

"You may not be Exe, but if you're her sister, then you ARE our daughter," Rove stated to Viva, who preened under this affectionate admonishment.

"Well, that talent's going to come in handy," Ella smiled shakily, taking the milk cup from Charley before he spilled it again in his excitement.

"FINALLY!" All three of Exe's younger brothers said in unison, dancing around Exe. Moth explained, "We've all been dying to talk to you about your magic, but we weren't allowed to unless you brought it up first."

Not allowed by Ella and Rove? Or by Velin? Exe wondered, as all of her brothers began pelting her with questions.

"Now is not the time to talk about her powers," Rove interrupted. "We still need an explanation as to where Exe has been all night. And where she found her twin. And everything else that's gone on these past few months. Now sit down and start talking. Both of you."

Exe immediately sat on the edge of the coffee table, but Viva hesitated, "What about the party?!" Rove stared her down until she sat next to Exe with a meek, "Yes, sir."

While Ella kept her inquisitive sons quiet, Rove spent the next twenty minutes debriefing Exe and Viva with efficient precision. The family sat in astonished silence when he was finally satisfied. Then he called out into the shadows by Exe's tower door, "Anything you'd like to add, Mister...?"

"Asher Verelustre. Exe and Viva's father," Asher introduced himself to a wary Rove, startling Exe. (*I can't believe I forgot that he was listening!*)

"Birth father," Rove corrected, hesitating a moment before grasping Asher's hand with an authoritative grip. Then he turned toward the shadows once again.

"I'm impressed!" Malina called, stepping out into the light. "I've never witnessed such rigorous and thorough questioning done so swiftly, not even from our most highly-trained interrogators. I'd love to learn your strategy."

"You two can discuss military tactics later. Right now, we have more pressing issues on the home front to discuss," Ella replied.

"Sirs and ma'ams," Easy interjected. "I understand that a lot of heavy things need to be discussed, but given all that Exe and Viva have been through, don't you think they deserve a little celebration? Viva mentioned a victory party going on in the field that connects our worlds..."

All four parents looked at Easy consideringly for a moment, then Ella relented, "Your sister may take you boys out to the party."

"Not that sister," Rove said, when Easy made to link his arm through Exe's.

Exe's brothers slowly followed Viva as she gleefully led the way into Exe's tower, glancing apologetically over their shoulders at Exe as they left. The moment the tower door closed, Rove and Ella turned to confront Exe, their overwhelming relief and mingled rage at all she had risked pushed them beyond words. They settled on wrapping her into a united hug instead.

"You've still got a lot of explaining to do, young lady," Rove broke away to fix Exe with a stern stare.

Ella's attention shifted to Asher, "I'll not let my daughter live with you in a land where people want to see her dead. I don't care that they've retracted that decree, or what you promise to do to protect her. She's a part of our family, and we won't give her up."

When Ella drew a deep breath to continue her tirade, Asher held up a hand, "Exe has already made it very clear that she intends to continue living here with you—although she will visit us in Anacapia. As a matter of fact, we need to discuss how best to incorporate our other daughter into your family. It seems Viva has bonded quite well with your sons, and she's asking to attend school with them."

"Oh. Well, of course she's welcome anytime. I'm sure we can work out how best to share our daughters," Ella smiled and relaxed her grip on Exe.

"And your sons. I think it's probably best as we move forward to consider ourselves one big, happy family," Asher replied.

"Absolutely! Now then, what can I bring to this party you're throwing?" Ella asked. "Easy's given me lots of practice at throwing last-minute celebrations together."

"As a matter of fact, I need help with refreshments. I've no talent for anything beyond doling out military rations," Malina said. "I've heard from Viva that you're a wiz at whipping up delectable dishes, which she said she heard from Exe. But I now realize she learned that from tasting your food."

"Yes, Viva definitely shows more interest in cooking, in baking particularly, than Exe ever has. That's how I knew she wasn't Exe," Ella chuckled. "Oh, I should've had the boys stay and help. It'll go faster with more hands."

"Let them stay at the party. I know a few tricks that'll make quick work of our cooking adventure. You know, I've always wanted a big family," Asher said conversationally, winking playfully at Exe as he followed Ella into the kitchen.

Unfortunately, Rove wasn't about to be put off. Fixing Exe with a withering stare, he said, "Of all the—You put your life on the line without even telling us?! What were you—With my military expertise—I, at least, should have been consulted, young lady! The next time you—"

"There won't be a next time without you knowing about it, sir," Exe executed a perfect salute with just enough of Charley's cherub cheekiness to soften him up.

"Why wouldn't you come to us if you needed help?" Rove demanded.

"There wasn't time to talk you into agreeing to our plan, Dad," Exe replied.

"Speaking of military expertise," Malina said, breaking the tension between them. "There's a few people I'd like to introduce you to, Colonel Parsell. I know our resistance could benefit from your input."

"Please, call me Rove. Perhaps Exe sought tactical guidance from a more experienced source," Rove said wryly, eying Malina's military uniform. "From the looks of it, you outrank me."

Acknowledging the compliment with a modest nod, Malina said, "Our leaders are debating our current strategy, in light of recent events. We could use a set of fresh eyes on our tactics and capabilities, especially from someone with your credentials."

Leveling Exe with one last 'We'll finish this discussion later' look, Rove followed Malina into Exe's tower.

Exe stared after them, breathing a sigh of relief that she'd temporarily put off accountability—but also completely bemused that after all that fuss, everyone had just left her behind. And for the first time, Exe didn't relish the privacy. Heading into her tower, she thought, *Easy would be proud; I actually want to be a part of the party.*

Exe gasped as she walked out of her tower door. Malina had transformed the barren, fenced-in field into a magical wonderland. After expanding the mirage's emerald grass out to the etched fence, she'd conjured up a storybook garden filled with delicate grottos, pristine pools, and private pathways to meander.

"Don't worry. Anyone outside the fence will still only see an empty lot," Malina murmured to Exe, after breaking away from a group of Sub Rosa members who were mired in a deep debate with Rove. As she admired the newly-grown garden, Exe noticed that her tower door was embedded within the outer hedge of a small maze.

"This is now a permanent connection between Nowhere and the mirage for both you and the Parsells to use. I've spelled it so that your family can use it without powers," Malina answered her unasked question. Turning a stern eye toward Exe's brothers, who were currently enthralled by Caulder's retelling of the trial, Malina added, "Your brothers have promised never to venture through the mirage. Can they be trusted? Anacapia is far too dangerous for people without powers."

"My brothers like to push boundaries, but they won't break rules that put people in any real danger, including themselves," Exe reassured her. "Aren't you concerned about creating a direct path to me? I mean, what if the Disimulata stumble on my door? This leads right into my bedroom."

"Only our family can use it. The Parsells and us," Malina clarified. "Anyone else who attempts to find out where this door leads will be in for quite a surprise."

"Now I almost hope someone tries it," Exe smiled, turning back to admire the garden Malina had conjured. Centered in front of the mirage, she'd erected a filigreed gazebo with several tables underneath that Ella and Asher were now filling with crazy concoctions and decadent desserts.

Glancing up at the banner fluttering above it, Exe burst out laughing. Instead of 'Welcome,' the sign read, 'Happy Exhumation, Exe!'

"Your brothers insisted that I change the sign to that," Malina smiled, obviously unsure as to why Exe was so amused. "They said it was an inside joke?"

"It is. I'll explain it someday," Exe replied, breathing a sigh of relief. "I can't believe we made it through. It's finally over.

And just beginning. I'm not sure what to expect now. But I know I'm not afraid to face it. Not anymore."

"I'm glad that you found a way to come home to us," Malina laid her arm across Exe's shoulders. "And I'm glad that your family is so open to welcoming Viva. I'm afraid that fighting tyranny hasn't allowed us to provide her with much of a home life. Spending time with all of you in Nowhere will give her a chance to just be a normal kid for once. It's what she needs. And Anacapia cannot provide it."

Exe thought that Viva would probably object to being called 'normal,' but she wasn't about to say so. Instead she stayed silent and leaned against her birth mom, content to relax in the safety of her embrace, if only for a little while.

"And don't worry about journeying back and forth between our worlds," Malina continued. "We'll work out a way for you and your sister to live safely in both worlds—without fear of Jettani or her Disimulata."

If anyone could make that promise so that Exe would believe it, Malina could. And she was pretty sure that Rove would insist on assisting with security measures too. Between all four of her parents, Exe was confident that they'd be able to keep her—and their whole family—safe.

"So you're the ones making all this racket," Velin groused, appearing beside them. "I've got this entrance into the Vale alarmed, you know. It's been going off incessantly for an hour now!"

"I know. How else was I going to get you to attend the festivities?" Malina teased. Although Velin glowered at her, there was a smile tugging at the corners of his mouth. Looking down at Exe, Malina said, "You owe this man a mammoth debt of gratitude."

"I know," Exe replied, grinning at Velin.

"We all do. Velin, you did more damage to Jettani's regime than you realize," Malina smiled as Velin grumbled and blushed.

"What do you mean? How was Jettani hurt by what he did?" Exe asked.

"By pinning all of Jettani's nefarious deeds on Demaine, Velin made her appear as if she was just Demaine's puppet, rather than a leader in her own right," Malina explained. "And Jettani couldn't very well claim otherwise. Not after Velin so clearly spelled out all of the dirty dealings that have happened under her regime. He forced her to choose between appearing weak or bearing the responsibility for eroding Anacapia's freedoms herself."

Velin nodded, "Jettani has devoted herself to cultivating a mystique of purity and honor, so she couldn't admit to the evil she's ordered done against her people in the name of obtaining ever more power and control. Doing so would have been the ultimate act of self-destruction. You'd do well to learn how to find and exploit your enemy's weaknesses, Miss Experience. Especially now that you'll be spending time in Anacapia."

"You'll need to learn how to discover and overcome your own weaknesses too," Malina added. "Out of control wish magic may be why you found your way home, but in the end, I believe you'll realize that it wasn't your biggest flaw after all."

"Impatience and impulsivity are your real problems," Velin nodded sagely. "Showing off your magic to that Bonnie girl without taking the time to discover that she was untrustworthy. Bullheadedly dashing off into Anacapia for answers that I would've eventually given you, despite knowing that it might cost you your life. Letting emotions drive your decisions, that's another character flaw you've got."

Exe bristled, but Malina shot her a quelling glance, "Acting before you think is a dangerous way to live, especially in Anacapia."

"We'll need to work on that in our training sessions, young lady. You should work on it with her in yours too, Malina," Velin said, suspiciously casual.

It took a second, then Exe gasped, "You're both going to train me?"

"Yes. You and your sister too," Malina beamed. "And probably Caulder. And Dodger. And Riven. Maybe more. I fear that we're all going to need to be ready to defend ourselves after the cracks that Velin put in Jettani's regime today. Double training sessions on top of school—it's going to be a lot of work. Think you can handle it?"

"Yes—Mom," Exe said.

Malina gave Exe's shoulders one last delighted squeeze before getting drawn back into the military debate Rove was now leading amongst several of the Sub Rosa members. Exe admired how Malina held her own in the discussion, clearly impressing Rove in the process. As she watched, she spied Rande watching her. He gave her a begrudging nod of acceptance before diving back into the debate. *That's the best I can expect from him,* Exe thought.

Exe couldn't help noticing that Velin was still beside her, shifting nervously as he surveyed the partygoers. *It must be awkward to mingle with people as an equal when you were once their revered ruler.* Exe tried to think of something, anything that would put Velin at ease. But she could only think of one question that had been nagging her for a long time. Startling him, Exe asked quietly, "Why did you let me go?"

"Last night?" Velin frowned at her. "Didn't seem possible to stop you from trying to save your sister."

"No, in the first place," Exe replied. "You could've stopped me from ever going into Anacapia, simply by telling me who I was and agreeing to train me. But you didn't. Even though you said that you had every intention of training me— eventually. You let me go. Why?"

Squirming uncomfortably, Velin said, "Because I finally realized what you were really searching for. All your blather about wanting to rid yourself of your powers, it took me a while to understand that you were actually looking for a place to belong. Everyone deserves to know who they are and where they're from. I couldn't take you there myself, but you had a right to go if you were willing to take the risk. So I did everything I could to ensure that you understood how great a risk you were taking."

"Thanks. I owe you a lot. But most importantly, thanks for trusting me," Exe said, swallowing hard when she saw the tears in Velin's eyes. "I'm not going to hug you."

"I should hope not," Velin replied, comically outraged.

As Velin turned to go, Exe said, "Just one last question?" Velin rolled his eyes and glowered at her as he waited expectantly. Exe continued, "Who reformed the presage? You or me? It felt like me, but you said—"

"You reformed that presage. I simply took credit to protect you. If you only listen to me one time, make it this one: Never let anyone know that you are an Unbindable. I learned the hard way how dangerous it is to let others know that you're more powerful than they are," Velin answered. Giving Exe a curt bow, Velin strolled off to enter the fray of the military strategy debate.

While the adults gathered in small groups to debate politics and resistance strategies, Easy and her brothers were in their element organizing games and activities for themselves and the Sub Rosa's children. Teaching the rules of tag to players who could volte was no easy task, but Easy managed to turn it into an asset by incorporating hide-and-seek into the game. By pairing each of her elders brothers with an Anacapian, and establishing an 'eyes on' rule instead of a physical touch, he soon had them all romping around Malina's garden as if they'd always been lifelong friends.

Viva hadn't joined in the game, though. Charley, Henny-Boy, and Moth had her cornered, begging her to perform various bits of magic for them as they gazed at her adoringly. When Rove noticed the way his young sons were pestering her, he called out, "Your sister is not a parlor trick, or a sideshow, or your personal wish-granting genie. Kindly refrain from asking her to use her powers for your personal gain and entertainment. That's an order."

Rove's command only deterred them for a moment, though. Once he was reabsorbed into a deep discussion, the boys were back to fawning over Viva and her magic. Viva sighed and rolled her eyes as if annoyed by their antics and attention, but she couldn't hide her secretly pleased smile.

Watching her family enjoy the celebration, Exe was relieved that they were handling their introduction to magic so well—and that the Sub Rosa were so open to embracing her Hoi Polloi family. In fact, judging by the number of people captivated by Ella's cellphone demonstration, they found the unpowered Parsells utterly fascinating.

Frankly, Exe was stunned by the number of Sub Rosa members who had come to celebrate her return—including those who had served on the concilium. The most shocking attendee was the bulbous slug Welmish. She waved lamely in return when he beamed a slimy smile in her direction.

Noting her reaction, Asher joined her and explained, "Quaere Welmish utterly fooled you, didn't he? The man has a brilliance to rival Velin's. He's the one who recruited Malina and I into the Sub Rosa, after arranging your escape from execution. Then he spent the next fifteen years positioning himself as a zealot seeking your death, so that he could ensure that it never happened."

"How exactly?" Exe balked. "He was rooting to have both Viva and me killed."

"There's the brilliance. When the opportunity arose to reverse your death sentence, he caved immediately. Given his reputation for intelligence and his rabid desire to see you dead, who else could continue the fight to execute you after he abandoned it? You'll find that many things in Anacapia are not what they seem on the surface. It's vital for our survival in this battle for freedom," Asher replied, beckoning several people over to meet Exe.

While she would've loved to join her brothers' games, Exe had little chance to play. So many of the Sub Rosa members insisted on drawing her into conversations to welcome her back. Careful not to reveal too much, Exe spent the afternoon retelling the trial to various groups and carefully sidestepping questions about her past. As much as the Sub Rosans wanted to know about her, Exe was just as eager to glean as much as she could from them.

Mahidable and Fusty were absolute fonts of information, and both promised to find time to answer all of Exe's questions about their lives and roles in Anacapia. Although she'd tried to avoid the bulbous slug, in the end Exe was most impressed with Quaere Welmish. His off-putting appearance, he explained to her, was cleverly crafted to mask his magnificent mind, razor-sharp wit, and fierce patriotism.

"Never underestimate the strategic value of letting your enemies underestimate you," Welmish shrewdly advised.

Serious talk waned as twilight came and the adults turned their attention towards celebrating. Conjuring up a host of twinkling lightning-fairies to illuminate the garden, and an orchestra of odd creatures (that absolutely delighted Charley and his new Anacapian friends), Asher led Ella out to dance. Rove followed suit, twirling Malina about in the gazebo. Then Rande joined in, dancing a girl with riotous red curls into the semi-privacy of a low-lit grotto. While the youngsters tore around the dancers in a no-magic-allowed game of tag, Exe's elder brothers found dance partners among the Sub Rosan girls. Fusty even got Velin to cut a rug with her, and soon almost all were dancing joyously in the rising darkness.

Caulder caught her eye across the merry crowd, an invitation to dance in his eyes, but Exe shook her head. With an overdramatic sigh, Exe communicated her need for a reprieve from the festivities—after a full day of being the center of attention.

Acknowledging his understanding with a nod, Exe was pleased to see him invite Viva to partner with him instead. *After all the attention from my brothers and now dancing with Caulder before I do, just let Viva try to complain about me stealing her spotlight.* Exe knew she would, though. On principle.

Seeking a little solace to unwind before rejoining the party, Exe stole up into the deserted mirage. Only it wasn't quite empty. She found Henny-Boy and Dodger engaged in a just-the-two-of-us game of super secret espionage— disarming imaginary bombs, stealing top secret documents, hiding from assassins in the shadows, and taking it all very seriously the way only fellow ten-year-olds could. When they spotted Exe, Dodger raised her nose in the air, muttered something about being infiltrated, and led Henny-Boy off into the maze to play catch-a-spy.

Sinking down on the mirage's boulder, Exe watched them skip away, overcome with nostalgia for the simplicity of childhood friendships. Not long ago, she'd been lamenting that she'd never had any. Now, watching her brothers so serenely embracing magic and their new Anacapian friends without complaint or obligatory disbelief, Exe realized that she'd had six solid, reliable relationships all along—eight if she counted Ella and Rove. Which she did. Whether intentional or not, a normal childhood had been Velin's gift to her. *Well, as normal as it could be, for someone like me.*

Lost in blissful recollections of growing up with the Parsells, it took Exe a minute to notice the low whistle coming from the cascade. Stepping to the gathering pool's edge to investigate, Exe almost fell in when she spotted a black-clad figure hidden within the waterfall. She choked back her scream when she recognized Riven. Glancing around to make sure no one would notice and follow, Exe slipped into the cascade and out into the Corpse Copse clearing.

Riven was waiting for her, leaning against a tree, half-shrouded in mist and tossing his coin, just as he had on the day they'd met. When Exe sank down on the twinkling midnight grass overhanging the milky riverbanks, Riven joined her, but neither spoke. A thousand thoughts collided in Exe's mind: thanks, queries, apologies, defenses. But in the end, she knew that after all they'd been through, the future of their friendship hinged on his answer to just one question.

"Why did you agree to take me into Vianelle last night?" (*Has it really only been less than twenty-four hours?*) When Riven hung his head with sheepish guilt, Exe continued, "You knew that Asher had a plan in place to save Viva, but you didn't tell me. Why didn't you put an end to it by telling me, instead of letting me browbeat you into taking me to the Portal? I know I didn't tell you that I intended on getting caught, but you knew the plan was to give my presage to Asher when you agreed to help me enter the Portal with it. Yet all along, you knew Asher didn't need my presage to save her."

"I never intended to take your presage to Viva's trial," Riven confessed, trailing a twig through the gently rolling river. "Once I'd volted you safely back home, I was gonna make you keep your presage. I convinced myself that it was a fitting parting gift."

"Why? Why risk so much just to give me that gift?"

"Because you deserved to have evidence of just how amazing and strong and extraordinary you really are," Riven jumped up to prowl restlessly. "I've been haunted by what I said to you in your graveyard that night. About being evil. I was so angry that night, and so sick of living in the shadows—that I was only thinking about myself when I answered you. I should've realized what you were really asking me. You are not evil, Exe. And you deserve to have absolute proof of that."

Reaching into his pocket, Riven withdrew her presage and held it out to her in the palm of his hand. Exe rose and took the delicate, spiraled glass with trembling hands.

"You took it?" she whispered reverently.

"I had to," Riven replied, shoving his hands into his pockets. "After all you risked to get it, I had to make sure it came back to you. And I couldn't risk anyone else viewing it. Especially not Jettani. Or my mother."

Though subtle, Exe caught his hint. "Did you view it?"

"That's privileged information, locked securely away in a little vault that only I can access," Riven's slow, intimate smile gave Exe her answer. Only a few people knew that Exe was an Unbindable, *but Riven knows*. That shared knowledge electrified the air between them.

Clearing his throat, Riven said, "You'd better go. You're the guest of honor, and you'll be missed. I wish I could come celebrate with you, but I'm still stuck in the shadows. Most of those Sub Rosans would panic or attack if I set foot in there right now. Because they don't know that I'm a double agent, and it needs to stay that way."

"I really wish you could—come out of the shadows. Maybe someday."

"Yeah," he replied, not believing it.

"We'll make sure of it. Remember, just yesterday I had a death sentence hanging over my head. And my parents were ready to seal me away in the Vale forever because they were certain Anacapia would never be safe for me. And now I'm free to return as myself, not Viva."

"Between you and Velin, you got me a whole lot closer," Riven chucked her under the chin. "My mother was raging after the damage your trial did to Jettani's image of selfless benevolence. It'll be a lot harder for them to hide their underhanded efforts to turn Anacapia into a totalitarian nightmare now. Trust me, toots, behind-the-scenes, Jettani is terrifying."

"I hope I never find out."

"Me too."

Saluting Riven with her presage, Exe said, "Thank you. For everything."

Riven returned her salute with his coin. Then, after hesitating only a split second, he tossed it to her and said, "Just in case. Or just because..." Holding her with his eyes, Riven strolled backward into the volting tree and vanished.

Exe's return into the mirage went unnoticed by everyone—except Caulder. Somehow she wasn't surprised to find him waiting for her, sitting on the boulder, calm and curious. When Exe joined him, he leaned back, supporting himself on his hands so that his arm was almost around Exe's waist—but not quite.

"Everything okay?" Caulder asked softly.

Exe nodded, surveying the party with a bittersweet sigh that Riven couldn't celebrate with them. While many were still dancing, Viva was back to entertaining the youngsters with various magic tricks. Rove and several others had started a card game, while Ella fussed nearby over an irritable, yet secretly delighted Velin. Rande, her older brothers, and others had gathered around a campfire to laugh, sing, and tell stories. All making happy memories to fortify them in the face of an uncertain future.

Happy that she was free to make satisfying memories for herself too, Exe smiled.

"What's got you grinning?" Caulder gently prodded.

"For the first time in forever, I'm happy right where I am," Exe replied. "I'm not lamenting the past or afraid of the future. I'm content. And ready. For whatever comes."

"I'll say. The way you stood up to Jettani, I almost didn't recognize you," Caulder joked, then sobered. "So, I guess we will be seeing more of each other in the future. I can understand why that upsets you."

"What? Why would I—" Exe cut herself off and wrinkled her nose at him when she spotted the mischievous twinkle in his eye.

"Seeing more of me means seeing more of Viva," Caulder replied, feigning grave concern. When Exe laughed and leaned against him, Caulder put his arm around her waist for real. After a few peaceful moments, he leaned his forehead against hers and asked, "Are you worried about Jettani and the Disimulata coming after you now that you've challenged her so publicly?"

"No. I know that I'll be okay," Exe said, shaking her head against his. Leaning her cheek on his shoulder, she added, "I wished for it."

About the Author:

I had an awesome childhood, growing up as an '80s kid. Playground tag and snowball fights. Lazy afternoons at the public swimming pool. Riding bikes with friends until the streetlights came on. Saturday morning cartoons featuring the original (and best!) Smurfs, Scooby Doo, Garfield and even Pac-Man. Collecting stickers, playing with Strawberry Shortcake dolls, and trading Garbage Pail Kids cards. Crazy board games, noisy arcades, even video games at home like Burgertime and Tunnels of Doom. (My very first video game experience was the text-only adventure Deadline that came with "feelies!")

I was lucky enough to be the youngest of nine kids, too. True, half my siblings were out of the house by the time I was old enough to form lasting memories, but they left behind two decades of abandoned toys to stimulate my imagination. (Dawn dolls, Creepy Crawlers, Rock Polishers, and more!) They left behind their childhood books, too. In those old stories, I learned that cookie was once spelled "cooky." I learned to make candy by pouring boiled molasses on fresh, clean snow. I learned that teens had much more active social lives than they did in my day (and today, too...) with sock hops, weenie roasts, malt shop dates, and rumpus room shindigs almost every weekend.

The mountain of books left behind by my siblings (and collected by my grade school principal dad and my school librarian mom) let me explore the world... and worlds unknown. From Neverland to Wonderland to the Emerald City. Icy Kingdoms hidden in wardrobes. Elves and dwarves at war with evil. Ghosts in globes and eerie mirrors. And girls with metallic eyes and telekinetic powers.

The vivid characters, settings, and adventures crafted by these masters of the imagination let my mind play long after I was sent to bed. I pray that my own creations will inspire young imaginations to explore and dream and achieve as my predecessors' works continue to inspire me.

Thanks for reading!

C.B. Arche

CBArche.com